(UN)RIVALED

A SECOND CHANCE, ACCIDENTAL MARRIAGE
ROMANCE

SAINT STEPHENS LAKE
BOOK 4

K.C. BROOKS

*To those who hide their soft hearts behind
reinforced steel walls.
May you find someone worthy of
letting down your guard.*

AUTHOR'S NOTE

This book contains on page, sexually explicit situations. It also contains elements of strained family relationships, childhood trauma and abuse, manipulation, and memory loss due to alcohol abuse.There are some chapters with on-page violence, kidnapping, and references to stalking and harassment.

While it is the author's intention to broach these topics with sensitivity, it could still be triggering for some readers. If that is the case, please skip this book.

Protect your peace, lovelies.

PLAYLIST

1. Right Person, Wrong Time- Henry Moodie
2. The grudge- Olivia Rodrigo
3. Guilty as Sin?- Taylor Swift
4. Little Do You Know- Alex & Sierra
5. I'd Run to You- CJ Starnes
6. Give Me Love- Chris and Bri
7. Hold on Tight- Forest Black
8. Surrender- Natalie Taylor
9. Start a Riot- BANNERS
10. Who We Are- Tristan Prettyman

PROLOGUE

"Why the hell is there a ring on my finger?"

Under normal circumstances, the sound of a strange man's voice in my room would cause me to bolt up, grab my taser from my purse, and try to remember everything I learned in kickboxing.

Today, however, none of those were an option.

From the moment I opened my eyes, my brain felt like someone was sawing it in half. It was painful even to breathe, much less move more than an inch. And the worst part? I had no one to blame but myself.

"Oh my God," I groaned, rubbing at my temples with my forefingers. How much did I have to drink last night? Considering I usually capped myself at two glasses of wine, I didn't have the best tolerance, but this hangover was worse than anything I'd ever had in college. Forgetting about the man lying next to me, I crawled back under the comforter, desperate to keep any source of light as far away from me as possible. Maybe if I shut my eyes extra tight and kept them closed, this would all reveal itself as a bad dream.

There were only two reasons why someone would be in my

room right now. Either I was going to become a dateline special about a serial killer preying on hung-over women, or I'd had a one-night stand. The former was almost more likely. In my twenty-five years on Earth, I'd never had a one-night stand. No shame to those who did, but I wasn't wired that way. Having anonymous sex meant being impulsive and dropping my guard, two things I was incapable of doing.

"Holy shit," the same deep tone groaned. It was gravelly and pained—just like how I'm sure mine would sound if I attempted to speak. I squeezed my eyes closed even harder, but that just amplified the pulsing in my skull. Was it too late to beg him to kill me? Because that might be preferable to dealing with this pain. But I kept my mouth shut as I felt the bed shift, and I sunk more into the middle of the mattress. Oh God. Was this what death felt like? It had to be. There was no way I could go on living if the tension in my skull didn't let up soon.

When I heard the shower turn on, I cracked one eyelid open, practically hissing at the stream of light breaking through the curtains. *The blue curtains.* Forcing my head to rise, I realized not only was I not in my hotel *room,* I was pretty sure I wasn't even in the same *hotel.*

Gone were the deep reds and Roman-themed accents from my hotel. Instead, everything here was bathed in a dark blue, like we had been plunged into the depths of the ocean. Mirrored silver furniture lined the walls, and in the middle sat the ornate bed. As I looked up, I saw my reflection in a large mirror plastered on the ceiling above the bed. Well, I certainly looked as shitty as I felt.

Maybe another day, I would have taken the time to try to figure out how I ended up in this position, but today, I had one goal: get the hell out of there before my new buddy left the bathroom.

Walk of shame, here we go.

I shifted in bed. Okay, walking might be out of the question. Was there such a thing as a crawl of shame?

After a deep exhale, I forced my legs to work and stumbled to grab my discarded dress. Luckily, I still had my underwear on, so maybe last night didn't go as far as I thought. Usually, there was some sort of physical indication I'd slept with someone. I mean, at least when it was enjoyable. Today, it was hard to tell. My entire body felt like a giant bruise, and all I wanted to do was crawl back into the bed and stay there forever.

How the hell had this even happened? This weekend was supposed to be about *work*. I was only in Las Vegas to attend a national legal conference. My new firm had paid for the trip, citing associates' need to make connections within the legal community. While the practice was prominent in New York, times were shifting. The old rules no longer applied, and many old shops were struggling to adjust to the modern, digital era. Apparently, our firm's revitalization strategy included shipping some of its junior associates across the country to attend all the major legal conferences as walking advertisement. The governing committee chose ten of the associates to attend the one this week, including me, and selfishly, I knew this was my opportunity to prove myself. My boss was a hard-ass, but I respected him. He got me excited to practice law and use what I'd learned to help others.

While the others had chatted on the plane ride about what clubs they'd hit up after the conference, I balked at their immature antics. I might have been in Las Vegas, but it was just the backdrop for work. The city wouldn't tempt me.

Oh, poor past Devyn. What a naïve little fool you'd been.

I groaned and rubbed my eyes with the heels of my hands. *Why did I decide to go out?* The past twelve hours were a blur. All my memories ran together, leaving me with a confusing highlight reel of the night's events. The last thing I remembered was walking out of the conference after it wrapped up, counting down the minutes until I could collapse into bed and binge-read while my colleagues got shit-faced.

In my attempt to untangle the previous night, I must have missed the sound of the shower turning off. Because as I muttered to myself, haplessly trying to sort out my memories, someone cleared their throat behind me.

"Running out on me, Ace?"

My entire body stilled. I was pretty sure my heart missed a beat, too focused on the man standing behind me to function properly. With that one sentence, some of my memories snapped into place, recalling my name being called out from across the casino and finding someone staring at me like I was a ghost.

Grayson Anders.

When I saw him across the casino last night, I immediately rushed over and pulled him into a tight hug. It had been years since we'd seen each other in person, but time didn't dull how much he meant to me. Gray was my first real friend, the one who stuck by me through my awkward and tense teenage years, my first love and first subsequent heartbreak.

It had been almost three years since we were in the same room together. After we moved away to college, our friendship was never the same. It faded gradually until it was nothing more than missed calls and texts. I would have loved to pinpoint the minute everything changed, but in truth, it was a million different moments. Time and hidden feelings had messed with our bond, but no one would have known looking at us last night.

And just like when we were kids, it had been impossible to say no to Gray, especially when he asked me to stay for a drink. One drink turned into ten, and before I knew it, his entire baseball team was cheering us on, clinking glasses until we kissed.

"Gray..." I whispered as I turned around. He stood only a

couple of feet away from me, his lower half wrapped in a white terrycloth towel. His body was cut— defined from years of playing professional baseball. My eyes traced the tattoos drawn around his wrist and started to climb both of his arms. Maybe if my eyes were in better shape, I could've made out the designs, but right now, all they looked like were black swirls. His long, dark blond hair was loose around his shoulders, already starting to form waves. Even after all this time, he was still the most attractive man in the world.

The blood drained from my face as I looked from him back to the bed. Had I spent the night with Gray? *God, this was even worse than I thought.* After years of wanting Gray, knowing he'd never see me as more than a friend, I'd finally gotten the chance to be with him, and I was too drunk to remember a moment of it.

"What happened last night?" I croaked out, running my hand over my clothes and desperately trying to keep from making eye contact with Gray.

"No fucking clue," he grumbled, rubbing his hand over his face.

As he did, the sight of something on his ring finger made me sick. A thick black band stuck out against his lightly tanned skin.

I raced into the bathroom, purging everything I'd eaten last night. By the time I finished, Gray sat at my side, handing me a damp washcloth. Scooting back until I hit the wall, I covered my face with my hands. "Gray, please tell me nothing happened between us. I couldn't live with myself if you cheated on your wife—"

"I'm not married," he huffed from my side. His face fell as he looked down at the ring. "Don't think I am, at least. Woke up with this on my finger."

I pulled up slightly, resting my head on the toilet seat. Disgusting, maybe, but in this moment, nothing could have gotten me to lift it any further. "You don't remember putting it on?"

"No. Memory's pretty fucked," he grumbled as he lifted up my left hand. A spark ignited where we touched, and it took everything in me to keep my body calm. It had been so long since I'd been this close to Gray, unable to stay in his orbit and risk my heart breaking again. But even though we were practically strangers now, the same sensation rocked through me: longing, lust, and complete comfort, wrapping around me whenever he was near.

But all of that faded away when he reached for my ring finger, and I felt something there, something I hadn't noticed in my haste to get out of the room. I glanced down at the delicate, braided silver band on my finger. Gray followed my line of sight and twisted the ring with his thumb. Then, he held up his ringed hand, putting it next to mine. The two bands were polar opposites, much like we'd always been, and yet...they worked together.

Another round of nausea pulled the thought from my head, and Gray backed away to give me some space. He returned a couple minutes later with cans of ginger ale, some saltine crackers, and his phone.

"C'mon. You should eat something," he said, helping me to sit against the wall. I pushed away the crackers, unwilling to even think about putting anything in my stomach, but when he held out the ginger ale, I snatched it greedily. "Slow sips," he warned. As I did as I was told, Gray leaned back, running his hand over his gruff beard. "What do you remember about last night?"

"Not much," I answered, dropping my head down to my knees. "The last thing was leaving the bar and going somewhere with your teammates. They were cheering about something?"

"They were cheering about us," Gray said, his tone low. He

pulled out his phone, showing me a video playing on the screen. It looked a lot like the two of us standing on an altar, exchanging promises to each other. Gray watched my face the entire time, waiting for me to process what I'd seen.

I shoved the phone back to him. "I don't understand."

"Ace..." Gray's voice was soft, softer than I'd ever heard it. That should have been my first sign of trouble. He ran his hand over his face and sighed. "I think we got married last night."

ONE

Devyn

You know when people talk about those out-of-body experiences? The moments they can feel their hearts beating in their chests—knowing air is coming in and out of their lungs, but they can't feel any of it?

I always thought that was a gross exaggeration, little more than a feeling people made up to cover their panic, needing something to blame when all their senses failed to save them. No, I was too strong for that, too hard-headed to ever let something like emotions derail me so spectacularly.

All it took were two words for my entire view to change.

Two little words from Grayson Anders, and my entire body went *numb*.

For most of my life, people had referred to me as cold. Because I didn't wear my emotions on my sleeve, many assumed I didn't have any, but it wasn't true. I felt a lot below the surface, but I was never very good at letting people know.

This was the first time I felt like all my emotions had been switched off, leaving me little more than a shell with a pulse. Feelings, sensations, and even sounds were powerless against the weight of his words, knocking my world off its axis for the first time.

My wife.

That bastard.

All at once, as my ex-fling Jack's Mercedes rushed down the street away from us, everything came flooding back to me. The lights of Grayson's bar were too bright, and the quiet, sleepy town was now nothing more than a dissonance of melodramatic noises. Even my heartbeat, which should have been the most soothing sound in the world, was too much.

Especially when Gray turned to face me, his sparkling steel eyes soft as he met my shocked expression. "You okay, Ace?"

Okay? Not even a little. I might be having a stroke, a heart attack, or everything in between. He'd outed our secret without so much as a second thought, and now, I was left wondering how in the hell we'd ever put back those pieces. Because a secret like this—one with the power to detonate everything around you? There was no way to put that back into the bottle.

All I could do was nod, not trusting my voice to carry what I needed to say when he was looking at me like that.

Grayson Anders.

My husband.

My voice tried to come up with an answer for how I was feeling, but it all came to a screeching halt when my sister, Calla, stepped between us. Her hand clamped down on her hips, steam practically boiling out of her ears as she stared at us. She pointed her finger at Gray, but her eyes never left mine. "I'm sorry, but did he just call you his *wife?*"

My eyes widened as they met Gray's, and I could see the moment he realized his mistake. It deflated a little bit of my rage, knowing he never meant to betray me, but then again, Calla wasn't staring at him, demanding answers with her scowl.

Seeing such hurt in her expression almost killed me. I hated being the cause of her pain. My little sister was my whole heart, and typically, I would do anything for her.

However, my emotions had already been through the wringer tonight, and I wasn't about to expose all my fraying nerves for the world to see, not after spending the last few hours avoiding Gray, trying to pretend like we were little more than strangers. I glanced at him, and his gaze had yet to break away from me.

As he looked at me, a painful truth washed over me. I missed him. It was hard enough occupying the same space as him, knowing we'd never get back to what we once were. But seeing him now? Staring at me like he actually cared? Hearing him refer to me as his wife? It poured pounds of salt into an already-painful wound.

I shook my head as I looked at Calla. "I can't do this right now."

"So it's true?" she whispered. Hurt marred her usual smile, her eyes already brimming with unshed tears. "You got married?" She exhaled slowly, bringing her hand up to her stomach. "When?"

I closed my eyes, knowing the answer wouldn't make things any easier. "Five years ago."

Calla let out a soft cry, a strange blend of laughter and a sob. "Five years? You've been keeping this from us–*from me*–for five years?" She shook her head. "What the fuck, Devyn?"

"It's not on her," Gray said, stepping to my side. While I knew he had the best intentions, it was the absolute worst timing. I almost snorted. That was practically the theme song of my life with Gray: always the wrong time.

Calla's eyes snapped to him. "Don't you even start with me, Grayson. We've seen each other every week for *months*, and you never thought to mention that you're married to my sister?" She stared back at me. "So clearly, this is some messed-up joke, because you two have barely been in the same room since high school."

"It was a mistake," I said at the same time as Gray said, "It's a long story."

I shook my head, reaching out to take my sister's hand, but she just stepped out of my way. My head ducked down to my chest. This was the exact reason I never told her. I never wanted to see that look in her eyes. It was hard enough knowing I loved her former boyfriend; I never wanted her to know I'd actually married him. Even though our marriage license was the only thing that still bound us together, I never wanted anything to shake my sister's faith in me.

"I can explain," I said. "Just not tonight, Calla. Please. I can't get into this right now."

"Fine," Calla snapped, turning into her husband, Theo's, embrace. "I've been in the dark long enough. What's a little longer? But you need to figure this out, Devyn. Because I would love to know why my sister is not only married, but married to a guy I thought you hated."

"I don't hate Gray," I insisted, stepping forward.

"Good to know," my husband pushed out at my side.

"Not now, Grayson," I bit back. I turned back to say more to Calla, but she was already in the parking lot, climbing into Theo's SUV. Everyone else had dispersed during our argument, probably not wanting to get in the middle. But now that I was standing here, watching my little sister drive away, it was like the last piece of my fractured heart had shattered at my feet.

Just as my sadness started to rip a hole through my chest, Gray placed his hand on my shoulder. "Come on, Devyn. The least I can do is get you a drink."

I snorted, shoving his hand off me. "Are you fucking serious, Gray? How could you do that?"

His steely eyes hardened. "What the fuck did you expect

me to do, Devyn? Stand there and watch as that asshole put his hands on you?"

"Yes!" I snapped. "I had everything under control."

"Oh, bullshit," Gray scoffed. "Lie to them, lie to everyone else in the world, but don't lie to me, Devyn. I know you too well for that."

I shook my head. It was too much. Gray was too close. Too many emotions clouded my mind. Typically, my best trait was my ability to switch off my feelings and focus on the task at hand. That was what everyone at work had always told me. But right now, staring at the man who captured my heart decades ago, I didn't feel like that cold, callous woman. No, I felt like a teenager again, standing on my front porch, begging the universe to let my best friend notice me.

Echoes of our past leeched under my skin, snapping me back to the moment, closing my heart yet again to the man in front of me.

I jabbed my finger into his chest. "No, you don't. Not anymore. And this marriage was nothing more than a mistake. You and I both know that. You should have signed the divorce papers *years* ago, Gray, and none of this would have ever happened."

His gaze only hardened at my words. "It's not that easy, Devyn."

"And you say I'm full of shit," I scoffed, shoving my purse up on my shoulder. I turned around, stomping toward my car. As I pulled the door open, I called out, "This changes nothing, Gray. Sign the damn papers so we can get out of each other's lives for good."

Gray just stood there, running his hand through his long, wavy hair. It made the muscles of his forearms flex, and I wondered if he'd added any more tattoos to his collection. What the fuck? That was the last thing I should be thinking about. I refused to meet his eyes, not knowing what I would find there. Because even though I said the words, the idea of living without Gray sank in my chest like a lead balloon. Our paths had barely crossed over the years, yet I still kept him close to my chest, like a baby blanket you've held onto even as it became tattered and frayed.

I shook my head as I climbed into the driver's seat, more than ready to head back to the city. This town had a habit of messing with my mind, making me remember things I would rather forget.

But when I reached the end of the parking lot, I slowed my rental car to a stop before turning onto the street. I adjusted the rearview mirror, finding Gray still watching. I closed my eyes, working hard to close the doors his appearance had forced open. It took everything in me to shift my foot to the gas and pull away.

As the car headed out of town, I thought of any other way I could convince Gray to sign the divorce papers, but nothing I'd offered seemed to entice him, which only made me angrier. He was the one who ended things; he was the one who walked away when I was willing to try. And now, he was holding out on signing the papers, like some bizarre twist where he didn't want me but also didn't want to let me go.

Over the past five years, I'd tried everything to rid my mind of Gray. Distance, no contact—nothing seemed to sever the strings tying me to him. And while I hated that he had so much power over me, I couldn't deny being around Gray still affected me.

That was the problem with giving your heart away before you're old enough to know better. You don't realize you might never get it back.

TWO

Grayson

"Great," I said as I dropped my keys on the front porch. "Just fucking great."

I tried to grab them quickly, hating that the alarm was already blaring at full force, but the damn things had lodged themselves behind my mother's planter, making me stretch as much as possible to reach them.

Closer.

Closer.

Got 'em.

Scooping them up, I pushed the door fully open, scrambling to find the glowing alarm box on the wall. Elsa, my golden retriever, barked at my legs, trying to say hello like normal, but with the alarm bells, I could only focus on pressing the numbers as quickly as possible. I must not have been fast enough, because by the time I hit the last number, the phone trilled to life.

I rushed into the kitchen, grabbing the old yellow landline hanging from the kitchen wall. The damn thing had to be over thirty years old, but my mother refused to get rid of it, even with my offer to upgrade their wireless service provider. She didn't trust cell phones, especially not in the middle of the woods. She claimed the cell towers would all go out one day, and we'd all be here, begging to use her ugly yellow phone.

I didn't have the heart to argue with her.

I grabbed the phone, pulling the receiver to my ear.

"May I have your code word, please?"

"Ace of Hearts," I muttered, hating my mother a little for picking that phrase, especially tonight.

"Thank you, sir. Have a good night."

I hung up with the security firm and took a steady breath. Elsa jumped excitedly at my feet, reminding me she had business to take care of. Reaching down, I scratched her head and led her through the kitchen. "I know, girl. Come on."

I pushed open the back door, and she rushed outside, staying close enough that I could see her, even without the porch light on. Usually, we'd spend some time out here so she could stretch her legs, but considering the dropping temperature and the late hour, we were both ready to get back inside. I grabbed her favorite toy from the counter, depositing a few treats inside before letting Elsa wander back to her spot by the fireplace. She happily played as I crossed my nightly chores off my list, hoping it would be enough to lull me to sleep when the time came.

As I poked my head up the staircase off the living room, I said a silent thank you to the universe for my parents not waking up. However, once I stepped back into the kitchen, footsteps creaked along the floorboards. I turned, spotting my mother as she entered the room, wrapped up in my dad's old, tattered robe. When she got close enough, I pulled her into my arms, kissing the top of her head. "Sorry about that. Dropped the keys, so I couldn't put the code in on time."

"Happens," she shrugged. "I was up anyway."

"Everything okay?" I asked, pulling back to look her in the eyes. My mother, Marta Anders, was the strongest woman I knew and could handle anything life threw at her. But the past year had worn heavily on us all, and we both knew the days were taking their toll. She was exhausting herself, and I hated that she wouldn't ask for help.

"Everything is fine," she hushed as she moved to where she kept the tea bags. She grabbed the kettle from its place on the stove, filling it with water before returning to turn on the burner. "Your father had a rough night, but we worked it out. I had to give him a little medicine to get him to relax."

"You should have called me, Mom." I pulled out one of the stools and took a seat on the island. "I'm here to help."

"We're okay, Gray. You have your own life, and you need to live it. I hate that you already gave up so much to be here for us."

"It's not enough." I looked down at my hands, knowing the sacrifices my parents had made to help me live my dream. I'd started playing baseball in middle school after one of my friends took me to the batting cages after school. Something about the rhythm of the machines, focusing on the ball, helped me silence the noise around me. When I was in that metal cage, nothing else mattered. After a lifetime of being unable to focus, it felt like a sign I could tune out the rest of the world as soon as a bat was in my hands.

After that day, I begged my parents to let me join every team. I was on travel teams, rec leagues, and every intramural I could find before I was finally able to join the modified league in eighth grade. And as much as it strained them, my parents were at every game and sacrificed everything to make sure my dream became a reality.

It was the kind of love you could never pay back, but I would be damned if I wasn't going to try.

My mother reached out, taking my hands in hers. "You're

here, Gray. That's all I could ask for. I know you should be back in the city, but selfishly, I love having you home."

"Even when I set off the alarm in the middle of the night?"

She leaned back and shrugged. "Kind of reminds me of high school, when you and Devyn used to think you could sneak out without us finding out."

"You knew?"

My mother leaned her head back and barked out a laugh. "Of course, we knew. God, did you actually think you'd gotten away with it? There were plenty of nights your father followed you, making sure the two of you were safe, even though we knew you would be."

"Why?"

She gave me one of her usual smirks, the one that showed she knew much more than the rest of the world. "Because you were with Devyn. You'd never let anything happen to that girl."

Her words cut deep, knowing I'd caused Devyn more pain than anyone else in her life. It was like a wound that never healed right, constantly aching when it should have faded away years ago. Some days, it was a dull throb, but nights like tonight, when she was so close yet so distant, it felt like someone was carving me up from the inside. I stared up at my mother, and my guard dropped, letting the weight of the evening finally settle around me.

She stared through me, just like she did when I was younger. So many days growing up, I'd sit in this same spot, my mother giving me the same look. Just a couple of words from Marta Anders, and I'd fold like a cheap chair.

She leaned into the counter, interlocking her fingers together. "I know that face. Even better–I know who's usually the cause of it."

"It's a long story," I chuckled, but there was no warmth in the gesture. All I wanted was to rewind the night and take back the words that spilled out of my mouth. I didn't even know where that protective urge had come from. It was ridiculous. Devyn had never been my wife in anything other than name. But from the moment that asshole pulled up in his suped-up car, all my protective instincts came blaring to life. My mother was right about one thing—no one would ever hurt Devyn, not in front of me. I might have been the one to fracture us beyond repair, but that didn't change how I felt. I'd do anything to keep her safe.

My mother reached out and took my hands. "Look, Gray. I know you and Devyn had a special bond growing up, but maybe it's time to let her go."

I just shook my head, unable to say the words out loud. Honestly, I thought the same thing. Shit, I'd tried—more times than I could count. But the moment things started to get serious with anyone else, I'd shut down, unable to get Devyn out of my mind. "I don't know if anyone else is in the cards for me."

My mother started to interject when a loud crash echoed from the upstairs bedroom. Both of us sprang into action, dashing upstairs to find my father sprawled out on the floor, trying to get his bearings.

"Oh, Curt," my mother cooed, trying to help him to his feet. But instead of letting her guide him, my father swatted her hands away.

"I can do it," he hissed, shoving off to his feet. "I don't need your help."

"Honey, I'm just trying to—"

"Don't you dare call me honey," my father snapped, getting into my mother's face. "Only my wife can call me that. If she hears you saying that to me, trust me, she'll make you wish you never laid eyes on me."

"Okay," my mother sighed, holding out her hands. "I won't say it again. But please, Mr. Anders, let me help you into bed."

He stared at her for a long moment, and my heart ticked harder, hoping for a glimmer of recognition. Most days, my father was fine, his usual self, his memory intact. But these episodes were getting more and more frequent, especially if he woke up in the middle of the night. The doctors warned us that there might be a day when he was lost more often than lucid, so it was important to hold on to the good days as long as we could.

But I didn't want to measure my days with my dad in variables; I didn't want to wonder if today would be the day he forgot me forever. But Alzheimer's Disease didn't care about my wants or needs. It didn't care that I still needed my dad, still needed the man I knew him to be.

As my mother led him to the bed, my father looked at me, a slow smile creeping over his face. "You know, you look just like my son. He's down in the city, playing ball." His smile lit up his face. "You should see that kid pitch. He's incredible."

"Probably thanks to you," I answered, swallowing the lump in my throat.

"Nah, that was all him," my father chuckled as he laid his head against the pillow. "If you go to a game, make sure you tell them that Curt Anders sent you. My boy will take care of you."

"Will do," I said, taking my mom's hand as we left him to get a few more hours of rest. As I led her down to the spare bedroom she now called home, I pulled my mother into a hug. Her breath shuddered against my chest. These moments were challenging for me, but they were even harder for her. My parents started dating right after high school, and they'd never spent more than a week away from each other in the forty years they'd been together.

She pulled back, wiping her tears away on the back of her hand. "God, Gray. I'm so sorry."

I took her hand in mine. "You don't have to carry this alone,

Mom. I'm here for you." I stared harder at her. "But I think you should consider what the doctor said—"

"I'm not putting him in a home." She shook her head. "I promised to take care of him in sickness and health, and I mean that today as much as I did back then. I'm not going to send him away just because this is the hard part."

"It's only going to get worse—"

"Don't, Gray." The finality in her tone cut off my words. "Just...not tonight. Let me pretend for a little bit longer that everything will be alright. When we reach that step..." She swallowed slowly. "We'll discuss all of this later."

She stepped into her new bedroom, effectively ending any further discussions about my father's dwindling mental state. It was okay; I was fine with putting off this discussion a little longer too. I didn't want to live in this house without my father, needing to hear his laugh and the constant tinkering of his tools.

But the knowledge it would eventually end was always lingering there in the corner, just waiting for the moment when we were content to strike. That was the thing about living with a diagnosis like Alzheimer's: more days than not, it felt like a guillotine was waiting over you. And one day, much sooner than you ever hoped, the rope would finally snap, and everything familiar would get washed away. You'd be left with nothing more than memories of the person sitting in front of you.

And while I was beyond thankful I still had my father with us, I couldn't help that sting of bitter disappointment, knowing he was a shadow of himself. That one day soon, he'd look at me like a stranger while he would continue to be my hero.

I pushed these thoughts out of my mind as I walked down the stairs, waking Elsa from her place on the couch. She looked at me with tired, dark eyes but followed me into the garage, climbing the stairs to the attached loft. Originally designed as a mother-in-law suite, I'd moved up here as soon as I could in high school, excited for a slight hint of freedom. I never dreamed I'd be living here again at thirty.

While I owned a place outside of town, it felt wrong to stay there when my mother needed help, especially at night. My dad often woke up distressed, and she needed help keeping him calm. I felt more comfortable being close.

As soon as I opened the door, Elsa curled up on the queen-sized bed in the corner and closed her eyes. However, I was wide awake after the scene upstairs. Between that and my fight with Devyn, my adrenaline was at an all-time high. I walked over to my old bookshelf, the one that hadn't shifted in over a decade, thumbing through some of my favorite titles. I picked up a sci-fi novel I'd read so often, the pages were faded and bent. As I started thumbing through them, a piece of paper tumbled out from the center, landing at my feet. When I leaned down to grab it, the pictures stared back at me. Once I held the strip in my hand, I looked over each one and smiled at the memory.

Four images lined up on the paper, all of Devyn and me from one of the summer carnivals when the town sprung for a photo booth. For a moment, I looked at the younger version of myself, but Devyn was really what had all my attention. It was odd—she looked the same yet completely different at the same time. She had the same icy blonde hair pulled into a messy bun, her usually pale skin tanned from a long summer at the beach, the same dark eyes, too mature for our age but also filled with so much life. Now, all I ever got was a scowl; in these pictures, she looked so damn happy.

Devyn's bright smile was infectious, and I couldn't stop staring at all the images in a row. We must have taken fifty pictures that day. She had plopped into my lap, not thinking twice about our closeness. We never did back then. My arm was slung around her waist, holding her tight as we made goofy faces at the camera.

It was still early in our friendship, before the trajectory of our lives changed and forced us apart. As I looked at the younger version of myself, my stomach twisted. In every picture, I was staring at Devyn. God, I was already obsessed; I was just too young and dumb to realize it.

Muttering under my breath, I started to tuck the photo strip back into the book but paused. As I closed the cover, I put the book back in its rightful place but kept the photos out of it. Instead, I grabbed the tape from my desk, ripped off a small piece, and put it up on my mirror.

This was ridiculous. One night with Devyn, and I was already back to obsessing over her. But it felt too good to be close to her, to smell the perfume that always lingered a few seconds after she left the room. I wanted so much more, but there was no way she felt the same.

Shaking my head, I walked away from the mirror. I pulled my shirt over my head and shoved off my jeans before climbing into bed, too emotionally drained to even deal with a shower. As Elsa curled up into my side, I closed my eyes, dreams of a past life haunting me.

THREE

Grayson

TWELVE YEARS OLD

Someone had invaded my fishing spot.

No, not anyone. *She* had invaded it.

All I wanted was to go down to the ice and try to catch a fish before the sun melted it too much, but nope. That wasn't going to happen today, not when my favorite secret spot had been invaded yet again.

I toyed with the small rod in my hand, looking over my shoulder. There had to be other places to go. There was that one spot over by Guardian's Beach. But then again, someone had fallen in last week after a thin patch gave out. I shuddered, not willing to take that risk. No, if I wanted to get the practice in, it had to be here. After all, there were only a couple more weeks until Dad started going up north with his friends. I have to show him I could handle it—that I had the patience to sit and wait for the fish if I wanted to tag along this year. And let's be honest—I really did need the practice.

But from the moment I saw her sitting there, any plans of fishing left my mind.

Devyn Winters.

My mortal enemy.

Okay, so maybe that was a little harsh. It wasn't like she stole my toys or kicked my dog. There was just something about Devyn that *irritated* me. We'd known each other almost all our lives–an unfortunate side effect of our dads being best friends. It was no secret they hoped their friendship would pass down to us.

Good luck with that.

Devyn and I never got along, barely able to spend more than ten minutes in a room together without arguing. My parents had sat me down a ton of times, reminding me to be nice to Devyn, but nothing seemed to work. We were too different. Eventually, we'd learned to co-exist. Between weekly dinners and spending all our vacations and holidays together, we weren't given much of a choice.

Until her dad died, and then, everything changed.

Immediately after the funeral, her mother boarded up their rooms at the Isadora and traded them in for a ritzy apartment in the city. Devyn and her family still visited in the summer and on school breaks, but they stayed close to her grandfather.

But even though she was rarely in town, it seemed like our paths always managed to cross.

Standing at the tree line, I watched her pencil glide across the page. She briefly looked up, squinting to monitor a pair of birds that had landed on the ice. Most of the wildlife had fled before the snow started to fall, but these birds were stubborn, I'd give them that. Wisps of her ice blonde hair untucked from her braids, and she lifted a bare hand to swat them away, unwilling to break her concentration.

I smirked, an evil plan forming in the back of my mind. I crept closer, waiting until she was concentrating on her drawing again to sneak up behind her. But as I took another tiny step closer, my boot pressed into a stick buried in the snow. The resounding crack echoed across the space between us, and

Devyn lifted her head ever so slightly. "I know you're there, Grayson. You might as well come out."

My head dropped down to my feet, hating Devyn had managed to beat me. *Again.* I rolled my eyes as I stepped out. "I thought I told you this was my beach?"

"Oh, you were serious about that?" she said, still tracking the movement of the birds. "Guess you'll have to provide some evidence, and then I'll move along." She looked up at me with one of her smug smiles. "Until then, I think I'll stay. Besides, I was here first, and you know what they say about possession being nine-tenths of the law."

I ground my teeth, trying to hold back the words on the tip of my tongue. *This* was the exact reason why Devyn Winters and I could never be friends. Most people assumed it was because she was a girl, but I didn't give a crap about that. My best friend Wade said it was weird to be friends with girls, but I didn't see it like that.

No, I couldn't stand Devyn because she always needed to be right, always needed to prove she was the smartest person in the room. I swear, the girl was born with the ability to win an argument. No matter the topic, every time our paths crossed, she left me feeling dumb, which wasn't an unusual feeling for me.

I spent most of my days wondering what was wrong with my brain and why it was so hard to focus on anything, especially in school. For the most part, I was able to ignore that internal voice telling me I was stupid. But when I was around Devyn, a girl who was too smart for her own good, that whisper turned into a roar, sure she'd make fun of me if she knew the truth.

The sounds of the birds taking off pulled me back into the moment, watching as she muttered something under her breath. She turned, and her brown eyes cut into me. "Can you just go,

Grayson? Please?" A hitch caught in her throat. "I...I can't do this, not today."

I stared at Devyn, unsure what the hell was happening. This girl, seemingly made of Teflon, was breaking down in front of me, and I didn't have a single clue why.

But for the first time in my life, instead of taking the opportunity to get as far away from Devyn as possible, I plopped down next to her. We sat in silence for a while, not knowing how to even really talk to each other without trying to hurt the other's feelings.

I glanced over at her bare hands, her fingers still clutched around the pencil. "You should have gloves on. The wind on the lake gets really cold."

"I know that."

I sighed, dropping my elbows onto my knees. "I wasn't trying to be a jerk. We have some extra pairs at home if you need some."

Devyn turned toward me, studying my profile. I forced myself to keep my eyes forward, not sure if I'd like what I found if I looked back at her.

Eventually, she let out a dry laugh. "I can't believe you're still trying to scare me."

"Gonna get you one of these days," I said, letting go of some of my annoyance toward Devyn. Maybe it was because I knew how it felt to feel raw, or it was because I hated the idea of kicking her while she was down, but either way, teasing Devyn didn't seem right.

She chuckled and reached out to push me off the rock. Instead, I grabbed her wrist and pulled her in a little closer. Her deep, brown eyes widened when I held her, and for the first time, I noticed the different shades that made up the color. For as long as I could remember, I teased her that her eyes were like mud—nothing special at all about them. But now, I realized I was wrong. There was nothing flat or boring about the color. it was more like the mountains on clear summer mornings.

As soon as Devyn balanced herself on the rock, I dropped her hand, giving us some much-needed space. What the hell was in the air today? Why did I notice all these things about Devyn so suddenly?

"Why are you being nice to me, Grayson?"

"Told you not to call me that." I smirked to avoid her question. "How do you like it when I call you Devy?"

She shuddered, returning to the sketchpad draped across her lap. "That's not my name, but Grayson is yours. Just because you don't like it doesn't make it any less true."

"Still don't like it," I grumbled, messing with the ends of my hair.

She scowled up at my movements, tapping the brim of my hat with her fingers. "Are you going to keep growing it out?"

"Yeah. Gonna see how long it takes my mom to snap." I smirked, shoving my long hair away from my eyes. A couple of months ago, Mom declared I was old enough to decide how I wanted to style my hair, a choice she was starting to regret more and more each day. Now that it was almost past my shoulders, she liked to make comments at the dinner table, asking if I thought it was time to try something new.

Devyn pursed her lips then nodded, more to herself than to me. As her thumb danced through the last lines she'd drawn, I couldn't help but watch, mesmerized by each swipe. "Why're you doing that?"

Devyn frowned to herself, "I'm trying to make the shadows, but I can't get them right." Her voice cracked a little again, and she exhaled, as if trying to push all those emotions away. "David, my mom's new boyfriend, says my sketches lack depth, and I need to play more with dimension if I want to get taken seriously."

I laughed, but Devyn's face only tightened. "Wait...you're not kidding?"

She slammed the lid of the book closed, crossing her arms around her chest. Her eyes narrowed at me. "No, I wasn't. Why would I joke about my weakness?"

"Because you're in, what? Sixth grade?"

"Yup, same as you."

"Exactly," I chuckled, taking the pad from her hands. I thumbed through the pages, hoping she couldn't read the amazement in my eyes. Because hell, this girl was talented, more than I'd ever want to admit. But when I looked up at her, gone was the know-it-all-all who usually bugged me to no end. Instead, her lips rolled together, watching as I looked at each sketch. I closed the book and held it out to her. "He's an idiot."

Devyn barked out a laugh, and her face transformed. She looked nicer, softer. *Prettier.* She shook her head as she clutched her book against her chest. "You don't know what you're talking about. David *knows* art. He is an—"

"Idiot," I finished for her. I shifted the book so the front cover was visible. She'd sketched a woman crying, but her tears had transformed into a river, life growing out of her pain. "And probably jealous. You're just a kid, and he hates that you're already so talented."

"You think?" she asked, her puffy pink lips turning up at the sides.

"Hell yeah, Devy." I knocked her on the shoulder. "Gonna see your name up in lights one day. Get to tell everyone I knew you before you were famous."

"Yeah, right," Devyn chuckled as she settled on the rock next to me again, her leg bumping into mine. Despite the shivering temperature, heat rushed through me at the gentle touch. She nudged me with her elbow. "And what about you, Grayson? Where will you be?"

"Don't know," I said. "But I'm going to be somewhere far away from here, playing baseball, that's for sure." I laughed as I looked at her. "Who knows? Maybe we'll even be friends when we're old."

"Yeah, right," Devyn snorted. "Like you'd ever want to be friends with the 'most annoying girl on the planet'?"

I blushed, running my hand through of my hair. "You heard that, huh?"

"Yup," she said. I expected her to hurl more insults at me, to take off and run away, breaking this weird truce we had going on. Instead, she just rolled her eyes. "It's fine. I've called you worse before."

"Oh, yeah?" I smiled at her. "Like what?"

"Not gonna tell."

"C'mon, Devy. I promise not to laugh too hard."

She coughed a laugh then turned to look down at her feet, "I might have implied you think I'm a know-it-all because I use multisyllabic words, making it impossible for you to comprehend what I'm saying."

My cheeks flushed at her implication, and I hated that she'd picked up on one of my biggest insecurities without even trying. No one but my parents and teachers knew the extent of my failings. Even though they tried to help, it didn't make my brain work any better—it didn't make it any easier for me to concentrate.

Hating how raw I felt with her words, I hopped off the rock, trying to get as much distance from her as possible. "Gotta go."

"Wait," Devyn said as she rushed after me, taking my hand in hers. I almost jumped at her touch, and not only because her hands were like ice. Something pulsed between our fingers, something I'd never felt with anyone else. It was weird, almost uncomfortable. Without thinking, I pulled my gloves off, placing them around her hands before she could say anything.

She looked down at her now-gloved hands and frowned, as if no one had ever done something like that for her before. Maybe it was weird, but I went with it. Her wide brown eyes looked up at me. "I'm sorry. I shouldn't have said anything like that. Truthfully..." She sighed. "Truthfully, I've always been a little jealous of you."

"Of me?" I laughed.

"Is that so hard to believe?" Devyn spit out. "You're so...*nice*. Everyone likes you! No one thinks you're mean or rude."

"I don't think you're those things." Devyn narrowed her eyes. "Anymore."

"It's fine." She shook her head. "I know I can be abrasive at times. It's not like I try to be that way, but I just hate being talked down to. If I don't make people see me, then they treat me like a kid."

"You *are* a kid," I smiled, stepping closer to her.

"Semantics," she grinned back at me.

I shook my head. "Look, I know we've never gotten along before, but maybe we could try something new. Maybe try not hating each other?"

"Like a truce?"

"Yeah, something like that."

She paused, searching my expression for any clues of deception. Finally, after a long, tense moment, she nodded. "Fine." She held out her hand. "But only if I get to call you Grayson."

I placed my palm in hers. "Never gonna happen, Devy."

FOUR

Devyn

The text message from earlier this morning stared back at me, joining the dozens of other unanswered ones. It had only been a couple of days since the blow-up at the bar, and my heart ached from missing my sister. Would she ever hear me out? Did I even deserve that? Calla was usually the most forgiving person in the world, but this was a deep secret I'd kept from her for *years*.

But how was I supposed to tell her? Oh yeah, so you know your high school boyfriend? Yeah, I married him on a drunken whim in Las Vegas. And even though Gray and I had been friends first, she was the one he dated, the one he actually wanted. I couldn't bring myself to explain how I had been madly in love with him and was willing to settle for second place.

I would rather eat a tin of thumbtacks.

My phone chimed, and I instantly sat up, hoping it was Calla. But no such luck—just another text in a group chat with my law school friends. They were trying to arrange drinks, and usually, I'd try to make an effort, even though I'd most likely back out at the last minute because of some work emergency. But today, I didn't even feel like responding, too busy wallowing about being such a shitty sister.

The worst part was that there was a moment last year when I could have told her. It was right after I found out Calla was dating her older boss, even though it was against the company's rules. I thought it was going to end in disaster, but luckily for them, Theo was too stubborn to let my sister go. He loved her with a fierceness I only dreamed about. They were even expecting a baby this summer.

And while I was thrilled it had worked out for them, when I first found out, it hurt that Calla had lied to me, even though it had only been a couple of weeks. Add another check into the hypocritical column for me. We'd promised each other no more secrets. That was the moment I should have told her everything.

But I'd done what I always did: made excuses in my mind to hide the past with Grayson. Because as much as I wanted to tell Calla, she was the one person I couldn't admit the truth to. Not only because Gray had been hers first, but because I would hate to see her opinion of me change. She was one of the few people who saw the good in me despite my surly personality pushing most others to the periphery. Even back home, where she'd tried to pull me into the fold of her friend group, I felt like the outsider, like I was one quip or smart ass comment away from being excommunicated.

A knock sounded on my door, and my eyes darted up to meet the smooth smile of my favorite investigator. Tomas wasn't a tall man, probably just shy of six feet, but he was still one of the most intimidating men I'd ever met. His dark eyes were intense, able to make the most assured man question himself. His chocolate brown hair was shaved at the sides but longer on top, and a dusting of stubble covered his olive-toned chin and cheeks. He stepped closer, holding a stack of documents. I arched a brow, trying to hide my hopeful smile. "Please tell me that's what I think it is."

"If you were hoping it's photos of your client engaged in extracurricular activities with a woman who is not his wife..." he chuckled, passing me the envelope. "Then you're going to be very happy."

As soon as I held it in my hand, I ripped the envelope open, both horrified and delighted by what Tomas had captured on film. Glancing around him to make sure there weren't any lurking ears, I whispered, "You think you can get this to the wife's attorney without alerting anyone?"

Tomas clicked his tongue. "I'm insulted you even have to ask, querida. But I have to admit, this little assignment piqued my interest. Shouldn't you be helping your client keep his prenup in place?"

I stared back at Tomas, trying to keep up my stony veneer, but he'd always been able to see through me, even when we met years ago. The best investigator contracted by the firm—he was only supposed to work with the named partners. Luckily for me, our paths had crossed on one of my first days, and a particularly bad one at that. He must have seen something that gave him pause because, unlike the rest of my colleagues, he stopped and asked if he could help me. Typically, I would have said no, needing to prove I could do it myself, but he caught me at a weak moment, and to be honest, I needed the help.

As they said, the rest was history.

I shrugged my shoulders as I leaned back in my white leather chair. "I don't know what you're talking about. Obviously, someone on the wife's side must have gotten wind of the affair and leaked it to her attorney."

Tomas' wolf-like smile matched mine as he walked over to the corner of my office, thumbing over the top of my legal texts.

My office was small, but at least I'd moved up a few floors. It wasn't on the top, and most people forgot about me down here, but when I walked in every day, it made me proud to see my name etched onto my door.

"Does this have anything to do with the police reports the judge suppressed?"

I toyed with the rings on my pointer finger, trying to get the images out of my head, even months later. My client beat his wife within an inch of her life, and even after filing a police report saying he was the cause, she *still* wasn't granted a restraining order. And because of some bullshit technicality, the overseeing partner had gotten it thrown out of court, making it even harder for his ex-wife to get any support from him now that they were divorced.

While I tried to do my job and fight for my client, domestic violence was unforgivable in my mind. My client deserved to lose everything, but I also had to think of my future, hence the need for anonymity. Luckily, Tomas and I saw eye to eye on a lot of these cases, and he was always happy to throw in a couple of pro-bono hours for a good cause.

I handed the photos back to him. "Like I said, I have no idea what you're talking about."

As soon as Tomas took the folder and tucked it inside his leather jacket, I leaned back in my chair. My eyes closed, and I rubbed my lids, trying to push away the migraine that had been plaguing me all day.

"What's going through your mind, querida?" Tomas asked as he sat down, kicking his feet up on the end of my desk. I tossed a stack of Post-It notes at his feet, making him chuckle and put them back on the floor, but when he leaned closer, there was nothing but cold observation in his eyes. "You look tired, Devyn. Even more than usual."

"Isn't that just a euphemism for saying I look like shit?"

"You could never," Tomas shrugged. Once upon a time, his bold flirtations would have come across as more than a passing comment, but now, they were familiar. Besides, we worked well together, so we'd never crossed the line, a choice I was very grateful about. Not only would it have made work awkward, but we'd become good friends, and we would have never worked out as a couple, not when I couldn't give more than a few sleepless nights.

Tomas' voice broke me out of my haze. "Anything I can do to help?"

Only if you have a time machine and the ability to wipe people's memories. Maybe if the past forty-eight hours were gone, I'd be able to take a full breath. It was tempting to fill him in, but there were eyes everywhere, and even though I trusted Tomas, I didn't want anyone else in this building to learn my weakness. I'd seen firsthand how quickly loyalties could shift for the right price. No, this secret was mine to bear. And considering that my husband—*I shuddered thinking that word*—was currently at the top of my shit list, there wasn't anyone else I was willing to let in.

"I'm fine," I sighed, shifting forward to look over my caseload for the day, but Tomas just stared at me as if able to read the lie in my words. I sighed, dropping the glare for a moment. "I *will* be fine. As long as I don't have to talk about it, especially not here. I just want to do my job."

Tomas stood, and for a moment, I thought he was going to walk out of my tiny office without another word. But instead, he leaned forward on my desk, placing his hand on top of mine. "Remember why you came here, Devyn."

My jaw tensed. "Of course I do."

"Then focus on that. You're getting close, querida. I can feel it. And then, maybe once we close all this..." Tomas sighed, like he wasn't sure he believed his own words. "Maybe it's time to think about moving on. Start really living."

I narrowed my eyes at him. "I don't remember asking for tough love with my morning coffee."

"Might be tough love, but you need it," he shrugged. "I know why, but I've watched you kill yourself for years, Devyn. You're a damn good lawyer, but I want you to think if this is what you want the rest of your life to look like."

No. The voice in the back of my mind called out before I could stop it. From the outside looking in, it looked like I had everything I could ever want: the job, the fancy apartment, and enough money to live comfortably. But it was a hollow existence, and I probably would have left a long time ago if I'd had the courage to walk away.

But I wasn't ready to consider that. I was too focused on my goals to picture a life afterward.

I smirked as I looked over to Tomas. "And you waited how long to say something to me?"

"This is the first time I thought you'd actually hear me. Oh, and before I forget, there's a little something extra tucked in that folder. You might find it interesting." With a knock on the door-frame, he backed away, waving at me as he passed through the office door.

After it swung closed, I tried to keep my pulse calm as I searched through the file to find what Tomas had left for me. Underneath all the photos was a zip drive, and I let out an excited sigh. Peeking out into the hallway, I closed the blinds to my office and rushed into the corner to grab my personal laptop. It was a risk doing this at the office, but there was no way I could wait until I got home.

As soon as my computer booted up, I plugged in the external hard drive and made sure the Wi-Fi connected to my personal hotspot. When Tomas and I first started down this path, I talked to the IT director, flirting with him to see how I could work around our system in case I needed to access anything I didn't want my boss to see. I'm pretty sure he thought I was filming OnlyFans videos in my office, but that was better than the truth.

It only took a moment for everything to boot up, and the drive required an encryption code to access it. *Tomas and his spy games.* I guess I should be grateful. He was doing all of this to keep me safe, but it was hard to be thankful when I was memorizing fifteen different codes and pins a week.

As the data downloaded, I searched through each file, looking for anything familiar. Most of the pages were financial reports, ones I would really need to sit down and analyze to make sense of it all. But as I scrolled through a few more pages, a familiar name jumped out at me.

Saint Stephen's Lake.

"What the hell?" I muttered, scanning through that section. It was just a quick mention of a project, but it was enough to pique my interest. "What are you doing at the lake?"

A group of interns walked by my office, and I slammed my laptop shut, not wanting to risk getting caught. But after I tucked everything away and moved back to my desk, the silence around me became overbearing. I couldn't stop thinking about what the file said. Maybe it was nothing, but the idea of my investigation leading back to the lake made me want to crawl out of my skin.

Sitting wasn't an option, not with all this excess, frantic energy coursing through my veins. As I stood, I moved over to the window, watching the city below me. It was a world away from the lake, where time seemed to move slower. Even though I'd lived here for the past five years, it felt like I was still getting used to the noise, still getting used to how you could barely see the stars. Just the thought made me miss Saint Stephen's Lake. I hadn't lived there for over a decade, but it was still the closest thing I had to a home.

"Get a grip," I whispered to myself, rubbing my fingers along my brow. This nostalgia was nothing more than a knee-jerk reaction, residual emotion from my trip back to that fucking town. It always took me a few days to shake off the memories, to focus on the present, to forget about the past that haunted me so spectacularly.

And Gray.

It was always a kick in the stomach to see him, especially after a long span apart. Even though my head knew it was a mistake to give him an inch, my body always had other plans, wanting to be as close to him as humanly possible. And even though he graced my television screen often, seeing him in real life was a completely different story.

Being the sole focus of those steel eyes was like being pulled underwater, helpless to resist the call of the depths.

And that wasn't to speak about the rest of him. The man had been finely honed through years of hard work, baseball consuming his entire world since we were in high school. His tall frame was packed with muscles, every inch of him a finely tuned machine. I knew how dedicated Gray was to his craft, spending as much time in the gym as he did on the baseball field.

My office phone blared on my desk, and I was grateful for the reprieve. I needed to get my thoughts as far away from Gray as possible. But when I saw my boss' assistant on the other side of the line, I internally swore. Lifting the phone, I rested it between my shoulder and ear. "Hey, Teresa."

"Hey, Devyn. Mr. Turner would like to see you in his office."

"I'm just working on the Masters brief right now. Can it wait?"

She sucked in a sharp breath. "I don't think that's a good idea. He was very insistent you get up here as soon as possible."

That was her polite way of saying he was already in a foul mood and any stalling on my part would only poke the bear.

"Great," I sighed. "I'll be right up."

As I hung up the phone, I reached into my desk, pulling out a pad of paper from the top drawer. As I rifled through my belongings, I couldn't help but glance at the paper tucked inside the corner, taped so it would never shift and get tossed by accident. With one swipe of my finger along the strip of photos taken on a summer day so long ago, I straightened my back, hoping I could borrow a little strength from my past self.

FIVE

Devyn

FOURTEEN YEARS OLD

"I can't believe you don't have to wear a uniform."

I flicked my fingers along the hangers, trying to understand why Gray wanted to shop here. Usually, he was happy to wear whatever his mom grabbed from him, but over the summer, he'd declared it was time for a new look, trading in his flannel jackets and cargo pants for fitted shirts and jeans that clung to his legs.

So, here we were, spending the final days of our summer vacation at the outlet mall a few towns over. His mom was shopping down the block, so we'd been left to our own devices. The outlet mall was small, with no more than fifty stores crammed within a few-mile radius. Most were way out of our spending limit, but there were a couple that had what Gray was looking for. I didn't need much, considering my new prep school had a strict dress code. In a couple of weeks, I'd be trading in my shorts for a blazer and plaid skirt.

Kill me now.

I found a black lace top and held it up to my chest as I looked into the floor-length mirror. My mom would never let me wear something like this. Even when I wasn't at school, I had little control over my wardrobe. My mother hand-picked all our clothes, ensuring we all fit the mold our stepfather set for us. The three of us had specific roles to play. Laurel was the heir, being primed to take his place one day, I was the serious one, the future lawyer or state senator, and Calla was the precious little princess, being forced into frilly dresses that never suited my carefree sister.

So when Mrs. Anders dropped us at the front door and told us she would be back in a couple hours, I didn't know what to do. Luckily, Gray was at my side, like he had been all summer.

"I don't know," Grayson called out from the dressing room. "We're starting high school. Seems like a good time to change things up." Rustling noises came from the room. I stiffened, trying not to picture what was happening behind the black, gauzy curtain. "Plus, a lot of the guys on the team have been ragging on me about my clothes. I don't want to show up on the first day looking like a loser."

"You're not a loser," I snapped defensively.

"I know, Devy," Grayson said as he shoved the curtain to the side. I started to reply, but my words died on my tongue when he turned around to face the mirror.

Gone was the skinny boy I'd known my whole life. After a summer of playing baseball with the modified team, he'd grown into his body, new muscles emerging that had never been there before. My mouth dried up as I scanned his back. What the hell was going on? Was Gray...*hot*? I shook my head, trying to force the words out of my head.

Despite our rocky history, Gray was my best friend now. He was the one who held my hand when I was scared, the one I called when I missed my dad and couldn't hold back my tears. He'd seen me at my worst, yet he still stuck around, never bothered that I couldn't always keep up the perfect act my family demanded.

It was the best feeling in the world—like popping your head

out of the car window and letting your scream get lost in the wind. It made me feel alive, even when the rest of the world was trying to corral me into a tiny little box.

Gray turned around to face me, breaking me out of my thoughts. "I want a fresh start," he sighed. "I've been stuck with most of these kids since I was in diapers. I want them to see me differently, not..." He shook his head. "Doesn't matter."

I knew what he meant without him finishing his thought. *Not like I'm stupid.* And even though I'd told Grayson it wasn't true, that there were different kinds of intelligence, he never took it to heart. He might have struggled in school, but that didn't change the fact that he was one of the most brilliant people I'd ever met. He understood physics and body mechanics in a way I could never. He could take one look at an engine and figure out how to take it apart and put it back together. It was the kind of life skill I would kill for.

I turned toward the dressing room, propping my hand on my hip. "You know if anyone else talked about you like that, I'd punch them in the throat."

"Oh yeah?" Gray chuckled as he pushed open the door and stepped in front of me. "You gonna have my back, Ace?"

My nose scrunched. "Ace?"

"Yeah," he said; his eyes suddenly darted down to his shoes, and a blush filled his cheeks. At least, I thought it did. By the time he looked up again, it was gone. He shrugged. "Seems fitting, considering how smart you are. We both know you're going to kill it this year."

My cell phone rang in my pocket, and I looked at the screen. My mother's number glided across the front, so I tucked it back into my pocket without opening it. I shook my head, already knowing what she would say. She and my stepfather disapproved of my friendship with Gray, and I had no idea why. David, I could probably guess. The man hated our hometown and almost everyone in it, thinking they were all beneath him. But my mother was a different story. It was like when she married my stepfather, she'd decided to cut out everything from our former life, including the Anders family.

While our parents were no longer friends, Gray and I refused to let that happen to us. I'd already lost enough, and I refused to lose Gray too.

Gray met my far-off look in the mirror, the corner of his mouth ticking up. "You okay back there, Devy?"

"Yeah," I answered, swallowing to push those thoughts away, but the sight in front of me was just as distracting. It took a significant amount of effort not to drool over this new look, especially with his signature long hair tied in a bun at the base of his neck. Just once, I wanted to run my fingers through it, to feel what it would be like to have all Gray's attention. But instead of saying anything more, I just cleared my throat and shook my head. "Just think this is a very different look for you."

"Too much?" Grayson asked, turning around to face me. His hand slid down the front of his shirt, accentuating the muscles in his forearms. Was that a thing? I wouldn't really know. Honestly, most of the boys in my school were fellow trust fund brats, more obsessed with their clout than their muscles. The only thing they regularly flexed were their mouths. But Gray was always different from that world, more down-to-earth and centered. Maybe that would change as we started high school, but I wanted to hold onto that feeling for as long as possible.

"No," I said, looking up to meet his steely eyes. "Not bad, Grayson."

He rolled his eyes, taking a step away from me. "Told you not to call me that, Devy."

I chuckled as he tucked back into the dressing room, tossing the shirt over the door. I closed my eyes, trying not to picture what was on the other side. "It's only fair. You've gotten away with far too many Devys today. You're lucky I'm distracted."

"What's got you so distracted?"

"It's nothing."

Gray emerged from the dressing room and stepped into my space. He looked down at me and arched his brow. It was ridiculous, but I was unable to lie to him, even when I wanted to. I flinched, stepping away to catch my breath. It was hard to focus with Gray so close. "Besides the usual stuff with my mom and David? There's this kid back home who has been bothering me, and he got my cell number." I pulled my phone out of my pocket and showed him the messages. "He keeps texting me that I should smile more. It's annoying."

Gray rolled his eyes as he thumbed through the messages. "He's hitting on you."

"By being a dick?"

"Yup," Gray enunciated. "Some guys think that's the best way to get a girl's attention."

"That's stupid." I took my phone back out of his hand. "And it's not even true. He just likes to get under my skin. He did it all last year too. He would see me in the halls at school and yell at me to smile."

"Want me to talk to him?"

I snorted as I turned to walk away. "I don't need you to fight my battles, Gray. I'm perfectly capable of handling one jerk."

But before I could get too far, Gray caught my elbow, pulling me back toward him. "I know you don't need my help, Ace, but I've got your back, just like you have mine. No one messes with you and gets away with it." He smiled down at me. "Besides, I like that you don't smile too much."

I glared at him. "Why is that?"

"Because when you smile at me, I know you mean it. It's like you're saving them all for me."

Later that night, I snuck back into the hotel, taking the service elevator up to our apartment on the top floor. My family had owned the Isadora Hotel for over a hundred years. It sat on an island in the middle of Saint Stephen's Lake, only accessible by twin bridges on the north and south sides. When my great-grandfather first opened its doors, it had only ten rooms and a small lobby. Now, over a hundred years later, it was a massive compound, complete with several guest houses all over the property.

When we lived in Saint Stephen's Lake full time, my parents always talked about buying a home away from the hotel but never got around to it. Secretly, I was glad. People often gave me weird looks when they found out we lived here, but I loved it. It was like being a part of history. There were so many secrets hidden in these walls, and my sisters and I loved trying to discover them all.

But like everything else in my life, that all changed when my mother married David. Then, she decided we would move into his penthouse in Manhattan full time. Although we only came up for long weekends and summer vacation, my grandfather kept the apartment so we could come back to it anytime we wanted.

I pushed the back entrance of the apartment open into the kitchen. No lights were on—usually a good sign that the rest of my family was fast asleep. I was in no mood to deal with my mom tonight. Today had been too good, and I wanted to hold on to this feeling a little longer.

But it died a little as I passed the calendar hanging on the wall, our first day of school circled in dark red ink. I wasn't ready to even think about that, much less hear another lecture about my future. My mom and David were already putting so much pressure on me, wanting to make sure I was starting high school off on the right foot. Where most kids got four years to figure out their future, mine was already clearly carved, and anything else wouldn't be tolerated. But even though I knew it was a pipe dream, I still hoarded brochures for art school under my bed, counting down the days until I could apply and get out of this place.

I'd only gotten a couple of feet into the main part of our apartment when a throat cleared behind me. My insides instantly churned. As I turned, I met my stepfather's disapproving gaze.

Even though my mother married David last year, the man was practically a stranger. The only thing I knew about him was that he was cold and stubborn, demanding perfection from all of us. I'd gotten better about biting my tongue, but it was hard to be in the same room as him. The only good thing was that he hated coming up here, so usually, the lake was our refuge.

But this time, he'd decided to tag along, and I had no idea why. He'd barricaded himself in the office, only coming out to bark orders if we got too loud. Luckily, I'd managed to avoid him for most of the trip. Now, my luck seemed to have run out.

He glanced down at his watch, arching one of his thick brows. To the rest of the world, David might have been handsome once. He had classic American looks, like the son of a politician. But beneath the perfectly coiffed dark blond hair and cold blue eyes was someone obsessed with power and influence.

"Where were you?"

"With some friends," I said, trying to keep my voice calm. Out of all the girls, I had the most difficulty holding back my tongue, especially around David. Maybe I should have had more fear of the man who controlled my fate, but I wasn't wired that way. The more he tried to force me under his thumb, the more I fought back, acting the part in public but plotting behind the scenes.

David's eyes narrowed. "Your mother was worried."

I couldn't help but scoff. My mother knew better than to worry about me, especially up here. She trusted this town and knew nothing would happen to us. The other residents looked after each other, not like in the city, where your neighbors barely knew your name.

David moved to the side, opening the door to the study off the main living area. "We need to talk, Devyn."

I glanced down the hall, wondering if I could get to the exit before he caught me, but it would just be delaying the inevitable. It wasn't like I could avoid him forever, no matter how much I wanted to. I followed him inside the office, trying not to look around the room.

For so long, this was my dad's. He'd rented a little space downtown, but I'd never been there, mostly because he only used it to meet with clients. Everything else was done within these four walls. We'd be able to hear him all hours of the night, rehearsing his opening arguments for court.

When I was little, I'd hide in here and watch him work, laughing when he found me after a couple of minutes. He'd plop me in his lap and explain what he was doing, at least the broad strokes.

And now, this room, his legacy, was being systematically dismantled by the exact type of man he hated—the kind of man who would eviscerate anything in his path as long as his bottom line increased.

His stepdaughters included.

As I settled in the chair across from the desk, David cleared his throat. "Your mother tells me you've been spending a lot of time with the Anders boy."

"Gray?" I snapped, daring to look up at him. "Of course I am. He's my best friend."

"Is that it?"

My fingers dug into the thick maroon leather on the chair's arms. "Not that it's any of your business, but yes. We're just friends."

"Good," David settled into the large wingback chair behind the desk. "And this should go without saying, but it needs to stay that way. Under no circumstances will I allow you to get involved with someone of his caliber."

"Excuse me?"

David interlocked his fingers and leaned forward. "Make no mistake, Devyn. Your last name might be Winters, but you represent *me*. And with that comes certain expectations, including who you spend your time with." He pushed out a breath. "I understand you are getting to the age when you might look for companionship. Who you chose sends a message." He shoved his pointer finger into the top of the desk. "And it will be someone your mother and I approve of, is that understood?"

"You've got to be kidding me," I scoffed, unable to hold back a moment longer. My nails dug into the palm of my hand, sure to leave deep crescent-shaped marks later. But I could barely feel it, not when all my anger was aimed at David. "You've already dropped me into the school of your choice, I'm taking the classes you want me to take. And now you want to approve of the people I date?" I stood, turning my back to him. "Fuck you, David."

The words were barely out of my mouth when I felt something at my back, causing me to collide with the heavy wooden door. My face ricocheted off it, and I stumbled to the ground, my back resting against the bookshelf. As I looked around, trying to make sense of what happened, I could feel my face throbbing. I reached up and touched my nose. When I pulled my hand back, thick red liquid coated my fingers, and I stared at it in disbelief. "You..." I said, unable to get the words fully out as I looked down at my blood. "You..."

"Don't be ridiculous," David said from his desk. But he made no move to help me, not even phased by the blood. "You tripped on the edge of the rug. You really should be more careful, Devyn. Never know what could happen to you or those you care about."

As his words sunk in, my brain finally registered the pain. It radiated through my nose into my cheekbones. Shit, I really hoped I didn't break anything. But that was my secondary concern, too focused on his threatening tone.

I swallowed hard, ignoring the coppery taste at the back of my throat. "What are you saying?"

He sighed, giving me an annoyed stare, like my question was inconveniencing him. "You're a smart girl. I think you can figure it out."

With that, he exited the office, not sparing a single glance to check if I was okay. As I heard the door to his bedroom open and close, I sank down to the carpet, wrapping my arms around my legs.

David was an asshole, but he'd never laid a hand on any of us before. He dealt more in veiled threats. Once, when I dared to stand up to him at a company event, he mentioned he hated getting his hands dirty but had plenty of people who'd be willing to do it for him. Despite his words, I'd never really feared what he was capable of, not until right now.

"Or those you care about."

I almost vomited on his carpet. David's threat against me was bad enough, but to know he'd go after those I cared about to silence me? That was enough to make me purge my dinner.

And as much as I hated it, David's words had their desired effect. Calla and Gray were the two most important people in my life, and I'd do anything to make sure they were safe. When my little sister was a baby, my dad made me promise I would look after Calla. Even if I hadn't, I would *always* put her first.

But the idea of cutting Gray out of my life was worse than the alternative. Being without my best friend would be like walking around with only half of me. I needed him. I didn't think as I stood, needing to get out of the apartment to the only place that felt safe right now.

I ran right to Gray.

SIX

"We're letting you go."

My entire body froze as I stared across the broad, dark wooden table, meeting the blank gazes of the senior partners. The table was a clear line in the sand, separating them from me: the five men on one side, me, a lowly associate, on the other.

In the center was a man I knew all too well. Collin Turner, the firm's managing partner. He was younger than the others, with a charming smile and a full head of dark blond hair. He looked like the golden boy of legal ethics, the kind of person you would be glad to have on your team. When I first got the call about coming to work for him, I was thrilled, in complete disbelief my name had been plucked out of obscurity to land me an interview at one of the best corporate law firms in New York.

However, like too many things in my life, as time went on, it was clear the job came with golden handcuffs. But considering I was straight out of law school, I didn't think twice, for the sake of my burgeoning career.

As I stared blankly into Collin's eyes, the men at his sides started to shift in their seats. I knew all of them in passing, but few had bothered ever to learn my name. They looked like carbon copies of each other, all the same in a long line of stern, old white men who hated change and hated those who tried to implement it under their noses.

Awkward tension hung between us, and I knew it was useless to fight. My fate was sealed. None of these men would ever advocate for me, but I also never thought they'd bring the axe down on the back of my neck.

Fired. I was fucking getting *fired.* Years of hard work, sleepless nights, and ridiculous hours, and it was about to all be for nothing.

With my career officially in the toilet, I did the only thing I could think of.

I laughed, not caring about the uncomfortable stares and mutters about another unhinged woman. My cackle echoed off the walls of their stale, musty boardroom, ricocheting off the glass awards and pictures of million-dollar clients. By the time my gaze met theirs, I was near hysterical, and all I could do was push out the words, "Are you fucking kidding me?"

"That language is not necessary, Miss Winters," Cutler, one of the oldest partners, scoffed from the side of the table.

"Oh, it is necessary," I bit back. "I've been killing myself for years around here, and now you're going to fire me? For what?" I shifted forward in my chair. "Because if you don't have cause—"

"Jack Fischer."

My throat went dry when my ex's name left his lips. It was a shock, although it really shouldn't have been. There were no secrets in this city, not in the small group of people who ran in elite circles. Even with millions of people calling New York home, top echelons inevitably watched each other's backs.

Jack Fischer was a mistake I don't think I'd ever live down, a guy I'd hooked up with a couple of times when I was feeling low and lonely. I thought he was harmless enough, considering I'd met him through my brother-in-law, Theo. However, Jack had been plotting behind his back to take Theo's job and hurt my sister in the process. To me, that was unforgivable, so when Theo approached me about getting some revenge, I dove in without a second thought. It was stupid and short-sighted, but there was nothing I wouldn't do to protect my sister. But I never thought it would get me fired.

How did they even know about Jack? There wasn't any connection to the firm, and I'd been as careful as I could be. Hearing his name rattled me to my core, but I refused to let it show. Instead, I gripped the bottom part of my chair so hard, I was sure my nails were bleeding.

Collin studied my face, watching for any cracks in my impenetrable veneer. Just a few more minutes, and I could snap in private, take all my rage out on his shiny, stupid office.

When I refused to speak, he leaned in closer. "We have a complaint from Mr. Fischer saying you misrepresented yourself to some of his clients, convinced them his agency was under investigation for fraud and other ethical problems. And now, because of your actions, he is threatening to bring a suit against our entire firm."

"I—" My words died in my throat, knowing there wasn't much I could say. After all, almost everything Collin said was true. But while I might have toed the line, at the end of the day, I was still a damn good lawyer, which meant I had enough brains to make sure there wasn't any incriminating evidence to connect me to Jack's clients. Nothing in writing, no phone calls that could have been recorded. There wasn't a single shred of evidence. At least, nothing that would hold up in court.

But none of that mattered in this room, not with these men. Because the loyalty in their blood only extended to their bank accounts, and they would never understand why I would be willing to give up so much to defend my sister's honor.

I sat back in my seat, and the rage left my body as acceptance took its place. The men behind the desk looked at me like I was a ticking time bomb, someone on the verge of an emotional breakdown, as opposed to a lawyer who should have earned their respect over years of service. And while I might have messed with a line I had no business crossing, the same could be said for any of my associates. I knew plenty from lurking in their files—knew all too well how many ethical and moral lines they had danced around like they were nothing.

"You were never going to promote me, were you?" I finally asked after a long stretch of silence. I knew the answer, but I needed to see their faces, needed to know I had wasted years tolling away behind a desk under the guise of ambition.

Collin leaned forward to greet my eyes, almost as if enjoying this moment. "Give us a moment, please, gentlemen," he said without ever breaking his stare.

As the door slammed closed, his eyes almost twinkled. "C'mon, Dev, you knew what this was. Don't act like you're surprised now that you're no longer under his protection."

My blood reignited as I stared at him. My stepfather's face flashed in my mind, and it was almost enough to knock the wind out of my lungs. I should have known this moment was coming, should have realized it from the moment I discovered the real reason I was chosen for the open position years ago.

Like I said—the elite circles in New York consisted of a small group of men, and at the center? That would be my now-former stepfather.

Foolishly, it had taken me six months to realize this job was hand-picked for me. David had a deep connection to the firm and used them to get me a job where he could keep an eye on me. I should have looked closer at the partners before taking the job, maybe wondering why they wanted someone so green to join their firm. But I didn't question it, too thankful to have a job in this competitive market to think twice. It wasn't until I overheard a conversation at my family's Christmas party between David and Collin, my now former boss, that it clicked. As they joked about me, my heart dashed into a million pieces, knowing I was nothing more than a pawn.

Ever since that moment, I'd vowed I would be the best damn lawyer ever to walk their halls, all while looking for ways to destroy the men who preyed on people like me. For years, I'd managed to do both, often hiding my side investigations under the guise of my work. But the answers I sought were still out of reach, inaccessible to someone outside the inner sanctum. I was hoping if I made partner, those doors would open, but now, I'd never know.

Looking over at Collin, I searched for the man who first interviewed me, the man who talked about his passion for the law, who wanted to ensure we were protecting people's dreams. Now, I would love to think I would be able to see through his bullshit, but at the time, I ate it up. I wanted to help shape this city, help shape the world. After all, I had already sold my soul to have this career, so I might as well make it the best version I possibly could.

There was no hint of that man now.

Gone was the charismatic man who charmed clients and crowds alike. Instead, I saw the snake lurking underneath, the one far too aligned with my stepfather's goals to have an ounce of my trust.

I shook my head as I stood. "And what? Now that he's no longer married to my mother, David has to find other ways to exert control over my life?" I pointed my finger at Collin's face. "You can claim this is because of Jack's bullshit threat, but we both know it's because David owns you."

"Maybe," Collin chuckled as he leaned back in his seat. "It's better to be on his side than be one of his targets. And you've made one too many mistakes, Devyn. Did you really think he was going to sit back and let you ruin him?"

I stilled as I stared at him, afraid to blink in case he tried something. But instead, Collin just stood, smoothing his hand over his jacket. "Good luck, Devyn. Something tells me you're going to need it."

SEVEN

Grayson

Ping.

The ball made a sharp, high-pitched noise as it collided with my aluminum bat. It was a different sound than I was used to, but not unwelcome. After playing with a wooden bat for years, it felt appropriate, another echo of how my life has changed.

But luckily, some things hadn't. The way my body moved, the way my arms swung, how the ball felt when it hit my bat, going 60 miles an hour. There was nothing else on my mind; everything was blank, and all I focused on was that little white ball colliding through space.

I swung the bat back over my shoulder, waiting for the next ball to roll through the machine. Thank God time hadn't changed the old batting cages.

Pete's Hideaway was another local legend, a pirate-themed adventure track tied into the mini-golf course across the street. It had definitely seen better days, but the owners were getting older and not putting as much money into maintenance as they used to. Technically, they were closed for the winter, but the owners knew me and let me come and hit a couple of balls whenever I felt restless, which had been happening more often than not lately.

Luckily, the temperatures had gotten a little warmer over the past few days. Even though it was barely fifty degrees, it was practically a heat wave after the long and draining winter. Almost everyone in town was out and about, taking full advantage of the warmer temperatures. In upstate New York, you never knew what the weather might be like during these transitional months. One week might be warm and sunny, and you could have a snowstorm the next. Mother Nature was a fickle bitch.

My ball slammed into the back mat of the batting cage, and I couldn't help but smile. This was what I missed from Saint Stephen's Lake: the memories of growing up, of days spent in the same cage, working on my swing before a big game. I came here almost every night in high school— nights where things were too much, too loud, too chaotic. It was the only place that could calm my racing thoughts. And now, on one of the most challenging days of my life, *the most challenging period of my life*, it was once again my quiet little hideaway.

From the cage next to me, Cole looked over, arching his brow at my last hit. When I called him earlier to say I needed to clear my head, he didn't question me, didn't even think twice about joining me, despite the dropping temperatures. Alex, Cole's wife, offered to keep my mom and dad occupied while we were out. I was beyond grateful, knowing my mom could use the distraction. After our doctor's appointment this morning, she was processing the best she could, probably knee-deep in flour, determined to help Alex conquer her fear of baking.

I wanted to be there for her, but I couldn't, not while I was sorting out my own shit. It didn't help that we weren't seeing eye to eye on my dad's treatment plan. It would be good for both of us to take some space before we tried to talk about it again.

A sharp curse came from the cage next to me, pulling me back into the present.

"You good over there?" I asked, smirking as I lined up my bat for another hit.

"Don't know how the hell you do that," Cole said, shaking his head. "Especially right now. My hands are shaking too much to connect."

"Spent a lot of time in these cages," I answered, keeping my eye on the ball.

Cole just chuckled, mimicking my stance. That was why I called Cole; he understood my need for quiet. When I first came back home, it was jarring to see new people in the house next to ours. My entire childhood, that house had sat empty, just waiting for someone to find it and bring it back to life. Now, it looked like a home, complete with sunflowers during the summer and a bright blue door. But Alex and Cole were good neighbors and had become even better friends over the past few months.

They were practically family at this point, especially Alex. My mom loved having a girl to spoil and teach her ways. My dad loved having someone else who he'd show around this toolbox.

While Alex and I were friendly, I was closer to her husband. Cole and I had formed an instant kinship, a way of understanding each other without so many words. We were both quiet, both considered grumpy, and both preferred silence over the noise of a crowd. It helped when I needed to just exist without someone asking me a million questions about how I was feeling or what I wanted.

"So," Cole said between hits of his bat. "You gonna tell me why I'm freezing my balls off out here, or you gonna keep brooding over there all day?"

"Don't know," I said, shrugging my shoulders. "Kinda just felt like hitting something."

Cole sighed and resumed his swing, letting go of his question. As much as I felt bad for shutting him out, Cole understood and knew that I was a fort when it came to tough topics. If I didn't want to talk, I wasn't going to—just another thing we had in common.

But after this morning's doctor's visit, which my mom and I have been dreading all week, I need to get the words off my chest. And maybe, for once, it wouldn't be the worst idea to keep all my fears buried down deep.

"It's my dad," I finally said. In the corner of my eye, I saw Cole put down the bat and move over to the side of the cage. He stood there but didn't say anything, allowing me to continue my thoughts. "He's having a hard time. Doc says he's got about six months until he's going to need to have full-time help", I finally admit. "Six months left until he's probably going to have to live in an assisted living facility."

"Shit," Cole hissed. "I'm sorry, man. We had no idea it was progressing this quickly." He ran his hand over his face. "What about having someone come out to the house? Live in nurse?"

I shook my head, "My mom's not comfortable with that. But at the same time, the idea of putting him into a home makes her cry. So I'm kind of stuck. I don't really know what to do. "

"I'm sorry, man," Cole said, scuffing his feet along the turf. "I thought he was doing okay."

"He is," I said. "Most days. But the good days are becoming fewer and further between. And he's having a harder time keeping his memories straight. Last night, he thought I was in high school, fully convinced that he missed one of my baseball games. The doctor wants us to consider our options but also urged us to think fast. There's no telling what might happen when he declines more."

"What do you mean?"

This part was the most difficult to say out loud, so I kept it to myself. Even though the doctor never said it outright, I could pick up his insinuations. He was afraid for my mom. My dad was a big man. Even as he got further into his sixties, he was well over 6 feet and over 250 pounds of packed muscle. My mom was a waif of a woman, barely reaching his chin. If something was to happen, there was no way she'd ever be able to get him to safety or, god forbid, subdue him.

In his right mind, we all knew that my father would rather harm himself than ever put my mother in danger. But that was the thing. When he woke up in the middle of the night, he didn't recognize any of us. It was hard enough getting him to calm down when I was in the room, and I had him by a couple of inches. While I had to trust that my father would never hurt my mom, accidents happened every day.

Just the thought seemed ridiculous. And even though I knew it was wishful thinking, I couldn't imagine that no disease, no matter how dangerous it might be, would ever come between them. At the same time, I wasn't a doctor. I didn't know about timelines or disease progressions, or anything other than what I'd read online. I could only speak for my own lived experiences.

But I keep all that to myself, not wanting to burden Cole with all of my anxieties. I'd already shared more with him than I had anyone else in my life.

There were only three people in town who really knew about my father's sickness outside of our family. Well, six, if you counted their wives and girlfriends, because my friends could not keep any secrets from them.

Theo was the first one I told. It was the morning after Cole and Alex's engagement party, the day after I found my dad wandering through town with no memory of who I was. He'd said he was going to the bathroom, and none of us thought anything of it. Not until twenty minutes later, when we still couldn't find him. I spent hours driving down each road, fearing the worst. Eventually, I saw him sitting on a bench on Main Street. But the moment I approached, I knew something was horribly wrong.

After I drove him home and got him to bed, my mom broke down and told me about the diagnosis. She was trying to hide it from me until I had gone back home and was back in my routine. But from the moment I saw my father's scared and frantic face, I knew that my life would never be the same. I knew that I could never walk away and live with myself. Could never live with the guilt if I left my dad when he needed me the most.

So, without thinking, without hesitation, I went to Theo, who had only been my agent for a handful of months at the time, and told him I needed out of my contract. If I had any doubts about the guy before, that moment silenced them. He didn't ask questions, didn't need to know why, and didn't do anything other than be a sounding board for my fears and worries.

And all he said after I rambled on for an hour about my father and the treatment plans and everything else was that he would take care of it. That was all. But the next week, I was out of my contract, back in town, and living in the apartment above my parents' garage. It's not where I saw myself on the cusp of 30, but it's where I needed to be.

I glanced over my shoulder at Cole, making sure he was still there. He was there, a silent sentinel watching me, making sure I wasn't going to fall.

"I don't know what to do," I said quietly.

"We'll figure it out," Cole said. "Whatever you guys need, you know we'll all be there for you."

I had no doubts about that. They'd all been there for my

family since the moment I told all my friends about our deepest, darkest secret. I'd sworn them to secrecy because my mom wanted to deal with my father's illness privately, and I knew that they would keep it safe. They were great, constantly checking in on my mom and making sure she was okay. They also went out of their way to spend time with my dad, making sure that they filled his days with as much love and laughter as possible. They were incredibly patient, especially Alex and Cole, even on the days when it took a while for him to recognize their faces.

Even though these people would never give my family by blood, that moment alone had cemented their role in my life. There was nothing more I wanted but to make my dad's diagnosis disappear. Without that as a possibility, all I could ask for were good people in his corner, making sure he was supported for the rest of his days.

And my friends, *my new family*, had stepped up for that.

"Appreciate it," I huffed, toying with the bat in my hands. "I've got to talk to my mom. See what she wants to do next."

"But what do you think?" Cole said.

"I don't want to give up yet. I know that there's no cure, but there has to be something, anything, to give him more time. My dad's a fighter, and he would never want us to sit back and watch him deteriorate."

Cole scratched the back of his head, "What about one of those trial things?"

"Clinical trials?" He nodded. "There's a couple for early onset Alzheimer's. One of the most promising ones is down in New York, so I've been talking to some of the doctors down there. Problem is, it takes months to get an open spot. Some of them take even years."

I sighed with annoyance, knowing how many hours of my life I'd wasted looking at different trials, hoping for a miracle.

There were several that claimed they could heal him for a sizeable fee, but all of those weren't linked to reputable hospitals.

His best bet was in New York City, a trial at one of the best hospitals in the country. But the selection process was complex, and it was hard to get into. Not only was it costly, which I had covered thanks to my baseball career, but it was very, very hard to even get into the doctors.

Maybe if I had an in at the hospital, I could manage to get him into the trial. Unfortunately, I didn't know any of them. I was just nobody, a name in the crowd. And while most people might recognize my name from my baseball career, it didn't help me with this. In the world of New York's elite, people lived or died by their last names and their family connections. It was a hard club to break into and something as fickle as a sports career that would never open the doors I needed.

"Maybe," I said. "We're meeting with the doctor again next week to go over his latest scans, so maybe he'll have some more options for us."

As the machine wound down with a sad, whirring sound, I placed the bat back in my bag and left the cage. Cole met me on the other side, handing me back his bat as well. But as I stood up straighter, he clapped me on the back.

"You know, whatever you need, Alex and I are here with you. All of us. We're all in your corner. "

"I know that," I said quietly. "Means more than you know."

EIGHT

Grayson

FIFTEEN YEARS OLD

"Are you serious, Grayson?"

I turned my head from my spot on the dock, twisting to see my best friend heading my way. Her hands were clenched at her side as she stomped toward us. Her blonde ponytail swung happily with each step, a stark contrast to the look on her face.

"Oh, shit." Wade, my other best friend, smirked from my side. "You're in trouble now, Anders."

If you could've felt my heartbeat, you would have thought the same. But the fire in Devyn's eyes only made me smile, loving she let me see underneath her usual mask. It'd been up too much this past year, settling in almost permanently after she'd showed up at my house in the middle of the night last summer, claiming she'd walked into a door.

I knew it was a lie, knew it as much as I knew my name. But no matter how much I tried to push her, she refused to tell me what really happened. All Devyn wanted was a safe place to land, and she'd come to me.

After that night, I thought we'd be closer than ever, but it was the opposite. Ever since she went back to the city at the start of the school year, she'd started to pull away. We usually talked every day. Now, I was lucky to get her on the phone once a week. If I did manage to get a hold of her, our conversations were tense and brief.

At least things seemed to get better after she came back into town this summer. We spent almost every day together, laughing and hanging out like we used to. But I could tell Devyn was holding something back, like there was a wall she'd built to keep me out. I hated she felt like she had to hide anything from me.

But there wasn't any hiding right now—she was pissed. She stomped toward me, her pale top practically glowing against her tanned skin. It was a big point of contention between us. Because of my background, I tanned easily, soaking up the summer rays as quickly as I could. Devyn was the opposite. She'd go from pale to burnt, then, after a lengthy healing period, back to pale. But the last month on this very dock had finally given her some lasting color, and I hated how much I liked it.

She stepped up to the edge of my blanket, and I had to grip the edge to keep from reaching for her. When the fuck had that started? We'd always pushed and teased each other, but lately, I'd wanted more, things I shouldn't want to do with my best friend.

She arched a brow at me, oblivious to my turmoil. "I am going to kill you. You left me to fend for myself against Mrs. Dorset. You know she wanted you to be the one to drop off her lunch."

"Because she's always insisting I stay," I chuckled, rising onto my elbows to smile at Devyn. She'd started picking up shifts at the Lost Tavern this summer, and despite her initial fears, she was doing a great job. Still, there was a part of her that was holding back, relying on me to deal with any complaints or questions. That wouldn't do. I wanted her to feel confident. "You can handle her, Devy."

She tried to hide her smile, but the edge of her lips ticked up. "I hate you."

Wade chuckled, dropping his sunglasses back down to cover his eyes. "You fucked up this time, Anders. She's going to kill you."

"Nah," I said, smiling to meet Devyn's frown. "She loves me too much to stay mad at me."

As the words came out, anxiety crawled into my chest. Maybe love was the wrong thing to say, especially as we navigated this new normal. I waited for her to freeze, to change the subject, but she just smirked at me.

"You're testing that theory."

I hated how relieved that made me. Just hearing Devyn tease me was a welcome surprise, making me think we'd get back what we once had.

I forced myself to move, shifting so I could face Devyn fully. I leaned back on my haunches so she could see the sincerity in my eyes. "I'm sorry, Ace. I knew if I went with you, all the customers would look to me for answers." I smiled up at her. "I want them to see you as someone capable, someone with authority. And I meant what I said; I knew you could handle it."

Devyn stared at me, her hands plastered to her hips. Her fingertips tapped along the pockets, bringing my eyes down to check out her outfit better. Her denim shorts ended only a couple of inches below her hands, cut shorter than anything I'd seen her wear before. She wore a billowy white shirt over them, covering up the bikini shining through the opaque fabric—just enough of that bright blue color to tease what was hiding underneath.

Fuck. I needed to get it together. This was *Devyn*, my closest friend, practically a sister to me. At least, that was what everyone else always assumed. We'd grown up together, so people thought we were like siblings, but I'd never felt that way toward her. Friends? Hell yes. She was my best friend in the world.

Now, I was picturing so much more than friendship. This summer had been painful. It was hot, even more than usual, so we spent most of our time at the dock and in the water. Almost every day, Devyn wore some bikini that left little to the imagination. While I tried my best not to be a creep and check her out, I couldn't help it. Her body had changed over the past couple of years and was softer, more feminine. Her long legs led to some serious curves, the kind I had no right noticing. But it was impossible to look away, and every day, the urge to touch her became stronger and stronger.

"Gray!" Devyn snapped, nudging me on the shoulder. "Have you heard a single word I said?"

"Sorry," I chuckled. "Didn't get a lot of sleep last night."

She rolled her eyes. "Let me guess; you were up until 2 am trying to perfect your fastball?"

"Not 2 am," I grumbled. Devyn arched a brow. "Only midnight."

Wade hissed a curse under his breath as he stood and started grabbing his gear. "I'm gonna get out of here before she tosses you in the lake, Anders." He started walking away but stopped when he got close to Devyn. He smiled brightly at her, and for a moment, I forgot we'd been friends almost as long as Devyn and me. I practically snarled when he said, "You're looking good, city girl. Maybe you want to watch the fireworks with me later?"

"She's gonna be with me," I snapped, tempted to shove my other best friend's head underwater and hold it there.

Devyn blushed, ignoring my words. She tucked a piece of hair behind her ear and said, "It's kind of our thing." She looked over at me, chewing on her bottom lip. "But maybe you could come hang out with us. We always watch from the cove behind Guardian's Beach."

"Yeah?" Wade asked. "I'd like that. I'll see you there, Devy."

"Don't call her that," I muttered, ignoring the glare Devyn sent my way. "She hates it."

Devyn settled next to me, stealing Wade's place. She sighed as the sun hit her face, stretching out like a content kitten. "What was that about?"

I shrugged. "I didn't like how he was talking to you."

"Because he was being nice?" Devyn smirked at me. "The horror."

"He wasn't just being nice," I grumbled, rubbing my hand over my face. "Sorry, I'm exhausted, and it's making me more of a dick than usual."

"You should have called me," Devyn said as she reached out to take my hand. "I hate the idea of you being out there alone. Besides, you know I'll take any excuse to escape from Hotel Hell."

I turned to stare at her, noticing the dark circles under her eyes. "David still giving you a hard time?"

"It's fine. I can handle it."

As Devyn tried to turn away, I held her hand a little tighter, keeping her close to me. "You can trust me, Ace."

Her brown eyes sparkled as they searched mine. "I know that."

"Then talk to me," I insisted. "I know something's going on with David, and I hate that you're dealing with this on your own. So talk to me. Let me help."

Devyn stared at me for a long minute, then her gaze dropped down to her hands. "I don't know what to do. For a long time, I thought he just wanted to break my spirit, and that was hard enough. But now, David's turning his attention on Calla." She flipped onto her back and stared up at the sky. "I was willing to take the brunt of it to make sure he left her alone. He keeps threatening to send her away to boarding school, and I swear, if he does, that's it. I'm running away and never looking back."

"Not alone." I squeezed her hand. "I'm coming with you."

"Your mom and dad would kill you if you tried to leave," she said as she tilted her head toward me with a sad smile. "Besides, you have so many good things going on. You're not giving up baseball because my stepdad's an asshole."

"Hey," I said. "You and me versus the world, right? That means you leave, I leave."

Devyn's eyes searched mine, and I held my breath. Something twisted in my chest, cementing our bond without another word. Over the past couple of years, I knew we'd gotten close, but I never realized how much she meant to me until right now. If she asked me to leave, I'd go without a second of hesitation. Sure, life would suck for a while, but it was still a better option than staying here without her.

Devyn's eyes watered for a moment before she pushed toward me, wrapping her arms around my neck. She held me close and whispered, "You and me, Gray?"

"Always."

THE ANNUAL FOURTH of July celebration was a staple in Saint Stephen's Lake. It was held every single year, no matter the weather. My dad liked to tell a story from twenty years ago, when a strong hurricane sent heavy winds and hail our way. The town came together in the high school gym, refusing to let the year pass without their annual tradition.

While I loved the carnival and all the other events of the day, my favorite part was always the fireworks. Devyn and I found the best view years ago, watching the whole show from a small cove on the east end of the lake. It was hidden, far from the usual beaches and sights the tourists crowded every year. Ever since our parents decided we were old enough to go off on our own, we'd watched here—only the two of us.

Until tonight.

I glowered at my two best friends huddled together on a log. Wade said something, and Devyn threw her head back and laughed. The sound was like an anvil to my chest. As much as I wanted to watch the fireworks, I was too busy watching them like some creep. I swore, if Wade touched her without her permission, I'd—

"Wow. If that's how you look at your friends, I'd hate to be your enemy."

My head turned to the chair next to me, finding Calla draped over it, twirling a Twizzler in her hands. Devyn's little sister was only a year younger than us, and the girls were as close as they could be. I almost felt bad for their older sister, Laurel, who always seemed to be the odd man out. But there was something about Calla and Devyn, a bond that no one else could replicate.

Despite their closeness, the girls were as different as they could be. Devyn was shy, her words quiet but also cutting. Calla was one of the kindest people I'd ever met, always willing to go above and beyond for anyone. Where Devyn played her cards close to the chest, Calla was an open book.

Her auburn hair was tied in a ponytail and secured with a red, white, and blue ribbon. She was wearing a similar outfit to Devyn's but traded in the black top Devyn favored for one in a vibrant red. Just like her sister, Calla had grown up a lot this past year, looking more and more beautiful every day. And maybe, in another life, she'd be the girl I wanted.

But no, I was too busy fixating on my best friend, the one

who had been pushing me away for months, who now had blown off our most sacred tradition to hang out with Wade.

Calla smirked and pointed the candy at me. "That face. Right there. Damn, Gray. I honestly didn't know you had it in you."

I scrubbed my hand over my face. "I'm not trying to. I just don't get it." When did they start spending time together? I wanted all the details and none of them at the same time. When Wade asked her to hang out later, I thought it was spontaneous. But now that I saw them together, I wondered if I'd missed something. While I was watching Devyn, maybe Wade was too. Unlike me, though, she seemed to be looking right back at him.

Calla slid her seat closer to me, leaning in conspiratorially. "You know she's had a crush on him for *years*, right?" When I shook my head, she continued. "Yeah, ever since he grew a foot and joined the team. Devyn's got a type."

"What does that mean?"

Calla stared at me then leaned back, shaking her head. "Are you seriously telling me nothing has ever happened between you two? It seems like there's something there, something more than just friends."

I heard Devyn laugh, and once again, my eyes instantly went to her. It was so light, so airy. She sounded happy, and my heart sunk. I was being such a shitty friend. No matter what I felt, at the end of the day, all I really wanted was to see her smile. After everything that happened over the last year, that was all I could ask for. If Wade was the one to make that happen, I should be happy for my best friend.

Maybe that was all we were meant to be. We were friends. *Best* friends. And even if my head was all messed up right now, I knew I always wanted Devyn in my life. I wouldn't risk that because she was the most beautiful girl in the world. I'd rather be her friend than nothing at all. It was enough for me. It would always be enough for me.

I nodded, turning back to Calla. "Yeah, we're just friends. I've never thought of her like that." I cleared my throat. "Plus, Wade's a good guy. Devyn deserves someone like that in her corner."

Calla grimaced. "Good thing you said that, because otherwise…" She nodded behind us. "Otherwise, that might be hard to see."

I knew what had happened before I even shifted. But like a true masochist, I couldn't help but watch as Wade placed his hand on Devyn's neck and pulled her in for a kiss. It was tentative at first, and they jumped apart like they'd been shocked. But after a moment, Devyn leaned forward and kissed him again.

Fresh, burning agony seared through my chest, and I forgot how to breathe. This was ridiculous. Devyn wasn't mine, and I wasn't hers. So why did it hurt so much to see Wade kiss her? I closed my eyes and shook my head. *Friends. We're just friends. Keep saying it until you remember it.*

"Oh man," Calla sighed, dropping her head to her palm. "I want someone to kiss me like that."

Maybe it was because my heart had just been battered—maybe it was because I was too young and dumb to think about my choices—but I leaned over and said, "I can help you with that."

And I pulled her in and pressed my lips to hers.

NINE

Devyn

"What *the hell* happened in here?"

Calla? My eyes flicked open at the sound of my sister's voice, praying this was some sort of alternate dimension. After weeks of missing her, I might have been desperate to see her, but I was hoping it would be once I'd gotten my shit together.

In the two weeks since I was fired, I'd been holed up in my apartment, alternating between obsessing over the files Tomas found and wallowing in the pitiful state of my life. Maybe this was some sort of stress-induced hallucination? But as I shoved up my eye mask from my spot on the couch, it became painfully apparent that was not the case.

Calla's eyes bulged out of her head, and her mouth hung open as she took in my apartment. The last time she was here was right after she moved back upstate, and the place was pristine. There was not a single thing out of place, thanks to my daily maid service and the fact that I spent, at most, three to four hours here each day outside of sleeping.

"Shit," I hissed as I scurried off the couch, banging my knees on the coffee table, which was definitely *not* where it was supposed to be. *I think.* Honestly, at this point, the coffee table could have come to life in the middle of the night, and I would have just shrugged it off. "Calla...what are you doing here?"

"I got nervous. Considering you were calling me fifteen times a day after leaving the lake, it was a little worrisome when you just stopped. We had to be in the city for Theo's PT appointment, so I thought I'd do a welfare check." She shook her head in disbelief. "I should've come sooner."

I looked up at her. "I thought you hated me."

"No," Calla scoffed. "I could never hate you. Don't get me wrong—I'm still super pissed you hid something this major from me. But after everything you did with Jack, I can't stay mad at you." She held up one of the takeout containers, sniffed it, then turned a shade of green. "This is horrifying on so many levels."

"It's fine," I groaned, dropping my head back down to the pillow. As much as I wanted to engulf my sister in a tight hug, moving was not in the cards for me, not when every movement and sliver of light felt like it was a knife straight into my frontal lobe.

Calla shook her head as she reached down, taking my hands and pulling me to stand. "This is anything but fine, Devyn. Like the time you tried to cut your bangs because Donny Watkins called you a nerd bad."

"You're being dramatic." I rolled my eyes. "It's not that bad. It just needs a little...sprucing."

"Devyn..." Calla drawled as she turned around to face me. "We're a couple of takeout containers away from me bringing in the crew from *Hoarders*."

As I looked around my formerly immaculate apartment, I grimaced, hating how right she was. Magazines, junk food, and empty bottles of wine covered my counters. My practically brand new whisk was still tangled in the chandelier above the dining room table, a remnant of my break-out performance on the coffee table last night, where, after several shots of tequila, I convinced myself I was the next iteration of Taylor Swift. Even my couch had transformed into a shapeless pile of blankets, acting as a fort to keep the rest of the world away.

And none of this had anything on my outfit. Calla's nose scrunched again as she looked at me, taking in the mismatched neon knee highs and my RBG classic tee. I'd piled my hair on top of my head in a haphazard bun, held together by a leopard print scrunchy that probably belonged to Calla at some point.

And maybe, in the past, all this would have been a source of great shame for me.

However, on this cold, dreary Tuesday morning, I could not give a single, microscopic fuck.

Usually, at this time, I would have already been at the office for hours, my blurry eyes attempting to read through yet another brief, hoping to impress senior management. As a senior associate, my life was a balancing act. On one side, I had to stay under the radar enough not to earn any of the partners' wrath while also trying to stand out from the crowd. However, with twenty other associates hoping to do the same thing, there was a lot of pressure to stay on top of your game. Too many of my colleagues resorted to back-handed tactics—morals and ethical dilemmas be damned. Those attributes tended to be more of a weakness than an asset in our world. Being a young lawyer is a dog-eat-dog world, and looking at me now, I was definitely yesterday's meal.

"Okay, I totally came down here to chew you out for keeping something so huge from me," Calla sighed. "But clearly, you are in desperate need of an intervention."

"I am *fine*," I insisted, shifting my hair down from the top of my head. Okay, yeah...that's just a little bit crusty. I shook off the thought, throwing it all back up in a bun before she could notice. "I am just enjoying this time of transition, exploring all the new possibilities that await me."

"Are you high?"

"No, Mom," I scoffed. "I am not high. I am...weightless." I shifted past her into the kitchen. If I was going to get a lecture from my baby sister, I was going to need a very, very strong drink. As I dug through my fridge, I continued, "I have been stuck at that fucking bloodsucking law firm for years. And now, for the first time in as long as I can remember, I have nothing to do: no work, no demands, no bullshit commitments. So yeah, maybe I'm taking some time off from my usual self, but is that really so bad?" I snapped my fingers—big mistake. The pounding in my head now resembled a pack of wild horses. I rubbed my eyes, then looked at Calla, a false confidence filling my veins. "Maybe this is the fresh start I needed. Devyn 2.0! The cuddly, friendly version, who shits rainbows and hugs babies."

My sister wrapped her arms around me, and for the first time in days, I felt my body let go of all the weight. I sagged against her, not waiting before squeezing her around the shoulders. It was the kind of embrace you needed when your world was crumbling. We stood there as several silent minutes passed.

"I'm so sorry," Calla eventually whispered, holding me tight to her chest. "I hate that this happened to you because of me."

"I don't," I said, trying to keep my voice strong. "I don't regret what I did, not for one minute." I pulled back, steeling my voice before those traitorous tears tried to force their way out. Never going to happen. I hadn't cried in years, and there was no way this was going to be the thing that broke me.

I leaned away from Calla, hating the pity and empathy in her eyes. I knew she only meant it in the best way. My little sister was literal sunshine wrapped up in a gorgeous package, but right now, when my world felt like it was seconds away from shattering, it was hard to even look at someone so happy.

"I just need a new plan," I said, more to myself than anyone else. "I'm giving myself to the end of the week to wallow in self-pity, and then I'm going to figure it all out."

Calla sighed, looking at me like she wanted nothing more than to push past what I was offering. But knowing out of the two of us, I was the more stubborn one, she relented. "What are you thinking? Do you want to try to find a job at another law firm?"

No. My inner voice answered before I could even get the words out. "I don't think I do," I said quietly, not sure I believed the answer myself. Corporate law, on paper, was perfect for me. No messy trials, minimal emotional expense. Helping the rich get richer was never my mission; it was never the reason I got out of bed in the morning. But without that stable spine of my career, the options felt daunting, like free-falling without a para-chute. I shook my head. "Besides, you know everyone in this city talks, and if David's gone out of his way to get me fired, he's probably black-balled me from every reputable firm."

"I hate him," Calla said, crossing her arms over her chest. The move made me smile, exposing the baby bump that had finally emerged over the past couple of weeks. Now that Calla was into her second trimester, she was happy to share the news with everyone, but none of it felt real until I saw her with the bump for the first time. Thinking about my future niece made my anger melt a little.

Calla smacked me in the shoulder, "Are you even listening to me?"

"Sorry." I shook my head. "I was distracted. What were you saying?"

"That maybe you could come stay with us for a while."

I scoffed, reaching up to grab a glass out of the cabinet. As tempted as I was to pour a giant glass of wine, it felt kind of mean to do that to Calla while she couldn't enjoy one with me. So, instead, I grabbed the water pitcher and poured us a glass.

"No offense, Calla, but there's no way in hell that's ever going to happen. Not only because you live in a tiny, not very sound-proof apartment, but your space is already going to be invaded in a couple of months. I'm not going to impose during your last 'bout of freedom.'"

She rolled her eyes but didn't protest. A wicked smile curved on her lips as she turned to face me. "Then maybe you could crash with your husband."

I held up my finger. "Please don't start with this."

"Oh, I'm starting. You're lucky I waited this long to bring it up," Calla said. She took her water glass and climbed onto one of the island barstools. She intertwined her fingers and placed them under her chin. "I'm trying to wrap my head around this, Devyn, but I'm struggling. How could you keep this a secret for so long? Does anyone else know?"

"No one really knew," I said, rubbing my fingers over my throbbing forehead. It had been five years since that night, and I was still trying to figure out how everything got so tangled and messy. "It was a mistake."

"Was it?" Calla asked. "Because most people, if they think their marriage is a mistake, get divorced. And from what it sounds like, you and Gray are very much married, at least on paper."

I was all too aware of that fact. But when your husband was a stubborn asshole who refused to sign the divorce papers, even after you sent them *four* times, it got significantly more chal-lenging.

"Look, it's a very long story, one I'm not really looking forward to telling. Can we just drop it? At least for now. Once the other aspects of my life are no longer a dumpster fire, then maybe I can talk about that, but right now? I do not have the mental energy to get into it."

Calla pursed her lips, and I knew it was killing her not to

ask for more details. But I wouldn't budge, not ready to even think about Gray, much less talk about it.

"Okay, fine," Calla said, shoving off the counter. "But when my world was falling apart, you offered me some tough love and a place to land safely." Her hand fell to her abdomen. "And it changed my life for the better. So please, listen when I say this. I think you should come home, at least for a little while. Just long enough to figure out your next move. Down here, you're going to focus on your perceived failings, and I know you, Devyn. You're not going to be able to move on from that job, and it'll eat you alive."

I stared into her dark brown eyes, almost twins of my own. But where my reflection often felt cold and aloof, Calla's was full of warmth, like a tight hug on a winter's night. My baby sister was my whole heart, the better half of me. Maybe that was why I hesitated on the word *no*, unable to say the same thing I'd told every other living soul about moving home again.

Because, in truth, going home was the opposite of what she thought it would be. Moving on had never really been an option, not for me. Not when I'd closed my heart off after everything with Gray, and, despite my best attempts to forget him, he still held the key.

But as I glanced over her shoulder at my computer, I thought about what Tomas had found. Through my digging, I'd managed to unearth some information, but the dots weren't connecting just yet. All I knew was the files mentioned Saint Stephen's Lake, and I needed to understand why.

I smiled at Calla and nodded. "I'll think about it."

TEN

Grayson

After grabbing a cup of coffee at the local shop, Cole and I headed to the Lost Tavern, ignoring the brisk wind whipping through Main Street. This winter was holding up to its fickle nature, and after a few gorgeous days of sunshine, we were back to freezing winds and threats of snow.

"Shit," Cole said as he walked a little faster. "Remind me again why I moved here? California's sixty degrees right now."

"Might have something to do with that ring on your finger."

"Yeah." Cole smiled, looking down at his hand. "Being here with Alex is worth it, even if the winter never fucking ends."

I shook my head as we continued to pace through the parking lot. Ever since I opened up about my dad's struggles a couple of weeks ago, Cole had been checking in more, trying to join me at the cages at least once a week. It meant a lot—it gave me a moment to breathe. Plus, watching him try to match my speed was endlessly entertaining.

When we walked inside, I waved hello to the two servers on shift and walked around the bar. Most lunches were slow, and I didn't usually bother checking in. My parents' staff had worked at the Lost Tavern for years, if not decades. They weren't the most efficient crew, but that was part of the charm of small-town life. We weren't worried about Michelin stars, just good food and good company.

Michelle, one of our bartenders, clapped my back as I walked by her. "Hitting the batting cages again? Martin's gonna be thrilled someone's taking advantage of them."

"Yeah," I said as I dropped my stuff by the door to the back room. "Felt good to get back out there. Been feeling out of practice."

"Wouldn't know it by watching you," Cole chuckled. He sat down at one of the stools. "Not bad for a guy who always used a pinch hitter."

"Not my call," I grunted out. "Too much of a liability if I got hurt. If I had my way, I would have been up to bat as much as possible."

Just another reason why the glassy veneer of professional sports wasn't what I thought it would be. Don't get me wrong, I loved playing ball. Walking up to the pitch and hearing the fans calling my name were all highs I would never be able to replicate. But when I went pro, baseball stopped being about having fun and the love of the game. When you played at that level, you were always focused on getting better, on continuing to prove yourself. Even when I got to the top of the pack, there was so much pressure to stay there, I lost that passion I once had.

"Do you miss it?" Cole called out. "Playing in the majors?"

"Some days," I answered honestly. "I miss the rush." I didn't think it would ever go away—that feeling when you heard the ball hit the glove and you knew you had them. But the rest of it? The travel and being away from home more days than not? Definitely not. I shook my head. "It was time."

"Heard they offered you a big bonus to sign back up."

I almost choked when I heard the offer from the team's manager. He'd called right after I finished packing my shit, begging me to reconsider, but there was no changing my mind. I was a stubborn ass that way. Maybe in twenty or thirty years, I'd regret my choice.

But I doubted it.

The bell above the door rang, and we both turned to face it, finding our friend, Theo, walking inside. Compared to every other patron, Theo looked out of place in his designer jacket and shiny dress shoes. Even though he'd been living in town for months, he refused to give up his city style, which was constant fodder for the town's gossip circle.

I'd met Theo last year because of his wife, Calla. He was a talent agent who used to lead one of the largest firms in the country but got demoted after he fell in love with Calla while she was his assistant. Despite years of hard work, he'd decided he was done with that life, choosing his now-wife over his career. If you asked him, it was the best decision he ever made, especially now that they were expecting.

"Please tell me you still have those sliders," Theo muttered as he sat down next to Cole.

"Calla's got a craving?" he asked.

Theo shook his head. "Calla *always* has a craving, and they change constantly, so I like to have everything on hand, just in case."

"Sounds like a nightmare," I grumbled while putting his order into the POS system.

Theo leaned back, stretching his arms across the back of the chairs. "She's growing our daughter. Making sure my wife is happy and has what she wants is the least I can do." He nodded toward Cole. "You'll find out soon enough. Alex was asking Calla all about pregnancy stuff earlier."

Cole chuckled, shaking his head. "Not yet. I'm dying to have a kid with her, but Alex wants to wait until Fox Creek is in a better place. With all the renovations and hiring a night manager, our plates are already full." He smirked. "But hopefully soon."

"If my wife gets her way, all of them would be having babies at the same time." Theo shook his head, pulling out his phone. "Actually, Gray—can you add a blue cheese burger to that order?"

I narrowed my brow. "Calla hates blue cheese."

Theo shook his head. "It's not for her. Devyn is getting settled in, and she asked me to pick up some lunch for her too."

My pulse almost stopped at his words. I turned around, leaning over the bar. "What do you mean, settling in?"

Theo and Cole exchanged a look, like they knew they had said something that wasn't meant for my ears. Cole ran his hand over his face, "Look, we don't want to get in the middle of whatever is happening between you and Devyn."

"Speak for yourself," Theo added. "I very much want all the details of how you two got married and managed to elude everyone for so long."

My hands clenched the bar top, almost hard enough to hurt. I'd nearly forgotten I'd dropped that bomb in front of all our friends. Honestly, I was surprised it took this long to come up.

Cole silenced Theo with a stern look. "But we also understand we'd want to know if we were in your position. Have you talked to Devyn at all?"

"No, why?" I bit out. "She okay?"

"Yeah, she's good. Just some work stuff," Theo answered, his voice tense with something unspoken. "Calla convinced her to stay in town for a little bit, at least until she's able to clear her head. She's crashing with us for now..." He glanced at Cole. "But she didn't want you to know she was here."

My chest felt like it was about to cave in at his words. I was used to Devyn staying away, but that was when we were in the city. There, we had no history. But the idea of both of us being in town and not reaching out? That made my stomach sour. Even if I knew why she didn't want me around, it burned inside.

Theo's face turned contemplative. "Maybe you should reach out to her."

"I don't know what to say to her," I admitted. "Wouldn't even know where to start." My voice trailed off, unable to bring myself to say anything more. *She had every reason to hate me.* Despite how I felt about it, there was nothing I could do unless I told her everything. And that wasn't something I could risk, not yet. Pushing that thought out of my head, I glanced over at my friends. "Sorry you got put in the middle."

"No need to apologize to us," Cole said. "That's your private shit. Tell me, don't tell me. That's up to you."

Theo shook his head. "I agree. It might be fun to pretend otherwise, but this is your business, Gray. We're here for you." He crossed his arms in front of him, and his cheek twitched with amusement.

"What?"

Theo sighed, leaning forward. "Look, Calla would kill me for saying anything, but are you sure there's nothing between the two of you?"

I shook my head. "Not anymore."

"Your caveman stunt last month might say otherwise."

"I don't know what the fuck that was about." I ran my hand over my beard. "Never felt like that before, man." My blood pressure spiked just thinking of that asshole. I didn't know his history with Devyn, and I didn't want to know. But it killed me to believe she'd let someone like that close to her, someone who would dare put his hands on her. I swear, if he hadn't backed up, I would have killed him then and there.

"I get it," Cole shrugged. "You had to protect your girl. We've all been there."

"She's not my girl." The words soured on my tongue, but I

pressed on. "I don't know if she ever really was. And honestly, after everything we've been through, I have no right to think of her as mine."

Theo and Cole stared at me, as if hoping I'd elaborate. But my past with Devyn wasn't something I talked about easily, especially with the guilt I felt about letting her down. After all, I was the one who walked away first but then refused to sign the divorce papers when she asked. Because even if I wasn't sure I'd ever have her again, signing that line felt like a nail in our coffin, and I couldn't bring myself to do it, at least not yet. Maybe it'd be different if she met someone and moved on. But as far as I knew, she was as closed off as me and didn't seem to date people for very long. And while I hated the bitter taste that always accompanied the thought of her with anyone else, Devyn was clear. She didn't want to be married to me.

"You know," Cole muttered, toying with the glass in his hands. "When I first met Alex, she hated me. Never in a million years would I have thought I'd get to call her mine. I thought I would never deserve her, so I did everything in my power to stay away from her, everything to convince myself she wasn't for me."

"What's your point?" I snapped, feeling too raw.

"My point is that, sometimes, we can't see what's right in front of us." He shrugged. "Maybe there's a reason all this came out now."

"Yeah, my big fucking mouth," I groaned.

"Maybe," Cole said. "But I wouldn't count on it. And for Devyn's sake, I hope it means something good is coming. Girl's been having a lot of shit luck lately."

"Okay," I growled. "Someone really needs to tell me what the fuck is going on. Now."

Cole glanced over at Theo, waiting until he gave a nod

before continuing. "She got fired. Fallout from the whole thing with the guy from the bar."

"Jack," Theo seethed.

Cole nodded. "That's why she came home. Between losing her job and her stepfather kicking her out of her apartment, she had nowhere else to go. She's staying with these guys until she can figure out her next steps."

I didn't hear the end of his sentence, too busy imagining different ways I could murder those assholes— Jack and David, her stepfather—without going to prison.

Maybe Cole was right. The rational part of my brain wasn't processing any of this. But I knew Devyn, knew her better than myself. And yeah, she was pissed as fuck at me, but if she just lost her job, she'd be spiraling. She'd worked so hard for so long, and most people didn't realize why, didn't realize her dedication to the law was less about the practice and more about making her dad's memory proud.

"Okay, I get it now," Cole whispered to Theo.

"Get what?"

"Alex always says I get this primal, murder-y look when something happens to her. Thought she was full of shit until right now." He shook his head. "Before you grab your murder kit, Devyn is fine. We've got her back, and we'll make sure she's okay."

Theo nodded. "It's not the best situation with the baby coming, but she can stay with us as long as she needs."

"Wished she'd take us up on a cabin," Cole muttered. "Or she could have the apartment after Tori and Adam move into their new house."

"She won't," I said, staring at the wall. Pictures from our shared childhood filled almost all the picture frames. The years changed, but most of them were the same—Devyn and I together, no matter what. She was my person, the one I'd always protect. Maybe I'd failed in that mission over the last few years, but she was here now, and knowing her, she'd never willingly accept help.

"Can you lock up?" I asked Cole, tossing him the keys as I grabbed my jacket. My friends muttered something at my back, but I barely heard them, too distracted. I jumped into my truck and left the Lost Tavern behind me.

My body moved on instinct, not even acknowledging where I was headed until I hit my blinker, turning into the luxury apartment complex on the edge of town. It stood out among the rest of the buildings, no matter how hard the builders tried to match the aesthetics of the town, cheap, pre-fab crap that would be crumbling within twenty years. But Calla and Theo needed a place to rent while they finished construction on their forever home, and this was the closest place to town with open apartments.

Luckily, I'd been here plenty of times before, either checking on Calla or for our weekly poker nights. I pulled into one of the guest spots and raced up to the second floor, banging on their door.

As soon as I heard the doorknob turn, my heart raced in my chest. It was then I realized I had nothing to say and no real reason to be here. There were no words in my mind; I just needed to see for myself Devyn was okay.

As she pulled open the door, her eyes flared in surprise, shocked I would be standing at the door. For just a moment, I saw the girl I used to know, the one who looked at me like I hung the moon. But as soon as it came, it was gone, and her eyes narrowed, her lips turning into a frown. Devyn leaned against the frame, crossing her arms over her chest.

"Oh, honey. You're home."

ELEVEN

Devyn

Gray was standing in my doorway. Well, he was standing in *Calla*'s doorway, if we were being technical. I'd only been here for a couple of days, and apparently, I was already claiming ownership of her space.

The past week had been a blur. Between moving and cleaning out my old apartment, it felt like I'd left my heart in the city. If I was a crier, I would have bawled when I left the keys on the counter, looking out at the view one last time. It was so hard to take that first step out the door, to accept that part of my life was truly over.

I wasn't used to feeling this untethered. My life was a careful dance, each step coordinated to the minute. And now, instead of my packed schedule, there was just...nothing: no meetings, no trials, no more late-night investigations. I'd literally spent the last three days binging reality shows and letting Calla fill me in on all the gossip in town. I couldn't have picked most of the people out of a lineup, but I knew exactly who was warming their beds at night.

"You okay, Devyn?" Gray stepped closer. My name sounded too right coming from his lips, more of a breath than anything else. My fickle heart pounded in my chest, already sinking into his deep baritone. But no matter what reaction Gray elicited, he couldn't be trusted, not after everything.

My eyes narrowed at him. "Why wouldn't I be?"

"C'mon, Devy," he whispered. "Cole told me why you're here. I had to..." He cleared his throat, but his voice stayed soft. "I wanted to make sure you were alright."

The sincerity in his words threw me off, burying any snarky comment brewing on my tongue. I stared up at Gray, unsure how I felt about him being here. A large part of me was still so fucking mad at him for exposing us, for making me confront all these feelings I'd been avoiding so well.

But how could I stay mad when it was clear he raced over here, needing to check on me? Beyond Calla, it seemed like no one ever really worried about me, which was mostly my fault. When you spent your life proving to everyone you can handle anything, they tend to believe you.

The sound of a door slamming made me snap back to the moment, moving to the side so Gray could join me inside. He shucked off his wool coat, wearing an old Rebels hoodie. The star emblem was faded, almost unrecognizable after so much wear. I'd never admit it to him, but the same one hung in my closet.

He turned around, placing his coat on the hook and giving me an up-close view of his impressive back. Even with the thick hoodie, his shoulders were massive. His black joggers clung to his ass and thighs, making me almost groan in appreciation. Gray was *built*. He'd always been muscular, but this new version of him checked all my boxes. I wanted to touch him, to discover how much he'd changed over the years, to finally map those expertly honed muscles under my fingertips.

But considering the last time we'd spoken, I'd begged him for a divorce, that *might* send some mixed messages.

As he turned around and faced me, my thighs instinctively clenched. The man was too fucking good-looking; it wasn't even fair for the rest of us. With his long, wavy hair darkened with sweat and his grey eyes blazing a trail through me, it took everything I had to stand still and not show how I was trembling under his gaze.

Maybe this was a mistake. I never should have invited him in, not when it felt like the room had shrunken ten sizes since he stepped into it. But all my decisions lately had felt like the wrong ones. My life was in a complete and total clusterfuck—downfall, spiral, whatever you wanted to call it.

And now, my estranged husband was staring at me like he still cared.

"What are you doing here, Gray?"

He sighed as he stepped closer, studying my expression. "Already told you, Ace. I was worried about you." He walked past me and sat down on the couch—err, my bed. I cringed at the thought, hating that all it took to imagine Gray naked was that simple connection. I moved over to the armchair, propping myself on the edge. There was no way I was getting any closer to him, not when my mind and body were on such different wavelengths.

We're getting divorced, I reminded my libido, but she didn't care. Being around Gray always affected me, but this was an all-time low.

"I'm sorry," Gray said, breaking me out of my head. "For so many things, but mostly what I said last time. You were right. Whatever's going on between us, I never should have told everyone else. It was just..." He sucked in a sharp breath and leaned back on the couch. "Tell me you aren't with that guy."

"Jack?" I snorted. "Hell, no. I might not have a lot of self-respect right now, but trust me. I'd rather cut off all my fingers than ever touch him again."

"But you were with him?"

Anger rose in my chest. I stood, crossing my arms over my chest. "Yes, I was. Nothing serious, but we hung out a couple of times before he decided to use my sister as a stepping stone." I tapped my nails against my arm. "Do you really want to do this, Gray? Dig into each other's past hook-ups? Want to share the name of every woman you've been with lately?"

"Don't go there, Devyn. Not with me," Gray shook his head. "You want a fight, I'll give you one." He stood, walking over to me. "But right now, I just want to make sure that asshole can never come near you again. I don't give a shit about your past, Devyn, but your safety? That's something I do care about." He leaned in. "So promise me he's not going to show up here looking for you."

I tilted my head back, needing a break from the intensity of his gaze. Gray's steel eyes had turned into molten silver, almost like the thought of someone causing me harm brought out another side of him. I always thought I was safe with Gray in the past, but seeing it now filled some empty part of me.

I shook my head, my voice barely over a whisper. "No. He doesn't know where I am. We haven't spoken since that night."

"Good," he breathed, and I felt it like a caress on my cheeks. My hands thrummed with the need to touch him, to feel Gray's heart beating in his chest. This was the closest we'd been in years, and now, I remembered why I needed distance between us. It was too hard to keep my word when only inches separated us and I was aching to hold him again.

But he snapped the tension between us when he stepped back. I would have thought it was one-sided, but there was nothing calm about the look on Gray's face. If I knew him like I thought I did, he was barely holding onto his control as well.

"Get your coat."

"What?" I bit back in surprise.

"Get your coat. There's something I want to show you."

"No thanks, Anders," I scoffed, walking back to the couch. "This momentary lapse in judgment doesn't mean I want anything to do with you. You saw me. You know I'm fine. Now, go away and leave me in peace."

Gray chuckled, moving closer to me. "Like I said, don't lie to me, Devy. You are anything but fine. If that's what you need to tell everyone else, go for it. But don't think I'm buying it for a moment."

"God, you are infuriating."

"If you think that now, just wait."

"Wait for—"

But my words were cut off as Gray picked me up and slung me over his shoulder, just like he used to do when we were kids and I was stubborn. I'd never told Gray, but I'd always loved being handled by him—probably why I'd often fought him on things I really didn't care about.

However, that was at a different time in our lives, and right now, the last thing I needed was Gray's hands on me. It was fucking with my head. Standing in the room with him had been hard enough. With him caressing my thighs as I stared at his toned ass, I was about to start purring—but I couldn't let him know that. I had a reputation to uphold, you know.

My hands smacked into his back, which—*holy shit*—was even more muscular than I thought. "Put me down, you asshole."

"No can do, Ace." He smirked over his shoulder. "Now, hold on. We're going for a ride."

Fucking hell.

TWELVE

Devyn

SIXTEEN YEARS OLD

"You're doing it again."

Wade shifted his arm away from my shoulders and sat back in the red vinyl booth. The arcade downtown was a relic, a staple of the community since the sixties. Usually, I loved coming here with Wade. We'd play for hours, spending all the quarters we could find, and then split a plate of disco fries before heading home.

But tonight, what had started as a typical Saturday had shifted into a double date, and everything had felt off since we walked through the door. And the worst part? I only had myself to blame.

I could feel Wade's annoyance at my side. Despite an inner urge to soothe his worries, I couldn't bring myself to focus on him, too consumed with watching my best friend and little sister playing a game of air hockey across the arcade. With one smooth move, Calla sank the puck into Gray's goal and let out a loud whoop of victory. He moved to the other side of the table in three strides, pulling her up into his arms. Despite losing, he looked like he was having the time of his life.

Which was the complete opposite of how my evening was going.

"You've been watching them all night."

I shook my head, forcing myself to look back at my boyfriend. Wade and I made things official at the end of last summer, and despite spending most of the year apart, our relationship continued through the school year. It was easy being with Wade. He was funny and kind, and he made me feel special in a way I hadn't experienced before. But ever since I came back into town, something had felt off between us, and despite our best efforts to ignore it, it was continuing to grow.

Even tonight, when I should have been focused on him and enjoying our time together, I was too busy worrying about Gray and Calla to give him much thought.

I gave him my best fake smile and tucked my hand into his. "I'm sorry. I'm just trying to keep an eye on Calla."

"Right," he scoffed, pulling his hand away. He paused, letting out a long exhale before meeting my eyes again. "I don't think I can do this anymore, Devy."

"Don't call me that," I snapped, hating how it sounded coming from his lips. It sounded juvenile, like he was talking to a child instead of his girlfriend.

"That's exactly the point." He nodded across the arcade again, where Calla and Gray had moved to a new game. "You have no problem when *he* calls you Devy, but when I do it? You hate it."

"It's our thing," I tried to explain, but the words felt hollow. He was right; Gray was the only one I let call me that. And because he was the one who started it, it felt like it was something special between us, something Wade couldn't replicate, no matter how hard he tried.

"And that's the problem, Devyn." Wade sighed. "When we first started hanging out, I thought I could handle the whole you and Gray thing. I knew I'd never be your first choice, but I was here, and I liked you, wanted to give you the world." He shook his head, "But it's never going to be enough, not while Gray's around."

"He's my best friend," I bit out defensively. "I've told you that so many times."

"I keep waiting for you to really mean it," Wade bit back. As if taken aback by his tone, he sank back in his seat and shook his head. "I'm sorry, Devyn, but I want to be with someone who sees *me*, who puts *me* first. Maybe you're just friends with Gray, but he's always going to come first. No one else has a chance."

"He's my best friend," I repeated, but this time, my words were weak, lacking the force I usually put behind them. That simple label would never be enough to describe our relationship. Yes, Gray was my best friend, but he was also so much more. He was the voice in the back of my mind, the person I turned to whenever my world got too heavy. He was the first person I'd call with good news, bad news, and everything in between.

And while I loved him as a friend, there was a part of me that wanted so much more. For a long time, I could pretend it was nothing more than a crush. Objectively speaking, Gray was one of the most attractive guys I'd ever met. Of course, I'd notice that. But lately, it had shifted, no longer feeling so innocent. This light-hearted crush was harder to ignore, shifting from a slight ripple to a tidal wave, threatening to pull me under whenever we were in the same room.

Guilt threatened to consume me, and I hated myself for letting myself get carried away. Not only did I have a boyfriend I cared about, but Gray was officially dating Calla now. She'd come to me months ago and said they had gotten close, wanted to know if I'd be okay if they went out on a date. Of course I said yes. I just hadn't expected it to feel like my heart was being ripped out whenever I saw them together.

I looked down at my hands, toying with the small silver ring on my thumb. "I'm sorry, Wade. I never meant to hurt you."

He smiled sadly at me. "I know, Devy. I was willing to fight for you when I thought there was a chance, but there isn't, is there?"

I stared into his hurt expression, wishing more than anything I could give him what he wanted. Wade was a good guy—one of the best—the kind of guy I should want to be with, the kind who looked perfect on paper.

But there was no spark between us, nothing like the fever that overcame me every time Gray smiled in my direction. While Wade made me feel safe and comforted, Gray set my whole soul on fire. As much as I wanted to settle for less than that, I knew I couldn't.

"That's what I thought. I'm going to head out." Wade stood and turned to leave before looking back at me. "You should talk to him about this, Devyn. Think he'd want to know." He chuckled dryly to himself. "And now that we're broken up, maybe he'll stop trying to kick my ass."

I stared at him. "Why would he do that?"

"We both know the answer to that," Wade chuckled. He squeezed my shoulder. "Tell him, Devyn. Before it's too late."

As Wade walked out of the arcade, I sat back in the booth, dragging my hands over my face as a ringing echoed in my ears. The rest of the arcade faded away, leaving me alone with my racing pulse. That was it. Wade and I were over. And even though I knew it was coming, that it was best for both of us, I still hated this lingering ache in my chest. It wasn't quite heart-break—not that I knew what that felt like—but it was more like guilt, guilt for hurting someone I cared about, even if I never meant to.

I pushed a breath through my lips, forcing myself to sit up before anyone noticed me. In a place this small, gossip always traveled fast, and I didn't want to be the talk of the town over breakfast tomorrow.

As I grabbed my purse and ran my fingers under my dry eyes, I felt something else slide in next to my guilt. Relief. God, did that make me a shitty person? That I was almost relieved my relationship was over when I should have been devastated?

My relief had nothing to do with Wade. He wasn't a bad guy, but no matter how hard I tried, I couldn't fall for him. I didn't think I'd ever forget his face when he told me he loved me for the first time and I couldn't say it back. I *should* have loved him. Wade said everything right and did all the right things. But no matter how much I cared about him, I couldn't bring myself to say the words.

I looked over my shoulder, watching Calla and Gray joke as they moved between games. They had an ease between them, one Wade and I never seemed to have, even when we were good. That was what they both deserved. My sister was the kindest person I'd ever met. She deserved to be loved by someone like Gray—two people who loved with their whole chest, unlike me.

That last thought struck a bolt of pain in my chest; I was unsure if I'd ever be able to love someone like that. I had barely said the words to anyone but Calla in years, unable to bring myself to open up. Not when my life was surrounded by people who always wanted something from me, who wanted to shape me in their image. Maybe it was a side effect of my mother's toxic, loveless marriage. Watching her wither away in David's shadow had already jaded me to most relationships, but maybe I'd sealed my heart off more than I thought.

With one last look at my sister smiling brightly at Gray, I turned to the door, needing to get away from here. I couldn't go home, not while David was staying at the hotel for the weekend. It was hard enough living with him during the school year, but these summer months were supposed to be our safe place. Now, he'd invaded it, making himself all too comfortable in our home.

I forced the thought out of my head, deciding I'd head down to the beach for a couple of hours. There was a great view of the stars over the lake, and it always made me feel better when I could stare out at the open sky like I could be anywhere else in the world for a moment.

However, when I placed my hand on the exit, someone lightly grabbed my elbow and turned me around. Gray met my eyes, his brow furrowed in confusion. "Where are you going, Ace?"

"Home," I sighed, not willing to tell him my plan. "I'm ready to call it a night."

Gray kept staring at me, the crease in his forehead only deepening. "It's not even nine."

"That's late."

"Coming from the girl who never closes her eyes before midnight?" He shook his head as he stepped back. "I'm not buying it. Did you and Wade have a fight?"

"You could say that," I chuckled, rubbing my arm where his hand just sat. "We, uh, we broke up."

Gray's eyes flickered with some unknown emotion, and he swallowed before choosing his next words. "Are you okay?"

"Does it make me a bad person if I say yes?" I played with the strap of my purse. "Maybe it hasn't sunk in yet, but I'm actually doing okay."

Gray stared at me for so long, I started to squirm. Usually, he couldn't get under my skin, and I'd match his intensity with my own. But tonight, I already felt too raw, like the weight of my secrets was threatening to tear me apart, and with Gray staring at me like that, it made my mind wander, wondering if I should follow Wade's advice and tell Gray how I felt.

But before I could make up my mind, Gray pushed the door open behind me. "Then c'mon, Ace. Let's go for a ride."

"Where's Calla?"

He jutted his chin out behind us. I turned and found my sister in a large group of girls, laughing as they started up the old dance game. "A bunch of the camp counselors were coming to celebrate the end of the first session. She's going to hang with them tonight." He walked outside and held the door open for me. "So let's get out of here, Ace. Just me and you."

"HOW ARE you so good at that?"

Standing on the edge of the lake, I watched as Gray tossed his rock with surprising ease. The thing skipped almost four times before dropping down into the water. I glared down at the stone in my hand. No matter how many times Gray tried to show me what to do, I couldn't make it move like him.

Gray smirked at me over his shoulder. "Maybe it's from all those drills Coach made us run last week. He's been on my ass about pitching and trying different styles."

He moved to the edge of the woods and called me over to join him on a fallen log. I loved this place, this secret cove that seemed to belong just to the two of us. During the summer, tourists invade our beaches at all hours of the day. While the town needed their patronage to survive the winter months, it was sometimes hard to deal with, especially on nights like this, when I just wanted to clear my head away from the rest of the world.

Gray waited until I sat down at his side, then stretched out his arms behind us, leaning back so his head dropped between his shoulders. He'd already yawned a couple of times, exhausted from his early morning practices.

I stared at him, noting the dark circles lurking under his eyes. But despite his exhaustion, a small smile played at the corner of his lips. "How are you liking it?" I asked as I fidgeted with my bracelet.

This past year, Gray had become the breakout star of the high school baseball team. I wasn't surprised, not with his talent and work ethic. He spent almost every single day training to better his skills. But when this past season started, the coach decided to switch him from third base to the pitcher's mound. When he first made the change, Gray hated it but trusted his coach to do what was right.

It turned out, it *was* the right call. Gray was a natural on the mound, having near-perfect control of the ball. College scouts had already been asking about him, offering all sorts of incentives to get him to visit their schools. He'd put them off this summer, enrolling in a pitching clinic instead, but it would be coming up soon, with only two more years until graduation. The thought instantly made my hands tighten into fists. I tried not to think too much about how our lives would be going in different directions soon, but there was nothing I could do to stop it.

"It's getting better," Gray eventually admitted. "It's a lot of pressure, but I think I like that." He kicked the rocks at his feet then turned to study my face. "We gonna talk about baseball all night, or are you going to tell me what happened with Wade?"

I furrowed my brows as I shifted to face the water. I couldn't talk to Gray about this, not yet. Not when my mind was already so jumbled and I had no idea how to unravel it. So instead, I tried to play it cool. I shrugged. "I told you. We broke up."

Gray let out a half-hearted chuckle. "Yeah, Ace, I got that. I meant more about *why* you broke up."

"It just wasn't working," I said, unable to look at Gray. "He wanted us to get more serious, and I wasn't ready for that."

"What do you mean?"

Gray's tone forced my eyes up to meet his. There was a dark storm in his expression, and if it was anyone else, I would have been terrified.

"Gray?"

"Did he try…" He shook his head and clenched his jaw. "Was he pressuring you—"

"Oh God, no!" I said, forcing out an awkward laugh. "Nothing like that. I meant emotionally. He told me he loved me…" My voice trailed off, realizing I'd already told Gray more than I meant to. I didn't want anyone to know what had happened that night. It was already hard enough, knowing I'd hurt Wade so badly. The last thing I wanted was for anyone else to know about it. But I trusted Gray, more than I trusted anyone else in this world. I needed to talk it out before my self-loathing became a permanent scar. I sighed as I turned back toward the water. "Do you think I'm capable of it?"

"Of loving someone?"

I nodded, feeling that familiar prickle in the back of my throat. I closed my eyes, soaking in the night breeze and the sound of the water rippling along the shore. "I think there's something wrong with me. No matter how much I wanted to say the words, they wouldn't come. I haven't said them to anyone, not in a long time. I don't know if I even can."

But before I could spiral further, Gray took my arm and turned me until I faced him. His hand fell to my cheek, brushing away the one lone tear that managed to escape. "You're more than capable of loving someone, Ace. It just needs to be the right person."

I shook my head. "It's easy to say that—"

But Gray cut me off, shifting his fingers to my chin and lifting it so I was forced to meet his eyes. "Maybe you don't see it, but I do. You are the most loving person I've ever met. Maybe you don't say it with your words, but I see it in your actions every single day. With your sisters, with your friends." He swallowed. "With me. You protect your heart, Ace. You don't give pieces of it away easily, but once you do, you're in for life."

I bit my lip to keep from crying. I'd never heard someone describe me like that, never had someone see me so clearly. The rest of the people in my life seemed to pass over me, always believing what I projected on the outside. With the exception of Calla, no one made the effort to see past my prickly exterior, never made the effort to really get to know me.

But in just a few words, Gray proved he knew me better than anyone else. And to see he not only noticed it but appreciated me, exactly how I was? It broke the last wall around my heart.

I loved him.

The words rushed out in my mind, as if they couldn't hold back for another moment. This wasn't a crush. This wasn't a weak moment. I was irrevocably in love with my best friend. That was why I could never say it to Wade, why it felt like a kick in the teeth every time I saw him with Calla.

I was head over heels in love with Grayson Anders.

There the words were, right on the tip of my tongue, practically begging me to tell him. But before I could let my emotions get the best of me, Gray's phone rang. He searched my expression, as if waiting for me to say something. But once I dropped my eyes, he let me go and stepped away.

He clenched his jaw as he looked at the screen. "It's Calla. I promised her I'd give her a ride home."

That poured icy water through my racing heart.

While I might have been in love with Gray, he wasn't mine to love. He was with someone—my sister, of all people. I'd spent my life trying to protect my little sister. I refused to be the cause of any of her pain.

No. I couldn't tell Gray, not when my feelings could destroy not only our friendship, but also my relationship with Calla.

As Gray started to say something, I jumped off the log and started walking back toward town. I wrapped my arms around my middle, trying to push down the nausea rushing through me. "You should go."

"No," Gray insisted as he chased me further down the beach. "I'm not leaving you here by yourself. It's late, it's dark. I can give you a ride home too."

"It's fine," I said, keeping my back to him. "I'm not ready to call it a night, and I want to walk. Besides, you know nothing ever happens in this town. I'll be safe, I promise."

He grabbed my hand, the touch electrifying. Sparks traveled through my veins, igniting me like never before. I'd spent months with Wade, and it had never been like this, like a simple touch had the power to consume me.

But he wasn't mine to claim.

Reluctantly, I released his hand, swallowing down the pain with each step. "I mean it, Gray. I promise, I'm okay. You really should go and make sure Calla gets home okay."

Gray stood there, still staring at his open palm.

"Devyn, I—"

I held up my hand, cutting him off. No matter what Gray wanted to say right now, it had to wait. "Go. I know the way from here." He stared at me for a long moment, as if trying to read the lie in my words. But I blocked them before iron-enforced walls, refusing to let him see how much this was killing me. "I promise, I'll be safe. If anything happens, you'll be my first call."

"Promise me, Devy."

"I promise, Grayson." I tilted my head toward his truck. "Go."

With a long sigh, Gray eventually nodded, walking up the

rocky shore toward his truck. It hurt to watch him walk away, worse than when Wade broke up with me. Maybe I was a bit of a masochist, though, because before Gray could climb into the driver's seat, I called out to him. "Hey, Gray?" He paused and looked back at me. "Thank you. Not only for being here, but for what you said. It...it means a lot to me."

He smiled, and I could feel it all the way down to my toes. "Always, Ace."

THIRTEEN

Devyn

Gray's truck ambled down Main Street, and I stared out the window, continuing to pout about being forced into this drive. Okay, maybe forced was too strong of a word, but given the harsh look Gray gave me when I tried to head back inside, it felt like I really didn't have a choice in the matter.

Besides, my curiosity was piqued. You know that saying about the cat? That was me. I never met a mystery I didn't want to solve. Maybe that was why I was so drawn to the law. Each case was a puzzle, and I was the one who had to connect all the pieces. Granted, most of the time, I was helping large corporations hold on to their sizable bank accounts, but it still soothed something inside me.

We drove past the Lost Tavern, and I couldn't help but sigh, wishing we were heading there right now. I would have given anything for one of Curt's burgers.

"You should go," Gray said, as if he could read my thoughts. "They'd like to see you."

"Not sure that's true."

There were a lot of things about being back in this town that I hated, but seeing the disappointment in Marta and Curt's eyes always cut like a knife. In reality, they were more my parents than my actual parents. With my dad dying when I was young and my mom being well, my mom, they'd taken me in and given me more love than I knew possible. Marta and Curt were the kind of warm, hearty people who took you under their wing and never let go.

Honestly, cutting ties with Gray hurt twice as much because it also meant cutting ties with them. I missed their easy smiles, comforting hugs, and whispers of "it'll be alright."

Gray shook his head. "They miss you, especially my mom. She never says it, but she always holds out hope you'll come in with Calla."

I rolled my lips, turning to look out the window. "It was hard, you know, to see them after everything. At first, because they tied me to you, and then..."

"You didn't want to lie to them."

I nodded. "I didn't know if you told them about our situation or not. It was a gamble I wasn't willing to take."

As the restaurant faded into the background, I tried not to picture Marta with her bright smile and constant support. It would gut her to know I was staying in town and didn't bother to come by. It had been far too long since I had walked through those doors, resorting to sneaking their food in to-go containers.

Like so many places in this town, that restaurant had formed me. It was my first job, hostess-ing on hot summer nights. I'd spend every extra moment behind the bar, learning how to mix drinks and fix the antique cash register. The walls were lined with pictures of me over the years, right alongside the rest of the family.

"I miss them too," I whispered, more to myself than Gray.

"Do you?"

I wiped my head in Gray's direction. "Of course I do. Don't

think any of this has been easy for me. When you tore us apart, I lost a lot more than you, so don't sit there and judge me."

"I deserve that," he muttered. "I didn't mean anything by it. It was just nice to hear." He hit the blinker, turning off onto one of the smaller county roads. "I know you care about them. I'd never question that."

We let the silence brew between us after that, only the quiet crooning on the radio filling the truck cab. I expected the space between us to feel tense and brittle. Chalk it up to my anger and the years of distance. But despite my best intentions, I found the same ease I always felt around Gray. It didn't matter how many years passed between us; we always fell into the same routine. Maybe our bond was stronger than I thought, forged during our formative years through memories and mistakes.

Maybe it was even strong enough to survive the pain we'd caused each other.

We drove past an old shack on the corner of the road; the walls were painted a hideously bright shade of blue. I gasped when I saw it, putting my hands on the door and lifting it to get a better look. "Please tell me the Blue Cow is still open. I haven't had ice cream in forever, and I still dream about their Key Lime Pie cup."

"You got a few months until their doors open," Gray chuckled.

"I'll be here opening day. No matter where I'm living, I'm going to be the first in line."

Gray shook his head. "Doubt you'd even remember how to get back here, city girl."

"Please." I rolled my eyes. "I walked here every day for almost ten years. It's not a hard place to find."

Gray just hummed, not saying anything else. With his focus on the road, I took a moment to study my husband—ugh, that word. It was the first time in a long time I got to openly admire him, taking in the changes over the past few years. He'd aged well, growing into his rugged good looks. Thank God he'd kept the beard, though I'd never tell him that. A couple of gray strands stuck out of his dark blond hair. Was it weird it made me proud I'd seen him at so many stages of his life? We'd gone through our childhood and the awkward teenage phase together, even though I'd say Gray got off much easier than I did in that area.

And now, here we were, stuck together in the town we'd both once called home. While no one would tell me why Gray moved back—they insisted it was his story to tell—it was clear something significant must have happened.

As I tried to picture what could have caused Gray to end his baseball career early, he turned down a dirt road, heading deeper into the mountains.

One of the things that made Saint Stephen's so beautiful was its location in a deep valley in the heart of the Appalachian Mountains. While the town itself was relatively flat, once you left the central part, gorgeous peaks surrounded you. There were plenty of hiking trails with stunning vistas, but they were all closed for the winter months. As Gray drove us further into the woods, my heart started to race, unsure of where we were heading.

But there was no doubt in my mind Gray would keep us safe. I might not trust him with my heart, but with my safety? I'd put my faith in him every time. He'd proven time and time again he'd rather risk himself than ever let anything harm me.

Eventually, he pulled onto a driveway, following it for almost a mile before a house came into view. Well, a cabin, really. It wasn't much, blending in with the wilderness around it. The walls were made of thick logs stacked on top of each other, leading to a pitched roof. Tall, thin windows broke up the walls. They were lined with black metal borders, a sharp, modern contrast to the rustic ambiance of the rest of the place. A small front porch led up to what I assumed was the main door. The house was bare; no decorations or signage gave any clues as to why we were here.

The snow was a thick blanket up here, and the tires crunched as he pulled in front of the porch and shifted the truck into park. I studied the home through the window as Gray got out, walking around to my side and opening the door for me. But I remained in my seat, crossing my arms. "Whose house is this?"

"Mine," Gray bit, holding out his hand for me. "C'mon, Ace. It's fucking freezing out here."

I reluctantly took his hand and let him pull me out of the car. He walked up to the porch, pulling out a set of keys from his pocket. My eyes instinctively went to the small leather keychain attached to the ring. It had faded over time, but it was still there, looking rougher than when I gave it to him years ago.

Without thinking, I reached out, touching it to make sure it was real. "I can't believe you kept this."

It wasn't anything special, just a token I'd made for his seventeenth birthday. Calla helped me stitch the tag out of an old baseball glove of Gray's, one he thought he'd thrown away months earlier. But I knew how much it meant to him; even if he didn't want the whole thing, he should still have a small piece of it with him. He almost cried when he saw it, and it made my world stop spinning. I assumed it had been lost or thrown away over the years, not sitting on his keys to this day.

Gray studied me for a long moment then pushed forward, opening the door without comment. "Shit," he muttered as a blast of cold air hit us. "Something must be up with the heat." He pushed off his heavy jacket and handed it to me. "Gonna go check it out. Stay here."

Nodding, I took his coat and draped it over my shoulders,

which was a mistake. As soon as it closed around me, I was overwhelmed by the scent of Gray. Memories from a lifetime ago, when he'd hug me after winning a game, flashed through my mind. I shook my head, refusing to let myself get lost in my memories, not when I was dying to look around Gray's home.

Maybe snooping was the wrong thing to do, but let's be honest: Gray knew better than to leave me alone in his house. My curiosity always got the best of me. If I really wanted to rationalize my actions, I could argue half of this place was technically mine. Not that I'd ever do that to Gray, but it made me feel better as I moved further into his space.

The front entrance was blocked off from the rest of the home, almost like a mudroom. But once you got past the doorway, the whole space was wide and open. The kitchen was ahead; on the other side of the room was a living space and a large dining room table. The walls were painted a pale green, which helped break up the dark wood furniture. Almost everything in here looked like it had been carved by hand, and I hated imagining how long each piece would take. It was beautiful, classic, and understated, just like Gray. There weren't any frills, nothing more than what he needed.

When I turned the corner, my hand flew to my mouth as I let out a little gasp. I spoke too soon. The entire back wall was made of glass windows framed in the same dark metal as the front. Beyond the glass panes was a large patio with a fire pit in the middle. But that wasn't what stunned me silent. No, that was the view. I knew we'd gone up one of the mountains to get here, but I didn't realize how high up we were. The entire valley was below us, and you were almost able to see the whole town.

I couldn't help but move forward, stunned into silence by the world surrounding us. With the light snow falling, it felt like we were trapped in a snow globe. I'd always loved winter the best as a kid, savoring the snow and icy temperatures. Maybe that was odd, considering our lakeside town survived because of the summer tourists, but I liked moments like this when the world felt quiet.

I could tell why Gray picked this place, knowing he was more people-phobic than me these days. Even though the town adored him, he'd always kept his distance, not wanting anyone to pick up on his perceived faults. This was his refuge, his sanctuary, and I didn't want to think too deeply about why he'd chosen to share it with me.

With a loud bang echoing from the other side of the house, I heard a muttered curse before Gray finally emerged. As he walked toward me, I swore I felt the heat kick on, but that might have just been how it felt to be his only focus. Each stride was purposeful, as if there was nothing he wanted more than to be next to me.

I swallowed, shaking away the thought. God, I had to get out of this town. After years of locking down my emotions, they were all being brought to the surface quickly. Too quickly. It left me spinning, like I was finally emerging from the darkness, and I wasn't ready to take on the light just yet.

When Gray approached me, I said nothing; I just crossed my arms over my chest. "That should do it," he muttered. "The unit is older, and I haven't had a chance to replace it yet. That's first on the list for the spring."

"Gray," I said slowly, hoping he'd pick up on the annoyance in my tone. "What are we doing here?"

"Showing you the house," he said plainly as he walked right past me. He pointed to the room off the living room. "Primary and guest bedroom are down there, both the bathrooms. They're not the biggest, but there's a little study off the kitchen. Couch pulls out in there if you need it."

"What are you talking about?" I said as I hurried to catch up to him.

He entered the kitchen and opened the fridge. "There's not much in terms of food, but there are enough staples to keep you fed for a day or two before you have to go to the market. I've got an extra truck parked under the awning. She's a little rough, so you'll have to be patient, but she'll get you where you need to go."

Gray tried to step around me, muttering something about salting the driveway. But before he could, I jumped in front of him, placing my hands on his chest. "Stop. Just stop for a moment. What are you talking about, Gray? Why do I need to know this?"

He stared at me like the answer was obvious to everyone but me. "Because you're going to stay here."

FOURTEEN

Grayson

Devyn stared up at me, her bright brown eyes locked onto mine in confusion. But after the longest pause in modern history, she ripped her hands from my chest and laughed, full-on belly laughs like I was the most ridiculous thing in the world.

"*Me?*" she squealed. "Stay *here?* Why the hell would I stay here?"

Good question, one I hadn't really put a lot of thought into. I was acting on pure impulse. Ever since I saw Devyn's belongings piled up in the corner behind the couch, I'd been trying to keep myself in check, knowing Devyn wouldn't respond well to my anger.

I moved closer to her, noticing how her eyes widened as I approached. So maybe this feeling wasn't as one-sided as I thought. Being around her ignited a fire in my chest, one that had died down but had never fully gone out. Every part of her called to me, like a craving I couldn't satisfy. From her long blonde hair draped along her back to her plump bottom lip, all I wanted to do was lock the doors and explore every inch of her.

How the hell had I spent so long denying what I felt for her? Even when we were kids, I knew she was beautiful, but there was something so much more to her. She was the moon, constantly orbiting in my atmosphere. I'd spent enough time trying to ignore her pull.

Devyn must have noticed me zoning out, because she stepped closer, waving her hand in my face. "Grayson Anders, do you hear me?"

"No," I said, walking back over to the door to grab the spare set of keys. "You need a place to stay, and I have one. Seems simple to me."

"I have a place to stay."

"And now you have a better one."

Devyn threw her arms up in the air. "This is why I didn't want anyone to tell you. I knew you'd bulldoze back into my life and try to fix things for me. Well, newsflash, Grayson: I'm not sixteen anymore. I do not need or want you to save me."

"Too fucking bad," I snapped, stepping closer to her. "Like it or not, we're married, Devyn, and I'll be damned if my wife sleeps on a couch when I have a perfectly functional house she can use."

Her eyes flashed for a moment, but she quickly shuttered the emotion. "Calla's place will be fine. It's only for a couple of weeks."

"And you think you'll last that long? I can't imagine it's been fun sharing 1,000 square feet with your sister and her husband."

"And their paper-thin walls," Devyn mumbled before scrubbing her hand over her face. "Okay, it might not be the ideal setup, but like I said, it's temporary."

"So is this," I shrugged. "But at least here, you'll have some privacy."

Devyn stared at me, her mouth agape. "I am not staying with you, Grayson. That will *never* happen."

"I'm not staying here," I answered. "I've been crashing at my parents. They need the help. This would all be yours."

Devyn's mouth fell open and then closed, but even without words, I could see her brain working in overdrive, trying to figure out an excuse to turn down my offer. She was stubborn, I'd give her that, but I was always worse. As she stared up at me, I just stood there, hoping she'd say yes. Other than for the reasons I'd already stated, I didn't know why I wanted her here so badly. But I needed her here; I needed to know she was safe and content. Devyn never needed anyone, but if she did, I wanted to be the one she called.

She looked around the room, chewing on her lower lip. I almost had her. Devyn walked over to the window, sighing as she looked outside. "I'm paying rent."

"No, you're not," I said. "I bought this place outright. There's no mortgage. I don't owe anything on it. And trust me, I don't need your money." I walked over to her. "Save it for yourself."

She looked over her shoulders, and her lips pursed into a tight line. "I don't need your charity."

I snorted. "That's not what this is, Dev. I know you better than that. This is me helping a friend."

"We're not friends," Devyn snapped.

"Fine," I grumbled, rubbing my hand over my beard. "Look at it this way. You need a chance to catch your breath and figure out your next steps. I need someone here so I don't have to worry about all my hard work turning to shit in the cold weather, and you know I'm not letting a stranger into my home." I shrugged, trying to come off more casual than I felt. "This helps out both of us."

She turned, taking in the room again. As she looked it all over, I stared at her. She was still so familiar yet different at the same time. Her long blonde hair was tied up in a ponytail, and it swung along her back as she walked around my space. Her slight fingers trailed across the back of my couch, tracing the leather. It was hard not to flinch, not to explain everything I had picked and why, to just let her explore, knowing her dark brown eyes always saw more than I wanted.

When I bought this house two years ago, I never meant for it to be my main home. I always expected to stay in the city or maybe settle into something in the suburbs right outside Manhattan, but life had a funny way of showing you what you needed, and it led me right back here. From the moment I found this place, I knew it could be something special with some money and effort.

But it never felt like home until Devyn stepped inside. I ran my hand over my face, trying to get my shit together. Even if she did decide to stay here, she'd made it clear she didn't want anything to do with me. I should have taken her at her word, but I couldn't help but hope she changed her mind. From the moment Devyn came back into my life, I wanted more. Craved what we used to have. I couldn't help myself when it came to her. Devyn was as much a part of me as the scars on my hands and knees.

After a long moment, she finally turned back toward me and said, "I need to think about it."

"That's all I ask."

I DROPPED Devyn back off at Calla's and then immediately headed to the Lost Tavern. Since my dad had been having more episodes at night, I'd taken over dinner service for my mom, making sure my phone was nearby just in case.

After parking my truck in the back lot, I walked inside, waving hi to the bar regulars. The restaurant wasn't big, but my dad had wisely divided it into two sections years ago. The front was an aged bar, the walls lined with wooden panels. The back was a bright dining room, trading the wooden planks for light bricks and other rustic accents. Although there had been a lot of updates over the years, the general feel of the place always remained the same, a testament to my parents' hard work. It was comfortable, the kind of place people came regularly, both for simple meals and to celebrate life events. A lot had happened behind the doors of the Lost Tavern, and I was honored to be a part of its history.

I checked in with Maggie, our general manager, before heading into the back. I flicked on the light in the back room before turning toward my desk, where I found a neat pile of receipts waiting for me. My mother must have stopped by after I left to get Devyn. I looked over her notes as I pulled off my jacket and draped it over the back of my chair.

A couple of the servers popped in as I worked, but they kept to themselves. My team was good about giving me space while I was trying to work, even though we all shared the same area. Due to a lack of space, the restaurant's office was combined with the storeroom, laundry room, and break room. It was narrow but decently sized and ran along the length of the restaurant wall.

In the far corner, my dad had set up a small desk before he opened. Over the years, he'd always talked about getting a better setup, but we knew that was all talk. He hated being confined to an office, preferring to bring his work to the bar so he could chat with patrons while checking in on everything. He prided himself on serving the community and wanted everyone to leave with a pleasant experience.

It was hard to imagine what the restaurant looked like when my dad first started. He'd poured his whole heart into making this place something special, and you could feel it every time you walked inside. The Lost Tavern was his legacy, and even though I never thought I'd work here, it was an honor to continue his work.

Forcing my dad out of my thoughts, I filed away the receipts and turned on the computer. It had to be a decade old; they hadn't replaced it since I was in high school, but luckily, it worked most of the time. I leaned back in the chair, twiddling my thumbs as I waited for it to boot up. All I needed was to finish the week's orders before I could head to the dining room.

And the scheduling.

And shit, I needed to grab my dad's medication.

The cursor blinked at me on the screen, and suddenly, everything overwhelmed me. My dad, Devyn being back in town, all the things I tried to keep buried suddenly pressing down on me, leaving me depleted. I leaned forward, and my elbows dropped to my thighs. I cradled my face in my hands as anxiety raced through me, reminding me of all the ways I was failing everyone around me. It was too much.

As the sounds blurred and my vision turned black, a sudden noise broke through my haze. The concurrent pings of an incoming text pulled me out of my spiral, and the room came back into view. I inhaled slowly, reminding myself of my surroundings: the receipts, computer, Dad's old Rebels mug. Each slow, steady breath helped center me. Eventually, my hands relaxed, releasing their tight grip.

I pulled the phone off the desk and found an unknown New York City area code had texted me. Curiosity got the best of me, so I opened the chat.

UNKNOWN NUMBER

Hey…it's Devyn.

Sorry. Don't know if this is okay, but I got your number from Calla.

I couldn't help but smile. Devyn had texted me. Jesus, this was ridiculous. You would have thought I'd just won the lottery with how that made me feel. But each step with Devyn was a battle, and her reaching out felt like my first major win since she'd come back into town.

Another text came in as I was debating what to write back.

UNKNOWN NUMBER

Never mind, forget it. Momentary lapse of judgment.

Wait. Was Devyn nervous? She was rambling, which was usually a sign she was. Maybe that shouldn't have felt good, but I liked that talking to me affected her. I leaned back in my chair, my panic receding as I stared at her messages.

ME

Hey, Devy.

Glad you texted. What's up?

As three dots appeared on the screen, I saved her number, unable to resist labeling it with her old nickname.

ACE

About earlier...I never thanked you for the offer

ME

You don't have to thank me, but you should take me up on it.

That's actually why I'm texting...

Does it still stand?

The house is yours for as long as you need.

Thank you, Gray.

Stop thanking me. You're helping me out just as much.

Trust me, that's not true.

Came back and found Calla and Theo in a
compromising position in the kitchen.

There are some things you can't ever unsee.

So, if you're cool with it, can I start moving
things in tomorrow? After I bleach my eyeballs,
of course.

I stared at the chat and suddenly needed to hear her voice. Pressing her contact information, I brought the phone up to my ear and listened to the line trill.

"Please tell me you haven't changed your mind already," Devyn grumbled on the second ring. "I've already started packing."

"Nah," I said. "Just hate texting."

Devyn laughed, the sound lighter than I remembered. She wasn't someone who showed her emotions easily, often hiding them behind a tough façade. But those little moments when I got to see the real her? Those were everything.

"Should have remembered that," Devyn chuckled. "You've always been technology averse."

For a moment, I thought about telling her the truth: I just wanted to hear her voice. After being starved of it for so long, I was desperate to talk to her, to listen to all her thoughts. Even when she was annoyed with me, it was better than not talking to her at all. I chuckled, keeping all that to myself. "Not as bad as I used to be."

"Good to know," Devyn sighed. "Because if you didn't have cable or Wi-Fi at your house, this whole deal might have been off. Calla's got me hooked on all these reality shows, and now I'm just as addicted. If I miss a *Real Housewives* reunion, there will be blood."

I laughed, the sound filling the room. "Don't you worry,

Ace. I've got both set up for you. No need to get blood on my new rug."

The line paused, and for a moment, I thought she was going to ream me out for calling her Ace. I'd done it a couple of times today already. The first time was a slip of the tongue. It was too easy to fall into old habits with Devyn as if no time had passed. But after that, I was almost testing the waters, waiting to see if she'd say anything about the nickname. Each time she let it go only emboldened me, wanting to know how much further she'd let me in.

She cleared her throat. "I should get going. I want to make sure I have everything ready for tomorrow. Can we meet at the house at 10?"

"Works for me."

"Cool..." she sighed. "I'll see you then."

Disappointment filled me at how our conversation ended, hating we'd only talked for a couple of minutes before I ruined it. But before I could pull the phone away from my ear, I heard her voice call out. "Thank you, Gray."

I smiled to myself. "Stop thanking me, Devyn. It's not needed."

"Yes, it is," she insisted. "There aren't many people who'd do something like that for me. Just Calla, maybe Laurel, and they're obligated because they're my sisters. But you..." Her voice trailed off, and I wished more than anything she'd finish the thought. I needed to know where her head was and how she felt about being around me again. She cleared her throat. "So thank you, Gray. It means more than you know."

"Anything for you, Devy."

FIFTEEN

Grayson

EIGHTEEN YEARS OLD

"Baby, please..."

My eyes darted down to the brunette wrapped around my waist and grimaced. We'd barely been at the party for two hours, and I'd already asked Emma to stop touching me multiple times. At first, she'd listened and backed off a little, but with each drink, my boundaries were becoming more and more a joke to her.

"You're no fun," Emma pouted. Maybe that was on me. I should have known why she asked me for a ride to the party, but I didn't really know for sure until I walked into the kitchen earlier and listened to her brag to her friends that I was going to be her summer conquest.

Never going to happen.

The party raged around us, almost our entire senior class filling the small lake house. It belonged to the parents of a guy on the baseball team. They'd gone on a cruise earlier in the week, and he decided to throw a huge party for graduation. No one was more grateful to be done with high school than me, but parties like this weren't my scene. However, this was the last time I could celebrate with my team. While we might not be best friends, we'd worked well together, making it all the way to the state championship this year.

During the past four years, baseball had been my life. While at first, I used it to help me learn how to focus, now, it was everything. There was something about being out on the ball field, where I could zone out everything else. When I was at school, I had to spend so much time and effort trying to drone out all the extra noise. But once my mitt was on my hand, my focus was singular: strike out the batter, get a home run, move as fast as my legs would physically let me.

Luckily, all that effort—early morning practices, sprints in the afternoons, extra time with the coaches—had paid off. I'd gotten a slew of offers from different colleges, but decided to head to Seattle. Not only did they offer me a full ride, but I liked the program and the coaches.

As much as I hated the idea of leaving home, starting fresh somewhere new sounded pretty fucking amazing. Growing up in such a small community meant I'd known most of these assholes since birth, and I was ready to meet some new people. Besides my parents, there was no one else I'd really miss, no one else I'd care about leaving behind.

Well, my parents and one other person.

"You ssshud taske me up shere," Emma mumbled, pulling me away from my thoughts. She giggled as she flicked my earlobe. Yup, definitely not into that. "Wez have sosh much fund."

No fucking thank you. Maybe that offer would have tempted other people, but I had no interest in going anywhere with this girl. In fact, I'd decided I was good with dating after Calla and I broke up a couple months ago. It was mutual, both of us agreeing we were better off as friends. We probably never should have dated, but Calla was fun, and that was what I needed for so long. She was great about getting me out of my routine, forcing me to enjoy my last years of high school. I would always love her, but I never felt like I was in love with her. There was never any drive to take things further than surface level, never any need to cross any lines. In fact, beyond a couple of drunken make-out sessions, we'd barely touched, settling into a routine that worked.

But as high school graduation grew closer, it seemed like we were both ready for something more. Calla wanted to be all in with someone, and I wanted to focus on baseball when I went to school. Considering the sizable scholarship I'd gotten from Seattle, it was the least I could do.

I shifted on the couch, trying to give Emma some space. "You should drink some water, try to sober up."

"Thatsh stuhphad," she pouted again as she climbed into my lap and tried to nuzzle my neck. I abruptly shifted, dropping her in the lap of one of my teammates. Lucky for me, it was Mike Dougan, who'd always had a thing for Emma anyway. He was a good guy and would make sure she got home safe.

As I stood, I looked around the room, hoping to find someone else to talk to. But given that everyone had been pounding shots for the better part of an hour, the party was already becoming a giant fucking disaster.

Maybe it was because I'd grown up behind the back of a bar, but I didn't see the appeal. Not only did you make a fool out of yourself, but the following day was always a nightmare. I wasn't interested in that, not when I spent every morning on the pitch, trying to perfect my fastball.

I'd just pushed open the back door when I heard someone call my name. Wade sat on a lounge chair on the other side of the back porch, playing with the beer bottle in his hand. For a moment, I debated going back inside, pretending I hadn't heard him. Wade might have been my best friend at one time, but our friendship changed after he dated Devyn. Even after they broke up, there was tension between us. I'd tried to get past it, but he made it clear he wasn't interested. We were teammates, nothing more.

Wade glanced up at me, his expression stormy. "Can you believe we're out of here in a few months?"

"Nah," I said as I took a seat in the chair next to him. "Feels strange."

He nodded, understanding what I meant. This was a small town, one most of us had lived in our entire lives. The most time I spent away from the lake was when my family went to Washington for a week last summer. But that was about to change. In a month, I'd be in a big city, on the opposite coast.

"Everything's going to be different," Wade sighed, taking a pull from his drink. He glanced over at me then looked back down at the bottle, like he was ashamed of his next question. "Where's Devyn going?"

"Columbia," I answered. "Pre-law program."

"Good for her," he said, and the words seemed genuine. "How are you guys going to handle that? Being on opposite sides of the country?"

"What do you mean?" I bit out. "We're friends. Best friends. Distance won't change us."

"Okay," Wade snorted.

I leaned forward, my voice lowering to a lethal level. "You know nothing about us, about our friendship."

"Seems like I know more than you." He shook his head. "There was a time when I almost felt bad for you two. You've been circling each other for so long, but neither one has the balls to make the first move."

"What the fuck are you talking about?"

He shifted to sit up, meeting my narrowed stare head on. "If you haven't figured it out yet, you're never going to, Anders."

Wade stood and tossed his empty bottle into the recycling

can. I stayed in the same spot, barely hearing him head back into the party. His words echoed in my mind, making me question my future with Devyn. It was hard enough knowing we'd be apart for the next four years, but to think we'd lose touch? That almost knocked the wind out of me.

Truth be told, the last few months had already felt different. We were just as close as always, but our schedules kept us apart. Between my constant baseball and her demanding extracurriculars, it seemed like we were always missing each other.

Hopefully, it'd be different when Devyn came back for the summer. I'd circled the date on my calendar months ago, marked off each day as it passed. Now that it was less than a week away, I was getting impatient, needing to see her again.

I glanced over my shoulder at the party still raging behind me, but I was done. Emma had moved on, happily snuggling with Mike on the couch. At least he'd gotten her to drink water, which was probably in both of their best interests.

Standing, I walked over to the gate at the far end of the porch, lifting the latch to get out to the driveway. Maybe I should have gone home, but Wade's words kept playing in the back of my mind, and I needed to work out all this extra tension.

Jetting down main street, I cut across the field to the local mini-park. The owners were only seasonal residents, coming back for the summer rush of tourists. The rest of the year, they lived in a senior community in Florida. Like most people in town, they were close to my parents, so they'd given us a key before they left for the winter. Even though they were back in town now, they had no problem with me coming by to use the batting cages as long as I was smart and didn't make a mess for them to pick up in the morning.

After I started up the machine, I grabbed a helmet and my favorite bat, then stepped inside the cage. I paused, waiting for the rhythmic movements to wash away the world around me.

After a lifetime of trying to block out all the extra noise surrounding me, this was the one place I didn't have to try. The whirring of the machine soothed me, giving my mind something to focus on.

But today, it wasn't working. The extra noise was all inside my head. Between Wade's comments and Devyn's distance, everything felt like it was closing in on me. For years, I'd pushed aside my feelings for Devyn, first because of her relationship with Wade, and then because of my own with Calla. This was the first time in a long time we were both single, but I still wasn't ready to confront how I felt about her.

Maybe it was cowardice, but with so many other changes happening in my life, I wasn't ready to risk our friendship too. I needed Devyn. She was the other half of me. She was my port in the storm, my safe place to land.

She believed in me like no one else, not even my parents.

A flash of her smiling infiltrated my mind, the image so gorgeous, I had to step away for a moment. It was bad enough she'd crept into my mind the last few times I'd gripped my cock, but now, I couldn't stop thinking about her spread out for me, letting me taste her supple skin. Just the thought made my cock harden, and I cursed as I willed it away.

I had no right to think of her that way. But even though we were just friends, in my mind, no one compared to Devyn. She had always been pretty, but in the past couple of years, her confidence had grown, making her downright stunning. And not just because her body was a work of art, worthy of lining the pages of her sketchbook—no, it was because her smile lit something inside me. It could be the worst day, but if I got one of Devyn's rare smiles, it made all the difference in the world.

Maybe it was selfish to hold on to her so tightly. After all, Devyn had the world laid out at her feet. She was so fucking smart. Even though she struggled with the decision to go to law school, I was so fucking proud of her for getting into Columbia. There was no doubt in my mind she'd make an incredible lawyer one day.

Meanwhile, I only had one skill, and if baseball didn't work out, I had no idea what I was going to do. Come back here and work for my dad? I might not have any options. There was No Plan B, not for me.

Fuck, I was spiraling. A ball rushed through the air and almost hit me because I was in the wrong position. Cursing under my breath, I moved to the side of the cage and pulled off my helmet, dropping my head into my hands. I needed to get it together. Maybe things were changing between Devyn and me, but I wasn't going down that easily.

Reaching into my pocket, I dug out my phone, searching for my best friend's number. But as the line trilled, the familiar ringtone echoed in the darkness. I brought the phone away from my ear, turning around to meet Devyn's smile.

"Hey, stranger."

"Hey yourself," I chuckled, ripping off the helmet and exiting the cage. Before Devyn could say anything else, I pulled her into my chest, letting her loop her arms around my neck. As she held me close, I buried my face in her hair, smelling the familiar scent of her shampoo. This was what I needed, the only thing that could keep me calm when my world unraveled.

I pulled back and searched her expression. "Thought you weren't coming until next week?"

"Finished finals early." She shrugged. "Decided to take the train up and surprise you."

"You took the train?" I said, shaking my head. "You should have called me. I would have picked you up."

Devyn smacked my shoulder. "I can handle myself, Grayson. Besides, I was excited to see you and didn't want to wait any longer." She smiled up at me. "What's it been? Five months?"

"Five months, one week, and three days." I winked at her. "Sorry, Ace. Lost track of the hours."

She rolled her eyes. "Can't believe you remember that."

"I remember everything when it comes to you, Devy."

Ducking her head, she tried to hide her blush, but I could still see it on her cheeks. She walked over to the door of the cage, twirling my bat in her hands. "So, your mom says you've been coming down here most nights. Are you trying to blow out your shoulder?"

"Not gonna happen," I chuckled, taking the bat from her. I swallowed, trying to ignore how much I wanted to touch Devyn, wanted to keep holding her tight. I gripped the bat, hoping it would keep me from doing something stupid. "Helps me clear my head before I go to sleep."

"I need to find something like that."

I smirked down at her. "You wanna try?"

Devyn shook her head. "No way. I am sports-adverse. I had to play volleyball in PE and almost broke a girl's nose."

I grabbed her hand, tugging her into the cage with me. As she looked around the space with wide eyes, I reached down and grabbed my helmet. Turning toward her, I placed it on her head, bopping the rim. "C'mon, Ace. I thought you weren't afraid of anything?"

"Whoever told you that is a bold-faced liar," Devyn chuckled. "And yes, I am terrified of balls flying at my face at sixty miles per hour."

"Careful saying that out loud. Some guys might take it as a challenge."

"Ha-ha," Devyn deadpanned. She glanced at me. "Don't you need a helmet?"

"I'm fine, Ace. Better to protect that big brain of yours."

Devyn stared at me for a moment then shook her head, but she stopped arguing and let me lead her behind the batting line. As soon as she stepped up to the mark, all her bravado faded away. Her eyes widened as she looked over her shoulder at me. "Tell me what to do."

"First, you're going to need this." I held out the bat, guiding her hands to the correct position. "Okay, now, bend your knees a little."

"Like this?"

I nudged the back of her knee with mine, letting my front rest against her. It was the closest we'd ever been outside of our usual hug, and something about it felt way too natural. I cleared my throat. "Is this okay?"

Devyn nodded, not saying anything as I moved even closer, bringing her against my chest. My hands wrapped around hers, mimicking the swing of the bat. "When you swing, make sure you follow through with your hips."

She swiveled against me, her ass grazing my dick. *Fuck.* Now that was all I was thinking about. What would she do if I slid my hands down further and pressed them along the top of her jeans? Would she stop me, or would she let me touch her like I wanted? My hands tightened, just a fraction, but before I could make another move, Devyn looked at me over her shoulder.

She inhaled a shaky breath. "Okay, then what?"

"Make sure you hit the ball."

"What?" Devyn snapped right as the first ball came flying past us. She muttered a curse as she tried to get back into position, nestling against me like I was meant to mold into her. A second ball snapped right past us, Devyn not swinging until it was already long past the base.

"Son of a—" she sighed. "I told you I couldn't do this."

"Just breathe, Ace. Ignore everything else around you." My

hands tightened against her, and she relaxed into my touch. I dropped my head, bringing my mouth close to her ear. "Now, keep your eye on the ball. You're going to have to gauge the speed to determine when you should start swinging."

"You make it sound so easy."

Nothing about this was easy. Being this close to Devyn was making me question everything, not sure if I could hold my rapidly dwindling self-control.

"You've got this, Devyn," I whispered, my voice hoarse and low. "Just let go."

Devyn

EIGHTEEN YEARS OLD

When I was ten, my mother took me to the Met for the first time. I remembered looking at all the paintings, stunned into silence by the talent surrounding me. It was like the rest of the world had been washed away, all that was left me and these masterpieces. I thought it was a once-in-a-lifetime feeling.

And yet, here it was again. But instead of a priceless portrait, I found it in my best friend's expression, the smile that only shined so brightly when Gray looked at me.

"You've got this, Devyn," he said as he stared down at me. "Just let go."

He made it sound so simple, as if I could think of anything other than him. Where his hands touched me, how his fingers were digging into my skin. All I wanted was for him to move them lower, to touch me like I always dreamed he would.

Ever since I realized I was in love with Gray, there'd been a delicate line between us. I had to keep those emotions buried deep, especially when he was dating my sister. Even though they had broken up, it was still a line I couldn't cross. It was bad enough that I'd fallen in love with my sister's boyfriend; what would she say if I told her I wanted to be with him?

I shuddered, not wanting to imagine how that conversation would go. No. If my loyalty to Calla wasn't enough to keep my feelings in check, my friendship with Gray was. I couldn't risk losing him, not when he was one of the few people in my life I trusted completely.

Shifting in his arms, I tried to pass the bat back to him. "I can't do this."

Gray placed his hands on top of mine. "Give it a couple more tries, Ace. I know you can do it."

I rolled my eyes and muttered under my breath, "You're going to feel like a dick when I walk out of here with a broken nose. Or when I seriously injure you. Consider yourself warned, Grayson."

Before I could get back into position, Gray put his hands on my hips and turned me to face him. When he looked down at me, there was not an ounce of humor in his expression. He reached up, brushing my cheek with his thumb. "I won't let anything happen to you, Ace."

"You promise?" I asked, my heart thumping a steady pulse under his touch.

"To my last breath," he quietly admitted. He shook his head after the words came out. "Sorry, it's something my parents always say to each other. I don't know why I just said that."

"Don't be sorry—I liked it," I said quickly. "Sounds like the best kind of promise."

"Always the best for you, Devyn."

For a moment, I swore his eyes darted down to my lips. We leaned in at the same time, our faces closer than they'd ever been before. My heart beat wildly in my chest, dying to know what Gray's lips tasted like.

But before we could connect, a ball released from the machine, hitting the cage behind us. The sound made me jump, almost crushing Gray in the process. He chuckled as my breathing returned to normal, shifting me so I could see the trajectory of the machine better.

What the hell was I doing? Hadn't I just told myself nothing could ever happen between Gray and me? And not even ten minutes later, here I was, about to kiss him like my life depended on it.

Luckily, the machine broke the moment between us, and Gray looked like he realized his mistake as well. I wasn't who he wanted, and it was best if I remembered that. There was a reason nothing had ever happened between us, and it would only cause everyone pain if I pushed us on this path now.

I cleared my throat, trying to give him a normal smile, but it felt flat. "Maybe we should call it a night."

"Not letting you get out of this that easily." He pressed the bat into my trembling hands. "Come on, Ace. I know you can do this."

I nodded, letting his faith in me steel my resolve. That was the thing about Gray: he didn't pass out idle praise or gratitude. He was willing to push when needed but always ready to catch you if you fell.

I stepped up to the line, throwing the bat over my shoulder like I watched him do a thousand times. It seemed easy enough: watch the ball, wait for it to get close enough, then swing the bat with all your might. But when the ball launched toward me, all those lessons left my mind, and I completely missed.

I looked over at Gray, who was smirking from his position on the other side of the grate. "Don't even say it."

"Wouldn't dream of it, Devy." He nodded toward the machine. "Incoming."

I hissed a quick curse word as I tried to figure out my stance in time, but it was useless. My poor coordination was no match for Gray's athletic genes, and with each missed swing, I felt my cheeks glowing hotter and hotter. If there was one thing that got under my skin every time, it was feeling like a failure. I'd already gotten enough of it at home. Every grade was dissected, each assignment checked for "room to grow." Even my art, which started as an escape after my dad died, was losing its appeal now that my mother and stepfather had started using it as a cute little anecdote for their high society friends.

I could still hear their laughter at their last dinner party, taking a piece I'd poured my whole heart into, metaphorically melting it down into nothing, their rebellious daughter who once thought art school was a viable option for college. They'd pat each other on the back, commending each other for breaking my spirit, happy I'd given in to their demand to attend an Ivy League university. My body sagged with defeat as another ball passed me by, and I dropped the bat at my feet.

"I can't do this," I whispered, heading over to the exit. But before I could shove the gate open, Gray was there, an intense look in his eyes. There was no way to move past him, not with him blocking the only way out. However, I didn't feel afraid. When I looked up at Gray, his eyes softened, searching mine for answers.

"Where did you go, Ace?" he quietly asked.

I rolled my eyes. "Obviously, I'm right here. But this is stupid. I'm not going to be any good, no matter how long you stand there and laugh at me."

"Did you see me laughing?" Gray asked, encroaching on my space a little more. "Did you hear me say anything other than you can do this?" His hands moved up until just the tips of his fingers rested under my chin. He tilted it up so our eyes met. It was almost impossible to stand tall with the look in his eyes—one I had seen a million times on the baseball field but never directed at me. Raw intensity, the kind that made the world fall at your feet, reflected in his dark gray eyes. "You're telling your-self you look stupid so you're not even going to try. But my best friend? She's never backed down from a fight before, and she's sure as hell not going to let a machine beat her."

"Oh, it did," I laughed halfheartedly. "It won easily, I might add."

Gray shook his head, not buying into my deflection. He once again took my hand and led me back to the line. But this time, when I picked up the bat, he stood at my side. He wasn't as close as before; we weren't touching, but I could still feel him there. As I moved into position, he nodded, checking my stance before I lifted the bat back up.

"Bend your knees," he called out. "More."

"Good?" I asked, staring down at my feet.

"Perfect," Gray answered, his voice a little deeper than before.

I nodded, all words failing me. As the machine released the ball, I swung, feeling much more confident than before. But once again, I was a couple of seconds too slow, and the ball hitting the back net felt like the worst type of failure. "You're overthinking it," he said. "Tune everything else out and just watch the ball. When it crosses the base, swing out and connect."

"Oh wow, how come I didn't think of that the first ten times?"

"Breathe, Ace."

The bright yellow ball peeked around the corner, and I could feel his body stiffen, forcing me to focus. As hard as it was to ignore his weight at my side, I liked having him as an anchor, like I could face the hard things because I wasn't alone. When the ball cracked toward us, I kept my eye on it, exhaling slowly to help me focus. As it passed the mid-point, I started to shift, trying to remember everything Gray taught me.

And this time, instead of the swoosh of the ball flying by, it made the most satisfying cracking sound when it collided with the bat. The ball ricocheted into the other side of the cage, ratting the metal rings. It was by no means a beautiful hit, but it counted, and it was mine.

Without thinking, I whipped around, throwing my arms around Gray's neck. I held him tight, practically jumping to wrap my legs around him. "I did it!" I squealed, crushing him a little tighter. "Holy shit, I can't believe I did it."

Gray smiled back at me, and for a moment, all I wanted were more days like this, days spent nestled in his arms, his bright smile aimed only at me. I wanted to see all his sides, to know every piece of his heart. But as hard as it was to pretend otherwise, it was the smart move to say no. I wanted Gray in my life, and anything more than friendship would risk that.

But it was hard to remember that when he stared at me with such pride. Without thinking, I lifted myself further into his embrace and placed a soft kiss on his cheek. "Thank you for believing in me," I said.

His resulting smile was the brightest I'd ever seen. "Always, Ace."

SEVENTEEN

Devyn

Steam spilled from the top of my coffee mug as I stared out across the valley below. Even after two weeks of living in Gray's house, I still couldn't get over the view. It was the perfect way to start my morning, enjoying a cup of coffee while watching the world go on. After spending so much time running through life, I was doing my best to appreciate these quiet moments.

Flurries filled the air, making it even more surreal. Winter should have been wrapping up soon, but you wouldn't know it by looking around our town. We still had mounds of snow lining the streets, a deep chill lingered in the wind. At least the skies seemed to be a little brighter, letting go of the murky gray that plagued us all winter.

As I finished the last couple sips of my coffee, I emptied the mug in the sink and moved over into my living room. Shit, not mine. It was too easy to forget that while living in Gray's mountainside escape. I'd never imagined living somewhere like this, always assuming I'd buy something in the New York City skyline when I eventually made partner. But to my surprise, I really liked living here. It had only been a couple of weeks, but I felt at peace, settled.

Maybe it was because I'd never given myself time to nest in my old home, but it never felt like mine. Sure, I was attached to it, but I never let myself really settle in. It might have been some sort of self-preservation, knowing David's blood money had purchased it, that it was mine in name only. It was only borrowed.

Kind of like this place.

I pushed the thought away, knowing David and Gray couldn't be more different if they tried. David held everything over people's heads, using his money and connections to help so it burned more bitterly when he eventually snapped it away.

Gray might seem gruff to most people, but in his heart, he was selfless. I'd heard over the years about his selflessness, donating a sizable portion of his salary to various charities. That was Gray, though. He could never let himself enjoy all the money, not while others were suffering.

I pushed thoughts of my husband out of my mind, focusing instead on the papers covering the coffee table. True to his word, Gray had kept his distance since I moved in. While we texted multiple times a day, he hadn't shown up here since that first day. And while I hated to admit it, I missed him. It was the strangest thing. For years, I was able to ignore the ache his absence had left behind. Maybe it was because I wasn't as busy, or maybe it was because I was in our hometown, but it was harder to ignore him here.

I jumped as my phone rang, the sound breaking the silence around me. I chuckled as I saw Tomas' name on the screen, bringing it up to my ear.

"Please tell me you found something."

"I found you," he chuckled. "That's a feat in and of itself. A lot of people have been asking about you, querida."

I bristled at the insinuation, hating that only a few words

made me vulnerable. Sucking in a short breath, I tried to keep my nerves together. "And what have you been telling them?"

"Not a damn thing," my friend chuckled. "I thought you knew me better than that. After all, discretion is a requirement in my line of work."

"Thank God for that," I sighed, sitting on the carpet in front of the coffee table. I placed the phone on speaker and started to look over my work in progress. Five years of work covered the surface of the table, five years of tracking down leads and attempting to follow the money. Reports from forensic accountants, private investigators, former disgruntled employees—anything I could think of to prove my stepfather was the monster I knew him to be.

But nothing seemed to turn the tide. At least, not until I bumped into Tomas in the halls of my old firm. We'd worked together on a couple of cases, and I knew he was the right-hand man for many of the partners. When you needed a break on the case but required unconventional methods, Tomas was the one to call. And even though he'd handled some shady dealings, only after a few short months of friendship, I'd divulged my secret side project. He immediately asked to help, all too aware of the risks. But like me, he'd seen the devastation my stepfather left in his wake.

One night, when we'd shared a bottle of wine as we dived into old financial records, Tomas told me one of his first clients was a woman looking for her sister. She'd been an intern at one of David's sub-companies and had gone missing shortly after filing a sexual harassment report. While there was never any evidence, her sister and Tomas believed the problem had been taken care of by one of David's business partners. Even though he'd never been able to get justice for the woman, he'd held onto that rage and used it to drive his business, hoping he'd get a chance to take down David and his partners once and for all.

It was a lucky break he crossed paths with someone who wanted to see David punished just as badly.

"Did you look over the file I sent you?" he asked through the speaker.

"Yeah," I sighed. "But I can't make any sense of the purchases. I can see it's tied to this town, but that's all. The names and dates don't make sense."

"That's what I figured," Tomas sighed. "I'm going to try to hack into their digital records and see what I can find."

"Good luck with that," I snorted. "This town is a bit behind the times. They just started using an app so people could pay for metered parking. There's no way files from thirty years ago are fully digitized."

I could hear Tomas smile through the phone. "Good thing we've got someone on the inside then."

"Yeah, right," I said. "I've avoided this town for years. If I start sniffing around, asking questions, red flags will be raised."

"Maybe it's time to call in a favor with your little sister."

The thought of involving Calla in any of this made my stomach lurch. No, I hadn't spent years being David's target only to pull her into his web now.

The only other people who knew David's dark side were my mother and my older sister, Laurel. My mother was the most obvious choice. She'd been involved in enough of her own shady dealings that she knew which palms to grease. But she'd also just finalized her divorce from David, finally getting the courage to leave after Calla cut her out of her life. Although they were attempting to mend their relationship—*we all were*—there was still a good amount of strain between us. There would always be a part of me that loved my mother, but I'd be the first to admit I didn't trust her.

My elder sister was also a stern no. Out of all of us, Laurel was the only one immune to David's abuse growing up. But then again, she'd welcomed him with open arms, whereas Calla and I never warmed up to him. Laurel became his protégé, eager for any opportunity he offered. Her bond with him had ruined my relationship with her, and I wasn't about to trust her now.

No, as much as I wished I could get someone else involved, the responsibility laid on my shoulders. For my mother, for my sister, and even for myself—I would see that bastard's kingdom come crumbling down. No matter the cost. No matter the consequences.

Even if I had to lose myself along the way.

"Querida?" Tomas asked, pulling me out of my daze. "You okay over there?"

"Yeah," I pushed out quickly, brushing the strands of hair from my face. "I'll see what I can do on my end. What's next for you?"

"I have an insider who might be ready to talk. Wants to clear his conscience apparently."

I chuckled. "And what did you say to that?"

"You already know, Devyn. No man who dirties his soul like that—"

"Their conscience is never truly clear," I finished for him, knowing the words by heart. He usually said it more as a warning, trying to keep me from dirtying my hands too much. But he'd stopped saying it months ago, probably aware there were few lines I wouldn't cross in the name of justice.

The sound of tires crunching on the snow pulled my attention away from the table. "Shit," I muttered, dashing over to the window. Gray was climbing out of his truck, his dog, Elsa, in tow. My blood ran cold, looking back at everything covering the table. I scurried back over, shoving all the papers into a pile. Without thinking, I shoved them under the couch, hoping Elsa wouldn't find them. Otherwise, this evening would be taking a very unpleasant turn.

"Everything good?"

"No," I huffed. "Gray's here."

"The husband?" He swore under his breath. "You decide if you're going to bring him into this?"

"Absolutely not," I bit back. "None of this touches Gray."

"Fine," Tomas said, annoyance tinting his tone. We'd had this fight when I first told him I was going back home to try to find more answers. He thought Gray might have some powerful connections we could exploit, especially considering so many of David's friends had ownership stock in Major League teams. But just like Calla, Gray was my line in the sand.

I shook my head, not in the mood to get into it again. "I've gotta go. Let me know if your lead gives up anything useful."

"Same to you," Tomas muttered, hanging up the phone just as Gray turned to me through the window. He smiled at me, waving a gloved hand in greeting. Just the sight of him was enough to soothe my unease. I tried to ignore the feeling, the pull I felt toward him, even though it had been years since we had been close. But every day I spent in his home, I felt the walls crumbling around me.

I glanced at the bottom of the couch, knowing I needed to keep my distance. Despite his kindness in opening his home to me, I still didn't fully trust Gray, and I definitely didn't trust myself around him. He knew me too well, knew all the ways to get me to forgive him.

And while it was tempting, I couldn't go there, not while so many other questions lingered in my head, not while I was working on taking down David. There were too many risks, and I didn't want any of this to blow back on Gray.

No matter what has happened in the past, one thing would always be true. I would never let any harm come to Gray. Not if I could prevent it.

EIGHTEEN

Grayson

From the moment the front door opened, I knew something was off with Devyn. By now, I was used to her mask and could tell when she locked it into place, but this was different. Devyn stood in the hallway, blocking my view of the rest of the house. She crossed her arms over her chest and fixed her face into a familiar scowl. However, her eyes were wild, almost like an animal caught in a trap.

Before I could ask what was wrong, Elsa rushed into the house. She immediately bounded toward Devyn, jumping up into her arms. I expected Devyn to freak out and yell at the dog to get down, but instead, I was met with the most melodious giggle, a sound I wanted to bottle and replay for the rest of my days. Devyn beamed down at Elsa, engulfing her in a tight hug. Despite the snow and mud being dragged all over her, Devyn kept petting her, even following her to the floor when Elsa laid on her back for belly scratches.

"You are way too cute," Devyn said, her voice several octaves higher than usual. "It's making me forgive you for all the fur you left over on the couch. Yes, it does."

Elsa just nuzzled in closer, batting Devyn's hand with her

paw to get her to keep rubbing her belly. The sight melted me, but it also made me a little jealous. When was the last time Devyn touched me that freely? Jesus. I scrubbed my hand down my face. I was getting jealous of my fucking dog. I really needed to get it together.

But as soon as Devyn met my gaze, the walls slammed back into place, and all the warmth in her eyes melted away. She looked off to the other side of the room before speaking. "Gray... what are you doing here?"

I threw my thumb over my shoulder, pointing toward my truck outside. "We're supposed to get nasty weather over the weekend. Thought you might need some supplies."

Devyn stood, brushing off the pieces of snow Elsa had left behind. As she ran her hands along her shirt, I took the chance to study her. She wore a matching tan sweatsuit, her hair in a messy bun, more casual than I'd seen her in years. It was simple, a glimpse into her everyday life, but it made me hard as a fucking rock.

However, the next thought killed all my arousal, and made my stomach knot. *This was what it would be like if I'd done things right, if I was coming home to her for real.* It was almost a punishment, getting these brief glimpses of a life with Devyn. When we were younger, we'd never had this, not while we were both living under our parents' roofs. But now that we were adults, I realized how much I'd missed, how much I wanted to know all of her, wanted to experience different pieces of our lives together.

"Oh..." Devyn sighed, a rosy color filling her cheeks. "You didn't have to do that. I could have figured something out."

"I know," I shrugged, walking into the kitchen. From the looks of things, Devyn had barely used any of it. Not surprised. Even when my mom offered her cooking lessons years ago,

Devyn refused. Opening the cabinet, I chuckled when I saw the rows of instant soup and other quick meals.

I held up the box of macaroni. "You know this isn't a real meal, right?"

Devyn rolled her eyes and swiped the box from my hand. "It works. It's quick, easy, and I don't have to think much about it."

A crude comment sat on the tip of my tongue, desperate to break out. But considering Devyn was still warming up to me, I wasn't about to tempt her into kicking me out of my own house.

I shook my head, already forgetting this was my home. Something about Devyn fit here in a way I didn't, at least not alone. The rooms were too cold, the mountain too quiet. But with her smile and her quiet admonishments of me to my dog, it felt more like home than it ever had before.

She dug into the bags, pulling out the vegetables and fresh fruit. She wrinkled her nose when the kale and spinach came out, and I already knew they were going to get hidden in the back of the fridge. I nodded toward her, unable to resist a little teasing. "I've got a good juicer under the counter if you want to use it." I made a crush motion with my hands. "That kale blends down really nicely with the fruit."

Devyn's face blanched, and I took it to mean something hadn't changed over the years. She shook it off, frowning as she looked down at the produce in her hands again. "I can't believe you still drink that green stuff."

"It's good for you," I said. "Gives you all the vitamins you need."

"I'd rather live without them," Devyn drawled. She turned back toward the counter, and her whole face lit up when she saw what was waiting for her at the bottom. Her wide brown eyes lit up as she pulled the container out of the bag. "You didn't!"

Smug satisfaction washed over me as I watched her open the Lost Tavern container and gasp at the sight of the blue cheese burger and sweet potato fries waiting for her. She was practically dancing as she grabbed a fry. "This is the best surprise ever. So much better than the kale."

"I think you mean *thank you, Gray*."

"Thank you, *Grayson*."

I smiled, leaning forward to tap her on the nose. "You're welcome, Ace."

That move must have felt too familiar, because Devyn backed away, clutching the container in her hand like I would take it from her. She walked around the counter, sitting on the other side of the island, still watching me warily—like she needed the piece of marble between us to feel safe.

My hands fisted as I tried to hide my irritation at the abrupt shift. One step forward, thirty steps back. When I was around Devyn, it was too easy to fall into old habits, like we could gloss over the lost years between us and the hurt I'd caused. I could forget she was my estranged wife and just remember what it felt like when she was my best friend in the world.

But it would never be that simple. We weren't those same kids. She didn't know this version of me, and I barely knew her. We were practically strangers, and if I wanted that to change, I had to bide my time and prove to Devyn I wasn't the same scared kid who let her walk away.

All my thoughts died when Devyn took a bite of her burger, letting out a moan so sexual, it made my dick stand at attention. Jesus. I was never going to survive this if she kept making those noises. *Calm down*, I internally shouted, needing my body to understand the mission here. *Earn back her trust.*

As if my dick had a mind of its own, it shouted back—*and then can we fuck her?*

The mental image of Devyn sprawled underneath me,

making those same noises because of my mouth, because of my cock, made me uncomfortably hard, needing to shift to lessen the tension in my jeans. Thank fuck I'd changed out of my sweatpants before coming over here.

Devyn sighed, put the burger down, and wiped her hands on a napkin. "You know when you've missed something for a long time, and then you go back and try it, and it's not nearly as good as you remember?" She pointed down at her burger. "It's the exact opposite here. I am kicking myself for refusing to have one for so long."

"You didn't have to stay away because of me," I said, leaning forward on the counter to steal a fry.

"Yes, I did," Devyn said, averting her eyes. She shook her head. "But seriously, Gray. Thank you for this." She eyed the front door. "If you have to go..."

"Nah," I chuckled, reaching into the bag to grab the last container. I pulled out my grilled salmon and vegetables, and Devyn's nose crinkled. I chuckled at her expression. "Even though I'm not in the league anymore, some habits die hard. I've been on the same diet for a decade." I shrugged. "It's worked so far."

"And you're eating it here?" Devyn asked, staring at me like she was trying to solve a puzzle.

"Yup," I answered, shoving a piece of asparagus into my mouth, mostly trying to keep myself from saying anything else. Like many things with Devyn, it was different. Keeping quiet had never been one of my problems. My dad always taught me to think before I spoke and to weigh out the value of my words before casting them on someone else. I took that to heart, keeping my mouth shut until I knew what I wanted to say.

And then, there was Devyn.

The moment those brown eyes hit me, I wanted to spill everything, to talk to her until my throat ran dry. I wanted to give her my every thought, wanted her opinion about every choice in my life. After going years without her, I'd grown numb to the constant pain in my chest, but now that she was in front of me, it was a sharp ache, like someone had my heart in a vise grip.

"Okay, what is this?" Devyn snapped after several minutes of silence between us. I almost chuckled, loving that she was the one to break the tension between us.

"Friends have dinner." I lifted my fork, motioning between our containers. "This is us, having dinner."

"Since when are we friends, much less friends who share a meal?" she said. "If this is some attempt to get me in your bed, you've already failed." She pointed down to her almost-demolished burger. "Because this might be amazing, but nothing is that amazing."

"One." I smirked. "Technically, you're already in my bed."

"Your *guest* bed."

For now.

"And two," I added. "That's not what I'm here for. I want to spend time with you, Devyn. Get to know this new version of you." I chuckled, pushing away from the counter to grab a glass of water. "Shit, haven't you ever just enjoyed a meal with someone with no ulterior motive?"

I realized my mistake as soon as I looked over my shoulder and saw the cold indifference in Devyn's expression. I shook my head, stepping over to her. I placed my hand on top of hers. "I'm sorry, Devy. I didn't mean anything by it."

"It's fine," she said, a little too quickly to be true. As I continued to stare at her, she sighed in defeat. "It's one of those things you don't realize until it's too late. Over the past few years, all I've done is work. It's taken over every part of my life. Expensive meals, high-end restaurants? I can't remember a single bite, all because I focused too much on the clients and making myself look good." She shook her head, shrugging her shoulders. "All of that noise to say, no. I haven't done this in a while." She exhaled, forcing her eyes up to meet mine. "But this is nice...being here with you, no ulterior motives."

With that simple sentiment, my heart almost burst from my chest, feeling stronger than it had in years. It felt like the best kind of victory, one hard-fought and hard-earned, like my first World Series tournament, when we only won because of the seventh game. Maybe it was ridiculous, but this moment with Devyn felt more monumental because I was unsure it would ever come.

She shook her head, pulling her hand out from under mine to resume eating. "Okay, Grayson, now that we've established what this is, tell me." She arched her brow. "What do you want to talk about?"

I smirked, lowering to my elbows so I could watch her better. "How about what you've been up to over the past five years?"

She stared at me. "That's a long story. How much do you want to know?"

"Everything."

NINETEEN

Devyn

"You are such a liar!"

I clutched my stomach as it ached from laughter. Gray sat on the opposite side of the couch, laughing almost as hard as me. After we finished eating, I thought Gray was going to make an excuse to leave, but he surprised me by asking if I wanted to hang out for a little while longer. Despite my initial hesitation, I couldn't convince myself to say no. After almost a week of limited contact with the outside world, it was nice to spend time with someone. It was even nicer because it was Gray.

We moved into the living room and scrolled through one of his streaming apps on the TV. Outside, the world had gone dark, and it was impossible to see past the porch. But even with the hours ticking by, neither of us attempted to move.

"I'm the liar?" Gray squawked, turning around to face me fully. "You made me watch Legally Blonde every single day that summer. I was half-convinced you only became a lawyer to re-enact that courtroom scene."

"If only," I muttered under my breath. "But it's not like I wanted to be Elle Woods; I just liked her confidence. She knew what she wanted and didn't let anyone else define her worth."

Gray's smile faltered for a moment, and I thought I said too much. I didn't want to break this moment between us; I needed this levity more than anything. After everything with my job, my stepfather, and uprooting my entire life, an evening of laughing and reminiscing was perfect.

Gray must have been able to read that on my face, because he nodded and took a pull from his beer. "Makes sense. Plus, no offense, Devy, but if you showed up in an all-pink outfit, I would have thought you were trying to send out a distress signal."

"You saying I can't rock an all-pink outfit?"

Gray mock glared at me. "You know I'm not. You could wear anything and still be a total fucking knock-out."

My throat dried up at his words, not sure how long I'd waited to hear something like that from him. When we were growing up, Gray was never short on compliments, but I took them for granted. I assumed they'd always be there, that I would always hear his words. And while other people I'd dated had dished out compliments, it wasn't the same as hearing them from Gray. His deep voice was like hot tea on a cold winter night, making me feel cozy and warm.

It made my heart ache, wishing we could go back in time. What would our lives have been like if we had never fallen apart? If we hadn't let distance ruin what we once had? Would we still be here, two people tied together by an accidental marriage? Or would we be here by choice, meaning the words we'd drunkenly mumbled all those years ago?

"Hey," Gray said, scooting on the couch to get closer to me. "Where did you go?"

"Nowhere," I said, swallowing to hide the catch in my throat. "Just trying to remember all of your embarrassing secrets."

Gray relaxed and leaned back against the couch. "Don't have any."

"The time you bleached your hair?"

He shook his head and laughed. "You dared me to do it."

"I didn't think you actually would!"

"It was worth it to see the look on your face," he chuckled. "Besides, nothing was as bad as when you tried to dye your hair black."

My face paled as I remembered the horrible orange tone that replaced it once the black dye washed out. That was the first and last time I tried to dye my hair by myself. "That was a terrible decision."

"Eh." Gray shrugged. "I kinda liked it. But it reminded me a little too much of Laurel."

I shook my head, realizing he was right. My older sister started dying her hair dark back in high school, probably to stand out from Calla and me. While my baby sister had auburn hair like our mother, Laurel and I shared my dad's dark blonde. But while she'd covered it up and never looked back, I'd gone the opposite route and started bleaching my hair to make the blonde even brighter.

Silence fell between us, but neither of us rushed to fill it. Gray continued flicking through the different apps, eventually stopping on a highlight reel from the last baseball season. Sneaking a peek out of the corner of my eye, I watched as his face fell. After a couple of minutes, I couldn't help but ask, "Do you miss it?"

"Every day," he answered. "The game, not everything around it. I miss the weight of a ball in my glove, that moment when you knew the batter was going to strike out. I miss that. Mostly, I miss playing a game for the sake of it, not for the money or the contract."

"You could still play if you wanted," I offered.

Gray shook his head. "Nah, it's not in the cards anymore.

I'm good with my choice. I don't regret walking away when I did."

I shifted on the couch, curling my legs up underneath me. Turning to face Gray, I asked. "Why did you walk away?"

His expression shuttered, and my heart sank. For a moment, I thought he wouldn't answer, or worse: shut me out like I'd done to him too many times. But Gray dropped his head back on the couch. "My dad's sick." He ran his hand over his face, as if willing the words to come. "Alzheimer's."

"What?" I said as I brought my hand to my mouth. "But he's too young–"

"Early on-set," Gray sighed. "Came out of nowhere. As far as we know, he doesn't have any history of it in his family, so it was just an unlucky hand."

"Shit," I whispered, covering my face with my hand. I knew something was going on with Gray. My sister had alluded to there being a bigger reason he'd come home after so many years away, but I'd assumed it was something about his contract, maybe his former team. His dad was sick... My stomach soured with the thought. "How is he?"

"Depends on the day." Gray leaned forward, resting his elbows on his knees. He toyed with the edges of his beer label, no longer looking at me. "Can we talk about something else? Not trying to be a dick, but this is the first night in a while when I've forgotten about everything going on at home."

"And you want to hold on to it a little longer?"

He nodded. "Just...play pretend with me for a few more hours, Devyn. Please."

He had to know I was helpless to resist him when he asked like that. That moment drew me back into the past, and I was looking at my best friend when he needed me the most. Maybe if we were playing pretend, I could extend that to the rift between us. We could ignore the distance and pretend it was just another night, two best friends watching a movie like we used to do all the time.

I grabbed the remote from his hand, putting on a movie we used to love. "Yeah, Gray. Let's pretend."

TWENTY

Devyn

As the credits rolled on our third movie of the night, I looked at Gray. His eyes were closed, but he was smiling peacefully in his sleep. He looked younger—like he did before the weight of the world had fallen on his shoulders.

I rubbed my fingers over my eyes, trying not to think too hard about what Gray had confided in me. Curt had Alzheimer's. The words sank in, and it took everything to keep from crying. Curt had practically been my second father, stepping up after my own had passed away. He was my dad's best friend, and Curt loved to tell me stories about him. He'd taught me how to drive, comforted me when my mother married David despite our concerns.

And now, when he needed me the most, there was nothing I could do to save him. No money and no amount of knowledge could stop the inevitable, and that was a bitter pill to swallow.

Almost as bitter as the realization I had wasted years with him because I was angry with Gray.

Shaking my head, I lifted myself off the couch, grabbing my wine glass to bring it to the sink. I also took Gray's empty water glass; he'd stopped drinking hours earlier because he needed to drive back home.

As I placed the glasses on the dish rack, Gray groaned painfully in his sleep. Before I even realized what was happening, I rushed back to his side. His peaceful expression was long gone, replaced by a furrowed brow and some light perspiration on his forehead. I took one of his hands in mine and placed the other on his cheek.

Shit, what were you supposed to do during a nightmare? You couldn't wake people up if they were sleepwalking, but was it the same if they were having a bad dream? I wasn't risking it. Instead, I just stayed at Gray's side, holding his hand a little tighter each time he mumbled under his breath.

After a few minutes, Gray suddenly shot up, taking my hand with him. I almost stumbled off the couch, but Gray reached out to steady me, holding me closer than before—closer than I'd been in a long time.

"Devyn?" he asked, his chest heaving with exertion.

"You fell asleep," I said quickly, hoping it would explain my closer proximity. "I think you were having a bad dream, but I didn't know if I should wake you up."

I glanced down at our joined hands, and Gray released me, moving back to his end of the couch. Rubbing his hands over his eyes, he stared off into the distance. "Sorry if I scared you. I've been having nasty dreams since my dad got diagnosed."

"I'm so sorry, Gray."

"Don't be." He shifted back toward me. "Thanks for being here."

"Always," I said, not realizing what had slipped out before I said it.

Gray's eyes flared to life at the simple term, the one that always meant more between us than any other promises. The word was our bond, but neither of us had said it in years. He swallowed slowly, and I couldn't help but watch the muscles in his throat move.

He reached out, placing his hand on top of mine. The tattoos covering his forearms stuck out from underneath his sleeves, and I glanced down at them. I'd seen some of his artwork over the years, usually only peeking out of his uniform. The hint of the designs made my mouth dry up, wondering where and how far they traveled. I wanted to trace them with my fingertips, wanted to know why he'd chosen each one.

As I studied his forearms, Gray reached up, placing his hand on my cheek. The first stroke of his thumb against my skin was like a lightning bolt through my chest, bringing me back to life after years of going through the motions.

"Devyn..." he whispered as his eyes dipped down to my lips.

All I wanted was to feel his mouth on mine, to seal this moment with a promise for more. I craved his hands on me, needing to know what it was like when we came together. He was so close. All it would take was one move, and I would finally remember how his kiss tasted.

But my bruised heart wouldn't let me.

I jumped back, needing as much space as possible. This wasn't just anybody —it was Gray. My former best friend, my "landlord," and my husband. If we were to cross that line, it would mean something, at least to me. Maybe Gray could hold that line between physical and emotional, but there was no way I could. There was too much history between us for it to be casual.

I stood up, darting over to the kitchen. As I went, I called out over my shoulder, "You should probably get going. It's getting late, and you're already tired." I grabbed a coffee pod from the cabinet. "Do you want me to make—"

My words cut off when Gray's hands found my waist,

keeping me trapped between him and the counter. His chest was against my back, and I could feel his heart pounding almost as hard as mine. "Why'd you run from me, Ace?" he whispered in my ear.

I shook my head. "I didn't."

"What have I told you about that?" I could feel his hands tighten against my skin. "Don't lie to me, Devyn. Even if it hurts, I want your truth."

I sighed, forcing myself to breathe. It was hard when he was this close—when his hands were on me. Being around Gray was already a struggle, and it was getting harder to remember why I was so upset with him. All I wanted was to move his hands between my legs, to show him why I was internally panicking.

"I don't know how to do this," I admitted. Gray released me, turning me around so I faced him. I dropped my eyes to the floor, unsure I'd be able to get the words out if he kept looking at me like that. "There's this...pull between us, and it scares the hell out of me."

"Why?"

I dared to glance up at him. "Because I don't know what we're doing, Gray. Every time we've gotten closer, I..."

"You've gotten hurt," Gray said. His hands left my waist, instead grabbing the counter behind me. "I've made a lot of mistakes in my life, Devyn," he whispered, reaching to brush my hair back from my face. I hadn't even noticed it had fallen out, too distracted by my husband. "And all the ones that haunt me the most? They all revolve around you."

My lip trembled as I looked up at him, trying to hold on to this moment of rare vulnerability. What would it be like to let this resentment go? To let go of the past and let Grayson back in? But as much as I wanted to, I didn't trust him, not with my heart. It might have been a battered, tired little thing, but it still beat in my chest. I couldn't risk any more damage at Gray's hands.

His thumb swiped along my cheek, brushing away a tear I hadn't noticed. "I've missed you, Devyn, more than I ever thought possible. But if you're not there yet, or if you don't think you can forgive me, I understand. You want me to sign the divorce papers? I'll do it. You want me to get out of your life and never see me again? Done. If that's what it'll take for you to be happy, just say the word, and I'll make it happen." He lowered his face, bringing both hands to my neck. "But if there's even a chance for more, I'm going to try. We've never given this a real shot, and I'll be damned if I let you go without a fight."

Was that what I wanted? If you asked me a couple of days ago, the answer would have been a resounding no, slamming the door on any possibility of Gray and me. But so much had shifted in my life lately, and this was the one place I felt safe. Despite our past, Gray was still here, still looking at me like I was the same wide-eyed girl who had fallen for him years ago.

And while I wasn't completely ready to let go of our past, I was so tired of holding it all in, so tired of secrets and guarding the fractured remnants of my heart. What would it feel like to just ride through these emotions with Gray?

He must have seen the conflict in my expression, because Gray sighed and took a step back. It was already too cold without him close. He grabbed his coat, turning back toward me. "I'm going to give you some space to sort things out. You know where to find me when you figure out what you want."

He leaned forward, pressing his lips to my forehead. I instinctively leaned into him, my fingers brushing against his chest. Gray squeezed my hand once, and then he was gone, calling for Elsa as he walked out the front door.

As soon as the door closed, I dropped my head to the counter and growled in frustration. How the hell had I gotten myself into this mess? For years, I was so angry with Gray, hating how we'd come together just to be ripped apart all over again. But from the moment I stepped back into this town, Gray had been lowering my defenses, making me remember why I'd fallen for him.

But I wasn't a naïve teenager anymore. I wouldn't let past feelings, no matter how strong, blindly lead me. Because yes, it had been hard to live my life without Gray in it, but I'd survived. And honestly, if we got close and I lost him all over again...I didn't know if that would still be the case.

I was still standing in the same spot, worrying about all the outcomes, when Gray stormed back inside, snow covering his hair and jacket.

"Shit." He shook his head as he looked at me. "There's easily two feet of snow out there. I'll be out of here as soon as I dig my truck out, but it might take a bit."

My eyes widened as I looked out the door behind him. The snow was up around Gray's truck tires, and even with its height, there was no way I'd want him traveling down dark, windy roads in this weather.

"You should stay," I said, not even sure where the words came from.

Gray paused, watching me like he was waiting for me to take the words back. He swallowed heavily as he came a little closer. "Are you sure?"

I nodded. "You have a bedroom here. I'd rather you stay and know you're safe." I glanced out the window, noticing the heavy snow falling behind him. "You shouldn't be driving in this weather."

Gray's eyes flickered with understanding. My dad died in a car accident while driving late at night on roads like these. All it took was one slick spot, and his car had veered off the road, colliding with a tree. He never stood a chance.

It had taken a long time to conquer my fear of driving. I still wasn't completely comfortable behind the wheel, especially in bad weather. That was fine in the city, but up here? I'd probably have to figure out something eventually. Either that, or I'd be house bound from October to March.

Gray's eyes met mine, and he nodded. "Okay, Ace. I'll stay."

TWENTY-ONE

Grayson

Two days.

It had been snowing for two fucking days, and there was no sign of it stopping. I cursed as I dug into the mound on the front step, determined to clear at least that much. But the rest of the driveway was going to have to wait. There was too much, and it was accumulating too quickly to make a difference. Whose bright idea was it to buy a house in the middle of nowhere? Oh, right. *Mine.* Initially, its isolation from the rest of the world was a selling feature. Now? Not so much.

With no one else around to help dig us out, Devyn and I were stuck here for the foreseeable future. Knowing how the town operated during a blizzard, the main roads would be the focus in case of any emergencies. The plow trucks would eventually make it up here, but it wouldn't be a priority until it stopped snowing so heavily.

The silver lining was that my phone service had returned, so I could check in with my parents. Alex and Cole were taking turns staying with them while the other tried to take care of things at the Lodge. From what Cole had told me, everything was going smoothly, and my dad was in good spirits. Small blessings, I supposed.

With my parents taken care of, I had plenty of time to focus on my other issue: Devyn. I shook my head, staring out at the miles of white. Ever since she'd asked me to stay, she'd been avoiding me, acting as if our moment the other night had never happened. I should have known I was pushing for too much, too soon. While I was determined to make Devyn realize how good we could be together, she'd always needed to come around to things in her own time. The more I pushed, the more she'd dig her heels in.

That didn't make it any less frustrating. I'd promised her space, but it was getting harder to keep my word. But for Devyn, I would do it. I could wait her out if that was what it took to get her back. Years of missing her had made me a stubborn fuck, and I meant what I said. There was no way I was letting her leave town with this tension still simmering between us. She made me feel alive, more alive than I had in years. Maybe she could ignore the spark between us, but I was done doing that. I'd already wasted too much time without her in my life.

At least, I hoped I could hold out. That theory was easier when we weren't sharing a house. Her bedroom was right across the hall, so close, I could hear her shower from my room. I spent half my days with my straining dick shoved into my jeans and the other half with it gripped in my hand, trying to ease the tension. I'd almost snapped when she came out of her room this morning in her pajamas, a silk tank top and matching shorts that cut off at the tops of her thighs. I'd cursed, trying to think of anything but her smooth skin. Eventually, I'd come out here just to get a break. The cold weather soothed me a little, but it wasn't enough. I needed more. I needed Devyn. Considering she ran out of the room every time I walked into it, that was not going to happen anytime soon.

As I simmered in my thoughts, the front door popped open, and Devyn looked out at me. "Any luck?" she called.

"There's a front step," I mumbled under my breath. "But we're not getting out of here anytime soon."

"Shit," Devyn whispered as she dropped her head.

"Got somewhere to be, Ace?" I said, climbing up the stairs to the front door. Devyn tried to avert her eyes, but there was nowhere else for her to go. Maybe trying to give her space was a stupid plan. Time and distance had never been our friends, so why the hell did I think it would work now? Plus, I knew Devyn, knew she could talk herself out of any situation. She'd probably come up with another fifteen reasons why we'd never work in the past two days.

Fuck space. If Devyn wanted to panic, I'd be right there, reminding her why we were still in each other's lives after all this time apart.

While I took off my winter gear in the hallway, Devyn darted into the house with Elsa on her heels. My dog had barely looked at me since we arrived. She and Devyn formed an immediate connection, and she slept with my wife the past two nights. I was pretty sure that when it was time to leave, Elsa was going to put up a fight, wanting to stay with her new best friend.

I meandered into the living room and found Devyn on the couch, holding a sketch pad in her lap and a stack of unopened romance novels in front of her. Apparently, Calla had sent her off with a bunch of her favorite romance novels in case she got bored. She'd been reading them nonstop, but now, she'd switched over to drawing. I smiled as I watched her. It had been too long since I saw Devyn with that serene smile, the one she always got when she was creating something. But as soon as she saw me watching, she closed the notebook and tucked it away.

When I approached, Devyn met my stare, chewing on the corner of her mouth. I arched my brow at the move, knowing she only did it when she was hiding something major. It was excruciating to hold back and not ask questions about it. But pushing her to face her feelings for me was one thing. Everything else? I could wait until she was ready. Her trust was something I took for granted once, and I never would again.

"You didn't answer my question," I said. "Is there something you need, Ace?"

"I'm going stir crazy," she admitted as I settled on the couch opposite her. "I'm not used to having so little to do. I've always thrived on being busy." She shook her head. "I'm going out of my mind."

"You could talk to me."

Her eyes narrowed in my direction. "I think you've said enough for both of us."

The fire in her words made my head spin, twisting to catch her back as she stood and walked away from me. *Again.* Well, fuck that. I followed her into the kitchen, waiting until she paused to speak. "If you've got something to say to me, Devyn, I'm right here."

She placed her hands on the kitchen island. "You promised me space."

"And I've given it to you. But if you think I'm tiptoeing around my own house because you want to pretend there's nothing between us—"

"There is *nothing* between us," Devyn snapped. "You made sure of that."

My chest heaved, her words cutting like a knife through my chest. But I'd already backed away too many times, believing Devyn's words when I knew she didn't mean them. I'd denied my feelings for her for almost a decade because I convinced myself I couldn't lose our friendship, and I still lost it in the end.

I moved closer to her, enough that she could feel the tension radiating off me, but I gave her enough space so I wasn't crowding her. "Yeah, I fucked up, Devyn. Convinced myself I was doing the right thing by walking away from you. But we both know that was a mistake, one I'll regret for the rest of my life." I lightly touched her hand, waiting to see if she'd pull away. When she didn't, I took it and placed her palm on my chest. "You feel this. I know you do. And if you're not ready to accept that, I understand, but don't you dare say that there's nothing here." I released her hand back to her side. "When you're tired of fighting this, you know where to find me."

She blinked her eyes as tears gathered in the corners. "And if you can't wait that long?"

I shook my head. "I've already waited all my life for you, Devyn. I'll keep waiting as long as you need. I'd wait a thousand years if it meant I got to spend a few days with you."

Before she could respond, I turned and headed into my bedroom, the one place I knew she wouldn't follow. I might have promised her space, but right now, I was the one who needed it. Being this close to Devyn, wanting her so badly but being unable to touch her, was the worst kind of torture.

"Fuck," I hissed, heading into the ensuite bathroom. Maybe a shower would help clear my head. When I first started renovating the cabin, I started with the bathroom, needing a place all to myself. I'd spent way too much money on the glass-enclosed shower, making sure there were enough shower heads to reach every single sore muscle. It was my retreat, and after everything with Devyn, I needed it more than ever.

But even after I stripped and let the water fall over me, all I could see was her.

The way her lips parted when I surprised her, the little flush to her cheeks when I encroached on her space. Devyn might have acted like she couldn't stand me, but there was always heat in her eyes when I leaned in close, like she didn't know if she wanted to destroy me or burn together.

I wondered what would happen if I held her against me, if I placed my hand on her pulse point. Would her heart be beating as heavily as mine? If my fingers drifted lower, would I find her wet? Would I finally get to feel how much she wanted me? Would she lean into my touch, letting me control her the way I wanted? Devyn was headstrong and bold, but there was also a softer side to her—one I wanted to explore more than anything. I wanted to feel her loosen in my arms, to see her completely unravel at my touch.

My dick stood at full attention, loving the idea of having Devyn compliant underneath me. My hand gripped my base, tugging myself roughly at the thought of her moaning, begging for me to fuck her. And God, I would *fuck* her. I would imprint myself inside her so no other man could ever give her what I could.

"Shit, Devyn," I groaned, imagining it was her soft lips surrounding me instead of my rough and calloused palm. Would she be able to take me deep? Yeah, I bet my girl would take me all the way to the back of her throat, loving it even as tears filled her eyes. "Fuck, Devyn, baby. Just like that."

A familiar tingle crept down my spine, and already, I knew I was about to come harder than I had in years. But before I could finish the job, the door pushed open, and Devyn stood in the doorway, her eyes wide as she took me in.

Maybe the smart thing would have been to stop, to pretend I wasn't just choking my dick at the thought of her. But I was so close, and with the real woman standing there in front of me, I couldn't bring myself to stop.

I wouldn't have blamed Devyn if she ran out of the room, if she screamed at me for putting on such a lewd show. But she just stood there, one hand on the doorknob, like she couldn't decide what she wanted to do.

Deciding to tempt fate, I twisted, facing her with my dick

still in my hands. It throbbed, needing release, and shit, did I want it to come from Devyn. She still hadn't moved a muscle, her eyes staring at my cock like it was the first one she'd ever seen.

"Devyn," I groaned, continuing to torture myself. "Fuck, baby."

Her eyes flared to life at my words, as if emboldened by the sound of her name on my tongue. She stepped forward, closing the door behind her. Her eyes never left my hand, watching as I stroked myself closer and closer to the edge.

"You like what you see?" I croaked out.

"You're..." She swallowed, looking up to meet my gaze. "You're a masterpiece, Gray. The kind not even the best artists could get right."

"Nothing compared to you," I grunted out. "You have no idea how fucking sexy you are. I'm going to come just by looking at you. You don't even have to touch me, and I'm losing my fucking mind."

"Show me."

My eyes flared at her words, and she stepped even closer to the glass. Even with the panel between us, I felt the heat in her eyes, could sense how turned-on she was. Her tongue darted out as she licked her lower lip.

"Show me, Gray. Make yourself come, and scream my name when you do."

Fuck. That simple command snapped the band inside me, and I exploded, roaring Devyn's name as I painted the wall between us. By the time I finished, I could barely hold myself up, dropping my forehead onto the glass.

It took a moment for my heartbeat to slow, for my eyes to focus back on the room surrounding me. I was ready to pull Devyn into the shower with me, to give into this tension between us.

But when I looked up, the doorway was empty, the pocket door having slid perfectly back into place. It was like she'd never been there, nothing more than a figment of my imagination. However, when I stepped out of the shower and pulled my towel around my waist, I could smell her perfume lingering in the air. Maybe I hadn't imagined her after all.

Devyn

After being trapped inside the house for four days, I was officially losing my mind. I'd never done well with feeling stuck, especially now that it meant sharing a space with my husband. The husband I watched touch himself the other day, demanding he say my name as he came.

I waited until I heard Gray exit his room and head down to the basement before I made my move. I grabbed Elsa's leash and shushed her as she excitedly yapped, all too happy to frolic out in the snow for a little.

As soon as the winter air nipped at my exposed skin, it felt like I could finally breathe. I wanted nothing more than to take the truck and drive into town. This would be the perfect moment to confide in Calla; I needed someone to set me straight. But then again, she was the biggest hopeless romantic; she'd be convinced Gray and I were meant to be. Scratch that plan. Calla was the last person I should talk to right now.

I walked down the driveway with Elsa, and any dreams of leaving came crashing to a halt. The plows had apparently come through, but they'd piled the snow up in front of our only exit. Perfect. Gray only had a couple of shovels in the garage, and it would take me hours to dig out all this snow. I was trapped for at least another day or two.

"Shit," I whispered as Elsa tugged my arm, wanting to go further on our walk. "Yeah, yeah. I'm coming, girl. Just trying to figure out why the universe hates me so much."

I couldn't lie— watching Gray stroke his dick with my name on his lips was the hottest thing I'd ever seen. It took everything in me to stay on my side of the shower wall, wanting nothing more than to see what those strong hands could do to me.

I meant what I said— the man was a masterpiece, the kind artists would sculpt to immortalize. Tight muscles covered his frame, all with deep cuts and grooves. It was the kind of fit that showed Gray knew how to move his body, fluid enough to play the sport he loved but strong enough to toss me over his shoulder and have his way with me. Once I got past his muscles, I noticed the tattoos covering his arms and chest. Those were all new. The last time I saw him shirtless, he'd barely had his half-sleeves, outlines of a forest covering his wrists and forearms. And while I couldn't make out the designs through the steam and condensation, I wanted to know every single one.

And his cock... I swallowed at the thought. It was thick and long and looked like it would be so heavy in my hands, the kind that would leave the most incredible ache after a night together.

"No," I snapped, hitting my forehead with my hand. This had to stop. I was supposed to be in town to find out more about David, to figure out why he had documents with my town's name on them. But being in proximity to Gray was making me forget my mission.

At least Gray had been true to his words and given me plenty of space. Even though we were inhabiting the same small cabin, our paths barely crossed. Gray spent most of the last two days in his room or in the basement, which I hadn't bothered to check out before he arrived. From the sounds of clunking weights and other machinery, I assumed there was a gym and maybe some kind of shop down there. Curiosity almost won out this morning, but I couldn't bring myself to do it, too mixed up about my feelings for Gray.

All he wanted was a chance.

And that scared the hell out of me.

I'd be lying if I said I wasn't tempted. Despite how much he hurt me in the past, I still liked being around Gray. He made me feel like a better version of myself—like my faults weren't flaws, but something to admire.

As Elsa tugged me back toward the house, apparently done being cold and wet, I tucked my lip between my teeth. I mean, we were technically married. Would it be the worst thing to give in to this heat between us?

Yes, Devyn. Yes, it would. Remember the last time you started thinking this way, and Gray abruptly changed his mind, leaving you reeling for years?

And now, it would be so much worse if things soured between us. Would I have to leave town? *Definitely.* And then there were our friends to think about. Gray was an integral part of our social circle, arguably bigger than me. He was their friend, whereas I was just Calla's sister, tolerated for her sake. It would be a simple decision on who to kick out of the group and who should stay.

And if those reasons weren't terrifying enough, letting Gray in would mean I'd have to tell him about my investigation into David, something I promised a long time ago I wouldn't do. Would he even hear me out? Would he understand my need for vengeance against the man who'd tried to take everything from my family? I had changed a lot in our years apart, no longer the naive girl he once called his best friend.

He wants to know this version of you.

"Ugh," I groaned as I crossed into the front hallway. I kicked off my boots and placed my coat on the hook. Why did this have to be so difficult? Once upon a time, I trusted Gray with my life, but our history had twisted into this brittle, painful thing. I pushed out a breath. Maybe that was where we needed to start —as friends, see if the bond we'd had as kids was still strong.

Before I could think too much about it, I went to the basement door. Pulling it open, I descended the stairs, following a blaring alternative song to find Gray. I took a steadying breath before I walked down the hall, turning into the room I assumed was a gym. But when I opened the door, I wasn't prepared for what was in front of me.

The room was on the smaller side, and several workout machines filled the space. There was a treadmill, a full row of weights, and several benches. Other than that, the room was sparsely decorated, a muted, pale gray on the walls. The only thing that broke up the color was a row of long mirrors fixed to face the machines. Across the room, floor-to-ceiling windows showcased the valley below. The gym must have been right below the living room, because the view was the same. With the deck hanging over the windows, it felt like we were part of the mountain itself.

While that view was gorgeous, the one on the other side of the room really took my breath away.

Gray's head was down as he twisted, pulling a cable with his arms. His muscles strained with each tug, and it made my eyes trace every inch of him. Every *shirtless* inch. Even though I saw him naked yesterday, the glass obscured my view. Now, without any barriers, I could study him, from the way his muscles contorted to the colorful ink that covered most of his upper half.

To my surprise, most of his tattoos were landscapes, images of swirling trees and colors melded into a beautiful scene. It took me a moment to recognize them, but eventually, they all made sense. Holy shit. They were all my designs—my sketches brought to life. Every image marked on Gray's skin I'd drawn when we were younger, memorializing our hometown in the pages of my sketchbook. The trees surrounding Gray's childhood home covered both of his forearms, the dock where we'd spent most of our summers lounging covering his bicep. My heart tensed as I found our cove, our secret spot, over his ribs. He had inked our story on his skin.

I was concentrating on the designs when Gray's eyes met mine in the mirror. He furrowed his brow as he turned around. "Devyn?" He put the cable down and turned around to face me. "You okay?"

No. I wasn't. Not when my eyes fell to the left side of his chest, the same place he'd placed my hand yesterday. Because on the spot, just above his heart, was an Ace of Spades symbol, with our word, *Always*, written in script around it. And inked in the corner? Our wedding date.

Without thinking, I stepped forward, tracing the lines with my finger. "Is this..." I asked, unable to finish the thought.

Gray nodded, never taking his eyes off me. "I got it right after we left Vegas. Wanted something to remember the night, even if it's a blur."

"It's over your heart," I said.

"Where else would it be?" Gray's brow furrowed. "No matter what happened between us, it's yours, Devyn. It's always been yours."

My heart pounded at his words, not sure I believed what I was hearing. But the evidence was right in front of me, inked onto Gray's chest. It was a permanent reminder of what we'd lost, what he had walked away from. The blood roared in my ears, making me feel like I was being dragged down into the depths of the ocean. None of it made sense, not after he'd let me walk away once.

Despite my confusion, I couldn't help running my finger

over the date. "I thought our marriage was a mistake. You *said* we were a mistake."

He placed his hand on top of mine, sealing it against his skin. Gray's eyes blazed with intensity as he spoke, "Marrying you drunk and in Vegas? That might have been a mistake. But you, Devyn? You have never been one."

TWENTY-THREE

Grayson

"We fucking did it!"

Champagne coated us as my teammates celebrated our victory, popping bottles like there was no tomorrow. And honestly, for us, there really wasn't. We'd still work hard and be consistently training during the off-season, but as the newest World Series Champions, we'd earned a few days of rest.

Okay, now that I thought about it, rest was probably the last thing on anyone's mind this weekend. When my teammates suggested a bunch of us fly out to Las Vegas, I was hesitant. Not only because I wasn't really into partying, but because I was burnt. This season had been challenging in the best ways. It was only my second on the Rebels, and I was still adjusting to life in the major leagues. I'd gotten a bit of a break earlier this year, when one of the veteran pitchers was out for surgery. Nothing major, but it meant he'd be out for a few games, giving me a chance to show my skills.

Luckily for me, I'd pitched a no-hitter during my time on the mound, cementing myself in management's eyes. When our winning streak continued, they thrust me into the spotlight, and I could no longer hide behind the rest of the team.

My mom even sent me a photo of me on a magazine cover back home. As much as I loved the game, the attention was another story. My manager had already begged me for more events and interviews, but it wasn't going to happen.

I shoved that conversation into the back of my mind. We were only here for a few nights, and I was determined to push myself out of my comfort zone. After all, what better place to let off some steam than Las Vegas?

"Oh man," one of my teammates said at my side. "You see that girl? Fucking smoke show."

I couldn't help but follow his chin tilt, trying to find the woman in the crowd. It wasn't like I was hurting for company, but lately, everything had felt so hollow. After my name took off, a lot of the women who hit on me wanted a story to tell, to talk to their friends about the major league player who'd warmed their beds. Very few wanted to stick around after.

Not that I was looking for that. Not since—

"Devyn?" The blonde turned her head, and all my thoughts died. I had to close my eyes, making sure I wasn't hallucinating. But when I opened them again, there she was: my former best friend, Devyn Winters.

When we left for college, we'd promised we'd keep in touch, that distance could never come between us. But as time passed and our phone calls became less frequent, it was clear we were drifting apart. I'd even driven down to the city one weekend to surprise her, but when I got to the dorms, a guy answered and said he was Devyn's boyfriend. I didn't even know she was dating someone. I left without a word, heading back to school to lick my wounds. It was almost six weeks until she called again. I let it go to voicemail.

But seeing her now, all those hurt feelings faded away. I was too busy staring at the woman in front of me. God, had she always been this gorgeous? My teammate, Damien, who'd spotted her first, turned to me. "You know her, Anders?"

"Yeah," I said, climbing out of the booth to find her before she disappeared into the crowd. "She's my best friend."

I could hear my teammates clambering for details behind me, but I didn't care, not when I was the closest I'd been to Devyn in years. She rushed through the crowd, and I had to hurry to catch up. She was dressed professionally, as if she just stepped out of the courtroom. I knew from my parents Devyn had gotten a job at a major firm right out of law school. It didn't surprise me. The girl had more determination in her left hand than the rest of us had in our entire bodies.

Once I got close enough to reach her, nerves kicked in. Would she even want to see me? Even though there'd never been a defining end to our friendship, it had ended. It had been years since we'd last spoken. Maybe Devyn preferred it that way? *No.* I refused to believe that was true. If she felt at all like me, it was like someone had ripped out the other half of my soul. I wasn't complete without her.

Before I could second guess myself, I reached out and touched her elbow lightly. "Devy."

She instantly froze, hearing her name despite the echoes of the surrounding casino. As she turned around and her big, brown eyes met mine, it was like time had stopped. The air was sucked out of the room, and nothing else mattered but her. The world could be crashing around me; even so, all I would see would be her.

Gone was the girl I'd grown up with, replaced with the most beautiful woman I'd ever seen. Her pale blonde hair was curled around her shoulders, her brown eyes wide with shock. Deep red colored her plump lips, and all I wanted was to kiss it off her.

I always knew there was something between Devyn and me,

an instinct that hinted we were meant for so much more than friendship, but I'd never allowed myself to consider it, not until now.

My heart pounded in my chest as she stared at me, as if trying to see if I was real. But after a long moment, a slow smile crept onto her lips. "Hey, Grayson."

I stepped closer, matching her wide smile. "What did I say about calling me Grayson?"

"The same thing I told you about calling me Devy," she retorted, still staring up at me. "What are you doing here?"

"Celebrating with my teammates. Our team won—"

"The World Series," she answered for me, a blush coloring her cheeks. "Yeah, I saw."

I dared to step closer. "You watched the game?"

She nodded, tucking her lip between her teeth. "I watch every single one."

The quiet admission broke the dam inside me, and I needed her so much closer. I pulled her into my arms, holding her against my chest. She settled in my embrace and wrapped hers around my neck. That familiar scent of jasmine and sandalwood filled my senses, and I instantly felt at ease. *This.* This was what I was missing for so long. While everything else in my life was going well, nothing had seemed quite right until this moment, until Devyn was in my arms again.

She cleared her throat and stepped back, nodding behind us. "I think your teammates want you back."

I glanced over my shoulder, suddenly not giving a fuck that I was supposed to be bonding with the guys. I looked back at Devyn. "Come hang out with us."

She chewed on her lower lip. "I shouldn't."

"Devyn," I sighed, shifting so close, she had to tilt her head to meet my eyes. "I'm not taking no for an answer. It's been too long since I've seen you, and I miss my best friend." I held out my hand. "Say yes, Ace."

She rolled her eyes but placed her hand in mine. As I pulled her into our roped-off area, she bumped into me and said, "So you missed me, huh?."

I looked down at her and smiled as I led her inside. "You have no fucking idea."

A COUPLE OF HOURS LATER, the drinks were still flowing, and most of my teammates were ready to move on to the next club. I didn't care where we went—as long as Devyn stayed at my side.

When she first joined our group, she was her usual stand-offish self. Most people thought it was because Devyn was cold, but I knew her better than that. She was always apprehensive around new people, taking a while to let them in. But my teammates were a stubborn bunch of assholes, and they decided from the moment she came over that she was going to be their best friend. I had to give them credit—it was working.

Devyn laughed at Damien's side, and my instincts flared. He brushed something away from her shoulder, and I saw red. We were friends and spent many early mornings practicing together, but right now? I was one move away from breaking his throwing arm.

I walked over to Devyn's side. When she smiled at me, her pose a little wobbly because of all the drinks, all my anger rushed away. I glanced down at her, placing my hand on her back. "You okay, Ace?"

She beamed back at me. "I'm always good when you're here." She turned back to Damien. "Did you know I've loved this guy almost my whole life?"

He smirked back at me. "Is that so? This asshole?"

Devyn smacked him on the shoulder. "Don't call him that. Grayson is the best guy in the entire world."

But I barely heard any of that, too busy fixating on the words that had just come out of Devyn's mouth. I shifted, blocking Damien from her view. "You loved me?"

She rolled her eyes. "C'mon, Gray. You knew that. It's not like I was very subtle about it."

"No," I said, shifting closer to her. "I didn't. I thought you just wanted to be friends."

Devyn rolled her eyes again. "C'mon, Gray. You knew I was crazy about you. But then you dated Calla, and I..." She placed her hands over her face. "It doesn't matter anymore. Now, we're not even friends. And you're with Kelsey—"

"Who?" I spluttered.

Her brows furrowed. "Kelsey. I saw her on your Instagram." She flinched. "Okay, I might social media stalk you from time to time, but that's not the point." Waving her hands in the air, she continued, "You're with someone, and if she makes you happy, I am so happy for you."

"I don't have social media," I grumbled. "My manager set up an account, but I've never used it. I sure as shit didn't post a picture with a girl I barely know."

"Really?" she said, her smile wider than it'd been all night. "Does it make me an awful friend that I'm relieved to hear that? Seeing that picture..." Devyn shook her head. "I thought you found your person."

Her words echoed inside my chest, giving life to a feeling I'd tried to bury for so long. But standing here, with Devyn, after so many years apart, everything I'd tried to ignore became clear. She was the one I wanted, the one I had wanted for so long, heartache was an old friend. I had missed my chance before; shit, I had fumbled so many chances, I didn't deserve one now.

But I sure as hell wasn't going to risk her walking away without putting it all on the line, once and for all.

"Yeah, I did," I said, finally realizing it myself. "Years ago, on this beach, back home. She was so mad because these birds kept flying away when she was trying to draw them."

Devyn's eyes widened with recognition. "Gray, what are you saying?"

I reached out, pressing my hand against her neck. Her pulse flickered under my touch, the rhythm even more intoxicating than our drinks. "You're my person, Ace. It's you. It has *always* been you."

She pulled me in by my shirt, not caring who was around us. The first touch of her lips to mine was tentative, almost unsure if she should have done it. *Fuck that.* I practically growled as I pulled her hips closer to mine and slotted my mouth over hers. She let out a little gasp but sunk into the embrace, her fingers in the nape of my neck.

When I pulled back, I stared at her. "Holy shit, Ace, that was—"

"Pretty incredible," she answered for me. "This doesn't even feel like real life right now."

I reached up and brushed her hair away from her forehead. "You've always been the most real thing in my life, Devyn. I hate that I've wasted so much time with you." I kissed her once again, already consumed by how she felt pressed against me. "But I'm done wasting it."

Devyn giggled, the sound lighter than anything I'd heard from her before. "That sounds good to me."

"Yeah?"

She reached up, pulling me down until our foreheads touched. "I don't want to waste any more time either."

I couldn't help but kiss her, wanting to hear that little gasp from her again. Devyn was my dream woman—my best friend and the sexiest woman I'd ever seen, all bundled up into one. As she groaned against my lips, I pulled back. "Shit, can we get out of here?"

My team cut off her response when they started cheering behind us. "'Bout damn time Anders met his match," Damien called out.

I flipped him off behind my back, kissing Devyn once again before turning around to face them. Devyn curled into my side, and I put my arm around her shoulders, holding her close. "You never answered me, Ace," I whispered in her ear. "You want to get out of here?"

"I do," she said. "But this is your night with your teammates. We should celebrate with them first."

"The only celebration I want is my head between your legs while you scream my name."

Devyn's eyes widened, but the flush on her cheeks told me she was open to the idea. Thank fuck. But as my arm tightened around her, she paused me. "Later, Gray."

Several of my teammates' wives came over, pulling Devyn out of my arms to join them for a drink. She rolled her eyes, probably knowing the truth, just like I did. After two years of trying to set me up with all their single friends, they were probably dying to learn all about Devyn, the girl who owned my whole fucking heart.

Damien came up to my side and passed me a beer. "That was a hell of a kiss for friends, Anders."

I glared in his direction, not needing anyone else's input on my relationship with Devyn. We both knew friends would never fully encompass what we meant to each other, and that kiss sealed our fate. All my life led me to this moment—to complete clarity that I was in love with Devyn Winters, and I had been for a long time. And while that love had taken many shapes and roles over the years, it was always there, as steady as the beat in my chest. She was mine, and I was done waiting.

"Damn, you really got it bad, don't you?" He laughed and nudged me with his elbow. "You know, there's a twenty-four-hour chapel around the block if you want to make this thing official."

I choked on my drink, but for the first time, the idea of being married didn't raise red flags. Not when it was with Devyn. "Give me some time," I said, never taking my eyes off Devyn. "But it is fucking tempting."

Devyn

As Grayson recounted his version of events, it took everything in me not to fall apart. It was such a stark contrast from my last memories of him, of hearing him say we made a mistake, that it was hard to breathe. His side of the story was everything I wanted to hear after all this time. To know he had loved me just as much as I loved him... It made the remaining pieces of my walls shatter into dust.

"I don't remember any of that." My words came out whispered, shame coating each one. Maybe if I had, things would have been different between us. Maybe I would have fought for us instead of walking away.

"Figured that out the next morning." Gray smiled sadly. "And while most of the night's gone for me too, that, I do remember." He stepped closer, cupping my cheek with his palm. "I promised you I'd never let you go again, and I broke that promise."

"Gray, I—"

"No, let me get this out, Ace." He sighed, running his thumb along my cheek. "Letting you walk out of my life was the biggest mistake I ever made. I thought I was doing the right thing, but I was a fucking idiot. I should have fought harder for you."

"And that's why you never signed the divorce papers?"

He shook his head. "Maybe it was the coward's way, but I couldn't bring myself to do it, to sign away the last thing that tied you to me. And when you kept sending them, it almost became a game, trying to imagine your face when I found new ways to ruin them."

"I did like the time they came back shredded."

Gray chuckled. "Liked that, did you?" As I nodded, he moved closer, close enough that I could feel the heat emanating from his muscular frame. "Nothing's changed, Devyn. Not for me. I still know you're the one for me, married or not."

My words failed me as I stared up into his eyes, memorizing all the different dark shades. All I wanted was to say the right thing, to explain to Gray how much he meant to me, but nerves kept me tongue-tied.

So, instead of giving him my words, I reached up on my tiptoes and slammed my lips to his. He initially didn't respond, either too shocked or stunned to match my kiss. But as soon as the veil lifted, Gray met me with the same level of passion, his lips bruising mine with a possession I craved.

"Fuck, Devy," he whispered between nips of his teeth. "Told myself kissing you was a fluke, that there was no way it could have felt this right." He kissed me again, as if he needed it more than his next breath. "But fuck, baby. It's the best thing I've ever experienced."

"Better than winning the World Series?" I joked as I pulled him in closer, needing to feel more of him against my body.

But there was not a single trace of humor in his expression when he answered. "Without a doubt."

His rough hands found the strip of skin between my sweater and leggings, wrapping around my middle. His strong arms lifted me into the air then turned us around until we sat on his workout bench. I gasped as my core met his hardened length, shifting to feel more of him on instinct.

Gray's hands moved to my waist, stilling my movements. "Shit, baby. If you keep doing that, I'm going to come in my shorts." He wrapped his hand in my ponytail, forcing my eyes down, "And there's no way I'm coming before you are. So if you want to stop, tell me now, Devyn, because I'm already losing my mind over here."

For a moment, my mind got the best of me, reminding me what would happen if this all fell apart around us. Given our history—Gray and I had never gotten this right before—what made us think we could work this time?

As if he could read my thoughts, Gray tightened his hold. "Look at me, Devyn." When I forced my gaze up to meet his, he continued, "I'm sorry I hurt you, more than you'll ever know. And if you'll let me, I'll spend the rest of my life making it up to you."

"The rest of your life?"

"Every goddamn day."

The words unleashed something inside me, uncertainty I'd been holding back. Gray would never intentionally hurt me, our circumstances being a mix of misunderstandings and outside forces. He'd proven more times than I could count that I could depend on him, that he would lay his life on the line for me. Could I forgive one horrible moment after a lifetime of evidence to the contrary? Looking at the mark on his chest, my heart spoke for me. *For him, I think I could.*

I stood, moving out of his lap. Gray's eyes shuttered in disappointment as I moved backward toward the mirrors that lined the far walls. But before he could get up, I shook my head, wanting him right there, his eyes on me only.

"You want my forgiveness, Grayson?" He nodded, and I

reached to the hem of my sweater, lifting it above my head. His eyes dropped down to my chest, studying the curve of my breasts. I internally high-fived myself for picking out the pale lace bra and matching panties this morning, because Gray couldn't stop staring. "Try asking again," I said, moving on to remove my leggings. As I kicked them away from me, I grinned at him. "But this time? Try asking on your knees."

Gray didn't waste a moment before crossing the room. His lips collided with mine before he stroked down my body, his head dropping to my chest. "I've been dreaming of this for so long. The real thing is so much better."

He didn't give me time to respond, lowering himself to his knees as his hands wrapped around my waist. While one hand unhooked my bra, the other stroked my leg, leading to the apex of my thighs but never getting close enough to satisfy me. As I squirmed to get him closer, Gray chuckled, reaching out to lick a circle around my nipple. When I moaned at the touch, he pulled his head back, blowing gently on the now-hardened peak. "So responsive, baby. Like your body was just waiting for me." He repeated the move on my other breast, and I almost screamed out from the exquisite torture. "Can't believe I get to see you like this."

I shook my head. "Nothing you haven't seen before."

Grayson frowned, leaning back on his haunches. "What are you talking about?"

"Vegas," I said, trying to force him back to where I wanted him, but Grayson refused to budge. Annoyed, I let out a huff. "We woke up together, so I assumed..."

Grayson chuckled. "You assumed wrong, Devyn. I don't remember much, but I know we didn't have sex."

"We didn't?"

"Nope," he said, leaning in to press a light kiss to my stomach. "Not because I didn't want to, but there was no way I was taking you for the first time when we'd both been drinking. I wanted you to remember every single moment of our time together."

Hearing the sincerity in his voice made me want him even more, happier than I could explain that I hadn't missed out on this moment. I hadn't lost this precious memory. Because after years of pining for Gray, he was right. I wanted to remember this, wanted to recall every touch of his skin against mine.

I sighed happily, reaching down to brush his hair off his face. "Nothing is stopping us now."

Gray's smile was wolfish as his grip hardened against my skin. "No, there's not." With those simple words, he put his mouth on my breast, lavishing my nipple with his tongue. It felt incredible, only fueling the sparks growing in my core.

"Gray..." I whispered. "Give me more."

"I'll give you everything, Ace."

As he moved his mouth to my other breast, his free hand reached for my panties. First, I felt him pulling the fabric, then came a distinct rip and a gust of cool air against me. I gasped when I looked down and saw the fabric on the floor. "Grayson!"

He just chuckled as his fingers slowly stroked me, just enough to make my head swim but not enough pressure to get me where I needed. He nipped down my body before lifting my left leg onto his shoulder.

The way he stared at me made my heart pound in my chest, my mind already racing with reasons why this was a mistake. As his large hands caressed my sides, my insecurity got the worst of me. "Are we still playing pretend?"

Gray leaned back on his haunches, gripping my hips hard enough that it would leave marks. I relished in the exquisite pain, loving how his eyes flared with desire when he looked at me. "No, we're not. We never fucking were."

Wordlessly, I nodded, feeling the certainty in his tone. As

soon as I leaned my head against the mirror, he shifted down, spreading me further apart. His resulting moan of appreciation made my insides clench, loving how sexy it made me feel. His fingers toyed with my slit, pressing just enough to ignite the fire in my veins. "Been dreaming about this, Ace," Gray said, continuing his slow ministrations. "About getting to have you like this."

"Then you should have me," I said, bucking my hips to show my impatience.

But he just chuckled, nipping at my inner thigh. "Slow down, baby. I've been dreaming about this perfect pussy for a decade. Don't rush me now."

I was about to protest when his tongue brushed my clit, and my back instinctively bowed. Gray groaned, trying to slowly taste every inch of my core, giving me just enough to drive me wild. "Fuck," he groaned, pressing his forehead against my thigh. "I could come just from the taste of you." His hands tightened, and then I was moving, Gray lowering so his back was on the mat flooring while I floated above him.

"What are you doing?" I said, placing my hands on the mat for balance.

"Need you to ride my face, Devy." He tried to pull me down onto his face. "Can't get nearly enough of you in that position, and I want you to soak my tongue."

I sat back, chewing on my lower lip. "I...I've never done that."

"Thank fuck," Gray whispered. "Because I want to be your first, baby. Now get your sexy ass up here and ride your husband's face. Use me to get yourself off."

Maybe it was his words, or maybe it was the fact that this was Gray, and despite my resolve not to, I trusted him more than anyone. I took a breath before letting him guide me to the right position. But even as his tongue started to work me, I couldn't quite relax, terrified I would smother him.

Gray must have sensed my unease, because he pulled away for a moment. "Devyn, stop holding back and fuck my face. I've been dying for a taste of you, and this halfway bullshit is not enough."

"I don't want to hurt you."

"You won't. Now sit down and let me fucking eat. And trust me—if you were my last meal, I'd die a very fucking happy man."

As his fingers dug into my skin, I reluctantly dropped my weight, letting him continue to work me. For a moment, I was in my head, wondering if I'd ever be able to get there like this, too worried about him to focus on my climax. But as Gray's lips bunched around my clit, sucking deeply, my head fell back, suddenly unable to think about anything but the pleasure he was gifting me.

"That's my wife," Gray groaned underneath me. He trailed his fingers along the inside of my thigh before pushing them inside me, and I groaned at the sudden fullness. "God, you moan so beautifully. Can't wait to hear what it sounds like when you come for me."

I could barely hear him, too absorbed in the sensations. As his tongue continued to explore, tease, and fuck me, my hips finding their rhythm, grinding against him like it was my last wish. His beard scraped along my delicate skin, and it only added to the feeling of being utterly claimed by this man. Every swipe of his tongue, every crook of his fingers, I was barreling closer and closer to the edge, and once I fell, there was no chance I'd ever be the same.

Sparks danced along my spine as Gray worked me, and my body contracted, feeling like I was on the verge of a tsunami. But Gray never stopped, continuing to work my body like he was teaching a masterclass, needing to know all the things that drove me wild.

"That's it, Devy. Come for me. Be a good little wife and soak my face."

With a flick of his tongue, my body exploded, light flaring behind my eyes, drowning the world in a sea of bright whites. There was nothing in that moment, nothing but Gray and me. Nothing but the pleasure he made me feel.

He continued to work me through my release, and once I finally came back down, I collapsed against his chest. My breath was heavy as Gray's fingers stroked a line down my spine. I lifted my head, staring at the man below me. My best friend. My greatest ally. My husband. The love of my life. I waited for that prick of terror that usually accompanied the thought, but it never came. Not now. Maybe later, when I was alone, all my negative thoughts would return. But right now? I refused to let them ruin this moment.

Gray shifted his hands, rubbing his thumbs against my side. I flinched when he hit my tattooed skin, hoping he hadn't noticed. But Gray always noticed everything when it came to me. His hands found my hips, shifting us so I was underneath him. He lowered himself so he was at eye level with my rib cage, staring at the small bit of script transcribed there. No one else had ever seen it. I kept it covered, even when I wore a bra or my bathing suit, which was one of the few requirements I had when I made the appointment.

I waited for Gray to say something, but he continued to breathe heavily against my skin, his thumb running back and forth over the word. I tried to read his expression. It was one I rarely saw from him, only saved for those precious moments that indeed rendered him speechless.

"Always," he finally whispered, daring to look up at me. My throat caught when his eyes met mine, so much love and devotion pouring out of him.

"I wanted a piece of you with me," I said, my words barely

audible over my heartbeat. "Even after everything that happened between us…" I pushed out a breath. "Having a small piece of you with me gave me strength."

"I always was," Gray answered. "Even if it didn't seem like it at the time, I have always been on your side, Devyn." He sat up and pulled me into his arms. "I'm sorry it took me so long to get back to you."

My eyes dropped, guilt overwhelming me. "I'm sorry I made it so difficult for you, Gray."

Suddenly feeling too vulnerable, I motioned for him to let me go. Gray did easily but stayed close to me, even as I started to gather my discarded clothing. I pulled them on quickly, then crossed my arms over my chest. "You asked me to forgive you, but you're not the only one who made mistakes. The things I've said, what I've done… I've been so angry at you for so long, Gray. I convinced myself I hated you, all because…" I sucked in a sharp breath, looking up at the ceiling. "Because it was so much easier than admitting how much I missed you."

Gray stepped forward, brushing his thumb along my cheeks, catching tears I didn't even realize had fallen. "There's nothing to forgive, Devyn."

I dropped my head to his chest. "How can you move past this so easily?"

"Because it's you." I pulled my head back to meet his eyes. "And I know how much I hurt you when I didn't choose you the first time. I would never hold your reaction against you, Devyn." He brushed the back of his fingers along my cheek. "And now that you're here, I'm going to make sure you never feel that way again."

TWENTY-FIVE

Devyn

After my nausea subsided, Gray helped me up and walked me back over to the bed. I wallowed in my stupidity as he tucked me in, then listened to him call his teammates to let them know he wouldn't be joining them for the day.

My phone chimed away on the end table, and I groaned as I forced myself to look at it. There was a notification for my group chat with the rest of the associates on the trip. Technically, the conference ended yesterday, but my team had made plans to debrief before catching a flight home tomorrow. And by debrief, they meant go wild on the strip and make the most out of our limited free time in Vegas. However, considering I was still recovering from my last bout of impulsivity, I sent off a quick text, telling them I didn't feel up for it. No one bothered to reply, probably already betting I'd find some excuse to avoid them.

Gray walked out of the bathroom, scrubbing his hands on one of the hotel towels. Maybe we should have left this room to talk, but the idea of moving more than ten steps made my body want to explode, so I wasn't leaving this bed anytime soon. This stupid fucking bed, where I finally got to be with Gray, and my drunken brain decided to block it out. Score one for karma.

"Red or blue?" Gray asked, holding out two sports drinks.

"Red, please," I said, reaching out to grab it. As I did, my finger touched the band on his finger. We both recoiled. If it didn't hurt so much, I would have laughed at the ridiculousness of the situation. I was wrapped up in a fluffy white, terry cloth robe, sitting in a hotel with my childhood-best-friend-turned-husband. And despite the fact we hadn't acknowledged the rings after that first awkward moment, neither of us had removed them either.

Gray must have followed my thoughts, because he leaned away, clearing his throat. "So we should talk about next steps."

"Next steps?"

Gray leaned his phone screen toward me, showing me a picture of us kissing in the middle of a cheesy Las Vegas chapel. The officiant was dressed as Cher, being far more fabulous than anyone had any right to be. "Apparently, the guys have all the documents." He cleared his throat. "They didn't want us to worry about anything but the honeymoon."

"Just perfect," I sighed, dropping my head into my hands. "Is it possible that none of this is legal?"

"You're the lawyer," Gray grumbled, passing me the phone to swipe through his texts. "But looks that way to me."

My heart pounded as I looked through them all in quick succession. Outside of the first few pictures from the bar, I don't remember taking any of them. It was odd, staring at myself, looking happier than I had in years. And when I reached the ones at the chapel...if it was anyone else in the images, I would have thought the night was planned. Gray and I were beaming at each other. Not like drunken fools doing something stupid, but like two lovers who couldn't wait to be joined together forever.

I shook my head, continuing to thumb through the photos until I reached the one I was looking for. The marriage license. It looked legitimate, and my signature, although sloppier than normal, was there for all to see. What the fuck had I been thinking? Getting married was never one of my goals, never something I'd dreamed about growing up.

Before I think any more about it, I passed the phone back to Gray. "We're going to need to get those back if we want to annul the wedding."

"Annul it?"

Gray's face morphed into a frown, and I kept staring at him, waiting for him to say more. When he didn't, I reluctantly climbed out of the bed, needing space between us. I dug through my bag, trying to find a pen so I could write everything down. "That's what makes the most sense. Obviously, we weren't in the right frame of mind when we signed the marriage license, and any judge would agree based on those pictures."

Gray nodded, still staring down at his phone.

"Gray," I snapped. "I need you with me if this is going to work."

His steel eyes met mine with a fierce determination. It was a look I often saw when watching his games, right before he pitched an amazing inning. But now, it was aimed at me, and I felt it from my fingertips to my toes.

"What if we don't?"

"Don't what?"

"Don't get an annulment," Gray sighed.

I shook my head. "A divorce would be much messier and would go on our records. An annulment is more—"

"No," Gray said, stepping closer to me. "What if we...stayed married?"

I stared at him, my mouth hanging open at the suggestion.

When he didn't say anything more, I just shook my head. "You can't be serious."

I turned my attention back to my bag, almost frantically searching through it. This was too much; it was all too much. I had one goal when I set off this weekend: to improve my standing at the firm. Now, I was not only linked to my best friend, but I was legally his wife. And he had the audacity to think, what? That this could be a real thing? A real marriage?

As my thoughts continued to spiral, Gray placed his hand on top of mine. I exhaled slowly then turned to face him. Shaking my head, I said, "This is ridiculous, you have to know that."

Gray took my left hand with his other, his thumb toying with my wedding ring. "Maybe it is, Devyn. But it also makes more sense than anything in my life. I've been sleepwalking for years, and last night, I finally felt alive again. Because of you." He linked our fingers together. "You've always been the best parts of me, Devyn, and I don't want to waste another day without you."

My breath stuttered out of me, and I could feel tears pricking the corners of my eyes. My heart wanted to believe him, to think we could really do this, but my rational mind wouldn't let me. "Gray, we barely even know each other anymore."

"True," he admitted. "But this could be our chance, Devyn. Get to know each other again. No one fits me like you, Devyn. Nothing feels as good as when we're together, and I want to figure out why. Don't you?"

My heart wanted to burst out of my chest as I stared into his steel eyes, knowing he meant every word. If it was anyone else, I would think this was some elaborate practical joke, but this was Gray. No, I never saw myself getting married before, but if I did, it would have been to him.

But fear was a powerful beast, and despite my initial impulse to say yes, I couldn't quite bring myself to do it. I thrived on facts and numbers, having had too many unknown variables derail my life. No matter how much I wanted it to work out, being with Gray was a risk, one I wasn't sure I was willing to take.

Having to live without him was hard enough once, and that was when our friendship had a slow, gradual decline. What would happen if we gave into these feelings, only to find out we didn't work as a couple? That would devastate me.

"I need to think about it," I muttered, running my hand over my face. "Preferably after a large cup of coffee and the biggest breakfast burrito I can find."

"Take your time, Devy." Gray nodded, leaning forward to kiss my forehead. "You stay here. I'll grab you some breakfast."

"You don't have to do that."

"I know, but I want to." He released me and winked as he walked out the door. "Gotta take care of my wife."

Over an hour later, Gray hadn't returned, so I made myself comfortable in his bed. The TV blared in the background, but I didn't pay it any mind, too busy looking at my wedding ring as it caught the light.

Something so simple shouldn't have felt so significant. As I twisted my hand, small details started to stick out to me. There wasn't much to the ring, just three thin silver bands twisted together. Tiny diamonds were laid into the center band, making it sparkle.

The ring symbolized something I wasn't even sure I wanted, a marriage I'd entered when I was too drunk to even remember my actions. And yet, the idea of taking it off pained me.

I toyed with my fingers again, smiling as the stones caught the light. What if I didn't take it off? What if we really did this, and I wore my ring with pride, declaring to the world Gray was my husband?

Oh God, that sounded way too tempting.

Closing my eyes, I imagined what it would be like to show up at work with this new accessory and try to explain I'd gotten impulsively married. No one would believe me. While I'd only worked at the firm for a few months, I was known for being cold and aloof. I'd heard many of the other associates joke behind my back, saying I was heartless.

It wasn't the first time I'd heard these things. Growing up, the comment followed me like a second skin. Everyone thought that because I didn't automatically smile or exude bubbliness, I was mean. Even Gray hated me until he got to know me. He was one of the first people to put in that effort.

I smiled at the idea of being with Gray. It sounded too good to be true, which meant it probably was. If we did this, we needed ground rules. Maybe we should start slowly—dating before deciding whether to announce our marriage to the world.

Oh my God, we were going to do this. I was going to date Grayson Anders. After pining after him for most of my life, it was hard to even believe we were finally giving this a shot. I thought it would never happen, convincing myself he would never want me in that way.

I should have been terrified, petrified at the idea of loving someone else. Even though the fear was still there, happiness overwhelmed it. This wasn't anyone I was giving my heart over to—it was Gray, the person I'd loved most for almost all my life.

As I heard the lock click open, I couldn't hold back my bold smile. I climbed out of bed to greet him, desperate to tell Gray I wanted to try with him.

But as soon as his eyes met mine, my heart sank into my chest.

Even through his hangover, there had been a light in Gray's eyes before he left. Now, it was gone, ripped away like it had never been there in the first place. He softly closed the door, moving toward me before stopping himself. He ran his hand through his beard, and my pulse battered in my chest. Cold, icy realization washed over me, and I knew what he was about to say before he opened his mouth.

"Wow. That was fast," I scoffed. "Not even an hour, and you've changed your mind."

I pulled my robe tighter as I turned away, needing to get away from Gray. It was hard to breathe, each step feeling like a stabbing in my chest. It was only amplified with the heavy pulsing of my heart, so loud, it tuned out the rest of the world.

I shouldn't have been surprised Gray changed his mind. I wasn't the woman people pined for, the one who lingered in the back of their minds. Even with my family, I was always there for them, but beyond Calla, they put in no effort to do the same. The only person who paid me special attention was David, and that was because I refused to bend to his will.

My feet suddenly stuttered to a stop, and my hand flew to my mouth. Nausea flowed through me, and I almost emptied my stomach. What if this was about Calla? Was Gray still in love with her? When they dated in high school, I thought they were serious, but Calla insisted that wasn't true. She said they were better off as friends, never really falling deeply for each other. But what if that wasn't the case with Gray? What if he couldn't have the sister he wanted, so I was nothing more than a consolation prize? And now that he had a moment to clear his mind, he knew this whole thing was a mistake.

"Devyn."

I flinched at the sound of my voice, finding Gray staring down at me, barely an inch of space between us. God, it hurt to look at him, to know I'd allowed myself a moment to pretend, to imagine this incredible man could be mine. But that was never meant to be my story.

"Whatever you're thinking right now," Gray whispered, "don't. This has nothing to do with you. I..." He snapped his mouth closed and took a step back, running his hand over his beard. "I didn't think any of this through. We made a mistake–"

"It's fine." I tried to step past him, trying to keep my face from showing the depth of my pain. "Just give me a minute to grab my stuff, and I'll get out of your life again."

"Shit," he hissed, grabbing my arm. "Please, Devy. Don't leave like this."

Suddenly, my temper snapped, and I yanked my arm from his grip. "Don't leave like this?" I laughed bitterly. "Are you serious, Gray? An hour ago, you asked me to stay married to you like it wasn't completely insane. But when I actually start to think it's a good idea..." I shake my head. "Forget it."

Gray stood in front of me, his eyes flaring with something I couldn't place. "You were going to say yes? You wanted to give us a shot?"

"Does it even matter?"

Gray's jaw tensed so hard, I thought he might crack a tooth. For a moment, hope blossomed in my chest, like this was just a moment of doubt. God knew I'd had one when Gray first suggested we try to be together.

But that ember was smothered when he shook his head. "No, I guess it doesn't." His steely eyes met mine. "I never meant to hurt you."

"You didn't." The lie burned on my tongue. "You didn't hurt me. This is the right move. It never would have worked between us. Maybe this was the closure I needed, and now I can find someone else. I've wasted enough time pining after you, Gray. I'm moving on, once and for all."

"Moving on?" Gray's nostrils flared. "You're my wife."

I ripped the ring off my finger and dropped it to the floor. "A mistake I'm going to remedy as soon as I get home."

TWENTY-SIX

Grayson

After holding Devyn downstairs for a little while longer, we walked back up together, finding Elsa happily waiting for us. Her tail wagged as Devyn got closer, and she instantly snuggled into her side.

As I closed the door to the basement, Devyn exhaled slowly, crossing her arms over her chest. Now that the spell between us had broken, I could see her walls fortifying. She glanced around the space, trying to find some excuse to keep her distance. It wasn't going to happen.

I crossed to her with three long strides, crushing my lips to hers. God, how the fuck had I gone so long without a taste of her? Kissing Devyn was indescribable. It was like coming home after a long stretch away. It reminded me of when I was playing ball on those rare occasions I would get to come back into town for a couple of days. Crossing the border of Saint Stephen's Lake, I could always feel myself start to relax.

But that sensation was nothing compared to having Devyn in my arms.

She matched the ferocity of my kiss, moaning in the back of her throat when I pulled her off the ground. Shit, just that little noise made me hard. My cock had been stiff as a rod since our lips touched downstairs, and now, it was almost painfully throbbing. I needed Devyn, needed to fuck her until she forgot about our past, about my fuck-up, about everything other than the way I made her feel.

When I shifted my hands to her perfectly round ass, I ground her against my cock, needing her to know exactly how much I wanted her. Her eyes widened when she pulled away. "Is that all for me?"

"Only ever you," I muttered, holding her so close, I thought I might combust right here and now. God, I needed to get my head on straight.

Devyn chuckled and kissed my lips once again. "Bedroom?"

Fuck yes. God, just the idea of Devyn spread out on my bedspread was enough to make me see stars. But looking at her now, her eyes drunk on lust, I couldn't help but pause, hating there were still secrets between us.

"I want that, Devyn, more than anything," I sighed, dropping my forehead to meet hers. "But maybe we should wait."

Her eyes searched mine. "Are you having second thoughts?"

"Not in the fucking least," I said, capturing her lips once more. "I want you, baby, more than I have ever wanted anything in my whole goddamn life."

"Then why?" she asked, her voice almost trembling.

God, that cut so deep, I thought I was actually bleeding. Knowing I was the cause of her insecurity made me hate myself even more. I reached out and brushed some of her hair from her face. "I don't want there to be any secrets between us, Devyn, not if we're going to cross this line."

Her eyes flared, and for a moment, I thought it was fear. But upon second look, I could see there was something else under the surface: guilt. What the fuck did Devyn have to feel guilty about?

Her lips snapped shut, and she motioned for me to let her go, severing our connection. She swallowed heavily, dropping her gaze to the living room. I started to follow her eye-line, but she stopped me. "What secrets are you talking about?"

Her voice had gone cold, almost like I was talking to a stranger. It was concerning, especially given what we'd just shared downstairs. I thought that was the beginning of our fresh start, but Devyn's reaction made my spine stiffen, wondering if there was more I was missing. While I was fully ready to confess my sins, from the way she was looking at me now, she seemed like she had her own hidden demons, and she was in no rush to tell me about them.

Ignoring that, I went over to the couch and sat down. My elbows found my knees, and I clutched my hands together. My knees refused to stop shaking, anxious energy pulsing through me. Devyn reluctantly followed, perching on the edge of the coffee table instead of sitting by my side. Fuck, I hated that, hated that there was so much distance between us after finally getting the taste of her on my tongue.

It would have been so easy to backtrack, to forget there was more to the story, to keep hiding the truth from Devyn, and protect her from all the carefully crafted lies. But I couldn't, not when lack of trust and communication had doomed us before.

I looked up, exhaling slowly when I found her dark brown eyes boring holes into mine. "You don't know everything about what happened when we were in Vegas."

As soon as the words left my mouth, Devyn froze, all her muscles stilling. She looked like she was barely breathing, probably terrified over what I was about to say. After all, I was the one who suggested we give our marriage a real shot, only to pull the rug out from under her. And now that I'd exposed all those healing scars, I was about to reopen them all over again.

"Devyn." I took her hand in mine. I needed to touch her,

needed that contact to know she was still with me. "You need to know I never meant to hurt you. I meant every word I said. I wanted that to be our chance, wanted it so fucking bad, it killed me to walk away."

"But you still did," Devyn whispered.

"Because I thought I didn't have a choice."

Her brow furrowed as she cocked her head. "What do you mean?"

I shook my head. "There's a lot I haven't told you, Devyn, things I've done that I'm not proud of." I held her hand a little tighter. "But everything I've done, all of it was for you. I would do all of it again if it meant keeping you safe."

Her brown eyes went wide. "What do you mean? What did you do, Gray?"

I rubbed my hand over my face, squeezing the bridge of my nose. "It started years ago. You remember that one summer, the one when you came to my house in the middle of the night, your face all bruised?" She nodded. "You told me you walked into a door, but I knew you were lying. You were hiding something from me." I exhaled. "So the next day, I went to the hotel to confront David."

Devyn sucked in a sharp breath and tried to pull her hand from mine. "Gray, you didn't–"

"He wasn't there," I finished. "It should have been simple. I was going to confront him and convince him to leave you alone by any means necessary. But then, it all spiraled, and I've been trying to unravel myself from this mess ever since."

"Why didn't you tell me?" Devyn said, her voice trembling.

"It was part of the deal I made," I answered, dropping my gaze down to our joined hands. "You had to be kept in the dark, at least until we figured out our plan. And when we got married..." I cursed under my breath. "It fucked up everything. It put you back in the spotlight and made our connection too public. If we'd stayed together, you could have been caught in the crosshairs, and I—we couldn't risk that."

Devyn suddenly stood and paced the living room. She didn't speak, but I could see the gears turning in her mind. After a long stretch of silence, she turned back to me but kept her arms crossed around her chest. "Tell me exactly what you're involved with, Gray."

I forced myself to meet her eyes. "We've been investigating David for years, trying to tie crimes to his business dealings, find ways to punish him for all the pain he's caused."

"What?" Her face paled, and she held the edge of the table. "Wh—why?"

I stood, unable to hold back the fury coursing through my veins. "Because that fucker *hurt* you. He tried to destroy every piece of *you*, and no one else was willing to put him in his place." I shook my head. "When this first started, I was just a kid, and there was nothing I could really do. But once I had resources at my disposal, I invested as much as I could so we could take him down, to make his kingdom crumble."

She shook her head. "You shouldn't have gotten involved. David is dangerous."

"Fuck that," I snapped. "He put his hands on the woman I l—" I cut off before I said something I couldn't take back. "I would burn the world if it meant keeping you safe, Devyn. I don't fucking care what happens to me, as long as I know you're okay."

She stared before suddenly rushing over to me and throwing herself into my arms. Devyn kissed me like it was our last moment on Earth, as if she couldn't wait another moment. But all too quickly, she pulled away, staring at me with a new intensity.

"Wait—did you say *we*?"

TWENTY-SEVEN

Grayson

As the hotel door swung shut behind me, a wide smile formed on my face. Every part of my body hurt, mostly from the ridiculous amount of alcohol I'd consumed last night. I might have made a few questionable choices, but I didn't regret a single one, not when they all led me to Devyn.

My wife.

And maybe it was the lingering effects of all the alcohol, but I wasn't upset, wasn't nervous. In fact, marrying Devyn seemed like the first right thing I'd done in a long time. There had been a void in my world since Devyn walked out of it. We were meant to be, I had no doubt. There was no other explanation as to why we felt so fucking right together. I'd never admit it out loud, but I'd always believed in soulmates. You would too if you'd grown up with my parents. There was no way two people would connect like that if there weren't cosmic forces bringing them together.

And for a while, I convinced myself I wasn't made for that kind of love. I was too quiet, too set in my ways, but in truth, I'd met my soulmate before I even knew myself. I just had to wait for my brain to realize it.

Staring down at my wedding ring, I shook my head, loving the weight of it on my finger. Marriage was something I'd always imagined way in the future, after my career came to an end, something I'd find when I was more settled. If it was anyone else I'd married last night, I'd be already calling my lawyers, demanding to get out of this mess. But Devyn was the one who put this ring on my finger, and now, I never wanted to take it off. Fuck, I wanted to tattoo a band underneath it, making sure her claim on me was there for the world to see.

As I heard the television flick on in the room behind me, I pushed off the door, determined to get Devyn everything she needed. Day one of our marriage, and I was already planning on showing Devyn why I was a safe bet.

I walked down the hall toward the elevator. When I pressed the button to the lobby, my phone chimed in my pocket. I frowned as I pulled it out and read the text on the screen.

LW

He knows.

As soon as the words sunk in, my blood ran cold. My heart pounded in my chest as I walked into the elevator, slamming my hand against the far wall. There was no fucking way. The devil worked fast, but there was no way he could already know. Shit, Devyn and I barely figured it out, and we were the ones who exchanged vows. She had to mean something else. But no matter the meaning, we were fucked. If David had picked up on our investigation, nowhere would be safe from his reach. Our power laid in our anonymity. The moment he caught on to our schemes and plan, we were done.

I glanced up at the descending numbers, trying to figure out what the fuck to do. Shit, my head was in no state to process any of this. I should be in bed, showing my wife why we were perfect for each other. Instead, I was having a panic attack in the middle of an elevator, praying this was all a bad dream.

My phone rang, and I could see the same number calling now, probably trying to fill me in on the situation. I couldn't deal with this, at least not yet. I wasn't ready for reality to ruin the morning.

But all of that came crashing down when the elevator arrived at the lobby and the doors opened, revealing a very pissed off Laurel Winters on the other side. She pulled her phone down from her ear and narrowed her dark green eyes at me.

As she approached me, I searched for any similarities to my wife, but Laurel was so different from her sisters. Although they were all tall and slim, Laurel was sharper, like her entire frame was cut glass. She'd dyed her hair dark in high school, so her dark green eyes were even more striking. They made you feel like she could crawl inside your soul, learning all your darkest secrets without even trying.

Where my wife had the same calculated stare, there was always a flash of life in Devyn's expression. Not everyone saw it, but it was one of my favorite sights in the world. When her lips turned up in a smile, it was everything, but Laurel held none of that warmth. It had been whittled down over the years, her light dimming more the longer she was under David's thumb. It was like she was just going through the motions, her need for revenge the only thing keeping her going.

I sucked in a sharp breath as I walked out to greet her, wishing I could stop time and never leave the hotel room. From the look on Laurel's face, I knew this conversation was going to be a painful one.

"I hear congratulations are in order," Laurel said, tucking her phone back in her purse. "Or is it best wishes for the groom?"

"HOW COULD YOU BE SO STUPID?"

Laurel looked around the crowded bar, making sure no one was listening in on our conversation. She shook her head and took a long sip from her wine glass. It was too tempting to order a drink of my own, to try to ease my hangover a little bit. But I was already wasting time away from Devyn, and I didn't want to stumble back into our room smelling like booze. I needed my head clear if I had any chance of convincing her to give us a shot.

Laurel exhaled slowly and squeezed the bridge of her nose with her fingers. "You are supposed to be keeping your distance from Devyn."

"I know," I said through gritted teeth.

"That was your job. To make sure my sister stayed as far away from this investigation as possible. To make sure she wouldn't be collateral damage if this all blew up in our faces. So please, explain to me *how the fuck* that equates to marrying her?"

I shook my head. "I told you, we weren't thinking."

"No, shit," Laurel hissed from the other side of the table. "You're lucky I intercepted the message before David heard it. Gives us time to clean this up before he *ever* finds out." She emptied the rest of her wine glass and then signaled for another round.

I arched my brow at her third drink. "You sure you want another?"

"I don't remember asking for your opinion," she bit back. "And yes, I am sure. Considering I was in the middle of a major merger when I got the alert about my little sister's impulsive nuptials and then had to rush to this godforsaken city before you did anything else stupid, I think drinks are called for." She waited until the waiter placed her refilled glass on the table and walked away before turning back to me. "You need to end this."

"No," I ground out. "Not going to happen."

Laurel leaned forward. "Let me remind you, you came to me. You wanted to help take down David, and now, we're in this. Together. There's no deviating from the plan now. Not when we are so close."

Fuck. I hated that she was right. When I first crossed Laurel's path a decade ago, I had no idea what I was signing up for. All I wanted was to destroy David, to make him pay for hurting Devyn. I'd never be able to pull that image from my mind, the one of her broken and bleeding as she crawled through my window. I hated that all I could do was hold her and promise myself I'd make the bastard pay.

When I showed up in their apartment the next morning, David was nowhere to be found. Instead, I stumbled upon Laurel in his office, copying files from his private server. She tried to make an excuse, claiming she was working on a school project, but it was too late. I'd seen enough, and stupidly, I offered to help. Laurel was apprehensive at first, especially considering I was only a high school sophomore. At four years older than us, Laurel wasn't around much growing up. She wasn't as close to Devyn as Calla, probably because of their age difference, but something in my eyes must have called to her, because before long, we were working together and hiding what we were doing from her sisters.

"I'll talk to Devyn," I conceded. "Let her know what's going on. You know she'd want to help–"

"You don't think I know that?" Laurel said, her voice softening. "I've thought about telling her and Calla a million times. But imagine what would Devyn do with the information we gathered. Would she sit on it, or would she go running at David with no regard for her own safety?" I grit my teeth, too aware of the answer. Laurel sighed. "That's what I thought."

"I love her," I said, staring at the band on my finger, the one that had filled me with so much hope. Now, it felt like an anchor. But considering I'd already placed myself in the depths, it was instead dragging Devyn down with me.

"I know you do," Laurel said. "And for what it's worth, I love my sister too, more than she even realizes. That's why I refuse to risk her safety. We've both seen too much. We know what David is capable of. The only reason Devyn is in the clear right now is because she followed the family plan. If she shows up married to you, how do you think that will go for her?" Laurel leaned back in her chair. "I wish there was another way, Gray, but this can't happen, not now. There's too much at stake."

"I won't give her up," I said, still staring at my ring. "I can't."

"We've both had to make sacrifices for this, Gray." Her face faltered, and for a moment, I could see the woman hidden behind her mask. She was right. She had made more sacrifices than me, more than anyone. First, working for David's company as soon as she graduated with her MBA to letting him set her up in a relationship he approved of—one that would benefit him, not her. She'd kept her sisters at a distance, cut everyone out of her life so they wouldn't be a target. Her life revolved around her revenge against David for reasons she wouldn't reveal to anyone, not even me.

Laurel leaned forward, her voice softening to a careful whisper. "I know you love Devyn, Gray. It's been obvious since you stormed into David's office, ready to give him hell for hurting her. I admire that love, more than you can ever know, but love has no place in this mess." She shifted, her eyes darting around the bar. "The best thing you could do for Devyn is to let her go. She can't get involved. I won't let her. So please, Gray," Laurel said as she started gathering her belongings. "Help me keep her safe."

I stared down at my hands, my knees shaking violently under the table. "She'll never forgive me."

Laurel sighed, pausing for a moment to place her hand on my shoulder. "Maybe, but we both know she's better off angry than dead."

TWENTY-EIGHT

Devyn

As Gray finished his story, I stared at him, unblinking. This had to be a joke, right? It was hard enough revisiting one of the worst moments of my life, but to hear my older sister caused it? My emotions felt like a kaleidoscope, all fractured and shifting so quickly, I couldn't pinpoint just one.

Gray's eyes tracked my every movement, like he was expecting me to melt down at his admission. But I'd spent so long being angry at Gray, so long questioning everything that happened between us, finally knowing the reason why felt like a weight lifting off my shoulders.

I'd convinced myself he'd left because of my flaws, that I wasn't enough for Gray. And even though I tried to brush it off, those thoughts stuck with me, making my defenses even more guarded. After all, if I couldn't trust my best friend to accept every piece of me, how could anyone else?

But that wasn't the reason. Gray wanted our marriage just as much as I did, and that was enough to repair most of the cracks in my damaged heart.

However, my anger toward Gray redirected itself, aiming right at Laurel. *How fucking dare she?* I hated her for pushing

Gray to leave, that she decided for the both of us without even consulting me. Laurel and I hadn't been close since we were children. How the fuck did she know what I could handle? She should have trusted me. They *both* should have.

But as angry as I felt, I was also in awe of my older sister. I couldn't believe she'd worked against David for so long. It almost felt too insane to be true. For years, I'd harbored resentment toward Laurel. After our mother married David, she seemed to gravitate to his side, taking any opportunity to spend more time with him. When she finished school, she immediately went to work for him, climbing up the corporate ladder to become one of David's right-hand people. Between her loyalty to David, and her marriage to one of his lackeys, I'd always kept her at arm's length. Even after our mother filed divorce papers, she stayed on at David's company, making all of us feel like she was picking his side over ours.

But now? Knowing she was actively working to destroy him framed everything in a new light. My stomach soured, thinking of all the times I'd complained about her, icing out my older sister because I thought she couldn't be trusted. Yet, she was the only one strong enough to throw herself into the lion's den, hoping to keep the rest of us out of danger.

"Devy..." Gray said, squeezing my fingers. "Talk to me. What are you thinking?"

There were no words that could describe my ricocheting feelings. I didn't even know anymore. The past couple of hours had fucked with my head, and now, I felt like I was in a tailspin, with nothing to ground me.

At least, not until Gray reached out and took my hands. His simple touch brought me back down to reality. I sighed, intertwining our fingers. "I don't know how I feel. I'm just..." I sighed. "I'm trying to wrap my mind around everything."

"I know I fucked up, Devyn," he whispered. "And I'm not

trying to make excuses, but we felt like we were on the brink of taking David down. One wrong move would destroy the entire plan."

"And did it?" I forced myself to ask.

"No," Gray quietly admitted. "Despite everything Laurel gathered, we weren't able to find anything to connect him to a crime." He squeezed my hands. "We haven't given up. Laurel is still digging, and I've got an entire team on him. We are going to find something to pin on him, I promise."

I released his hand, standing. "You should have told me."

Gray shook his head. "I wanted to keep you safe."

God, those words made me want to rage. I hated that he kept so much information from me, all under the guise of keeping me safe. *Weren't you doing the same thing?* The thought made me freeze as I snapped my eyes back to the couch, my files still gathering dust. Other than a couple of brief conversations with Tomas, I'd barely thought about them since Gray came over. But if we were spilling our secrets, it felt like the time to bring mine into the light.

"I get that, Gray. I really do." I exhaled slowly and stepped over to the other side of the couch. "But we have to stop making decisions for each other. You can't hide things because you think I can't handle it." I lowered to my knees, reaching underneath the couch to grab the file still hiding there. I pulled it out and dropped it on the coffee table. Gray's eyes darted to the portfolio then back up to me, a question lingering in his eyes. "Especially when we could have helped each other."

Gray's gaze darted from the file back up to me. "What is this?"

I shrugged. "I might have also been investigating David."

"What?" Gray snapped, reaching out to grab my evidence. He took out each page, scrubbing his hand with his face as he read them. "Holy shit," he whispered. "How did you get this?"

"You're not the only one with resources," I said, feeling a little smug at his shocked expression.

"Why didn't you tell me about this?"

"The same reason you didn't tell me: I wanted to keep you safe." I shook my head. "Little did I know, you were already playing Watson to my sister's Sherlock Holmes."

"This is..." Gray shook his head. "This is amazing, Dev. I can't believe you did all this on your own."

"Thanks, but that's not entirely true. I had a lot of help. One investigator at the firm did a lot of the actual digging; I just put the pieces together."

Gray's eyes flicked to me. "And you're sure you can trust him? Collin is in David's pocket—"

"Oh, yeah, I'm well aware of that fact." I grimaced. "I trust Tomas. There's no way he'd ever sell me out."

"Holy shit," Gray whispered, unable to hold back his grin. "I can't believe this. We might actually have him, Dev. We might be able to take him down."

I walked over to him and lowered into his lap. Gray's hands rested on my hips as I wrapped mine around his neck. The relief in his eyes was enough to make my heart burst. "And this will be even better because we'll do it together, just like we should have from the start."

He studied me, his hands tightening on my hips. "You have no idea how good that sounds, Devy. But if you need space—"

"I don't want space," I said, shifting closer to him so my chest pressed against his. "I've had enough space to last a lifetime." I dragged my fingernails through the hairs on the nape of his neck. "Now, I want you as close as possible."

"God, Ace," Gray sighed. "You have no idea what you're doing to me right now. Plus, this whole vengeance thing you've got going on..." He hissed a sharp breath as I rocked my hips over his length. "You gonna judge me if I said it's turning me on?"

"It'd be a relief," I joked. "I thought you'd get pissed at me for not letting it go."

"Never," he blurted. "I'd never judge you, especially after learning more about what he's done. But I'm not happy you've put yourself in danger. Ace, if anything happens to you—"

"I'm being smart about it. Trust me, I've spent a long time looking into his world. If David hasn't figured it out yet, he's not going to." I leaned forward, pressing a light kiss to his lips. "But enough about my fucked up family values, not when there are lot more things I want to do with you tonight."

Gray brightly smiled back at me. "Oh yeah? What kind of things are you thinking about?"

I shifted against him again, relishing in how his grip tightened on my skin. "I think it's better if I show you. Maybe in your bedroom."

"Fuck yes," Gray said, suddenly standing with me still in his arms.

I chuckled as he rushed toward the primary bedroom. "Gray, slow down!"

"Not gonna happen, Ace. I've waited a long time to have you at my mercy. I'm not taking any chances now."

Grayson wasn't joking. From the moment we crossed into his bedroom, he was a man possessed, only focused on one thing. He dropped me onto his carefully made bed and stood at the edge, staring down at me with a tense jaw and fire in his eyes.

"Take off your clothes," he said, his voice low and guttural.

I didn't think. I just reacted to his domineering tone, wanting to see if I could make him break like he did in the shower. As my clothes fell to his floor, Gray took a sharp breath, his eyes roving over all me. Without a word, he shifted my arm, rubbing his thumb over the tattoo I'd gotten for him. "Mine," he said, more to himself than to me. "If we do this, there's no going back, Devyn. You're my wife. You wear my ring. And if you ever think about sending me those papers, I'm going to bring you right back here and remind you where you belong."

My throat dried up at his words, and I judged myself when they turned me on so much. I was used to being in charge, to being the one barking orders. If anyone else spoke to me like that, I would destroy them. But coming from Gray, all I felt was desire, the inside of my thighs becoming slick with need for him.

I sat up on my haunches, reaching out to touch him. But before I could, Gray's hand went to my neck, not tightening but holding me in place. "Not until I hear the words, Devyn. Tell me you're mine, and I'll make you come so hard, you'll see stars. But I'm not doing this if it means you're going to run from me."

I swallowed, looking up at his steel eyes. I expected a pang of fear, some sort of shadow of doubt from our past, but nothing came. I wanted to be his, wanted to wear his ring and call him my husband, in truth. "I'm yours," I whispered. "Only yours. *Your* wife."

"Fuck," Gray hissed, his fingers tightening on my skin. "You have no fucking clue what hearing that does to me. Good thing you're all I want, because you're *ruining* me, Devyn."

"Just returning the favor."

With that, Gray dragged me up, letting go of my neck in favor of my thighs. His tongue tangled with mine, as if memorizing my taste. There was nothing delicate or apprehensive about this kiss.

It was a claiming.

Just as I moaned into his mouth, Gray dropped me back against the bed. He shifted down to his knees and removed his shirt. Before I could say anything, he gripped my thighs, dragging me to the edge of the bed. As his tongue lapped at me from top to bottom, my head fell back, groaning at the sensation. How had it only been a couple of hours since his tongue was last inside me? It felt like it was too long, as if I couldn't function without his mouth making me feel this way.

As his fingers entered me, I squirmed, already feeling my orgasm building inside me. But as my walls clenched around his fingers, Gray stalled. Sitting up on my elbows, I glared at him. "Why did you stop?"

"Sorry, Ace." Gray smirked up at me as he stood. "Your next orgasm is going to be around my cock. I just wanted to make sure you were ready for me."

TWENTY-NINE

Grayson

As I stared down at Devyn, looking at me like she wanted to rip out my throat, I couldn't believe my luck. Somehow, despite my countless mistakes and fuck ups along the way, Devyn Winters was in *my* bed, naked and practically begging for me to fuck her.

God, how many times had I dreamt of this moment, fucked my fist to images of her, flushed and wanton under me? While I'd hoped like hell we'd end up here, doubts always plagued me. I didn't deserve Devyn, didn't deserve a second chance with her. But I was selfish enough to take it anyway. She was here with me, and she was mine.

My wife. My love. My future.

"Gray," Devyn snapped, wrapping her fingers in my hair and pulling. *Hard.* "If you don't finish what you started, I'm going to take matters into my own hands."

I pulled her hand up, pressing a soft kiss to her fingertips before bringing her arm above her head. "Another day, I'm going to hold you to that, wife. I want to watch you touch yourself, just like you watched me." I nipped at her neck as I brought her other arm up. "Did you like that, Devyn? Did you like watching me fall apart, calling out your name?"

"Fuck..." she sighed as my teeth grazed her collarbone. "I loved every second of it."

My hands ran along her soft thighs, relishing the way her body shivered under my touch. She was already so close to the edge, it wouldn't take long for her to fall apart. Maybe it had been cruel to stop her from climaxing, but I meant what I said. I needed to be inside her, needed to feel her release. The thought was driving me mad. Nothing on heaven or Earth could have stopped me from sinking inside her, needing to ruin her just as she'd ruined me.

But as I removed my jeans and grabbed a condom from my nightstand, Devyn's eyes met mine. "Can we..." Her gaze darted to the condom in my hand. "I have an IUD."

My hands clenched, needing to keep my head together as I processed her words. I swallowed. "Are you asking me to take you bare, Devyn?"

"I was tested a couple of months ago, and I haven't been with anyone else since." She chewed on her bottom lip. "So if you want to..."

"Fuck yes, I want that." I kissed her throat, working up her jaw as she squirmed underneath me. "I've been tested too, and it's been a long time for me, so I'm good."

"What's a long time for you, superstar?" Devyn teased, reaching up so she could nip the skin on my neck. "A couple of weeks?"

"Five years."

Devyn's mouth fell open at my confession. Her eyes darted down to the tattoo on my chest, the brand I gladly wore for her. "Are you saying..."

"There's been no one else since we got married, Ace." I shook my head. "I tried when I thought this would never work out, but the idea of being with anyone else like that..." I shuddered. "It wasn't worth it, not unless it was you."

Devyn stared at me, her eyes filling with tears. "I've made so many mistakes," she whispered, holding me a little tighter. "I'm so—"

I cut off her words, pressing my thumb to her bottom lip. "Don't you dare apologize for living your life, Devy. I didn't tell you because I was trying to make you feel guilty. I was the one who tore us apart. I'd never judge you for how you chose to build yourself back up."

She nodded, and I leaned her back, dusting my lips over her pale pink nipples. As I worked one with my mouth, I teased the other with my fingers. "But now that we're together, Devyn, there's no one else. You are mine, and I'm not sharing you."

"No one else," she repeated, a smile tugging at the corner of her lips. "I only want you, Gray. I want my husband."

"Fuck," I grunted, shifting in between her thighs. "You can't say things like that right now, Devyn. I'm going to try to start slow, make sure I don't hurt you. But if you keep saying that—"

"Fuck me, Gray," Devyn demanded. "I'm not going to break. Fuck your wife like you should have on our wedding night."

With her simple words, I lifted her, depositing her into my lap. She shifted, sliding her drenched pussy over my length. "Fuck, baby, just like that. Gotta get inside you soon, or I'm going to come all over your pretty tits."

"Maybe another night," Devyn teased. "But you've made some promises, husband, and I want to see if you live up to them."

I chuckled, loving the spark of challenge in her eyes. This was why no one else could ever compete with Devyn. She made me want to be the best version of myself, constantly pushing and encouraging me. Even when we were apart, she was the voice in the back of my head.

I gripped her hips and lifted her, letting her take her time sinking onto my length. Her hands rested on my shoulders, clutching when it started to be too much. I pulled her chest closer, taking one of her nipples into my mouth, teasing it with my teeth and tongue. As her head fell back, urging me closer, she finally took the rest of me, bottoming out with a little gasp.

I leaned back and brushed the hair out of her face, loving the lust and desire in her eyes. "You okay, Ace?"

"Yeah, fuck," she moaned, lifting herself experimentally. "I'm just so...full."

"Too much?"

"No," she moaned, lifting her hips a little more brazenly. "It's perfect."

With that, she slammed back down, finding her own pace. It was exquisite, watching my wife work my cock like it was made for her. And maybe it was, because nothing had ever felt this good before.

This was heaven. I would gladly die right here and now, with my wife's pussy clenching me like she never wanted me to let go.

As she rocked against me, Devyn's eyes darted down to where we were joined, watching as I claimed this last piece of her. I wanted to collect them all and hoard them away from the rest of the world. Because no matter what happened next, Devyn Winters owned every piece of my soul, and I wanted to own hers in return.

"Gray," she cried. "I'm so close."

"Tell me what you need, baby. Tell me what you need to get you there."

"Rub my clit."

I eagerly complied, circling her bundle of nerves with my thumb. A few strokes, and I could feel her explode around my cock, her nails digging into my shoulders. The little bite of pain was enough to throw me over the edge, finding my release along with her. We both stared at each other as we crossed over the line.

As our breathing slowed, we kept eye contact, neither of us willing to look away first. It was like we knew this changed *everything* between us. It was a knot at the end of the strings that bound us together, a promise we'd never drift apart again.

A promise I would rather die than break.

AS THE SUN filtered into my bedroom the next morning, I reluctantly opened my eyes. The first thing I did was check the space next to me. It would have stung, but I wouldn't have been surprised if Devyn snuck out in the middle of the night. Last night was intense for both of us.

But there she was, curled up on her side, the same content smile resting on her lips. Her hair was mused from sleep, her lips bruised from our rounds last night, but she was still the most beautiful woman in the world. I brushed the hair away from her face, secretly wishing I could start every morning this way.

She nuzzled into the pillows, stretching her arms over her head. It was just enough to give a glimpse of the word marked on her rib cage. The delicate script unleashed something inside me, knowing she'd gotten a permanent reminder of us. While my skin was inked with our story, I never expected her to do something similar, not after what I'd done. And while Devyn seemed like she'd forgiven me, I'd yet to forgive myself—I didn't know if I ever could.

But I'd happily spend the rest of my days making it up to her.

Devyn twisted in the sheets, letting out an annoyed little huff. She slowly opened one of her eyes. "God, if you're a morning person, this is never going to work between us. Might as well leave now."

"Says the woman who used to live at her office," I teased, pulling her closer so her back was against my front. My legs curled around her, and she squirmed, her ass rubbing against my dick. "Baby, if you keep moving like that, we're not going to be getting out of this bed anytime soon."

She smirked at me over her shoulder. "Oh no, what a shame that would be."

Devyn

"Oh my God," Calla sighed as she walked to the back windows. "I can't believe you've been holding out on me. Do you know what I would give to see these views every morning?"

I chuckled from the kitchen, watching as my sister continued to explore every inch of Gray's house. It was his turn to host the weekly poker game with his friends, and I'd offered to help him set up. He usually had everyone meet up at the restaurant, but this time, I offered to host instead.

He looked at me like I'd lost my mind, and maybe he was right. I wasn't the hosting kind, never having more than a jar of olives and bottles of vodka in my fridge. But after the past week of domesticity, I thought it'd be fun to try something else out of my routine.

"What the hell?" Calla shrieked from my room. "Have you seen this shower? Please, please, please, tell me you've experienced those jets." She groaned as she walked back into the main living space. "When I'm huge, I'm commandeering that bathtub."

"Making yourself right at home?" I asked, arching a brow at her. She settled at the kitchen island, propping her head up with her hand. As Calla stared at me, I furrowed my brow. "What's that look for?"

"I'm liking this version of you, Dev. All domesticated." I sneered at the word. "Okay, poor word choice. But you look happy, more than you were in the city."

I couldn't even try to deny it. I *was* happier. I felt like a different version of myself, one who wasn't weighed down by everyone else's expectations. Without the constant pressure of trying to prove myself, I could finally breathe, letting my walls and defenses drop.

And then, there was Gray. Over the past week, we'd created our own little routine, like a real married couple. It was weird how easily we sank into our roles. We woke up together then made breakfast before Gray planned to go to work. He hadn't made it on time once this week, all because our stolen kisses and touches turned into him bending me over the kitchen island more than once.

When we came down from our high, he'd head down to the restaurant, and I'd stay here with Elsa keeping me company as I continued to sort through our growing pile of evidence against David. As I worked, Gray would call to check in, and I hated to admit how much I looked forward to each and every call. It was...nice to have someone do that for me, to want to make sure I was taking care of myself.

It shouldn't have surprised me. Gray was always good at taking care of the people close to him. He'd looked after me for most of our lives, and now, he was doing the same thing with his parents. He tried to be stealthier about it with them, though. Both Marta and Curt were proud people, and it was probably hard for them to accept Gray's help. But he didn't mind, stopping over at the house every night before he came back here.

A part of me felt guilty he was staying here with me every night, especially after he told me more about his father's diagnosis and their possible next steps. Fear and regret tinged his words as he talked about the assisted living facility the doctor kept recommending. He was supposed to tour the facility with his mom in the next couple of weeks. He'd asked if I'd come along, but I wasn't sure if that was a good idea. It was a family thing, and I didn't want to take away from the purpose of the visit.

"What is that look about?" Calla's voice broke me out of my train of thought. "Your smile just dropped."

I sighed, putting aside the bowl I was absent-mindedly mixing. "I was thinking about Marta and Curt." I shook my head. "Gray asked if I wanted to go see them, but I couldn't bring myself to do it."

"Why?" Calla asked as she reached across the island and stole my whisk. She ran her finger along the side and moaned as she popped it into her mouth. "They both love you, and you've always loved them. You were practically their second kid growing up."

"I used to be," I insisted. "Who knows how they feel about me now? And with Gray—"

Calla's lips curled into a smile at my words, my cheeks filling with a warm blush. Her expression turned almost feline as she leaned in closer. "What with Gray?"

"Something happened with Gray," I said quickly, getting the words out before I could change my mind. "I, uh, I think I'm falling for him." *Again.* But I kept that part to myself.

Calla went quiet for a long moment, long enough that I started to move toward her. But as soon as I took a step, she let out a loud whoop. "I knew it!" Calla said as she smiled gleefully. "I bet Theo fifty bucks you two were going to get together, but I didn't think it'd be this quick! I doubled up, sure he'd make you wait at least a month before giving in."

"Okay, I don't know what I hate more: that you're making

bets about my love life, or that you thought *Gray* would be the holdout."

She shrugged her shoulders. "You know you love me. You just hate that I'm right."

"I'm not going to admit it," I said, rubbing my fingers over my forehead. "But things are good between us, Calla. Like really good."

"How good?"

"Good enough that I'm terrified," I chuckled, but it held no warmth. "It feels right, being with Gray like this. But what if that's just because it's new? Maybe I'm reading too much into it and it's not the start of anything, just some old feelings coming up." I swallowed heavily. "What if this is a fling, something to get this tension out of our systems finally? What if it's just closure?"

"Is that what you want?"

"No." I wanted *everything* with Gray, but without a plan for our future, I wasn't sure how it could even work. Being around Gray was as easy as breathing, but that had never been our issue. What we lacked was timing. Our lives were always passing ships, one having to give up something to be with the other.

"Devyn..." Calla said, her tone more serious than it was minutes ago. "I love you more than I can put into words, but we both know you're not good at letting people in. And if I know you like I think I do, you're probably running through every scenario in your mind, finding some way to convince yourself this will never work." She reached out and took my hand. "But you're forgetting one thing."

I swallowed. "What?"

"It's just—this is Gray, Devyn." She smiled at me. "*Your* Gray. He's always been your person, and you've finally found your way back to each other. Don't let the fear win."

"I wish it was that easy." I shook my head, remembering how we claimed each other that first night. He'd called me his, and nothing had ever felt so right—like the pieces of my heart were finally sliding back into place. I groaned. "I'm sorry. I probably shouldn't be talking to you about this. I'd get it if you hated me now. After all, he was yours first."

Calla rolled her eyes, and her hand fell to her belly. "I think we both knew that's not true. Gray and I might have dated, but it was never what you two share. It's taken me years to see it, but now that I have Theo and know what it means to love someone truly, it's so clear. Gray has always been yours, Devyn, just like you were always meant to be his."

"Were you scared?" I asked, hating the vulnerability in my words. "When you fell for Theo?"

"Terrified," Calla chuckled. "Theo was the *last* person I wanted to fall for. God, he'd never even been in a relationship before, and he was so damn grumpy." She smiled softly and rubbed her hand over her protruding belly. "For a long time, I tried to hold back, sure we would never work out. I've never been so happy to be proven wrong." My sister paused for a moment. "You want my advice?"

"Obviously. That's why I'm asking."

"And there's the smart-ass I know and love," Calla groaned. "But honestly, Devyn, take it day by day. Enjoy this time with Gray. Stop worrying about what could be and enjoy the fact that you two are together right now." Her smile faltered for a moment. "We both know how quickly circumstances can change."

The next day, I sat back in my chair in the dining room, staring at the images taped to the wall. After an hour of staring blankly at them on the table, I thought a change might help, so I decided to emulate some of my favorite TV detectives. But no matter how long I stared at the files, nothing seemed to connect. They were just a bunch of numbers and transactions that made no sense—not without the key to how they all connected.

The closest I'd come to anything about Saint Stephen's Lake was a shell company's PO Box with the same zip code, but that was a dead end. There weren't any business listings, no other addresses, no other financial records. It could have been nothing, but my gut wouldn't let it go, not until we'd pulled on every single loose thread.

The door opened, and Elsa jumped up at my feet, barking to greet Gray. "Hey, Ace?" he called out. "You home?"

Home. The simple term brought a smile to my face. How was it only a month ago, I was so desperate for Gray to sign the divorce papers and free me from him? Now, the thought made my stomach drop. I hated the idea of severing our marriage, no matter how unconventionally we started.

"In here," I answered as I stood from my chair.

He walked into the dining room holding out a bag of take-out. Before he looked at all the documents covering his space, he leaned in, pressing a soft kiss to my lips. It was nothing Earth-shattering, but it still made my heart want to soar. It was the kind of kiss that promised a lifetime of greetings just like this one.

Gray leaned back and brushed a couple of strands of hair away from my face. "You look like you've been busy."

"Wish that was true," I groaned. "I keep looking over all of this stuff, hoping something magically jumps out at me."

"No such luck?"

"None at all," I groaned, reaching for the take-out bag. "God, this smells amazing."

"Yeah," Gray sighed as he took off his coat and hung it on

the hook by the door. "My mom was making dinner when I stopped by and insisted I take some with me."

Guilt sank the elation in my chest, and I rubbed the spot, hoping to soothe some of it away. I cleared my throat, moving into the kitchen to grab some plates and utensils. As I dug in the drawer, Gray wrapped his arms around my waist, inhaling the spot beneath my ear. "Fuck, I love coming home to you, Ace. Look forward to it all day long."

"Me too," I said, but my tone betrayed me.

Gray's hand tightened on my hips, shifting me so we were chest to chest. He gazed down at me, then ran his fingers along my jaw. "What's going through that head of yours?"

I tried to embody my sister's courage, knowing it wouldn't do us any good if I buried every uncomfortable feeling that came up. "I feel bad," I admitted. "You came back here to help your parents, and now you're here with me all the time. I don't want to distract you, not when they really need you."

"You're not distracting me from anything, Devy."

"Aren't I?" I asked, daring to meet his steely eyes. "You've been spending all your nights here, and I know you worry about them, especially your mom. If you want to go stay there, I'd completely understand."

Gray reached around my waist and pulled me into a loose hug. "I know, Ace. And I've been thinking about this a lot too." He pulled back to meet my eyes. "I talked to my mom about it today. I'm happy to go there as much as she needs, but we both agreed—I can't stop living my life either. Before you came to town, my entire world revolved around my dad's diagnosis and his treatment plan. As much as I wanted to help, it was leaving me feeling hollow." He squeezed my hips. "I needed to find balance, and you've helped me with that. So yes, I'll keep going to all the appointments and checking in during the day, but we're going to hire a night nurse to help my mom."

"Are you sure that's what you want?"

"More than anything," Gray said. "I want to enjoy this time with my dad, not be so worried about his meds and everything else that I miss those moments." I reached up, placing my hand on his cheek. He took it in his grasp, turning it to kiss my palm. "And I really fucking want a life with you, Devyn. I *want* to be here."

His words thrummed in my chest, and I felt the promise written in them. These were more than pretty words, more than just a promise to ease my doubts. This was the start of something that could be wild and beautiful, just like the flowers that covered these hills after the snow melted away.

"I like the sound of that." I lightly pressed a kiss to his lips. "I like having you here too."

"Yeah?" he said, letting his fingers trail along my exposed skin. "Do you like being here?"

His words gnawed at me like I was about to expose something I didn't even know how to admit to myself. When I first came up here, it was supposed to be a temporary solution, a place to rest my head while looking for more clues about David's dealings. It should have been a stop along the way, but now, Saint Stephen's Lake felt a lot more like my destination. It had been my first home, the place I met Gray, and the backdrop for so many of my best and worst moments.

This small, quiet town was the opposite of the big city future I had imagined, but it fit me. At least, this new version of me. The idea of going back to eighty-hour work weeks with no time for anything personal made my skin crawl.

I loved this quiet version of my life, especially if it included a tall, tattooed former baseball player at my side.

"Yeah," I said, my words hushed and low. "I think I love it here."

Gray's resulting smile was almost blinding. He pulled me

into his arms, lifting me until my feet dangled off the ground. As I wrapped my legs around him, Gray chuckled, "Does that mean I get to move your things into my room?"

I rolled my eyes. "The room is literally across the hall from yours. Does it really bother you if my stuff is in there?"

"Hell yes, it does," Gray said, kissing my neck. "If we're doing this, we're doing it for real, Ace. You're gonna be tucked against me every night, and I'm gonna wake up to you every morning."

I toyed with the hair that had slipped out of his bun, smiling like I hadn't in years. "I guess that could be arranged."

"Good," he chuckled, walking us out of the kitchen into *our* bedroom. "Just got used to having you in my bed, Ace. Don't think I could go back if I tried."

THIRTY-ONE

Grayson

"Are you sure this is a good idea?"

I glanced at Devyn, who was squirming in my passenger seat. She plucked at the edge of her seatbelt, her eyes darting to the side window and back to the front. Her anxiety was coming out in waves, and honestly, it was starting to make me nervous as well.

No, I wasn't sure if this was a good idea. A knot had burrowed itself into my stomach from the moment we left the house. I knew at some point, Laurel and Devyn would have to cross paths, but for some reason, I expected it to be when we had something to share. When I called Laurel to tell her Devyn knew about our investigation, the last thing I expected was for her to demand a meeting with all of us, Tomas included, to discuss our collective findings. The order had irritated me. It completely pissed off my wife. Devyn was not used to being bossed around, and I had a feeling it would only get worse when the sisters were face to face.

I reached across the console and took her hand, bringing it up to my lips. As I pressed a kiss to the back of her knuckles, she gradually relaxed. "I'll be with you," I promised, "the whole time. And if you don't want to do this, we can turn around right now."

"Laurel wouldn't like that," she deadpanned.

"Fuck what Laurel wants," I bit out. "You're the one I care about. You don't have to meet with her unless *you* want to. I'll make sure of that."

She hummed in agreement but said nothing else, continuing to stare out the window. However, that overwhelming anxiety was no longer seeping out of her pores, making the drive a little less tense.

Devyn squeezed my hand as we followed the directions, turning onto a dirt road about twenty miles outside of town. While most of the snow from the storm had melted, it left behind slick conditions, and even my truck was struggling to stay on the right side of the road.

"Distract me," Devyn said, her voice soft and tense. "Please, Gray. Tell me something that's going to make me think happy thoughts and not about dying in a fiery car wreck."

"Shit, Ace, you think I'd let that happen?" I shook my head, about to promise something I could never uphold. But I'd picked this truck for a reason, and it was made for handling this kind of terrain. Plus, with Devyn in the passenger seat, I was being extra cautious. Not only because driving made her nervous, but because I was savoring every minute we had together.

"Please, Gray," she pleaded, her hand so tight around mine, she was cutting off circulation.

Fuck, now I had no choice but to comply. Something shifted in my brain when Devyn said the word *please*. I would do anything if she asked. Toying with her fingers, I smirked in her direction. "Keep thinking about you in the shower last night. I'm never going to go in there again without getting hard. The way you took me, baby..." I sighed, looking over at her. "You're going to be the death of me, Ace."

"Happy to be of service," she chuckled, but the sound was forced. She glanced behind her, then turned back with a sly smile. "You know, that back seat looks very roomy. Maybe we could pull over and test that theory."

Without another thought, I turned the steering wheel and brought my truck over to the side of the road. My hand moved to the back of Devyn's neck, dragging her over to kiss me. Her lips collided with mine, and I held her tight, needing the feeling of her against my skin. Devyn was my addiction, and I had no interest in being cured. She tasted like cinnamon and vanilla thanks to her latte from earlier, and the sweetness of home. It was perfect. Everything about this woman was, even the things that drove me insane.

I forced myself to pull away, even though my entire body rioted in complaint. "I meant what I said, Devyn. You don't have to do this, but I think it would be good to clear the air with Laurel, figure out how you two can work with, instead of against, each other."

"Fine," she groaned and dropped her forehead to my chest. "I know it's the right move, but the idea of seeing Laurel..." Her voice trailed off. "I don't know how I'm going to react. I'm still so pissed at her. I'm afraid I'm going to say something so hurtful–" She looked up and searched my eyes. "What if I say something I can't take back, and she never forgives me?"

I held her tight, bringing her head back down to my chest. Her hands gripped my shirt, holding me so close, I barely knew where she ended and I began. Kissing the top of her head, I said, "You have every right to feel that way. And if you feel yourself getting upset, let me know, and I'll get you out." She nodded against me but made no effort to move. So, I kept holding her, willing to stay there as long as it took. "I have you, Ace. Always."

ABOUT HALF AN HOUR LATER, Devyn calmed down, and we got back on the road, getting closer to our destination. I didn't know if it was our talk or just us stopping to breathe for a moment, but my wife was back to her usual self, busting my balls and mocking my shitty taste in music.

The GPS signaled our next turn, telling us we were approaching our destination. We both froze, staring out at the antiquated motel in the distance. It looked like something out of an old horror movie, with its seventies-style sign flickering in a random rhythm, and the muted orange tones. It was enough to make me slow my truck down before pulling into the entrance, suddenly unsure if this plan was such a good idea.

Devyn chuckled at my side. "Don't tell me you're getting cold feet now."

"I just..." I sighed, running my hand over my beard. "I need a minute, Devy."

She crawled over to my side, pressing against the center console so she could get as close as possible. "Hey, all the same things apply to you. If you want to go, we go. No explanation needed. I have your back just as much as you've got mine."

I nodded as I took her hand. "You and me, right?"

"Now, he's getting it," she chuckled, bringing my knuckles to her lips. "You know, maybe what we both need is an incentive to play nice during this meeting."

"Incentive?"

She smirked at me. "I meant what I said about testing out that theory. We've fucked on almost every surface of your house, but we haven't tried your backseat yet. Maybe that could be our reward after the meeting."

I reached out and dragged her to me, capturing her lips yet again. Not only was the image of her sprawled out in my backseat making my dick impossibly hard, but I also just needed to touch her. To feel her. To remind myself why we were in this fight, what I had to lose.

She placed her hand on my chest and pushed me back slightly. "I said *after* the meeting."

"I know, Ace," I said, dropping my forehead to hers. "Just to feel you, to remember this is real. That you're here with me."

"Always," she promised. "But we really should get in there. I'm already stressed about having Laurel and Tomas in the same room."

"Fine," I groaned but smiled at her so she knew I was teasing. "But I'm holding you to that promise."

"Good."

As I shifted back onto the road, a thought washed over me, making my stomach clench in jealousy. I had no right to know how Devyn spent her time when we were apart, and I meant what I told her earlier. I'd never begrudge her for living her life, but I also needed to know what I was walking into.

"So Tomas..." I sighed, focusing on the road ahead of us. "Did you two ever..."

"No," Devyn blurted out. "We flirted on my first day but quickly realized we didn't have any kind of spark. I care about him as a friend. That's it." My shoulders relaxed at her words, glad I wasn't going to have to sit across the table from one of her past lovers. The one I'd already met was enough. "Honestly, I only dated a couple of people after you," Devyn said quietly. "And nothing serious. It was too hard when..." Her voice trailed off, and I dared to look at her.

"When what, Ace?"

"When I compared everyone to you," she answered. "It was like you were there in the back of my mind all those years, and no one could live up to you."

"And what about the real me?" I teased.

"You're even better."

I turned and stole a glance at her. Devyn was staring at me without any trace of humor in her expression. She meant that. God, how could I have ever survived without this woman? With only a few words of praise, I was on cloud nine, ready to take on the entire world.

But despite that feeling, there was one thing I couldn't get out of my head. "What about that Jack guy? He seemed to think the two of you were pretty serious."

Devyn snorted. "If he did, he was delusional. I think he liked the idea of me more than the actual version. We only hung out a few times, and I was clear I wasn't looking for more from him."

"He didn't seem like your type."

"This is going to sound really bad." Devyn paused, and my heart thundered in my chest. But just as I was about to ask her what was wrong, she continued, "Do you remember going to a Gala at the New York Museum last year?"

I furrowed my brow, trying to think back on my former social calendar. *Oh, shit.* It suddenly clicked. It was one of those major fashion house events every celebrity wanted to attend, and my former agent set me up with some actress. I'd already fired him at that point, tired of him selling my secrets to the press. I would have canceled, but her agent begged me to keep up appearances, not wanting her embroiled in a scandal right before her newest movie released. It was a long night, not only because the press was hounding me, but also because I started to believe the "date" wasn't as innocent as I was led to believe, especially after the actress stuck her tongue down my throat right in front of all the cameras.

"Vaguely," I answered. "That was a long fucking night, so I've tried to forget it."

Devyn toyed with her hands, turning to look at the passenger side window. "I was there too."

"You were?"

She nodded. "It was right after Calla went to work with Theo, before you came on as a client. She was nervous about going with him, so she asked me to tag along as a buffer."

I shook my head. "No. I would have seen you there."

"No, you wouldn't have," Devyn said sadly. "We were only a few feet away from each other, and you didn't notice me. You were too wrapped up with your date." she sighed. "And I hated that seeing you affected me so much. So, I decided if you could move on, so could I." She shook her head. "But I felt even worse after, so I stayed away from him...until Alex and Cole's engagement dinner."

My blood stilled, remembering that moment all too well. Devyn met my eyes from across the room, and it was like all the air escaped my lungs. It was the first time we'd seen each other in person since Las Vegas. At least, that was what I thought at the time. I wanted to talk to her, wanted to explain, wanted to say something that would erase the hurt in her eyes, but before I could make my way through the crowd, she was gone.

"It was too much," she said. "Being in town, being in the same room as you. It felt like the walls were closing in around me, so I did something stupid to try to escape." She laughed, but the sound lacked warmth. "So now you know some of my worst mistakes." She turned, giving me a sad smile. "Still sure you want to be with me?"

I took her hand. "Devyn, we've both made plenty of mistakes. We're human, we're going to fuck up. I'm not here with you because I expect you to be perfect. I'm here because I see you, flaws and all, and I'm crazy about you." I squeezed her hand a little tighter. "Plus, I've met the douchebag. I don't feel sorry for him at all." She let out a bright laugh, and I took it as a sign she was feeling better.

I let go of her hand and hit the blinker, forcing myself to pull into the parking lot. As I shifted the car into park, I turned back toward her. "But do me a favor, Ace?" I kissed her one last time before turning off my truck. "You ever need to fuck your feelings out again, make sure it's my dick you're using."

She smiled so brightly at me, it rivaled the sun. "That I can do."

THIRTY-TWO

Devyn

Every step toward the motel room felt like another step toward my execution. After confirming the room number with Tomas, my heart started pounding in my chest, trying to keep up my calm façade, not wanting to alert Gray to my rising stress.

Maybe I was being dramatic, considering we were meeting with my older sister and close friend, but I felt it all the same, at least about seeing Laurel. I was pretty excited to see Tomas and make sure he was okay. For years, we were a two-man team, and even though we'd brought more people into the fold, he was still someone I trusted. Laurel, on the other hand, was a different story.

Maybe it was hypocritical to be angry at Laurel after I forgave Gray so easily. But Gray had worked hard to earn back my trust, and there was a lifetime of moments to back it up. Most of all—I knew if he were given the chance, Gray would never do it again.

As much as I wanted to say the same for Laurel, I didn't really know her. I knew her public-facing persona, the doting daughter and wife she pretended to be. But this vigilante, determined to take David down at any cost? She was a stranger.

As I brought my fist up to knock on the motel room door, Gray reached out, placing his hand on my elbow. I furrowed my brow as I turned to look at him. "Remember what I said, Ace. One word, and we're gone."

"You sound like you're expecting bloodshed," I chuckled, trying to hide my nerves. But Gray didn't laugh, didn't even crack a smile. Instead, he continued to glare at the door, as if it offended him.

"The Laurel you and I know are very different people. She's a lot harsher when she doesn't have her mask in place. I just want you to be prepared."

I placed my free hand on top of his, stroking it with my thumb. "I've handled worse, I'm sure. Have faith in me, husband."

"Fuck," Gray groaned, pulling me in for a quick kiss. "You can't say that shit to me, Devyn. Gets me hard."

"Good," I chuckled. "I like having that control over you."

"You always have," he muttered, reluctantly releasing me. As I started to push the door open, Gray called out, "I do." When I turned around, he continued, "I do have faith in you, more than anyone else in the world. You've been slaying dragons by yourself for a long time, Ace, and I know you can handle anything life throws at you alone." He walked closer and took my hand in his. "But you don't have to, not while I'm around."

I could only nod, not sure how to articulate what that meant to me. For so long, I felt like a one-woman army, refusing to let anyone see how lonely I felt. It was worth it to know if any of this went south, the blowback would be on me—and me alone. But hearing Gray say those words made my chest lurch, wanting to gift him words of my own. Three words, to be exact, ones that had been on the top of my tongue for days.

There was no doubt in my mind. I loved Grayson Anders

more than anything else in this world. It was the kind of love that had the power to destroy me, but despite our past, I trusted my heart in his hands.

But now was not the time for confession, not with my sister waiting on us. So, instead, I lifted onto the tips of my toes and kissed him. "Thank you."

<hr>

BEING AROUND LAUREL WAS STRANGE. When I spent time with Calla, I instantly relaxed, knowing she was practically the other half of my heart. But standing around Laurel...it was almost unnerving.

I didn't realize how far we'd drifted apart until this moment, when we stood on opposite sides of the room, staring at each other. Looking at the two of us, there was no question we were related. We had the same sharp lines on our faces, the same curve to our nose. We even had the same careful, blank expressions.

But that was where the similarities ended.

The air was tense inside the small room, little more than a bed and a couple of end tables filling it. The walls were covered in a beige, patterned wallpaper, the edges starting to curl with either age, neglect, or both. There was a large window that faced the parking lot, and that was where Gray stood while the rest of us stood more in the middle. Laurel hadn't stopped pacing since we walked in, taking up the back of the room with her annoyed steps. Tomas laid on the bed, the only one of us who didn't seemed phased by all the frenetic energy filling the air around us.

As Tomas turned his laptop toward me, I stepped forward and started to talk. "This is where we last left off. We've been trying to tie different off-shore payments from shell companies to David's funds. This last one here...The Condor Account, that was the last one we tracked before I left the firm."

"That's great, Ace," Gray said, his eyes sparkling with pride.

"*Great*," Laurel huffed. "I cannot believe you are allowing her to get involved in all this. Have you thought about the risks? Have you thought about what could happen to her?"

"I'm right here," I insisted, ready to say more, but Gray beat me to it.

"I'm not telling Devyn what to do. She's a grown woman, and like it or not, we need her. Besides, you might feel comfortable manipulating people to get your way, but I'm not doing that to her. Ever." He crossed his arms over his chest. "I'm following her lead from now on, and either we all work together, or we walk out that door and take our findings with us."

I think I fell a little more in love with him.

Laurel stared at my husband, her eyes narrowed to a lethal point. I reached out and took his hand, not willing to let her target all her rage at him. "You've done enough behind my back, Laurel. We've both been at this for years separately. It's time we try something new."

Laurel's eyes widened, as if she was seeing me for the first time and I was finally seeing her. Gone was the air of propriety, her perfectly crafted attire and smile. I hadn't seen any emotion but quiet contentment from Laurel for years. But now, the mask was eviscerated, and despite the hostility, I *liked* seeing this side of her. It was better than thinking she was an unfeeling clone of my mother, worshipping at my tormentor's feet.

"Fine," Laurel snapped. "We'll try your approach."

"Oh, good," Tomas said as he sat up. "As far as team-up speeches, it wasn't the best, but hopefully it got the point across. Now, can we finally end the pissing match and get to work?"

Laurel narrowed her eyes in his direction. "She can stay, but I still have my doubts about you. Who exactly are you?"

"Tomas Molina, best Private Investigator on the east coast," His eyes traced her form, and he smirked when he looked up at her scowl. "Does that work for you, gorgeous?"

"Not in the least," she said as she turned back to face me. "Any other surprises, or is the Scooby Gang all here?"

"Ouch," Tomas said, bringing his hand to his chest. "I think you wounded me." As he walked to the boxes lined up along the wall, he leaned down and smirked at the detailed work. Over the years, we'd made copies of everything as a fail-safe, nervous digital copies could go missing if someone caught on to what we were doing. As he reached the last one, he smirked over at Laurel. "Luckily for you, I like my women mean. Turns me on."

I rubbed the bridge of my nose. I was used to Tomas' antics, but it was a very different story when he was hitting on my sister. My *married* sister. "Tomas, leave my sister alone. I'm pretty sure Laurel would eat you alive."

"Sister, huh?" He looked between the two of us. "Those are some good genes."

"Watch it," Gray growled.

I placed a hand on his chest, stopping him from approaching Tomas. My friend just laughed, unfazed by the six-three giant glaring at him. "Glad I finally get to meet the husband." He winked at me. "Devyn's told me a lot about you over the last couple of months."

Gray's eyes flicked to mine, all the hostility fading to warmth. "You told him about me?"

"Maybe."

"If you two are going to act like horny teenagers, you're going to need to rent another room," Laurel said, her tone even and almost cold. She knelt next to the boxes, searching through the first one. "But the rest of us would like to destroy David, so either scurry off or help."

Tomas stared up at her with stars in his eyes. Maybe he wasn't kidding about the whole mean kink. He chuckled as he looked back at me. "Never thought you'd be the cuddly one in your family, querida."

"You should meet our younger sister," I said, joining his side. "She practically exudes rainbows and sunshine."

"He's not meeting her," Laurel said as she stood back up. She dusted off her hands before moving further down the line. Her focus was on the documents, but she said, "Calla is not getting involved in this, and that's final."

My jaw tensed, and I took a step forward. "And what gives you the right to make that call? Just because you're older doesn't mean—"

"I said no."

I shook my head. "That's something you are going to have to learn, Laurel. You are not in charge here. Yes, you work the closest with David, but that does not mean you get to make all the rules." My anger bit at my heels, a tangible beast. Maybe it was her attitude. Maybe it was finally being so happy after years of misery. But I was done playing nice, even if we were sisters. "Your rules already cost me—" I took Gray's hand in mine. "Cost *us* too much."

Her eyes widened, and for a moment, she looked truly remorseful. She shook her head and said, "I'm not going to apologize for trying to keep you safe. I've failed you and Calla plenty of times, but you need to know I've had your best interests at heart."

"Then you should have talked to us!" I yelled. "Instead of becoming someone we didn't even recognize!"

"You think I don't know that," Laurel bit back. "If I could

take it back, I would. I would have never agreed to any of this, not if I knew this was how my life was going to turn out. If I knew it meant sacrificing you and Calla, meant leaving home and never coming back…" She slammed her hand down on the box. "But this investigation—this is my entire life, Devyn. I need him to pay. I need to make sure he doesn't hurt anyone else the way he has hurt us. I can't—" Her voice broke, and she turned away from me, bringing her shaking hand to her mouth. When she turned back around, the crack in her veneer was gone. "I need him to pay for what he did to our family."

As I watched her, a cold sense of dread crept into my veins. While I hated David, this was so much more, a deep-seated need for vengeance. I searched through my memories, trying to think of anything David had done to my sister, at least in front of us. But there was nothing, not a single snide comment or uneasy situation. She was his perfect protégé, unlike Calla and I, who were thorns in his side.

"What did he do?" I asked, trying to keep my voice strong.

Laurel shook her head. "Trust me, you don't want to know."

"Tell me."

She stared at me, trying to read my expression. But stubbornness ran in our blood, and there was no way I was leaving here without some answers.

Laurel broke first, sighing as she turned toward the door. She reached down, pulling out a file folder sealed with a thick rubber band around the center. She passed it over to me, but before I could open it, she placed her hand on top of mine. "You wanted to know, but be prepared. Once you see what's in this file, you're not going to be able to walk away from this. So this is your chance, Devyn. Take your husband, and go live your life." She smiled softly at me. "All I've ever wanted was for you and Calla to move on past our crappy childhoods. So please, Devyn. Walk away."

I shook my head. "I can't do that."

Laurel sighed but lifted her hand, letting me pull the rubber band off the file. As I lifted the cover, the first thing I saw were photographs of different people, all attached to death certificates or missing person reports. My hands shook as I flipped through each one, and my throat dried out. My words came whispered when I asked, "Who are all of these people?"

"They are people who have either been killed or gone missing after interfering with one of David's businesses. Most of their deaths looked like accidents or natural causes, but it's too much of a coincidence to be true. People in David's orbit tend to die when they piss him off, and he has enough power and resources to keep them buried."

I reached the end of the file, and my hand stalled on the last picture. It wasn't a headshot, but instead, it looked like the scene of a car accident. Gray sucked in a sharp breath at my side. "Is that..."

But the rest of their words were warped as I looked down at the car, recognizing the frame despite all the damage inflicted—the same silver sedan that had been parked in our driveway when I got home from school, making me run a little faster to the door. The one I would wait up for on nights he worked late, hoping to get one last story before bed. The ringing in my ears almost pulled me under as I kept staring at the photo until I saw the red stain on the driver's seat. A vicious roar sounded in my ears as I stared at the dried blood covering the fabric.

It was only then that I noticed the name attached in the corner.

Peter Winters.

Our father.

When I let out a soft gasp, Gray took my shaking hand. It was frozen to the image, unable to let go. As he lifted my hand, he closed the folder, sealing the image away, but I already knew it would be seared in my brain for the rest of my days.

"That can't be—" I croaked out, my eyes still stuck on the place the photographs just sat. "Laurel…"

She looked up at me and nodded, the movement so subtle, I almost didn't see it. "David's been eliminating any threats for a long time, and I think our dad was one of the first."

THIRTY-THREE

Grayson

All the color drained from Devyn's face as she stared down at the closed folder. Her brown eyes were cold, as if she was still staring at the image through the papers blocking her from it. I would've given anything to reverse time, to erase that picture from her mind. Devyn would never have wanted that, though. Because this was fucked in more ways than I ever thought possible.

I knew Laurel had a grudge against their stepfather, but she'd never told me about the connection with their father. When we first started, we were just looking for something that might show insider trading or other shady business dealings, something the authorities could handle. However, as we kept digging, we uncovered darker secrets, some that haunted me in the middle of the night. We didn't know if David was responsible for all forty-eight deaths in that folder, but he was involved in some capacity. They kept me up at night, imagining who we'd have to add next. The worst nights were the ones when I imagined it was Devyn's picture being added to the top, and there was nothing I could do to stop it.

"No," Devyn said suddenly. "It's not possible. That was *years* before he ever came into town, before he knew any of us."

"That's not true," Laurel said. "I've found lawsuits filed by our father, blocking the sale of land in town to one of his subsidiaries. They named David as one of the defendants."

"It was an accident," Devyn insisted. "Bad weather. His car lost control—"

Laurel motioned to the file. "That's what we were *told*. But read the police report. There were signs of another car, like someone forced his car off the road. It reads the same as other cases in that folder."

Devyn just kept shaking her head, as if she was trying to keep the words from landing. "No, Laurel, this is insane! You're saying David is responsible for dozens of deaths? Including our father?" She ran her fingers over her face. "This is so much bigger than we thought."

"Which is why I didn't want you involved," Laurel said softly, the words hanging in the air like a silent plea. "From the moment I connected the first death to him, I tried to hide this from you and Calla. I couldn't risk him hurting you two."

"But you could risk Gray?" she snapped. "You threw my husband into the line of fire!"

"He knew the risks."

Devyn turned to me, tears filling her eyes. "You should have told me."

"I didn't know," I sighed, pulling her over to the side. "I know about some of the connections Laurel made, but I never knew about your dad. I swear, Ace."

She searched my eyes and then nodded slightly. I let out the biggest sigh of relief. "But now you know why I needed you away from this. I couldn't risk you—"

"You shouldn't have taken that risk either, Gray," Devyn snapped. "The moment this got too dangerous, you should have walked away. If anything had happened to you..." Her brown eyes searched mine. "You should have walked away."

"Would you have walked away?"

She snapped her mouth closed, and I had the only answer I needed. Devyn shook her head and walked back over to the bed, almost in silent agreement. We were in this, and neither of us was leaving without the other.

Devyn sat down on the bedspread and ran her hand over her face. "I don't have the mental capacity to even think about this, much less what you're implying." She looked up at Laurel. "You have the list of names, and I have all of David's financial records. If we combine what we both know, maybe we can find some kind of payment history."

"We can try," Tomas said, pulling out his laptop. "I've one of my best hackers digging into some of these offshore accounts, but we haven't gotten anywhere yet. Whoever is handling things behind the scenes, they're good."

"Or are they just better than you?" Laurel asked.

Tomas' eyes narrowed. "You want to make comments about me, go ahead, but not my team. They are the best, and I won't let anyone question that, especially not you."

I glanced at Devyn, who was transfixed by the argument unfolding in front of us. Tomas' tone had no hint of flirting—he was utterly still and solemn. Laurel stared at him, likely waiting for him to say something more, but he just continued to work, effectively turning his back on her.

"There has to be something," Devyn mumbled as she stood, looking at all the boxes. Her voice was low, as if talking more to herself than the rest of us. "I refuse to believe he's committed perfect crimes."

"Or he's just very good at burying the skeletons in his closet."

"Wait," I said, grabbing the folder Devyn had pushed aside. "Maybe we're looking at this the wrong way."

"What do you mean?"

"We've been trying to work backwards," I said as I dug through the file, trying to sort the printouts by date. "We've been looking at his most recent crimes, thinking they would have the most evidence, more information we could pull from different servers. But we should be looking at his oldest crimes, trying to connect those dots."

Laurel looked at me. "Why?"

"Because rookies make the most mistakes," I answered under my breath. "Think about it. David's business had to be built from the ground up. There's a long history here. And if he made mistakes, it would have been back then, before he knew anyone was looking. Before he made connections that could help him cover up his crimes."

Laurel shook her head. "I don't know. Some of these people have been missing for twenty years. What are we going to be able to find that the investigators missed?"

"We'll never know if we don't check it out." I shuffled through the papers, pulling out the one sticking in the back of my mind. "This man—William Garber. He disappeared in 2004 from a town only twenty minutes outside of Saint Stephen's Lake. I say we start with him and see if we can find something the cops overlooked."

Laurel's eyes narrowed at me. "It seems like a long shot."

"But it could be something," Devyn added, meeting my eyes with a proud smile. "Even if it ends up being a dead-end, it's a place to start. Better than spinning our wheels trying to dig through all these files again."

"Fine," Laurel sighed, pushing an errant hair out of her face. "You two try to track down more about William Garber. But if we haven't found something by the end of the week, we need to explore other avenues."

"Deal," I said. "It's getting late. We should head out before it gets too dark." I reached out to Devyn. "You ready, Ace?"

Devyn nodded and moved to my side. But before we could leave, she glanced at the files one more time. "We're missing something, I can feel it. There's some thread tying all this together, and we're missing it."

"I know, but we'll find it," I said as I leaned down and kissed her temple. We glanced over at Tomas and Laurel. "Are you staying in town?"

Tomas smirked. "You're looking at my digs. Staying here as long as it takes."

Devyn's eyes narrowed in his direction, "Are you sure it's safe?"

"Definitely," Tomas said, his tone taking a much more serious edge. I appreciated that he wanted to soothe my wife's worries and that he knew how to take certain things seriously. "No one knows I'm here but my team, and I paid cash. Also gave them a fake name, just in case anyone comes sniffing around."

"You come prepared," I grumbled.

"Perks of the job," he smirked. "Anonymity is part of the package. You learn quickly to keep yourself off anyone's radar."

I nodded over to Laurel. "What about you?"

She was so focused on Devyn, it took her a moment to process what I'd asked. "I'm staying at the Isadora with Mom. She needs some help redecorating David's old office, and I thought it might be a good idea to see if there's anything left behind that might be useful for us."

"How long does Harry think you'll be gone?" Devyn asked.

She gave her sister a sad smile. "Unlike your husband, mine actually prefers when I'm not home."

"Smart man," Tomas whispered under his breath.

But it wasn't quite low enough, because Laurel glared at him with as much vitriol as she could muster. He wasn't fazed, however, and just continued to stare at his computer screen.

Devyn looked up at me, suddenly looking exhausted under the weight of what we learned today. "I'd like to go help too," she said, turning toward her sister. "Maybe we could even ask Mom where Dad's old files ended up. Might be worth checking out to find a connection."

Laurel nodded, dropping her gaze down to the floor. "I'd like that."

THIRTY-FOUR

Grayson

The drive back home was almost completely silent, only the sounds from the GPS keeping us company. I was used to the quiet, thrived in it, actually. But having Devyn sit next to me in silence? That was lighting all my nerves on fire.

Even as we turned into the driveway, she said nothing, just continuing to stare out the window. Did she think she had to hold all this inside? Today was a lot, from seeing her sister to hearing Laurel's theory about their father. I wanted to reach out and remind her I was here, but the look on her face stopped me. She had to know that, right? That I wasn't going anywhere, no matter how challenging our lives got?

I pulled into my parking spot next to the front porch and put the car in park. When Devyn didn't say anything, I cleared my throat. "I should go check on my parents. My mom wants to talk about our visit to the care facility." Devyn nodded. "Do you..." I sucked in a sharp breath, bracing myself for rejection. "Do you want me to come back later, or do you need some time?"

She shrugged. "It's your house. You can come and go as you please."

"Hey…" I said, my voice taking on a more demanding tone. I put my hand on her thigh, and she turned to look at me. "Today was a lot, and I get it. If you need some time and space to get through it, I'll give it to you." Devyn's brown eyes widened for a moment, and I knew I said the wrong thing. She tried to pull away, but I held on, making sure she heard me. "Don't think this means I want to be away from you. I fucking hate the idea of sleeping without you. But if you need it, I'll do it. Even if I leave, I'll be right back here tomorrow morning like the needy bastard you've made me." I cupped her cheek. "I also don't want you to feel smothered."

"I don't," Devyn said, her voice soft and low. "Today would have been a lot worse if you weren't there with me."

"Then do you want me to stay?"

"Yes," Devyn breathed, her eyes meeting mine. "I want you to stay and make me forget, just for a little while. Help me feel something other than this ache inside my chest."

I brought her hand to my lips. "I can do that, Ace. Whatever you need."

She wasted no time climbing over the center console to settle into my lap. My hands flexed against her hips, loving how she felt against me. Her lips found mine, kissing me as if it was the only thing keeping her together. If she wanted to forget, I would make it my mission and not let go until she was pliant and satisfied in my arms.

Devyn leaned back, and I took her cue, unbuttoning her jeans and shimming them down her legs. As she tried to step out of them, she bumped her head on the roof. "Shit," she chuckled. "This was sexier in my head."

"Pretty fucking sexy to me," I growled as I rubbed my thumb along her soaked panties. "Gonna ruin this truck forever. Every time I sit behind the wheel, I'm going to picture you, all wet and needy for me."

"Yes," she sighed as I tugged the fabric to the side. "Touch me, Gray. I need you so fucking badly."

But I held back—keeping my movements light enough to drive her mad. As she let out an annoyed huff, shifting her hips to get more pressure, I pulled away. Her eyes narrowed. "Are you teasing me, Grayson?"

"You want something? Use your words." I nipped at her neck. "You know the right ones to make me do whatever you want."

She grinned back at me. "Fuck me with your fingers, Gray. Make your wife come all over them."

That was all it took. I ripped away her panties, throwing the ruined fabric in my backseat. As my thumb continued to circle her clit, my other finger entered her, already feeling her pulse around me. I added another, relishing in her little gasp as I stretched and filled her just how she liked it. Devyn's hands found the back of my neck, pulling me into a kiss as she rode my hand, soaking it with her desire. Her fingers dug into my neck as her walls constricted, practically crushing me by the time she fell over the edge. Her brown eyes met mine as she gasped my name, letting out one final groan before collapsing against my chest.

"Did it work?" I asked as I pressed a kiss to the top of her head.

"It was a good start," Devyn said. Her hands reached down, unbuckling my jeans and shoving them and my boxers down enough to free my length. I was already hard as a rock from watching her fall apart on my fingers.

"A good start?" I arched my brows. "That's not gonna do. Get your ass up here."

"And do what?" Devyn asked with a sly smirk. "You need to use your words, husband."

Fuck. I reached out and gripped her hair in my fist. "Get your ass up here and ride my cock like a good little wife."

Devyn tucked her lip between her teeth but then did as I asked, shifting so my tip lined up with her entrance. As she sank slowly down on me, my head dropped back. I wasn't sure I'd ever get used to how perfect she felt around me. It was heaven, something divine I could never put into words. There was no way Devyn and I weren't meant for each other, not when we felt so good together.

As she started to rise, then dropped again, fighting to lower herself even further. She shifted a few times, taking in more of me each time. It was slow, exquisite torture. Eventually, my patience snapped and I gripped her hips, pulling her all the way down. Devyn's fingers dug into my shoulder, so I lifted my hand and cupped her cheek. "You good, baby?"

"Amazing," she sighed. "You make me feel so good, so full."

"Fuck yeah, I do," I groaned, moving my hands back to her hips. While I wanted her to set the pace, I couldn't help but guide her through it, needing to feel my hands on her skin. "Who else fucks you this good, Devyn?"

"No one," she moaned. "No one fucks me like you do."

"Damn straight," I said, my fingers digging into her a little more. "And no one's going to have the chance. Not after me. You're mine, wife, and I'm never letting you go again."

"Say it again," Devyn groaned. I could tell she was close, her movements growing sloppier and more frantic. I helped her keep a hard and steady pace, just as I knew she liked.

"You're mine, Ace. My wife. No matter what happens, it's me and you. Always."

"Shit, Gray," Devyn groaned as her orgasm ripped through her. Her fingers dug into the back of my neck, anchoring me to her as she rode out her pleasure. With her body constricting around me, it took only a few more thrusts until I was following right after.

As we both waited to fall down to Earth, Devyn cuddled against my chest, her fingers absentmindedly tracing over her mark on me. "Thank you."

My eyes darted to her, loving how she looked pressed against me. I kissed her temple. "For sex in my truck? Pretty sure I should be thanking you for that one."

"No," Devyn chuckled. "Well, yes. That was pretty incredible." She gazed up at me, all humor gone from her expression. "For being there for me today, through all of this. It's been a long time since I felt like I was part of a team, and I really like being one with you."

"You don't have to worry about that, Devy," I said as I held her tighter. "Because I meant what I said. I'm not going anywhere."

THIRTY-FIVE

Devyn

Three days after our meet-up with Laurel, I found myself in my family's suite at the Isadora Resort, the hotel my great-great-grandfather had started over a hundred years ago. It was a staple in this community, the only high-end resort in this county. While many people flocked here for the summer months, I'd avoided it for a long time.

Calla used to joke that she'd always live here, at least until my mother unceremoniously kicked her out a couple of years ago. During my childhood, I felt the same. The Isadora was our home, and I thought it would always feel that way. But over the past decade, the feelings had started to twist and fray into something unpleasant. The Isadora felt haunted—not necessarily by spirits, but by unpleasant memories I'd rather forget. Being back in this place reminded me of a time when I was weak, when I didn't have the resources to fight for myself beyond my sharp tongue and faulty filter.

Calla nudged me in the side. "Are you okay? You've literally been staring at that wall for ten minutes."

I shook my head. "It has not been that long."

"Okay, maybe not exactly, but still. It was long enough that I was starting to worry."

"I don't like being back here," I quietly admitted so our mother wouldn't hear me. While she hadn't been the best example of maternal love growing up, at least she was trying to do better now, less pushing her ideals and taking more of an interest in our lives. But after being ignored by her for most of my life, I'd gotten used to existing without her, only hearing from her if she needed something. When Calla and our mother were estranged, it was the first time she reached out to me first. I thought she was attempting to get to know me better, but she was really just using me as a messenger. After that, I didn't let myself get too hopeful we'd ever have an ideal mother-daughter relationship.

But she was trying, especially with Calla, as she was expecting a daughter of her own. It gave them something to bond over, I guess.

I looked at my little sister, noticing her bump had fully popped. Although she was just entering her third trimester, she was still glowing. "How are you feeling?" I asked.

"Like a beached whale," she answered. "But good. I'm starting to get tired quickly, but I guess that's to be expected. Only a few more months to go."

"How's Theo holding up?"

Calla playfully rolled her eyes. "He threatened the contractor to make sure the house would be done on time but then decided we needed a state-of-the-art home security system, which might cause a delay." She rubbed her belly. "He's lucky I love him as much as I do. Otherwise, I don't know how I'd live with him."

"He's just excited," I said.

"Just you wait," Calla teased. "You think Theo is bad? Wait

until you get pregnant. Gray is going to cover you in bubble wrap and follow you everywhere."

"Excuse me?" I choked out. "That's not something we're even thinking about, much less actively trying for. I don't even know if Gray wants kids."

"I know, but it's fun to think about." Calla's face scrunched up. "Wait—do you want kids? I feel like you've never mentioned them before."

"I...I don't know," I answered honestly. "I've never really allowed myself to think about it. Before, when I was at the firm, I pushed it out of my mind, trying to convince myself my career was enough. It wasn't like I was with someone or even thinking about settling down."

"But now?"

"I don't know," I answered quietly. "I think I could see it if it's with Gray. I don't think I would have kids with anyone else."

Calla squealed and wrapped me in a tight hug. "I'm so happy for you, Dev. You love your husband! I know it's supposed to be that way, but you guys always did things a little out of sequence. Now look at you, married and finally in love."

"Okay," I said, patting her arm. "Yes, we are married, but we're not *married* married, you know?"

"No," Calla said. "I literally have no idea what that means."

"It means, yes, technically, on paper, we are married. But we missed all the steps. Dating, getting engaged, planning a wedding Cher didn't officiate." I stepped back. "It feels like we missed all those important moments—"

"Dev."

"And sure, I love Gray, and of course, I want to be with him long-term, but I also want all those things. With him." I groaned, dragging my hands over my face. "Does that make any sense?"

"Makes a lot of sense," a deep voice called out from behind

me. I stilled, instantly recognizing the deep timber of Gray's words. *Please kill me now and bury my body where no one will ever find it.* He stepped up closer to me, so close, I could feel his heat at my back. As he placed a hand on my shoulder, he said to Calla, "Mind giving me a minute with my wife?"

My sister just smiled at the two of us, beaming back like we were the cutest thing she'd ever seen. When she left the dining room, Gray shifted his hand down to my elbow and twisted me to face him. I kept my eyes down, too scared to look up. I didn't know what I would find there. Hurt? Confusion?

I didn't have long to think about it, because Gray's fingers found my chin and tilted it upward until our eyes were locked. I almost gasped at the fire in his expression, much like the first time we'd kissed. It was the kind of fire that incinerated my walls and destroyed any obstacle in its path. I might have been ice, but Gray was all flames, and I was happy to melt at his feet.

"Something you want to ask me, Devyn?"

"Nope," I said, my voice suddenly several octaves higher. "Just wondering what you're doing here."

"Thought I'd stop by and make sure everything was going well. You seemed nervous this morning."

I placed a hand on his chest and lifted to kiss his cheek. "That's sweet, but you didn't have to go out of your way. Things are going...as well as could be expected. Laurel's been with my mom the whole time, so Calla and I have been hanging out here."

He nodded then leaned in to kiss my forehead. "Never out of my way for you, Ace."

I soaked in his warmth for a couple more moments before my mother and sister came around the corner. My mother, Diane Winters, was not considered a warm woman. We had that in common. She showed minimal affection, deciding to show how much she cared by nitpicking and pushing her children toward unattainable goals.

So I was very surprised when she came over and hugged Gray. He must have felt the same, because, although he returned her embrace, his eyes widened in shock over her shoulder. After a long moment, she pulled back. "It's very good to see you, Grayson."

"You too, Mrs. Winters. And it's just Gray."

She clicked her tongue, probably because Gray had forgotten how much she loathed nicknames. My mother stepped closer to me and took my hand. "My daughter says the two of you are dating. I'm very happy for you. I always thought you'd end up together years ago, but I'm glad you both waited until you were old enough to know for sure."

"You did?" I asked. "But David said—"

My mother held up her hand. "He always had an issue with Grayson. For some reason, he never wanted the two of you together. But we won't worry about that anymore. We're cleansing him out of this home *and* out of our minds."

Calla furrowed her brow. "Wait, if he had such an issue with Gray dating Devyn, why didn't he say anything about me?"

My mother leveled a glare at her. "I thought we were going to ignore that elephant in the room."

"It's fine," I said, waving my hand. "I think we've all moved past it."

"Fine," my mother said. "If you must know, it was because he had no idea the two of you were dating. I never told him, and when he asked, I made excuses for Calla. He'd already driven a wedge between Devyn and Gray, so I didn't want any more issues like that. Besides..." She grimaced at Calla. "It wasn't like it was going to be forever, not with the way Grayson looked at Devyn. Sorry, dear."

Calla rolled her eyes. "Mom, we broke up over a decade ago, and I'm pregnant with another man's baby. Pretty sure I'll find a way to get over it."

THIRTY-SIX

Devyn

"This is weird."

The words escaped me as I stared out at David's former office, the one that originally belonged to my father. But there was no trace of my father in this room. All my childhood, the bookshelves were stuffed to their limits with legal tomes and classic literature. It felt warm, worn, like it was just as vibrant as the man who stood behind the desk. I loved coming in here, hiding behind the desk whenever I'd play hide and seek with my sisters. The aroma of antique papers and aged scotch was comforting, and I wished more than anything I could smell it now.

It was long gone, though, traded out for books on business and other enterprises, ones no one ever read but stayed to give the illusion of intelligence. In fact, everything in this room served that purpose, to make anyone who entered this space cower under the weight of David's presence. I glanced over my shoulder, looking at the space where my face had once collided. Phantom pains raked over me, as if I was still that scared little girl.

"You don't have to do this," Laurel said. "If it's too much,

Gray can take you home. I don't want to make you uncomfortable."

"That would be a first," I muttered, running my finger along the shelves. "At least you're giving me an option this time, not just running to Gray behind my back."

"You're right," she said. I paused, turning slowly to face my older sister as she continued to speak. "When I found out you married Gray, I was scared, Devyn. David had already made a lot of comments about you, and I was able to keep him at bay because you were doing so well at the law firm. He liked that, liked that Collin could keep you in line. You'd done a great job playing the role he wanted, so he was willing to back off." She paused, inhaling and exhaling slowly. "But there was always going to be a moment when the levee broke. When I could no longer keep him from interfering with your life. For some reason, he really hates Gray, so when I found out that you'd married him—"

"You thought he'd come after me."

"Or worse: use Calla to get to you," she sighed. "David knows she's your weakness, just like Gray. That's his real power —knowing what matters most and warping it until he has you in the palm of his hand."

Her eyes turned glassy as she whipped around, facing away from me. Sudden understanding made my stomach drop. "What did he take from you?"

"My sisters."

My stomach dropped, hating that it was true. At least, it had been for years. But the course that had been carved out for us didn't have to be the one we continued to travel. I moved closer to Laurel and put my hand on her shoulder. She turned around, her eyes widening in surprise. I smiled softly at her. "You haven't lost us, Laurel."

"Yes, I have," she said quietly. "We don't have a relationship, and the fault lies on my shoulders. After he figured out I would do anything to keep the two of you out of his world, he twisted it, making sure I was still on his side."

"I hate that you've been stuck with him all this time. I really thought you wanted to work with him."

Laurel chuckled, "Not even a little, but I'd do it all over again. It's given me better insight into his world." Calla laughed from the other room. Laurel sighed. "At least she's made it out unscathed. I just wish I could have done more to keep you out of it too."

"I don't," I answered. Laurel's brow furrowed as I continued. "David's done some unforgivable things to all of us, and he's going to pay the price. I want to know I played a part in his downfall. I need justice after everything he's done. I'm never going to be okay sitting on the sidelines. If you ever want us to have a real relationship, you need to accept that."

Laurel stayed quiet for a few moments, studying me for any hesitance, but it wouldn't come. I wanted this. I wanted to be there when David realized the girls he'd tried to stomp all over had beaten him, that we never let him break us.

"Fine," she eventually relented.

"And I have two more things to add to the addendum." Laurel arched a perfectly manicured brow and motioned for me to continue. "If you ever try to come between Gray and me again, I will cut you out of my life for good. He is my everything, and if you make me choose, it will be him, every single time."

"Done," she said. Her eyes dropped down to her hands. "I never should have said anything in the first place. I should have trusted you more."

"Yes, you should have. Which brings me to point number two—we need to tell Calla."

"Absolutely not."

"Laurel..." I groaned, rubbing my hand over my brows. "If

we keep her in the dark, we're just repeating the same mistakes we've made with each other." When she started to protest, I held up my hand. "Calla is a lot stronger than you give her credit for. Not only can she handle this, but we need her if we're going to figure out what's going on." I stepped forward. "And think about how much it'll piss David off when he sees the three of us standing together, knowing that, in the end, he never broke us."

The corner of Laurel's mouth quirked up. "I do like the sound of that."

"Then it's settled. We're telling Calla."

"Telling me what?" Calla asked as she walked into the room with our mother, carrying more garbage bags and empty boxes. Laurel met my eye and shook her head. Not the time. I couldn't blame her for that, not when my mother was standing in the same room. In my heart, I wanted to trust she wouldn't betray our confidence, but she'd been married to David for years. Even if they barely spent any time together under the same roof, they had a relationship. I didn't know if her loyalties would completely lie with us—or worse, she'd fall on his sword to get us out of trouble.

"We want to throw you a baby shower," I said, the only thing I could think of on the spot. "But we weren't sure if Alex wanted to host, so we figured we'd talk to you and see what you wanted to do first." I motioned over my shoulder to Laurel. "She was planning to keep it a surprise, but I thought we should see how you felt."

"Okay..." Calla said, giving me a look as if she knew I was hiding something from her. "Doesn't matter to me; I just want everyone I love to be there. Everything else is just extra."

"On it," I said as I grabbed a box and moved over to the shelves. Running my fingers over the titles, I couldn't hold back a question that had plagued me for years. "Mom, what happened to all of Dad's old files and stuff? If it's still around, I might want some of it for my office."

If I ever had an office again. I'd reluctantly told my family I was out of a job, and they all surprised me, jumping to my defense. With their confidence, my own started to build. Maybe it was time to put myself back out there, to find my legal footing in a world without corruption and greed. I'd gotten into law to protect people, to continue the fight my dad had started, but the waters had gotten so muddled along the way, and I forgot about that goal. Now that I'd had some time to clear my head, it felt like the right course, time to correct the ship to its original destination. No, I wouldn't be making as much money, but I could live a life I was proud of, one that allowed me to spend it with the people I cared about most.

"Oh..." my mom said, shifting behind the desk. "Well, any client files got signed over to another attorney in town, and his open cases were also reassigned. But his personal records I kept, anything that didn't pertain to one of his clients. Any notes, books, whatever he had stored here."

"You did?" Laurel asked, sitting up in interest.

"Of course," she answered. "After your father died, I couldn't bring myself to throw it all away. When David started coming around, he was insistent I get rid of his stuff, but I still couldn't, even though he'd been gone for years. So, I took his old office space downtown and used it as storage."

"What about now?"

"It should still be there," she said as she stood up straighter. She used the backs of her hands to push her dark red hair away from her face. "Before he died, your grandfather bought the building, and it was transferred into my name after he passed. I thought about selling it, but..." She sighed, smiling softly at us. "I didn't have the heart." As her voice trailed off, she turned back to the desk, opening the drawers methodically. "If you want anything, you're welcome to it. I have the keys in my office downstairs somewhere. Your father would have wanted you girls to have that stuff instead of it sitting there, waiting for someone else to find it."

Laurel met my eye, and I gave her a subtle nod, knowing we were both thinking the same thing.

It had been waiting for us.

THIRTY-SEVEN

Grayson

"This seems a little excessive," Devyn whispered at my side.

I looked over at her, dressed in all black, her hair tucked into a knitted cap. She looked adorable, even though she'd been on edge ever since we walked up to the office building.

As soon as Diane mentioned Peter's office, Laurel and Devyn started planning, wanting to get in there as quickly as possible. They were ready to drive right over and start digging into his files, but after talking to Tomas, they waited until tonight instead.

"Maybe," Tomas looked over his shoulder as he pushed the key into the lock. "But we're not taking any chances. We're already tempting fate by assuming everything is still in there."

Devyn huffed, staring up at the building. I reached out and took her hand. "It'll be there, Ace. I know it is."

She squeezed my hand back, but her eyes never strayed from the door. So much of Devyn's identity was tied to her dad's. He'd given her a love of the law and a strong sense of justice. Even though we were both young when he passed, his death had destroyed a piece of her. And even though I could never take away that pain, I wanted to try. I wanted to hold her in those challenging moments and remind her we had so many good things waiting for us in the future. *Our* future.

Tomas pushed the door open then moved to the side so Devyn could enter first. She gave me one last look as she let go of my hand and walked inside the back entrance of the building. As I followed her, I tried to take in the space despite the limited lighting. The air was musty, like what you'd find in the archives section of the library. Dust covered most of the surfaces, and each of our steps made a little more kick up into the air. After shutting the door behind us, Tomas handed us small flashlights and made his way to the front of the office space.

I could see how this place had sat silent for so long. It was still in the center of town but far enough away from the main drag that it got limited foot traffic. The building itself was in good shape, despite the shuttered windows and lack of life inside. Diane might not have come here, but someone was taking care of the building. There was no evidence of age or damage on the inside or out, which had been one of my major worries. In fact, despite the dust, it looked like it had been preserved, as if Devyn's dad would be walking back inside at any moment.

Devyn's phone chimed in her pocket, and she pulled it out, grimacing as she read her text. "It's Laurel. She wants to know if we've found anything yet."

Tomas snorted. "Doesn't have a lot of patience, does she?"

"She's been working on this for over a decade," I bit back, suddenly feeling a bit protective over Laurel. It wasn't the same as the feral need to make sure Devyn was safe, but after working together for so long, it was hard not to defend her. "She's ready to move on. We all are."

Devyn nodded at me then turned back to Tomas. "Where do you think we should start?"

He motioned for us to follow him further, stopping to look

inside each space. I glanced over my shoulder, expecting to see Devyn behind us, but instead, she was facing one of the walls, her flashlight pointed at something I couldn't make out from my angle. As I stepped closer, my breath hitched as I saw the etched glass: *The Law Offices of Peter Winters.*

"I keep thinking about him," Devyn whispered. "What he would think about all this. What he would think of me." Her wide eyes met mine. "Do you think he's ashamed of me?"

I pulled her into my arms and kissed the top of her head. "Never, Ace. Why do you think he would be?"

"I wasted so much time in corporate law, defending the people he abhorred." She looked back at the sign. "He told me the law was meant to help people, that we were responsible for keeping the world just and fair. And I failed that..." Her voice trailed off. "At least, I used to."

I brushed the hair away from her eyes. "What are you saying, Devyn?"

"I think I want to make a change." She inhaled slowly. "I want to be more like my dad, defending those without a voice." A tension lifted from her shoulders with each word, and I could feel how much this meant to her, how much it would have meant to her dad to see her walking in his footsteps. But that didn't matter to me, other than it mattered to my wife. All I ever wanted was for her to be happy, and if this was the way, I'd support her until my dying breath.

"Then we'll make it happen," I said, my word as my vow. "I'm with you, Ace."

She smiled at me then reached up, kissing me. While I loved her fiery kisses, the ones that led to us tangled up together and her screaming my name, I might love these more. She only intended them as a simple touch, as if she needed to feel my lips on hers.

Tomas chuckled as he approached us. "I appreciate a touching moment as much as the next guy, but there's something in here you're going to want to see."

Devyn and I followed him into an office off the side hallway, one with Peter's name etched on the front door. As Devyn stepped into the room, I held Tomas back for a second. "Please tell me this is good news."

He chuckled as he pat my shoulders. "Trust me, my friend, this is *very* good news."

I stepped inside and found Devyn in the middle of a sea of boxes, her hand covering her mouth. She turned toward me, a broad smile etched on her face. "They're here, Gray. They're all here."

Hours later, we were still digging through boxes, trying to make sense of the information. While Peter had a specific system in life, in death, Diane had piled everything into random boxes without labels. Without a case name or client information to go on, all we had were his notes, different things he'd researched while he was alive.

By the time morning rolled around, we'd figured out we were in way over our heads, especially me. While Devyn and Tomas had the background to filter out the critical information from the rest of it, I had no clue. Sitting and staring at papers was making my brain itch, and the effort it took to keep my attention on the page was exhausting.

"This is useless," Devyn sighed. "None of it makes any sense. He's writing in some type of code, and I can't figure it out."

"I'm going to find us some coffee," Tomas said as he stood

and stretched his limbs. "Please tell me somewhere in this town makes a decent cup."

"Yeah," I said. "Right on Main. Try a pastry too. You won't regret it."

Tomas nodded as he walked out the door, leaving Devyn and me alone with the ghosts of her father's life. She thumbed through one of his journals, her brow furrowing as she looked over each page. I reached out, placing my hand on top of hers. "We're going to figure this out, Ace."

"How?" she said, her voice hushed. "How are we ever going to figure this out? David's not just twenty steps ahead, but he's twenty *years* ahead. He's got unlimited resources, and it's just the three of us fumbling around in the dark." She closed the journal at the same time as she closed her eyes. "I keep waiting for this moment when the dots all finally connect, but I'm starting to feel like it's never going to happen. Like, I'm going to spend the rest of my life watching David continue to ruin people's lives, and there is nothing I can do about it."

I pulled her into my lap. "I know everything seems dark right now, Ace, but if anyone can solve this, it's you."

"You have too much faith in me," she whispered as she dropped her head onto my chest.

"Never," I answered, wrapping my arms around her. "You are the smartest person I've ever known, Devyn Winters. But you're so much more than that. You're clever and kind–" She snorted. "You are. Maybe you don't let the world see that side of you, but I do." I tilted up her chin. "And if it takes us a lifetime to put together the pieces, we'll do it. Together. Because I know you're going to figure it out, Devyn, and I want to be at your side when you do."

Her eyes searched mine, so full of emotion, it made my heart beat a little faster. The unspoken words hung between us, and I was desperate to give them life. Even though Devyn told Calla she loved me, I'd pushed it out of my mind. I wanted her to give them to me freely, to know if she fell, I'd be there to catch her.

"Gray," Devyn started to say. "You know I—"

My phone blared to life, breaking the moment between us. I wanted to chuck the fucking thing out of the window, but once I saw my mom's picture on the screen, I started to panic. Even though I stopped by their house every day, I felt guilty I wasn't able to be there for her as much as I used to.

I pressed the button, answering the call on speaker. "Hey, Mom."

"Don't you, *hey, Mom*, me," she said. "Do you want to know what Belinda from the FreshMart just told me?"

I groaned, running my hand over my face and along my beard. "I don't think I do."

As she spoke, Devyn crawled out of my lap, returning to the journal she'd just abandoned. Even though she still looked stressed, there wasn't as much defeat in her expression, as if our brief conversation had brought more fire into her veins. She traced each line with her finger, and I was content to watch her work—at least until my mother's voice blared through the phone.

"Well, too bad. She told me the reason you've been at your house so much is because *Devyn Winters* is staying there with you."

Devyn's eyes jumped up to meet mine, and then she rolled her lips together, failing to keep from laughing. As my mother continued to berate me, she mouthed, "You're in trouble."

I raised my brows. Two could play that game. "Yeah, Mom. Devyn is staying at the house with me. I was waiting until things calmed down a little before telling you." I smirked over at Devyn. "Actually, Mom, she's here with me right now if you want to say hi."

Devyn narrowed her eyes at me but leaned in closer to the phone. "Hey, Mrs. Anders."

"None of that Mrs. Anders nonsense," my mother tsked. "You know better, Devyn. I'll always just be Marta to you." Devyn nodded but let my mom continue. "Although I'm not pleased with you either. How long have you been in town?"

Her eyes widened, and she looked to me for help. I just leaned back, chuckling like she did when it was me. "A couple of weeks."

"*Weeks?*" My mother gasped. "And you haven't come down to see us?"

"Oh," Devyn said. "I meant to. We've just, uh, been busy—"

"I don't want to know how you and my son have been keeping busy, but I expect to see you. Are you free tonight?"

"Yup," Devyn said, glancing to me for confirmation. When I nodded, she continued, "We'll be there."

As she wrapped up the call with my mother, she passed the phone back to me with a glare. I held my hands up. "Don't look at me, Ace. She was bound to find out eventually."

Devyn twisted her fingers together. "Are you upset she knows about us?"

I reached out and pulled her hand into mine. "Not for a second. I'm so proud to call you mine, Devyn."

She smiled brightly back at me. "I am too." But a shadow passed over her face, dimming her smile. "I think we should keep the whole marriage thing to ourselves, though."

"Yeah, definitely," I said. My parents would be devastated if they found out we were married, accidentally or not. They would want to give us a real wedding, and I knew Devyn well enough to know she wasn't ready for that. But her words from earlier in the week stuck out to me. She wanted the traditional wedding, wanted a real engagement that wasn't lost to our drunken memories. More than anything, I wanted to give her those things.

As Devyn slid back to her spot on the rug and resumed her reading, a plan started to form in my mind, hopeful I could give my wife exactly what she wanted.

THIRTY-EIGHT

Devyn

"I don't think I've ever been this full." I groaned as I leaned back against the counter, my stomach delightfully stuffed.

Marta smiled at me as she passed me another dish to dry, "You know where to come next time you need a home-cooked meal, Devyn. No more of this staying away, you hear me?"

I tucked my head, hating it had taken me so long to return home. While I'd split my time growing up between my family's hotel and our penthouse on the Upper East Side, this house was what built me. It was filled with so many memories, ones I had tucked into a little box when Gray and I fell apart. But now that things were finally going well between us, I'd started rifling through them, letting the joyous moments of my childhood shine bright.

"So," Marta said as she turned off the water and dried her hands. "How long do we have you here?"

"Oh…" I tucked my head, hating to admit I didn't have a definitive answer. Ever since my conversation with Gray at my dad's office, my head had been spinning. While I'd come back to this town with an end date in mind, I had no desire to head back to the city now. Maybe this was exactly where I was meant to be all along. My dad's office had been sitting there all this time, waiting for someone to take over his practice. Why couldn't it be me? There weren't any legal practices in town, and most people had to drive almost an hour away to get quality advice. Even if it entailed more low-key cases than I was used to, I would be giving back to the community I loved.

Not to mention, I'd get to stay with the man I loved.

I glanced across the kitchen toward the living room, where Gray and his dad were talking. Seeing them together warmed my heart. While my own family life had never been ideal, Gray worshipped the ground his parents walked on, and they did the same for him. It was the kind of love I wanted for my future kids, the kind I wanted my family to be built upon.

The one I wanted with Gray.

That whisper of hope tucked in the back of my mind. I wasn't ready to speak it aloud, too afraid that the moment I did, everything would come crashing down around me. We'd managed to move forward despite the pain of the past, but I was still nervous things wouldn't always feel this way. Sure, Gray thought he liked the girl I used to be, but could he deal with the woman I'd become? Would he be able to handle me when I went back to work, often losing myself in cases and forgetting to focus on the rest of the world?

And then there was his father's declining health. Even though Curt was in good spirits tonight, the gaps in his memory were hard to ignore, no matter how much everyone at the table tried. There was no slowing down time, no stopping the clock now that his mind had started deteriorating.

It was selfish of me to want so much of Gray's time when he was needed here. I already knew he was living here before I came into town, needing to be close to help his mother. But now, he was only spending a couple hours a day with them, choosing to spend his nights at home with me. Would he eventually start to resent me for it? Was I impeding on his dwindling time with his dad?

God, I hated that I'd missed so much time with Curt over the years. He was practically my second father, taking on more of the role after my dad passed away. He taught me how to drive and threatened my first boyfriend to treat me right. Not to mention, he shaped Gray into the man I fell in love with.

Maybe there was some sort of hope, a clinical trial or something along those lines. Even though my mother and I weren't close, she owed me a lifetime of favors. I was her liaison between her and Calla for months while they were estranged. The least she could do was make a call to some of her friends on various hospital boards.

"I always thought you two would find your way back to each other," Marta said as she moved to my side. "Even when he was too young to realize it, my boy's been in love with you. Glad he finally got the courage to tell you."

"Oh—" I spluttered, turning away from her. "We haven't—we're *not...*"

Her words caused my heart to plummet to the depths of my stomach. I wanted to be honest about how I felt, but I hadn't told Gray yet. Of course, I loved him. I'd loved him before I even knew what the word meant. I thought Gray loved me too—I was almost sure of it. But after a lifetime of never knowing where I stood, not having the explicit words gave me pause. I'd gotten ahead of myself before, and it all blew up in my face. Even though I understood Gray's reasons for leaving, it didn't take away from the bitter sting of his absence. When we fell apart five years ago, I was devastated, and it had taken me all this time to open my heart again.

And that was before I got to feel Gray moving inside me, before I knew his touch ignited every fiber of my being, before I got to hear him call me his wife or ever got to know what it was like to fall asleep in his arms.

Before I'd fallen deeply, irrevocably in love with him.

Marta took my hand, tugging me further into the kitchen so the guys couldn't hear us. She studied my expression. "I know that look, Devyn."

"I don't know what you're talking about."

"Yes, you do," Marta insisted. "It's that look you get when you're scared, when those big emotions are threatening to pull you under, so you shove them into a box. It happened a lot when you were younger and you didn't want people asking too many questions about home. Now, you're doing it again, but it's about my boy." She squeezed my hands in comfort. "So talk to me. Even if Gray is my son, you know I have always loved you like a daughter. I'm here for you, just like I would be there for him."

I exhaled slowly. "I know I do—love Gray, I mean. But I'm not good at this. I'm terrified I'm going to mess everything up, or he's going to figure out I'm difficult and stubborn and not who he pictured being with." Tears threatened to fill my eyes, but I shoved them back, determined to make it through. "I'm so scared, I can't see straight, but the idea of walking away from him makes me nauseous. I don't know what I'm doing."

Marta smiled brightly at me. "Oh honey, you're definitely in love." She pulled me in for a tight hug. "It's scary being vulnerable with someone, giving them that power over your heart. But I promise, if it's the right person, it's worth the risk."

"What if it ends?" I quietly asked. "I don't think I'd survive it."

"All love stories end," Marta answered, giving me a sad smile. "Through mistakes, apathy, or time, every single one comes to an end. Look at Curt and me." She sighed and looked over her shoulder to where her husband sat. "When I met Curt, I never imagined we'd be here, with me waking up each morning praying he recognizes me. But even knowing that, I would still choose him, every single time. Because no matter how this ends, the journey made it so worth it."

Even though I wasn't a hugger, I pulled Marta in, holding her close for a few minutes. Someone clearing their throat made us break apart, turning to find Gray standing in the doorway.

"Everything okay in here?"

"Yes," Marta chuckled, swatting him with a kitchen towel. "Just catching up with my girl. How's your father?"

"Good," Gray answered. "Talking about playing cards. Are you cool if I have everyone over for a couple of hands?"

"Of course. The more the merrier."

Gray's steel eyes met mine, concern flickering in his irises for a second. But as I smiled up at him, it faded in the background. "What do you say, Ace? You up for a round?"

"You're on."

THIRTY-NINE

Devyn

Less than an hour later, the three of us transformed the living room from a cozy country home into a modern-day saloon, complete with the green felt poker table and a rolling drink cart. As soon as Gray said his dad wanted to play a couple of rounds of cards, all our friends drove over, happy to give Curt a fun night.

In fact, there was a new light in his eyes as everyone shuffled through the door, greeting every person by name and giving them a big hug. Curt was his usual self, and his memory seemed to be pretty intact. Gray watched him carefully, warning me he tended to get worse after the sun went down, but so far, he showed no signs of slowing down.

After we all grabbed drinks and settled around the table, we chatted as Curt and Marta set everything else up. At first, I felt a little uneasy, especially considering that the last time we were all in the same room, Gray spilled the news about our marriage. I thought there might have been a little animosity after the fallout, but everyone seemed to be just as welcoming as usual.

"It feels weird being out this late," Cole's sister, Victoria, chuckled from my side. "Usually, I'm passed out next to Emilia after reading her a third bedtime story."

Her boyfriend, Adam, looked over at her softly, knowing the days she didn't have her five-year-old daughter, Emilia, were tough. Even though she had an amazing relationship with her daughter's father, Victoria had an incredible bond with her child, and she missed her terribly when she was with her dad for the weekend.

"I know what you mean," Calla chuckled from across the table, one hand on her cards, the other on her belly. "I'm already struggling to keep my eyes open. Can't imagine it's going to get any better after she arrives."

"We'll figure it out," Theo said as he leaned in to kiss her shoulder. "Especially if you let me hire a night nurse—"

"Not happening, Sunshine," Calla smirked back. "We're going to be all hands on deck with this baby, midnight feedings and all."

"I know," Theo said, unable to hold back his smile. "I just worry about you."

As my sister turned to him and whispered something in her husband's ear, I returned my attention to the table, suddenly feeling like an intruder in their private moment. I turned to my other side, finding Alex and Cole chatting happily with Curt as he sorted all the poker chips. It was interesting to watch the couples sitting at this table. All of them had long journeys to find each other, but they were making it work, and it was obvious they loved each other.

As I glanced over at Gray, I found he was already looking at me, the same slight smile on his lips. What did they see when they looked at us? Did we look at each other like we wouldn't survive without each other?

"Alright," Curt said as he shuffled the cards. "Gotta let all of you in on the rules of poker in my house. No complaining, always make sure you have a drink in your hand before the flop, and aces are always high."

Victoria scrunched her nose. "I thought they could be low or high."

"In most cases, yes," Curt chuckled. "But not in this house."

"Why is that?" she asked.

He chuckled, looking fondly up at his wife. "Started with a bet. I was just a dumb kid, in love with this beautiful girl who saw me as nothing more than a friend. So, one night, a bunch of us were hanging out, and she brought out a deck of cards. Decided to play poker. Night goes on, and everyone goes out except the two of us. And then she decides she's all in, but I don't have the chips to match." He looked up at Marta, smiling softly to himself. "Remember what I said?"

Marta nodded her head, smiling at her husband, tears in her ears. "You had nothing to give me but your last name."

"That's right," he smiled. "And by some dumb stroke of luck, she thought it was a good enough line to keep playing. So, when it came time for the final card, we both showed our hands. Both of us had three of a kind, but she had an ace, and I had a king." He paused, shuffling the cards in his hands. "Technically, she should've won, but I wanted to see how she played it."

"You would have never known that at the time," Marta chuckled as she came around and stood at his shoulder. "The man was grinning ear to ear."

Curt reached out and wrapped his free arm around her waist. He stared up at her, and you never would have known they'd been married for four decades. Curt looked just as love-struck as he did in their wedding pictures. "I said to her, your choice—is the ace low or high?" He turned to the rest of us. "If she said low, I would've let it go, known she felt nothing for me but friendship. But then she said..."

"High. Always high." She leaned forward and kissed his cheek. "Guess I'll be taking that last name now."

Curt smiled like he was still there, looking at the girl who won his heart. "Gave it to her six months later. Called her my Ace of Hearts ever since." He sighed and looked out to the rest of us. "And now, it's the house rule: nothing ever rivals an ace."

My eyes widened as I looked over to Gray, who was watching me apprehensively. Years ago, he'd gifted me the nickname Ace, claiming it had something to do with my grades. But now, my heart hammered in my chest, knowing the truth without him saying a word. All the love I'd questioned, all the times I thought Gray saw me as nothing more than a friend, the answer had been there all along. I just never knew where to look.

"Could you excuse me for a moment?" I said as I started to head toward the bathroom. But instead of turning into the room off the kitchen, I kept moving, walking straight into the garage and up the stairs to Gray's old room.

As the door closed behind me, I leaned against it, holding my hand to my chest. My heart thumped an unsteady rhythm as my emotions threatened to overwhelm me. It was only made worse when I looked out into the space, and my past threatened to sweep me away. Ever since Gray moved out to the garage when he was sixteen, this room hadn't changed. I'd spent so many nights here when I couldn't stand to be home. It still had the same dark blue paint, framed posters on each wall. Photos lined the shelves, and I was in several of them, smiling at Gray like he was the center of my universe.

I walked over to the bed and ran my hand over the comforter. It was where I had run years ago, when it felt like the ground was about to swallow me whole. Gray held me, pressing an ice pack to my swollen face as I cried myself to sleep. I drifted off, listening to him promise I'd be okay, that he'd keep me safe.

Gray was my safe space, the person I'd always run to when the world was too scary and big to confront alone. And even though moving back was Calla's idea, I had to wonder if it was really the same thing. If all along, I'd been trying to find my way back to him.

Before I could examine that thought too closely, though, a knock sounded on the door.

"Ace, open the door."

FORTY

Grayson

I held my breath as the doorknob turned, watching as Devyn came into view. From the moment she walked away from the table, my heart sank, unsure how she felt about my dad's story. And even though she was in front of me now, I still couldn't tell, not with Devyn's mask firmly back in place. There was no betraying what was going on under the surface, if she'd put the pieces together about her nickname. Honestly, I'd forgotten all about how that saying came to be in our home, just knowing my dad always referred to my mom as his ace of hearts, that the Ace always represented the best of the best.

"Why?" she asked, still grasping the door handle.

"You know why, Ace."

"I need to hear you say it."

I moved toward her, and she shifted out of my way, allowing me into my room. It was weird being back in this space. Not so long ago, it was where I imagined living for the foreseeable future. But now, home was with Devyn, in our bed up in the mountains. While I knew I should feel guilty about moving out right after I came home, I couldn't, not when it meant spending each night wrapped in my wife's arms.

I walked over to the picture I'd placed on my mirror over a month ago, long before I ever thought Devyn and I would work things out. Tugging it free, I moved closer to her, showing her what I'd saved for so long. "When I first started calling you Ace, it wasn't even on purpose. It just slipped out. But I knew what the word meant to my family." I sighed, dropping down to the edge of my bed. I thumbed the pictures. "I've always loved you, Devyn. Sure, it was in different forms and ways over the years, but I loved you all the same."

"Gray..."

"No, I need to get this out," I said, staring down at the picture of her. I couldn't face my wife just yet, couldn't bear to look at her if she didn't feel the same. "But none of that compares to this time we've spent together, Devyn. I am *in* love with you. It's terrifying and consuming, but fuck, if it's not the best thing that's ever happened to me. I am so in love with you, and that's why I call you Ace. Because no one else in this life, or any other, will compare to how I feel about you."

I dared to look up, but it was too late. Devyn was already kneeling in front of me, wiping away tears I hadn't realized were falling. She smiled softly up at me. "Then it's a good thing I'm in love with you too, Grayson."

"Yeah?" I asked.

"I've been falling for you for twenty years, Gray. I love you. I am in love with you."

"Say it again."

"I love you, Gray."

I groaned as I pulled her into my lap. "Now say what I really want to hear."

Devyn smiled and pressed a soft kiss to my lips. "I love my husband."

"Fuck," I hissed, capturing her lips in a soul-shattering kiss. Relief coursed through my veins, beyond happy I no longer had to hold anything back. After a lifetime of poor timing and missed opportunities, Devyn and I were finally on track, and it was the best fucking feeling in the world. As I pulled back, I ran my fingers along her cheeks, loving how she leaned into my touch. My wife. *Mine.* This woman was everything, and now, she was completely mine. No more questions, no more doubts. Devyn Winters was mine in every way that mattered, and I would spend the rest of my life proving I was worthy of her love.

As I shifted her hips along my length, Devyn let out a sharp gasp. "Gray! Your parents and all our friends are downstairs."

"Don't care," I muttered as I dragged my lips along the column of her neck. "Got a new turn-on. Hearing you say you love me makes me so fucking hard, I can barely stand it."

She moaned as I thrust against her once again, her hips matching my movements. My hands clasped her ass, twisting us until she was underneath me. Devyn let out a little gasp as her head hit the pillow, and then she smiled up at me. I lifted her shirt, kissing my way up her stomach until I found her peaked nipples. My mouth encircled one while my fingers twisted the other, loving the way my wife responded to my touch.

"Gray..." she moaned. "We shouldn't."

"I'll make you a deal, baby." I climbed up her body, kissing her sternum and neck. "If you really want to head back downstairs, we can do that. Or, you can come for me, and *then* we'll join the party." I pressed my lips to her pulse point as her hand curled in my hair. "Your choice, Ace."

"Fuck," she groaned as she writhed against me. "Make me come, Gray. I need you."

Devyn sighed as my fingers found the button of her jeans. She lifted her hips as I leaned back and slid them down her legs. "What do you want, baby? You want my fingers or my mouth? Or do you want your husband's cock to fill you up?"

"Fill me," she whispered, arching up into my touch. "I need to feel you inside me right now."

"Good answer," I said as I unbuttoned my jeans, lowering them just enough to free my cock. My fingers traced her core, teasing and exploring to make sure she was ready for me. I nipped at the column of Devyn's neck. "Fuck, baby. You're so wet. This all for me?"

"Always for you," she moaned, shifting to seek more friction between us. I happily obliged, reaching underneath her to bring us chest to chest. Devyn gasped when my eyes met hers, and I could only imagine what she saw in my gaze. Longing and lust overwhelmed me. Even though it had only been a day since I had Devyn like this, it would never be enough, never convince me I deserved to have her in my arms. But I didn't care. She'd given me her heart, and there was no way I'd ever give it back.

As I lifted her to sink slowly on my length, I watched as every thick inch of me filled her tight heat. She worked me, swiveling her hips until we were fused, tight enough that no force could ever pull us apart.

My fingers trembled against her hips, guiding her in a steady rhythm. Without any secrets between us, that last barrier finally pulled down, it felt even more incredible inside her. Despite the group waiting for us downstairs, our movements weren't hurried, like we were content just to feel each other, to feel how well we moved as one.

But as my thrusts continued, Devyn's hips became more frantic, seeking her release. I brought my hand up to her hair, tightening until she looked at me. "You need my fingers, baby?"

"Yes," she gasped. "You know how I like it, Gray."

I tightened my hold on her hair. "That's not how you get what you want, Ace."

Devyn smirked at me as I increased my thrusts, making her walls squeeze around me, desperate to come. She pressed her fingers into my shoulders. "Touch me, Gray. I want to come on my husband's cock."

"That's my pretty little wife," I said as I brought my thumb to her swollen clit. "You're so beautiful when you're begging for me."

She gasped as I increased my pressure, and then she crashed over the edge, screaming my name as her walls crumbled around me. The pressure of her orgasm was enough to trigger my own, and I spilled inside her, desperate to mark her just as much as she marked me.

After our breathing evened back out, I shifted and laid Devyn out on my bed. She cuddled against my pillows, and I ran to the bathroom for a washcloth. I cleaned myself up and fixed my jeans then walked out to the bedroom to do the same for Devyn.

But as beautiful as she looked, lying on my bed and exhausted from our love-making, something was missing. Devyn's brow furrowed as I pivoted away from her, moving over to the dresser on the other side of my room. I opened the top drawer, pulling out the rings that had been sitting there since I moved back into my parent's house. Maybe it was ridiculous, holding on to the cheap rings we drunkenly picked out in Vegas all those years ago, gut they meant something to me—meant something to *us*.

"What are you doing?" Devyn asked, propping herself up on her elbows. I pulled her ring out of the box and held it up to show her. Devyn's hand flew to her mouth. "Gray... I can't believe you kept that."

I chuckled as I moved closer to her. "Of course I did, Ace. It was a part of you. And if you want to get rid of it, we can do that." I moved back onto the bed. "Get you something better when the time is right."

Her eyes sparkled as she looked up at me. "When the time is right?"

"Got plans for you and me, Ace."

"Gonna share those plans?"

I ticked my tongue. "Not right now. But until I can make good on them..." I held up the ring. "I know we didn't do this the right way, but I love you, Devyn, more than anything else in this world. Our marriage might not be traditional, but neither is our love story." I took her right hand in mine and traced her ring finger. "So for now, I'd like it if you wore this ring. Not on *that* finger, but on this one. As a promise between us that we're in this together."

Devyn smiled at me and held up her hand. "Always?"

I leaned forward as I slipped the ring onto her finger. "You already know the answer to that, Ace."

FORTY-ONE

Grayson

"Oh shit," I groaned as I woke up, my body and back sore from the ancient mattress. After the poker game ended, it was late, so Devyn and I decided to crash in my room above the garage. My parents didn't question it, just making sure we would be comfortable up here. I thought we would be, at least until I remembered this mattress was from the eighties and a far cry from the high-priced one I had up at the cabin.

It was still dark as I tried to stretch out my sore muscles, so I grabbed my phone to get the time. 2:28. I turned to check to make sure Devyn was sleeping okay when I found the spot next to me empty. Maybe it was everything we'd been working on lately, but my hackles instantly rose, unsure if our past had finally caught up to us. But there was no sign of a struggle, nothing missing except for my wife.

I climbed out of bed to search for her, and my heart hammered in my chest. In the past, I would have asked a million questions, wondering what I had done to scare her off. But now, I knew what we shared, and I knew both of us were all in. We both wore our rings, and despite them being on the opposite hands, they symbolized our unbreakable bond. Devyn wouldn't have gone far, not without me at her side.

As I pulled open the garage door, I heard a soft oof, and Devyn stumbled at my feet. I chuckled as I looked down at her and Elsa, who lay curled up around her feet. "Whatcha doing out here, Ace?"

She held up the journal and a flashlight in her hands. "Couldn't sleep. No offense, but that bed has seen better days." She brought the book back down to her lap. "Thought I'd get some more reading done, but I didn't want to disturb you."

"Never disturbing me, Devy." I sat down at her side, reading over her shoulder. The notes were hard to process at the late hour, especially considering half of them were written in code. "Getting anywhere with those?"

She shook her head. "I think I've figured out a couple of the symbols, but not enough to make any kind of progress." She pointed to one section of the page. "I'm 85% sure this is talking about meeting with someone. Can't make out who or why though, so it's pretty much useless."

I put my arm around her shoulder and brought her against me. After brushing a kiss on the top of her head, I took the notebook and closed it. "You're going to get it, Ace. I know you will. But you also need to rest."

"I know." She nodded, then looked up at me. "But since we're both awake, there's something I want to run by you." I kept quiet, letting her continue. "After going through all my dad's things, it made me realize how long it's been since I visited his grave. I think..." She sighed. "I think I want to go see him tomorrow. Maybe that will help me clear out all this brain fog."

"I think that's a great idea." I squeezed her a little tighter. "If you want, I can come with you."

"If it's okay, I think I need to do this by myself."

I tilted her chin up and stole a kiss from her lips. "More than okay, Ace. You need me after, I'll be there." As we stood, I glanced at the journal in my hand. "You know—there's someone else who might be able to decode these journals."

"Who?"

"My dad," I answered. "They were best friends, and your dad helped mine set up everything with the restaurant. If he's lucid, he might be able to help us with some of these symbols."

"Are you sure?" Devyn asked. "I don't want him to get upset."

"I'll tread lightly," I answered. "If he doesn't want to talk about Peter, I won't push it. But if it could help, it's worth a shot."

As we walked back into the bedroom, Devyn turned and wrapped her arms around me. "Thank you for being here, Gray. It means more than you know."

"Nowhere else I'd rather be, Ace."

THE FOLLOWING DAY, Devyn headed out early to check in with Laurel. Between the journals and their debate about including Calla in the investigation, they had a lot to discuss. While she was gone, I had a laundry list of tasks to do myself, such as helping my mom prep for the new night nurse's arrival and seeing if my dad could be any help with the code we'd found.

"Do you think she's going to need anything else?" my mom asked, looking around my dad's room. "Maybe some magazines or something to keep her occupied?"

The room had changed a lot over the past year, especially after my mom moved into the guest room down the hall. On one end, their bed sat where it always had. But on the other side of the room, they'd cleared away my mom's desk and sewing machine, exchanging it for a recliner and a small TV for my father so he didn't have to bother with the stairs if he was having an off day.

He sat there now, watching my mother as she fluttered around his space. My dad tried to get up and help a few times, but after my mom kept shooing him back to his chair, he gave up, all too happy to sit and watch her.

"Mom," I sighed, rubbing my fingers over my eyes. "She's here to work. You don't need to worry about anything else. She'll have it covered."

"I want her to feel comfortable," my mother insisted as she folded up another blanket and tucked it next to the chair. When she caught my eye, she shrugged. "What? It gets drafty in here, and I don't want her to get cold."

"Okay, Mom." I took the blanket from her hands and led her over to where my dad now stood. "Now, I know you like people to feel welcome in your home, but this is going a bit far, don't you think?"

"You know he's right, Marta." My dad pulled her into his arms. "Want to tell me what's really going through your mind?"

My mother sighed and dropped her head against his chest. "I hate feeling so helpless. When we got married, I promised you I'd be there in sickness and health. And now..." Her voice trailed off as she turned to the end table, where a picture from their wedding lived. "I've failed you."

My father pulled back and searched my mother's eyes. As much as I wanted to turn and give them a moment, I couldn't. I'd grown up watching them show their love in a variety of ways, never hiding for a moment how much they cared for each other. When I was younger, sure, it made me a little nauseous, but now that I knew these moments wouldn't last forever, I let them enjoy them without interruption.

"You have *never* failed me, Marta. Not once in almost forty years. You've given me a home, a son, and the best damn life I could have imagined. No matter what comes next, I wouldn't change a single damn thing."

As they parted, I walked forward and hugged my mother. "You're doing everything you can for him, but there's no shame in asking for help."

She smiled softly at me. "Maybe not, but I'm having a hard time accepting it anyway."

As she pulled away and continued her fussing, guilt washed over me. I was supposed to be here for them every day, yet I'd picked my own happiness over their needs. I could never regret the time I spent with Devyn, but the realization I'd abandoned my parents during the worst period of their lives made me sick. As far back as I could remember, my parents were my fiercest advocates, the loudest ones in the stands at every game. They never hesitated to support me, even when my dreams took me so far from home.

As my thoughts started to darken, my mother took my hand. "Don't do that, Gray. You've been here every single day. That is enough. You are doing more than enough."

"Is it, though?" I asked quietly. Shaking my head, I started walking toward the door. "I'll go make sure everything is set downstairs."

"Oh no, you don't," my father said, standing up to face me. Even with age, my father's height rivaled mine. His stature was always imposing, but once you got to know the man underneath, that all faded away. "I know things have been hard, but you need to know something, Gray. Neither of us ever wanted you to give up your life, not for us."

I shook my head. "But you need me—"

My father moved to my side and placed his hand on my shoulder. "All we've ever wanted is for you to be happy. For so long, I've watched you going through the motions, enjoying the game but not everything outside of it." He smiled at me. "And I know my mind's not what it used to be, but I've seen a change in you now that Devyn's come home." I swallowed as he continued. "She makes you happy, doesn't she?"

I nodded. "More than I ever thought possible."

"Then keep fighting for her, Gray," my dad insisted. "Fight for a life with the woman you love. We appreciate your sacrifice more than we can ever put into words. And maybe there was a reason all this happened the way it did, but now that you have Devyn back in your life—*live*. Don't waste a single moment of the time you've got together."

FORTY-TWO

Devyn

As I sat against my car, staring out across the cemetery, I waited for the urge to run to overtake me. For so long, I'd avoided this place, wanting to erase my last memories of it from my mind—memories of standing next to my mother, watching as they poured dirt over my father's coffin. I was too young to grasp he was gone, at least until I watched them lower his coffin into the ground. It was so final, so heartbreaking. To know my father, who was so full of life, was suddenly nothing more than a memory gutted me to my core.

For the last fifteen years, I'd avoided his final resting place. Not only because it was too hard to come back here, but because the whole idea of visiting cemeteries never made sense to me. It might have been where his body was buried, but he didn't reside there, not anymore.

But in talking to Marta about learning to let go of the past, I realized I'd never allowed myself to really grieve for the man I'd lost. For too long, when asked about my dad, I'd put on a placating smile and avoided the subject, not wanting to expose any of that lingering hurt. But that pain reminded me of how much I had loved him, how much I missed having him in my life. It was almost therapeutic. The scars that lived within us could never really heal if we left them for too long.

Once I started walking, it wasn't hard to find his marker. Even though it had been years since the funeral, the path was ingrained in my mind. But now that I wasn't weighed down with grief, I took in more of the surroundings, loving where my mother had chosen his final resting place. The last dredges of winter were starting to let go, allowing the world around us to fade from white and gray to a timid shade of green, almost as if spring wasn't sure if it was time just yet. Tiny buds lined the tree limbs, and birds called out to each other. It was peaceful, almost calm.

My dad always loved nature and everything the Earth had to offer. On days like this, when the sun wanted to peek out over the clouds, he'd go down to the main deck of the Isadora with one of his many books, enjoying the fresh air as he read.

After walking up to his headstone, I dusted the last layer of snow from the top. It looked different from the last time I'd been here; signs of age and wear started to show on the polished marble stone. I took off my scarf and wiped down the front, reading the inscription as I went.

Peter Winters. Devoted husband and father. Taken from us too soon.

My fingers traced each letter as my eyes started to water. *God, when did this crying thing start?* It felt like my tears were always waiting in the wings now. When I was satisfied his grave was clear of debris, I leaned back and sat on the patch of grass, using my jacket as a buffer from the icy ground.

"Hey, Dad." I pressed my hand on the ground in front of me. "Sorry it took me so long to come. Honestly, this still feels so weird to me."

I sighed and sat back, staring up at the sky. "But I've spent so much of my life feeling lost. For the longest time, I thought it was because of Gray. Don't get me wrong—that threw me off kilter, but I'm starting to see that maybe it started when we lost you."

I chuckled and ran my hand over my face. "God, that sounds so weird. We *lost* you, like you could somehow be found." I swallowed. "Because you really, you were taken from us. *Stolen.* Even if David wasn't involved, something happened that night. I keep looking into your death with Laurel, and the more I do..." My voice trailed off as another group passed, bringing flowers to their loved ones. "Remember when you used to read me fairytales, but you'd twist the endings? You'd ask me who the real villain was, and I had to guess." I smiled to myself. "And I'd get so mad because that wasn't how the story was supposed to go."

A memory ripped through me as my voice trailed off. It was one I'd pushed into the back of my mind, forgotten in my haze of grief and loss. About a month before he passed, my father arranged a camping trip just for him and his girls. While my mother stayed at the Isadora, he took us further into the mountains and taught us how to set up a tent and start a fire.

Laurel and Calla fell asleep first, leaving my dad and me alone around the fire as the stars lit up the sky. While I rested in his lap, he read me another fairytale, changing up the story like he always did.

"Why do you keep doing that?" I sighed as I rested my head against his chest. "When Mom reads it to me, she just says the words."

"Ah," my dad chuckled. "But where's the fun in that?"

"It's what you're *supposed* to do."

My dad closed the book and shifted so he was facing me. "Maybe you're right, Devyn. But there's also a lesson I want you to take away from these stories."

"That the story can change?"

He chuckled. "That's part of it. Sure, in stories, we always know the ending. The villain is exactly who you think it will be. But life doesn't work that way." He brushed some of my hair behind my ear. "One day, hopefully a long, long time from now, you're going to learn that lesson. People can hide the worst intentions behind beautiful words and actions." He stared down at me. "What I want you to learn, my brilliant girl, is how to see through the smoke and mirrors. That no matter what happens, you have the strength to overcome even life's hardest lessons."

"Is that what you do?" I asked. My dad's work fascinated me, and I loved to see him in his office, crafting arguments for court. He didn't work a lot of cases that went to trial, but he always acted like he was heading into battle, wanting each of his clients to get the best of his abilities.

"Sometimes," he chuckled and pressed a kiss to my forehead. "Lately, it feels like it's all I've been doing. There are a lot of people in this world who think they can use their money and power to hurt others."

"That's messed up."

"Yeah, it is," my dad agreed. "And as an attorney, it's my job to make sure that doesn't happen, to make sure everyone is held accountable to the law." He motioned for me to stand, and he grabbed a stick from the ground. "So right now, I'm working with someone who's going up against a giant." As he spoke, he drew images in the dirt. "And he tried for a long time to get someone to believe his story. But the problem is, he's going against someone who's very rich, and everyone believes he's the good guy."

"But he's not?"

"Not at all, Dev."

I frowned, staring at the drawing in the dirt. I glanced up at my dad, who was watching me with a keen eye. "But you believe him?"

"I do," he said. "I think it's my job to make sure his story gets told, that he gets justice."

I scrunched my nose. "How are you going to do that, Daddy?"

He chuckled and pulled me into a hug. "Good question, Devyn. Honestly, I'm not really sure. But I'm going to figure it out, no matter what it takes." As I stared up at him in admiration, he continued, "It can take one person to change the tides, Devyn. Just one person standing up for what's right to make lasting change."

By the time I come out of the memory, my face is drenched with tears. They streak down my face in waves, and as much as I dread what I look like, I feel free, like the ties of grief and doubt are no longer holding me down. These tears are the last ties to that broken little girl.

My father was my hero, and his quest for justice stayed with me all this time. I ignored its call for years, but Gray helped pull the veil away from my eyes. What had started as an inkling was now a call to action. It would be a shift, definitely a change in the way my life used to be, but I was no longer afraid; instead, I was honored to step into his footsteps.

As I thought back on that memory, something tugged at the back of my mind. I pulled out the journal in my bag, the one he'd written right before he died. I scanned through the journal, hoping the dates aligned. My thumb slowed, and I let out an excited chuckle as I found the same week as the camping trip, the one when my dad talked about the case he was working on. Playing back his words, I scanned the page again, searching for any hint of familiarity. There wasn't much, but one of the meeting notes called out to me. I stared at them harder, trying to match the symbols to the rest on the page. There were only two —likely initials, if my instincts were correct.

"Wait..." I said as I dug my phone out of my pocket,

searching Morse code guides in my web browser. We'd eliminated that from the rest of the words; there weren't enough characters to make up all the dashes and dots needed to create a message. But the symbol for the initials seemed to be made up of just that, the code reimagined into two distinct characters. I could've been completely off track, but after days of staring at the pages and getting nowhere, I was willing to try anything.

"B.....G...." I said as I tried to match the symbols. It wasn't exact, but they seemed pretty close. Maybe everyone else would think I'd lost my mind, but in my gut, I knew I was on to something. As I squinted at the symbols, I noticed a few more lined up in the margins. They were so faint, I'd brushed them off before as stray pen marks. I held up the book, following the dots and dashes until a pattern started to emerge. *A date.*

I shook my head. The pieces were there, waiting for me, but I wanted to check with everyone else before I continued down this path, wanted Gray at my side if this helped us turn the tides against David. I snapped a quick picture on my phone and sent it off in a group text before getting ready to leave.

As I stood, I placed my hand on top of my dad's grave. "Thank you, Daddy. For loving me and showing me the way. You'll be happy to know I found someone who loves me just as fiercely, who encourages and supports me, just like how you would have wanted. I'll visit again soon and bring him with me." I chuckled as I imagined my father's face if he knew I was married to Grayson. "I think you'll be a little shocked, but I promise, he's the very best man for me."

With one last goodbye, I put the journal back into my purse and started walking over to my car. But as I stepped closer, my blood ran cold, meeting the eyes of the last person I expected to see.

"Jack?" I called out, searching over my shoulder for anyone else in the area. My ex-fling was the last person I ever expected to see again, especially after our last meeting. Gray had threatened him into leaving town, and I thought Jack took that message to heart. I hadn't heard from him since he got me fired, and I had no idea what he was doing here now.

I meant what I told Gray at the time—I could handle Jack. At least, I used to think I could. At the time, I thought he was harmless, just another spoiled, rich man throwing a temper tantrum. But seeing him now, there was no sign of the slick executive I met last year. There was something about the way he was watching me that set me on edge. His appearance was disheveled, his eyes wild, like an animal that had just been let out of its long-term cage.

"Surprise, Devyn," he said as he stepped closer. "I think we need to have a little talk."

"Not interested," I scoffed as I stepped around him.

But before I could get to the safety of my car, he grabbed my arm and slammed me against the passenger side door. Jack snarled as he held my face in one hand, fumbling through his pocket with the other. "You seem to think you're in control here, Devyn, but it's about fucking time you shut up and listen."

"Fuck you," I snarled as I lifted my leg and tried to knee him in the crotch. Before I could make an impact, Jack twisted, turning so my knee slammed against the car. Pain radiated along my leg, but I bit it down, refusing to let him see any fear in my eyes.

"Here's how this is going to go, Devyn. You're going to take a little nap, and when you wake up, we'll talk." He pulled a rag out of his pocket, and I shifted, trying to break his hold on me. But no matter how hard I tried, I couldn't get away. As the cloth covered my mouth and nose, Jack whispered, "That's good. Just like that, Devyn. And if you even think about giving me any trouble, I'll make Calla pay the price."

Grayson

Later that afternoon, after my mom headed to the Lost Tavern, I sat with my dad in the living room. With a college baseball game in the background, it felt like a regular weekend, one we used to have all the time before he got diagnosed. If it wasn't for his moments of confusion, we could almost pretend everything was just as it was supposed to be.

Looking over at my dad as he shook his head at the umpire's call, guilt swept through me, hating that I was about to bring up his past. He was happy, happier than I'd seen in a while. But I'd made a promise to Devyn, and honestly, I needed to know for myself. After spending so much time investigating David, I was ready to be done. Ready to start my life with Devyn without his presence hanging over us.

I stood, grabbed one of the journals from the kitchen counter, and walked back into the living room. "Hey, Dad?" I said as I sat next to him. "Take a look at this for me?"

"I'll be damned," my dad chuckled as he thumbed through the pages. "Where the hell did you find this old thing?"

"Pete's office downtown," I answered as I looked over his

shoulder. "Diane kept it all these years, and we found all of his old notes and journals there."

My dad nodded as he thumbed through the pages. "I never took Diane as a sentimental type. I'm glad to hear it, though. Your girl deserves to have these."

I paused, watching my dad for any sign of distress. "Devyn's been trying to read them, but the codes inside don't make any sense." I pointed to a few of them. "Any idea what they mean?"

"Not a damn clue," my dad said as he stared at the pages in front of them. "But that was always Pete's game. He was paranoid, especially towards the end of his life. He'd always written in code, just in case anyone ever subpoenaed his files, but this was a whole new level." He turned the journal to the side, running his finger along the edges. "There they are." He laughed as he handed me the book again. "See those marks?" I nodded, following along with his finger. "He'd use those to indicate a case file or if he was meeting with a client he didn't want to put on the books just yet."

"Seems like a lot for a small-town lawyer."

My dad wrinkled his brow. "He wasn't always."

"What do you mean?"

He sighed as he backed up in his chair. "He didn't like to talk about it, but Pete was a hot shot in Manhattan for a long time. Only moved back up here after he reconnected with Diane. Before then, he worked as an Assistant District Attorney."

"What the hell?" I asked as I analyzed the book. "How come none of us knew about this?"

My dad shook his head. "He left that life behind when he married Diane. He didn't want his past convictions to come back and haunt him." His face fell. "At least, I thought he did."

"What do you mean?"

My dad stood, and I shifted around the couch to help him

steady himself. He waved me off and moved out of the living room toward the stairs. I followed as he headed upstairs but turned before he got to his room, instead going to the attic stairs at the back of the house. When he opened the door, I reached out, saying, "What are you doing, Dad? Maybe we should go back to your room."

"Gray, I know you and your mother are worried about me, but I'm fine. Let an old man help while he still can." I nodded and shifted out of his way. After he climbed the stairs, he hummed to himself and moved some of the boxes around. As we got further into the back and the boxes got heavier, he'd tap on the ones he wanted me to move. When we finally found some unmarked boxes in the back, my dad smiled. "Knew these were up here somewhere."

"What are they?" I asked, kneeling to open the first box. Dust coated the top, the insides musty and old. The handwriting was familiar, an exact match for the scribbles inside the journal. *Pete's files.* The evidence we'd hoped was waiting in his office had been sitting in my attic all along, right above my head for God knows how long. I sat back and covered my mouth with my hand. "I'll be damned."

"Before Pete died, he asked me to look after this stuff, that I hold onto it until someone we trusted came looking for it." He chuckled as he moved to my side. "Tried to open the box, and he made me swear I wouldn't go digging, that I would just store them until someone was able to follow the clues."

"Devyn," I whispered as I pulled out one of the file folders. It was almost identical to the ones Laurel had assembled for David's assumed victims. The first case looked familiar as soon as I saw it—a young woman who disappeared after filing a bunch of complaints against an executive at her office. We'd just added her to the pile. Laurel and I had missed her originally not seeing the connection until we followed the paper trail Tomas and Devyn laid out. Once we realized David was a major shareholder in the company and would have lost millions if the allegations were true, the dots started to connect themselves. But we would never have gotten this far, not without Devyn. A slow smile formed as I imagined the look on her face when she saw these boxes. "He was waiting for her."

"I wouldn't have been surprised," my dad chuckled. "He loved all his girls, but he connected the most with Devyn. Always joked about how he was going to have to share his office with her one day."

"She would have loved that," I said as I kept digging, finding more and more evidence on David. "I can't believe this. Everything we've been looking for—it's been sitting here all along." Once I reached the back, there were newspaper clippings, pictures of a road I instantly recognized. But the handwriting was different, seeing my dad's scribbled text instead of Pete's crowded loops. I held it up to him. "What's this?"

My dad took the file from my hand. He thumbed through it and shook his head as he handed it back to me. "I started to collect this stuff after Peter passed, but it never went anywhere. I never thought Pete's death was an accident. The man was never rattled, and when he came here with these boxes, he was scared. A week later, he was dead? On a road he'd driven a million times?" He shook his head. "Never bought that story. But once the cops said it was an accident, what could I do?"

I nodded as I stood, digging my phone out of my pocket. But before I could dial Devyn's number, my dad placed his hand on top of mine. "Are you sure you want to do this, son?" When I started to speak, he held up his hand. "I know how much Devyn means to you, and if you two want to pursue this, I'm not going to stand in your way. But this cost my best friend his life, cost Devyn her father. Think long and hard if this is a fight you can win."

"I already have," I whispered as I looked down at the boxes. So many folders, so many files, so many people whose lives were cut short for no reason. "I don't know if we can win it, but I also couldn't live with myself if we didn't try. These families deserve answers, Dad."

He nodded and began walking down the stairs. "Then I hope you find what you need."

As soon as he was back on the main level of the house, I pulled up Devyn's number and hit the call button. While it rang, I checked my watch. It had been almost three hours since she left. Surely, she was heading this way. But when her voicemail clicked on, I frowned. I pulled up my messaging app and fired one off in our group chat. Before I could hit send, though, I saw one waiting for me, a picture Devyn had sent almost an hour ago. Why the fuck hadn't I heard it? Shit, it must have been while I was talking to my dad. I turned my phone on silent because I didn't want to disturb him. I glanced at the image, seeing one of her dark painted nails pointed to the marking in the corners. I smirked. My fucking brilliant wife. She'd figured it out, even without my dad.

But that flash of pride was soon extinguished when I called her again, and once again, her voicemail greeted me. I frowned as I switched over to the group chat and sent a message.

ME

Anyone heard from Devyn? She should have been back by now.

LAUREL

Not since her last text.

TOMAS

Same. Did you want me to track her phone?

I paused, unsure how to proceed. Normally, I'd balk at the

idea of violating Devyn's privacy. However, it wasn't like her to take off without saying something, and my protective instincts were surging with the need to find her.

ME

> Yeah. Hopefully, she's just out of service range, but I want to be sure.

TOMAS

On it.

As I waited for another response from him, I paced the attic, unable to focus on anything until I knew Devyn's location. I couldn't even think about looking at the files, already feeling paranoid about my wife's disappearing act. When my phone rang out and I saw Devyn's name on the screen, I let out a long sigh of relief.

"Shit, Ace, you scared me. You okay?"

"No, I don't think she is."

The unfamiliar male voice made every one of my nerves stand on end. I stood, suddenly feeling like all the air had been sucked out the room. My pulse thundered as I squeezed the phone in my hand. "Who the fuck is this? And where is my wife?"

"She's safe," he said. "And she'll stay that way if you do exactly as I say."

FORTY-FOUR

Devyn

"Oww..." I groaned as my eyes reluctantly opened. My head throbbed, and my entire body ached with the need to stretch. But as I tried to move, my arms and legs wouldn't budge.

My eyes started to focus, and I looked around the room. Nothing was familiar. I wasn't home, wasn't curled up with Gray at my side. No, instead, I was in an old cabin, one that had seen much better days. The dark wood was overgrown with moss and grime, and the windows were cracked, allowing the cold wind to creep inside. A small fire glowed in the fireplace in the corner, but it seemed to be the only source of heat. How in the hell had I ended up here?

I groaned as I looked down, finding myself in an equally grimy chair, one that looked as old as the house. The metal arms attached to a solid base, and I squirmed to get comfortable on the hard leather seat. It was hard to move, especially with my wrists and ankles bound to the chair with thick rolls of duct tape. Fuck. Fuck. Fuck. I tried to pull my arms away, but the tape didn't budge, just ripping my skin.

After attempting a few more times to wiggle out of my

restraints, I groaned and dropped my head to the back of the chair.

"Breathe, Devyn," I whispered to myself. "You can figure your way out of this."

First, I needed to figure out where I was being held. I couldn't remember much from before my world went black, but I already knew I needed to get the fuck out of this place. Stretching to try and look out the windows, I didn't recognize anything, only seeing a forest outside. That didn't help. Thick forests surrounded Saint Stephen's Lake—if I was even still in town...

I tried to take a deep breath and do anything to calm my erratic heartbeat, but every passing minute only increased my anxiety. My ears buzzed as I strained to listen for anyone in the house. Whoever tied me up must have left. The only sounds I heard were birds singing outside the windows, celebrating the end of the long winter.

My head sagged, exhausted by the fear coursing through my veins. This wasn't how my life ended. It couldn't be. I'd spent so long by myself, closed off from the people surrounding me. I was finally learning to let people in, to depend on others instead of just myself. Yes, I was still determined to get justice for the people David hurt, but I wanted more than just that. I wanted a life.

I wanted a life with Gray.

I wanted the ridiculous wedding where our families bickered about the unimportant details. I wanted nights on the couch, arguing about who has the worst taste in movies. I wanted a baby with his dark steel eyes and his pure heart. I wanted it all.

I yanked my hands as hard as possible, letting out a primal scream from the pit of my soul. I didn't care who was around; if

I was going to die, it wouldn't be quietly. I'd fight like fucking hell to get back to my husband.

My muscles ached and my throat burned, but I kept going, needing to get at least one of my hands freed. If I did that, then the rest would be easy. *Right?* But nothing seemed to work, even as the sun faded behind the trees outside.

The chair still held me captive hours later, offering no way out. Attempting to get out of the duct tape for God knows how many hours had depleted all my energy. My arms were red and blistered from trying to escape. My stomach rumbled, and my bladder ached, but mostly, I just wanted to go home. Hope was failing with every passing minute, but I tried to hold out, praying that somehow, Gray would find me.

I whispered another silent plea for him as a car pulled up to the house. I winced as the headlights shone through the dirty, cracked window pane.

"Shit, shit, shit," I hissed, tugging and pulling my wrists, but nothing happened. Even though the tape had loosened a little, it was not nearly enough to pull my hands out. Why the hell did they always make it look so easy in the movies? I breathed out slowly, trying to calm myself when footsteps approached. At least now, I would know the face of the person responsible for my hellish afternoon, considering my memories were nothing but fuzzy black spaces in my mind.

At least, they were, until Jack Fischer pushed open the door with a wide grin.

"Oh good," he said as he placed his brown paper bags on the table. "You're awake. You were snoring so hard, I thought you'd be out all night and miss all the fun."

"Jack?"

He ticked his tongue. "I thought this might happen. Sorry for dosing you, angel, but I knew you wouldn't come with me otherwise."

"So you drugged me and left me here?"

He moved closer, rubbing his thumb over my cheek. "No, no. I was only making sure we could talk without interruption. I'd hate for your husband to show up and ruin all my fun."

I swallowed at the sound of Gray's name. Nausea rolled through my stomach, making it hard to breathe. "What did you do to Gray?"

Jack shook his head. "Nothing you need to worry about. Sent him on a little wild goose chase. Luckily for me, he was already looking in the wrong direction, so I just steered him a little more that way."

"What do you mean?"

Jack walked over to the table and grabbed a bottle of water. He cracked the lid as he stepped back toward me. "See, I've been watching you for a while, Devyn. I discovered something interesting about your little band of misfits. Turns out, we want the same thing."

"World peace?" I snarled.

"Nice try," Jack chuckled. "But no." He held the water bottle to my lips, and as much as I wanted to refuse, I couldn't. I held my mouth open, and he poured a little inside. "It turns out, we have a mutual enemy. Your stepfather."

"David?"

"You see, when I first came to New York, well, I was angry. Theo had taken something from me, and I thought, what the hell, it'll be fun to take something away from him." He pulled the bottle back and tapped me on the nose with it. "Your sister, Calla. I could already tell Theo was falling for her and thought it would be a lot of fun to break him like that."

I chuckled as I leaned backward in the chair, trying to meet his gaze. "Calla would never go for that."

"A lesson I learned a little too late." Jack moved behind me, and my pulse skyrocketed, hating I couldn't track his movements. He placed his hands on my shoulders, and I shuddered, wishing I could reverse time and take back all the moments I had spent with this man. There were only two nights, two nights I wished I could erase from my memories. But then again, they led me to Gray, and I would never regret the time we had together.

Jack's fingers trailed along my neck. "But then I met you, Devyn. I thought I could let go of my anger, let go of my resentment. Then, when your stepfather approached me with an offer, I knew I'd be a fool to refuse."

I bit my lips together, trying not to give him the attention he clearly craved, but my curiosity won out over my stubbornness. "What did he do?"

Jack leaned down and traced his nose along the column of my neck. "He offered me *you*, Devyn. He promised to help get you on my side and convince you we were a good match. And on top of that, he offered to help me become the head of the company. Said that with his connections and resources, I'd be untouchable. All I had to do was keep Calla away from Theo and get her back into the fold."

That motherfucker. I supposed I should have been happy he only wanted to control us, as opposed to how he usually handled his adversaries. But after spending hours stuck in this godforsaken chair listening to my ex-fling describe his master plans with my evil stepfather, I was finished being a pawn in someone else's game.

Please forgive me, Gray.

I melted into Jack's embrace, letting all my fear and dread wash over me. He glanced down at me, his eyes widening as he took in my submissive form. "And now what?" I asked, batting my eyes to push away my tears. "Why are you doing this to me?"

"Oh, angel," Jack said as he shifted in front of me. He crouched and ran his hands along my thighs. "Because you fucked me, and then you fucked me over. When I had nothing to give him, David took everything else from me. You left me in ruins, but he burned those down to ash. So he needs to know what it's like to feel helpless, to have someone else control your fate."

"Let me help," I whispered, staring into his dark blue eyes. Had I ever really looked at Jack before? Had I ever taken the time to get to see the man lurking underneath the smooth veneer of power? Because there was no warmth lurking in his expression, nothing but calm resignation, and that was the scariest thing of all.

"Devyn, angel," he said as he leaned forward and took my hands. "You *are* helping. Because with your death, I'll be able to do what no one else has done before. I will finally defeat him, send him off to prison for your murder." He shifted away from me and moved toward the fireplace. As he turned, he held up my phone. "After all, who could blame him? After everything you and your sister tried to blame on him? David, well..." Jack shook his head. "He just snapped. Really tragic, if you think about it."

"You've lost your fucking mind!" I screamed, pulling at my bindings. But my strength failed me, and I slumped down into my seat further. Hope seemed like a dwindling ember, one buried so deep, I couldn't reach it, no matter how hard I tried.

Jack smiled at me as he walked back toward the door. "Maybe I have. But you're the only one who knows that, and you're only going to be a problem for a few more hours."

FORTY-FIVE

Grayson

"Useless," I said as I shoved open the doors of the sheriff's department. "Absolutely fucking useless."

Tomas and Laurel stayed behind me, trying to smooth things over in my wake, but I had no interest in that. I was going full scorched earth, and if you weren't helping, you were in my way. I didn't care what bridges I had to burn to get Devyn back. Hell, I'd burn the whole town to ash if it meant my wife was back in my arms.

When I reached my truck, I smacked the side of my fist on the door panel, barely feeling the pain that followed. It had been almost five hours since we'd heard from the kidnapper, almost five hours since my heart exploded inside my chest. Every time I closed my eyes, all I could see was her, out there somewhere, waiting for me. I'm sure Devyn was afraid, but I also knew my girl. If anything, she was probably being reckless, unable to stop pissing off the person who thought they could take her from me. She wouldn't go down without a fight. I didn't know if that made me more afraid for her or unbelievably fucking proud.

Someone's hand landed on my shoulder, and I whipped around, ready to fight anyone who tried to get in my way. Tomas stepped back, holding his hands in the air. "Be cool, Gray. It's just me."

"Shit," I hissed as I leaned against my truck. I ran my hands over my mouth and beard. "I'm fucking losing it, man. I need her back."

"I know," Tomas answered. "We're going to make sure that happens. But we need help, and you threatening the cops isn't doing us any favors."

"They're not doing anything!" I screamed. "You heard them. There's no evidence, nothing that shows this was a kidnapping besides a call coming from Devyn's phone. They've already made up their minds that she just took off. That she left me." I dropped down, resting my elbows on my knees. All of this was too much. My guilt consumed me. Maybe if I had never pulled Devyn back into my world, maybe if I'd never brought her to my cabin, this would have—

I cut off that thought, because no matter what happened next, I would never regret a moment I had with Devyn, and I knew she would feel the same. I loved her, loved my wife more than anything in this world, and I refused to let this be the end of our story.

Laurel rushed over and crossed her arms as she studied the two of us. "Are you done wallowing? Because I just got a text from the kidnapper. It's their demands."

She held up her phone so we could see the message sent from Devyn's phone only minutes earlier.

DEVYN

All the evidence you've gathered in exchange for your sister's life. Midnight at the cove.

"Done," I said, moving to open my car door. But before I could climb inside, Tomas slammed it closed.

"It's not that simple," Tomas protested. "We don't even know who is asking for the evidence."

"Obviously, it's coming from David or one of his lackeys. He must have gotten onto our investigation, and now he wants whatever proof we have," I bit back. "He gets his freedom, and I get my wife back. Seems pretty fucking simple to me."

"Nothing about this is simple," Tomas insisted, his tone going soft. "I care about Devyn too, but there has to be another way, one that gets her back and keeps the ball in our court."

I glanced over his shoulder at Laurel. "Let me guess: you agree with him."

Her deep green eyes narrowed at me. "Absolutely not."

"What?" both Tomas and I snapped at her. Laurel stood there, her arms clasped around her waist. She glanced between the two of us, her expression harder than I'd ever seen before. It was rage, pure and simple, and I would have hated to stand in Laurel's way.

"Lord, give me fucking strength," Tomas muttered under his breath as he stepped back from me. "Let's get one thing clear— we are all on the same side. We all have the same objective. But we can't run in there, drop evidence at this guy's feet, and expect to walk away unharmed. Maybe he will give us Devyn, but it's just as likely he'll kill all of us. Is that what you want?"

"Obviously that's not what any of us want," Laurel sighed, turning her attention fully to him. "If you want to talk us out of this, you have four hours to come up with a plan. Otherwise, we're going to do what they ask and whatever else we need to do to bring Devyn home."

Tomas' gaze softened, and for the first time since the motel, pure admiration shined back. "Okay, we'll do it your way, gorgeous. We'll figure out a plan that keeps everyone safe."

"In case that doesn't happen, I'm running home to grab the files," I said as I pushed past Tomas and climbed into the driver's seat. I looked over to the other side of the bench, almost expecting to see Devyn sitting there, rolling her eyes about my overbearing tendencies. I didn't care. She could make fun of me for the rest of our lives after I got her back.

"Wait," Laurel said, her eyes glued to her phone. She answered an incoming call. "Hey, Calla, what's going on?" Her eyes widened when her sister spoke—she was so loud, I could hear her through the cracked window of my truck. "No, you made the right call. Stay where you are, Calla. Do not go back in there. I'll be there as soon as I can."

She hung up, tucking the phone into her back pocket. "David just arrived at the Isadora. Calla was visiting with our mother when he barged into the apartment, demanding answers. She got out through the exit in the kitchen and is safe in the parking lot, but she's really worried about our mom."

"Answers about what?" Tomas asked.

Laurel shook her head. "I have no idea, but we need to get over there. Now."

I nodded, knowing I would need to wait to grab the files. If David was the one responsible for Devyn's abduction, there wasn't much that could stop me from confronting him. But as I thought about his smug expression and the years he'd threatened my wife, a plan came to mind. "I'll meet you over there."

"What?" Laurel snapped. "No, we need to go *now*, Gray. Who knows what he's going to do to my mom."

"I swear, I'll be right behind you," I promised. "But I've been waiting to confront this asshole for a long time, and there's one thing I need to get before I can finally cross it off my list."

Laurel shook her head, muttering obscenities under her breath as she walked away from me. Tomas followed and grabbed her elbow, directing her toward his parked motorcycle. "C'mon, I'll take you. We'll get there faster on my bike anyway."

She locked eyes with me as she pulled on the spare helmet. "Five minutes?"

"I swear," I barked as I shifted my truck into reverse.

Because no matter what happened next, David was going to pay for what he'd done to my wife.

CALLA WAS the first person I saw when I pulled into the Isadora parking lot. Her face was tear stained, and her body trembled as she leaned against her large SUV. As soon as I put my truck into park, she rushed over and squeezed her arms around me.

"Hey, you're okay," I said, patting her back. "You're safe, I promise."

"I know, but you should have seen the look in his eyes, Gray. The man is losing his mind. He came in screaming about Devyn and some asshole trying to screw him over." She looked up at me, her wide eyes stained with fear and anger. "Gray, where the hell is my sister?"

"I don't know," I whispered as I released her. As she took a step back, I opened the back door to my truck and grabbed my bat. I hadn't swung the bat since Devyn returned to my life, but I was ready to show those guys why I'd gotten drafted. My hands tightened, feeling the wood in my grip. Shocking that it didn't splinter under the intensity.

Calla's eyes widened as she took in my bat. "Gray, what is going on? Where is Devyn?"

I wanted to answer her, wanted to soothe away her worries, especially with her being so late into her pregnancy. However, anything I could have said to ease her fears would have been a lie, so I gave her the only truth I could. "I am going to get her back. No matter what it takes."

Calla stared at me, her lower lip wobbling at my words. The poor girl had already been through a lot, and I hated adding to her stress level. But before I could say anything else, her resolve steeled and her eyes narrowed. "I'm coming with you."

"No fucking way," I barked, moving in front of her. "I'm not letting you in there. And pretty sure if you step foot inside that building, Theo's head would explode." I placed my free hand on her arm. "So if you don't want to stay here, do it for him. Do it for your daughter."

She huffed. "Low blow, Anders."

"Do what I can, Winters."

She squeezed my hand once then backed away toward my truck. "Bring her home, Gray."

"That's the only fucking option."

FORTY-SIX

Grayson

When I reached the floor of the Winters' apartment, Laurel greeted me by the kitchen entrance. The door was pretty hidden from the interior of the home, designed to look like another row of cabinetry if you didn't know of its existence. Laurel's brow arched when she spotted the bat in my hand. "That was what you had to get?"

I shrugged. "Back-up plan if you can't convince him to give up Devyn."

Laurel rolled her eyes as she pushed her key into the lock. "Do you really think that's the best course of action? Barge in and start breaking shit?"

"Works for me," I shrugged. "Where's Tomas?"

"He's checking in with security and local PD. He wanted me to wait for him, but I declined."

"Why am I not surprised?" I murmured as I stepped through the door.

"Wait," Laurel said, stepping in front of me. "I want him to pay as much as you do, but the most important thing is getting my mom out of there and finding where he has Devyn." She narrowed her eyes at me. "That means no spilled blood until we have control over the situation."

"Fine," I scoffed as I stepped into the kitchen, checking for any signs of life. Shattered dishes and overturned stools littered the kitchen, but otherwise, everything was in order. Laurel shifted behind me as we walked toward the dining room, listening for David and Diane.

As we moved further into the apartment, Laurel gasped and dashed ahead of me. "Mom!" She dropped to her knees as Diane came into view. She was lying on the ground, her arms sprawled out as if someone had struck her. When Laurel pushed her hair out of her face, a small amount of blood covered her forehead, enough to make her daughter shake with worry. While Laurel took care of her mom, I stalked the room, looking for any sign of David. Raised voices echoed from the office, muttering something I couldn't quite make out.

Laurel stayed at her mom's side, shaking her lightly until her eyes fluttered open. As soon as they did, Diane let out a stuttered breath. "Laurel, you shouldn't be here." She sat up, keeping her daughter's forearms trapped in her steel grip. "David... He's lost his mind."

"No shit," I hissed, keeping my eye trained on the hall to the office. "Are you okay?"

Diane nodded, and more blood trickled from her forehead. Laurel tried to lift her mother's bangs away, but she shooed her off. "I'm fine. It barely hurts. David shoved me when I tried to stop him from going after Calla."

"You should have run too," Laurel insisted.

Diane shook her head, looking her in the eye. "No, he threatened my girls. Said he would hurt you if I didn't help him find what he needs."

"He already did," I snarled as I stepped closer. "He has Devyn."

She shook her head. "No, he doesn't. He never mentioned Devyn when he stormed in here. Whoever has my daughter must be the same people threatening David. Somehow, they got documents about illegal actions at David's company and threatened to go public if he didn't pay them."

"What does that have to do with Devyn?"

"I don't know," she whispered as she turned toward Laurel. "Oh God. I didn't know, Laurel. I swear, I didn't know he was like this."

"We don't have time to get into this right now," she bit back, her eyes darting around the rest of the apartment. "Where is he now?"

"The office," Diane whispered. "Calla's okay?"

I nodded. "She's in the parking lot, worried about you. Go." I looked at Laurel. "I'll take care of David."

"Oh, bullshit," she hissed. "There's no way I'm leaving now."

"Get your mom somewhere safe, Laurel," I said, gripping my bat as I walked closer to the hallway. I didn't wait for them to leave, instead stalking toward the hallway. My steps were light, trying to keep David unaware of my presence. When I reached the double doors, I turned the corner, spotting him pulling books off the shelves. As they tumbled out around him, wads of cash fell from their hidden centers, landing at his feet.

Jesus Christ. There had to be thousands of dollars on the carpet. Yet David kept pulling things off the shelves, not bothering to look away from his task. When I was sure he didn't have a weapon or anything else on him, I stepped into the room, leveling my bat at his face. "Where is she?"

David jumped back at the sound of my voice. Fear was a strange expression on his face. For so long, he had been the puppeteer, ruining other people's lives to line his pocket. But now, he was the one out of control, the one trapped in someone else's web. If my wife weren't part of this asshole's collateral, I'd tip my hat to the blackmailing bastard. I'd never forget the sight of David flailing, looking like he was a half-second away from soiling himself.

But as soon as he locked eyes with me, David snarled, "What the fuck are you doing here, Anders?"

"Something I should have done a long time ago."

Before David could say another word, my bat collided with the side of his head, and he sank to the ground, his blood mixing with the piles of money he was so desperate to obtain.

***

"DID you have to hit him so hard?" Tomas groaned, motioning toward David on the other side of the room. "You're lucky you didn't kill him."

I shrugged. "My conscience is clear. David deserves a lot worse than that hit, trust me."

Tomas shook his head, plugging David's phone into his laptop. He muttered to himself as he worked, but I didn't care enough to make out the words, too focused on the man bound in front of me. We'd kept him in the office but tied him to one of the dining room chairs. Looking at the once proud man trussed up with his old gym socks stuffed in his mouth was almost enough to make me smile, but the ticking clock on the wall was a reminder that every moment he stayed unconscious was one less second we had to find Devyn.

"Fuck yes," Tomas smirked, running his hand over his mouth. "I was right—the kidnapper used a different burner to contact David."

"Can you track it?"

"I can't, but one of my associates can hack into the system and pinpoint the location for us. It'll take a little bit of time–"

"We don't have time," I growled. "Devyn doesn't have time."

Tomas glanced at his watch. "We have another hour, Gray. Let me try."

I nodded and moved back toward David. I used the tip of my bat to poke at his stomach and smirked when he groaned. His ruddy brown eyes opened slowly, and he cursed when he tried to pull at his hands. Muffled yells came from behind the socks tucked in his mouth, and I just shrugged. "Sorry, I didn't get that. Do you want to try again?"

David's body practically radiated with anger as he tried to lunge out of the chair to get to me. I stalked over, pointing my bat at his face. "If you want to walk out of this room, I suggest you do not fuck with me, David. I want to know everything the blackmailer demanded from you, including the drop-off location. If you tell me that, and it helps us find Devyn, then we'll let you go." I casually leaned against the bookshelf. "If you don't...I can't guarantee what'll happen next."

David groaned against the gag, and I leaned forward, taking it from his mouth. "Fuck you, Anders. You were a pain in the ass kid before, and you're still a goddamn loser—"

"Nuh, uh, uh," I said slowly, holding up the socks. "I said you needed to be helpful. That did not sound helpful to me." Pressing the socks close to his mouth, I continued, "You want to try that again, or should I use you for batting practice?"

"I don't give a fuck what you do to me; I'm not talking."

"Wrong answer," I said as I shoved the socks back into his mouth. I was about to make good on my threat when Laurel strode inside, Calla tight on her heels. She held a laptop, smirking as she set it on David's lap.

"Recognize him?" I couldn't make out the screen, but all the color drained from David's face. He screamed something against the gag, but Laurel continued without bothering to take it out. "That would be William Garber, a land surveyor who just happened to pass away from a heart attack a week after you two met. Coincidence, right?" She slammed the laptop closed. "I couldn't quite connect all the pieces, at least not until I got the files I needed from Gray's dad." She smirked. "Or should I say, *my* dad. Because not only did he trace the money to find the man you hired to kill William Garber, but he also figured out why you had him killed."

The air sucked out of the room at her words, all of us waiting to see what she would say. But the words didn't come from her. Instead, Calla spoke up, showing him a map of the town. "You were never interested in the land here, were you? At least, not for development." She turned the page, pulling out a financial transaction. "How long have you been using drug money to fuel your empire, David?"

My eyes widened as I stared at her. "That's what this has been about? Drug smuggling?"

"An extensive network of drug smuggling," Laurel added before cocking her head at her stepfather. "He's been buying up land, using them as drop-zones for cartels and other agencies. They're giving him a lot of money to keep their operations clear."

Calla stepped closer to David, her brown eyes narrowed in anger. "I don't really care why the fuck he did it. I just need to know one thing." She kicked him in the shin, and David cried out. "Did you have our father killed?" David glared at her, so she reached back, ready to slap him, but Laurel took her hand first.

She moved Calla back, and when I noticed how hard she was trembling, I wrapped my arm around her shoulders. She gave me a grateful smile and took a slow breath, rubbing her pregnant belly like it was the only thing keeping her from falling apart.

Laurel leaned forward toward David. "Now, all I want from

you is a yes or no. If you admit to killing our father and help us find Devyn, all this evidence can disappear."

"Laurel!" Calla gasped.

My hand tightened on Calla's shoulder, and she looked up at me. I tried to compel her without words, trying to convince her to let Laurel work. Luckily, Calla trusted me enough to nod, dropping her question.

Laurel leaned forward and tugged on the gag as her green eyes stared daggers into David's soul. "Are you going to help us, or should I send all this stuff to the NYPD, the DEA, and the SEC? You know they've been dying to make an example out of you."

David stared at her as if trying to see if she would break. I could only imagine what was going through his mind, watching the woman he thought he'd manipulated for so long control his strings. When Laurel's gaze never faltered, his head dropped almost imperceptibly in a nod.

"Good," she said, tugging the socks out of his mouth. "Then talk."

"Yes," David sneered, "I had your father killed. I tried to warn him to back off. I even tried to give him a payout to walk away from the case. But he wouldn't drop it." He leaned back in his chair. "I did what I had to do."

"And you just met our mother?" Calla asked from my side. "That seems like too much of a coincidence to me."

"Not a coincidence at all," David admitted. "I wanted to keep an eye on her. I didn't know if your father had told her about my operation, and she is a very beautiful woman, so..."

"And Devyn?" Laurel bit out, not showing any outward reaction to David's admission. While Calla looked like she was about to pass out, her sister was the opposite, looking almost bored as David confessed his sins.

"I don't know," he said, his voice taking a panicked edge

now. "They told me to leave the briefcase at the edge of the property, and they would send me the location of the files."

"That's what I don't get," Calla whispered. "What files could they possibly have? The only concrete evidence was locked in your attic for years. How could the blackmailer have found it?"

My eyes widened, and I moved around Calla to join Tomas. I picked up the phone and scrolled through the photos they'd sent David, the "evidence" they had gathered. "This is all ours." I showed the pictures to Laurel. "All the pictures are from Devyn's phone."

Laurel swallowed, glancing down at David then back up to me. "If he had nothing, what is the point of all this?"

I shook my head, my hands tensing with the weight of my thoughts. "What if this was never about money? What if that was just a ruse to get David at the scene of a crime? There has to be a reason they took Devyn before David ever got a message."

"We're about to find out," Tomas called out. "Because I just got the trace."

FORTY-SEVEN

Devyn

"Wake up, angel," a voice cooed in my ear. "It's almost time to go."

My eyes were hazy as they tried to open, exhausted despite my lack of movement. Every bit of my energy had gone into my escape attempt, but nothing worked. At one point, the duct tape loosened. However, in my excitement, I'd missed Jack walking through the door. He reinforced every piece before returning to my phone to check on the progress of his plan.

"Let me go, Jack," I whimpered. As much as I wished it was an act, I could barely speak at this point. My hoarse throat croaked out the word, "Please."

He ran his hands down my cheek, then along my jaw. "I wish I could, Devyn. Maybe, if you hadn't decided to ruin me, I would have considered it." His hand jerked back, gripping my hair so hard, my neck seized. "You only have yourself to blame."

As Jack pulled back, he reached into his back pocket and pulled out a knife. My body pushed back in the chair instinctively, wanting to get as far away from the blade as possible. When pressed with fight or flight, I geared toward fight mode, and I'd do whatever it took to get the hell out of Jack's clutches.

But when he brought the knife closer, I was utterly helpless, only able to sit back and watch.

"Stay still," Jack said. "Or this will go a lot worse for you."

I nodded, continuing my docile act. He sliced through the tape on each of my wrists, and my arms fell to my side, almost in pain from being in one position for too long. Then, he freed my legs, and it was so tempting to kick out and run, but there was no way I could escape him, not in my weakened state. As Jack helped me stand, my bladder cramped, and I folded over in pain.

Jack sighed as he dragged me up. "Get yourself together, Devyn. You just have to hold on a little longer, and it'll all be done."

"Bathroom," I croaked out, looking up to plead with Jack. "I can't hold it anymore."

He groaned, shoving me toward the door on the other side of the room. As I tried to settle on the toilet, I fell to my knees. Jack shook his head at my pathetic state. "Get up and do it quick. You have two minutes, and then I'm coming back in, whether you're done or not."

As soon as the door slammed closed, tears of relief formed in my eyes. Using the toilet as support, I pulled myself up and shook my legs to regain some strength. Although they were sore and cramping, I still had some energy left.

I looked around the room, hoping for some way of escape. As I turned, a small window came into view. It was barely big enough for my body to fit through, but I had to try. I rushed over and tried to open it, but it was painted shut.

"Come on," I whispered, running my nails along the cracks. "Please open."

I almost cried out when the paint started to flake off, opening a little more with each shake of my hands. When it finally came loose, I almost cried. One step closer to freedom.

"One more minute," Jack called out from the door.

That was barely enough time to climb out of the window, but I would do it or die trying. There was no way I was walking to my death like a good, obedient girl. With that thought, I pulled together all my remaining strength and climbed on top of the toilet.

I looked down from the window and saw a slight drop, but it wasn't enough to deter me. With one last look over my shoulder, I dragged my legs through the window, then fell to the forest floor.

"Fuck," I whispered as a bolt of pain climbed up my leg. I'd definitely messed up my leg, but it wasn't enough to stop me from running. Maybe it was the adrenaline, maybe it was determination, but either way, there was no way in hell I was letting Jack catch me. If I got far enough into the woods—

"Devyn!"

Jack's roar from the bathroom pushed me forward, and soon, I was running so far, the cabin was a distant memory. My bones creaked and my muscles ached, but I refused to stop, no matter how much I wanted to. I had to be close to someone. There had to be a house nearby. If they could only get me into town, I could get to Gray, and nothing would happen to me once we were together.

As I imagined his muscular arms wrapping around me, I failed to notice a branch jutting out of the ground. My foot caught it as I ran, sending me tumbling forward into the dirt.

Branches and rocks sliced through my palms and knees as I tried to cover my face and head. Once I eventually came to a stop, I stared up at the branches above me, willing another breath from my lungs. *Keep going, Ace.* I could feel his words skitter across my skin. *Just a little longer, Devy, you can do it.*

I nodded to the Gray in my mind, too afraid Jack was nearby to speak out loud. Pushing up from the ground, I tried to take another step, but my body crumpled to the ground before I could. The slight throb in my ankle now seared with agony, and I had to bite my lip to keep from crying out. Using my good foot, I scooted until my back hit a tree, trying to breathe through the pain.

Once it started to subside a little, I reached down and untied my shoe. Shit, it was already swelling. Not a good sign. Based on the amount of pain, I'd definitely broken something, and there was no way I could outrun anyone in this condition.

"Fuck," I cried as my head dropped into my hands. I needed a plan, some way to get further from the cabin. With each passing moment, Jack was probably getting closer. I tried to stand, but my weight immediately buckled. My hands stung as I landed back in the dirt. The distance started to waiver in my vision, the dark spots from earlier returning to the corner of my eyes. Every blink felt heavy, like I'd sell my soul to sleep soundly in my bed.

Don't give up, Ace. Gray's words spurred me on, and I tried to crawl toward the trees in the distance. My nails dug in the cold, hard ground as I dragged myself inch by inch. By the time I reached the trunk, my arms burned, but I was still so far from where I wanted to go. As my body collapsed against the icy surface, tears pooled in my eyes, destroying my already-blurry vision. "I'm sorry," I whispered to the universe, hoping somehow, they'd make their way to Gray. I tried. I really did. But when my eyes slowly closed, I was helpless to resist the incoming darkness.

FORTY-EIGHT

Grayson

"Tell me again how accurate this is."

I leaned against my truck and stared off at the patch of thick forest. The signal had lead us here, but this was the end of the road. If we wanted to get any closer, we'd have to go on foot. As Laurel and Tomas talked in the truck, I stayed outside, needing the cold, crisp air to keep me calm. My eyes scanned the tree line at the end of the dirt road, trying to see what was lurking in the distance. But between the late hour and the starless night, it might as well be another planet. Nothing could break through. All we had was a dot on a computer screen, a dot in the middle of the forest the only key to finding my wife.

"Normally, it's within a 2-meter radius," Tomas sighed from the back seat of my truck, typing on his keyboard as Laurel and I tried to figure out how to track Devyn down. "But up here? With these trees blocking the signal? Could be closer to ten. If I could get into the government link-ups, it would be dead on, but we don't have that kind of time."

Laurel arched her brow. "Government satellites? Is there anything legal about your operation?"

"Define legal," Tomas smirked. "We straddle the line, but

my morals override the law. If the choice is between someone's life and staying on the right side of the law, I know what I'm picking every time."

"Focus," I bit out. "Give me an area, and I'll find her. But we gotta move faster."

With only a few more minutes left until the deadline, this was our last chance. Before we left the apartment, we'd made sure David's binds were solid then left him with Theo and Calla to wait for the authorities. Despite Laurel's insistence that she was going to turn everything over to her stepfather, she had no plans to let him get away with his decades of crimes. Not only did she record his confession about her father's murder, but she'd also scanned all the damning documents and sent them to the right people. Maybe it wouldn't be enough for formal charges, but we'd done enough of the legwork to make the case stick. It was out of our hands.

Now, I just needed my wife to close this chapter.

"About one mile north," Tomas finally said as he closed his laptop and grabbed his gear. "We'd get there faster if we drove, but I don't want to let this guy know we're coming."

I was just about to agree when movement flickered through the darkness—a person running through the trees. Without a second thought, I took off. The terrain was steep and littered with rocks and roots, but I kept my head forward, grateful for my years of cardio. I didn't care if it ended up being nothing; I'd rather risk that than lose Devyn for good.

As I burst through one copse of trees, the figure ahead came into view as he leaned against a tree trunk. It took me a moment to recognize him as Devyn's ex, the one I thought I'd scared off months ago. But here he was, breathing the same air as my wife. My fingers itched, desperate to get a hold of him.

I took a step forward, but Jack pulled something from his phone. A dot flickered on the screen. Was he tracking someone?

Was he tracking Devyn? Pride spilled into my chest. *That's my girl.* If he needed to track her, it meant she'd gotten away from him.

"Come on, angel," Jack sighed, his voice weary with exertion. "I know you're around here somewhere."

He moved again, holding up the tracker like it was a compass leading him to gold. While he searched for Devyn, I found the largest branch and positioned myself behind him. One hit, one snap, and all of this would be over.

But before I could swing out, my foot caught a branch on the ground. The audible snap echoed through the woods, and Jack went still. He slowly turned, smirking when he met my eyes. "Figured it out, did you?"

Clutching the thick branch, I moved closer. "Pretty fucking pathetic, trying to frame David. Should have known he only cares about himself. You were never getting your payday."

Jack chuckled and ran his hand over his face. "Is that what you think this was all about? Money?"

"How it looks from here."

"It's about respect," Jack shouted, slamming his palm to his chest. "That whole fucking family tried to ruin me, and what? I was supposed to move on?" He chuckled as he glanced at the remote. "Never going to happen. Devyn needs to pay for what she did to me."

"You touch her, and I will destroy you," I growled. I lunged and tried to grab Jack, but he slipped past me. I might have had him in size, but he had me in speed. He darted through the trees.

As I started to run after him, Tomas came out of the woods, holding up a tranquilizer gun. "Where the fuck did you get that?" I snapped.

"Go bag." He shrugged. "Which way did he go?"

I nodded, following his directions. The forest was eerily

quiet, as if the universe knew I needed to focus. I leaned against one tree and closed my eyes, hoping for some sign of Devyn or Jack. As I breathed in slowly, Jack made his move and darted out in front of my hiding place. This time, there was nowhere for him to go.

I used my full force to collide with him, sending both of us into the dirt. The tracker flew out of his hand, far enough that I couldn't see it, but Jack tried to reach for it, desperately pulling at the ground beneath us.

Anger coursed through my veins, a feral need to protect my wife. Because as long as he couldn't find her, she was safe. At least, safer than she'd be in his hands. I didn't know what Jack planned to do with Devyn once he caught her. I wasn't going to take that chance.

My knee collided with his stomach, and he wheezed out a shaky breath. He tried to kick me off him, but I rolled with his move, using his momentum to get us face-to-face. I grabbed his jacket and slammed his head into the dirt. "Where is she?"

"Probably bleeding out in the woods," Jack spat at me. "You'll never find her without the tracker."

My gaze darted up, desperate to find the small device. As soon as I loosened my grasp, Jack threw a punch, knocking me in the jaw. It was enough to startle me, creating just enough room for him to get out from underneath me. Jack scrambled through the brush, finding the remote before my vision cleared. He smirked as he held it out in front of me.

"You know, I had something else planned for Devyn, but I think this might be even better." He dropped the device to the ground, then used the heel of his foot to smash it into small shards. "Now, she'll die out here, all alone, and there's nothing you can do to find her."

A roar came from the pit of my stomach, a sound I'd never made before. It was anger. It was grief. It was years of longing crashing over all my senses, eliminating everything but the threat in front of me. Nothing mattered, nothing in this world compared to Devyn. I'd stain my soul forever if it meant she'd get to spend the rest of her days in peace.

Jack tried to run, but I was too fast, fueled by uncontainable rage. I knocked him back into the dirt then climbed on top of his chest. He tried to shove off me, but I wouldn't budge, not when I planned to keep all my earlier promises. His nose crunched with the first hit of my fist, blood and other fluids seeping out of it. Jack's pained cries filled the surrounding woods, but I didn't care, taking out every moment of stress and anger on his rotten body. The man tried to hurt my wife, tried to take her away from me. In my mind, he deserved a slow, agonizing death.

My fist lowered again and again, until his entire face was stained with blood. I was about to hit him again when someone called out in the darkness. "I've got her!"

Relief washed through me like a tsunami, leaving only need in its wake. I looked down at Jack. As the red faded out of my vision, I reached down and checked his pulse. It was there but weakened. "Fuck," I hissed as I climbed off him. "Don't you even think about going anywhere, or I'll come back and finish the job."

With that, I burst through the woods, not stopping until I found Tomas huddled next to a tree. There was a small bundle wrapped up in a silver emergency blanket. Tomas' eyes widened as he looked down at my cracked and frayed knuckles. He arched a brow, and I shook my head. "Don't ask."

"Wasn't planning on it," Tomas answered, standing to give me some space. "I'll head back that way and make sure he doesn't go anywhere." He pulled out his phone and called Laurel, letting her know we found Devyn.

I nodded my head in thanks, unable to form any other words

as I stared down at my wife. When Tomas backed away, I sank to my knees and ran the back of my fingers down her cheek.

"Gray?" Devyn murmured. Her voice was much weaker than usual, but it was there. I didn't hesitate, pulling her into my arms. Tears spilled down my cheeks as the emotions and fears I'd suppressed finally erupted. She leaned back, her fingers tracing the lines of my face. "I knew you'd find me."

"Always," I promised as I took her hand in mine. Dirt covered her fingers and nails, but I didn't care. I wanted to kiss each one, wanted to promise I would always be there, no matter where life took us. "Are you okay, Ace?"

She nodded. "My ankle's a little messed up, but I'm okay. I just need a long shower and the biggest burger ever to fill my stomach."

I shifted the blanket back and lifted her jeans to examine her ankle. It was badly swollen, the skin red and torn. I ran my fingers along it, and Devyn winced. "First, we're getting this checked out, and then you can have as much food as you want."

Devyn rolled her eyes, giving me a tired smile. "Are you always this bossy?"

"Only when it comes to you, Ace." I leaned forward, kissing her forehead. I leaned back and searched her eyes. "You're sure you're okay?"

"You're here," she breathed as I stood and lifted her into my arms. "I'm always okay when you're around."

"That's good to know," I chuckled, starting the trek back to the truck. "Because you're stuck with me, wife, for a long, long time."

Devyn

EPILOGUE

Six weeks later

"You know, I almost miss the scooter," I said as I looked down at my new walking boot. Even though my injury happened weeks ago, I still felt phantom pains whenever I looked at my foot. Everyone tried to assure me it was expected, especially with injuries like mine. Apparently, your bones don't like it when you snap them. If it had been any worse, I would have needed surgery to fuse the bones, which would have meant more months off my feet. The doctors warned me it could take months and a good amount of physical therapy to get my mobility fully back.

But honestly, after everything that happened that weekend, I'd take a long recovery. Besides, physical therapy was hard work, but at least it provided some good eye candy. I glanced over at my husband as he pulled into the parking lot. In the days after my abduction, Gray had trouble leaving my side. We ended up meeting with a therapist Adam recommended to work through some of our concerns and anxieties. It helped soothe him a little, but Gray still insisted on coming to all my therapy appointments.

Gray chuckled as he parked then pushed open the driver's side door. He walked around the truck to open mine as well. He took my hand. "I don't know about that, Ace. That thing was a menace."

"Only because I ran over your toes once!"

"Twice," Gray said as he helped me down to the ground. When I was steady on my feet, he leaned down and kissed me softly. "You sure you're up for this tonight? We can always come back."

I nodded but held him close. "I'm sure. It feels like a good end to this chapter of our lives. Time to focus on the future."

Gray hummed his agreement, holding out his arm for me to lean on. As we walked through the parking lot, I tried to push the negative thoughts out of my mind and focus on tonight. After David and Jack were both arrested, we weren't sure if the charges against them would actually stick. While Jack was a little more cut and dry, David was another story, and we were afraid his powerful friends would help him out.

However, the SEC had apparently been investigating him for a long time. Shortly after his arrest, they charged him with a litany of crimes. Between the criminal, fraud, and insider trading charges, David would most likely spend the rest of his days in prison.

After getting the call from the DA earlier and my new walking boot, I was in the mood to celebrate. When we got to the storefront, Gray passed me my keys, holding up the shiny new silver one he'd attached last week. "Let's see how it looks."

I held my breath, not sure what to expect when I walked through the doors of my dad's old law firm. After everything that happened with Jack and David, I took a couple of weeks to decide what was next. The investigative part of my life was over, but I wanted to use my law degree to help people, not corporations. Once I knew I didn't want to walk away from being a lawyer, there was only one place I wanted to practice. Here, in the same office my dad used, in the town I loved more than words.

For the past two weeks, Gray had worked tirelessly to bring the office into the modern age. I tried to help, but he insisted on surprising me. If it was anyone else, it would have been terrifying. But Gray knew me—knew me better than anyone else in this world. In fact, when I told him about wanting to take over my dad's space, he just smiled, knowing I was going to do that before I even did.

"Oh my God," I said as I stepped into the new sitting area. They had scaled back all the shades of brown, now accenting them with white and pale blue. They replaced the antique chaises with a more modern couch, one very close to the one I had in the city. I squinted as I looked at it. "How did you know about this? You never saw my old apartment—"

The words were barely out of my mouth when the room erupted in a loud cheer of "Surprise!" I jumped out of my skin, almost losing my balance as I took in everyone. Everyone I loved was gathered in my new office, and I already knew what Gray had done.

He came up behind me and rested his arm around my shoulders. "Don't be mad, but they all wanted to help. I thought they should be here when you saw it for the first time."

I just shook my head. Anger was the last thing I found. For so long, I'd been an island, never letting anyone close for fear of getting hurt. However, as I looked around the room at my friends and family, I felt lighter than I had in months. Hell, it was lighter than I'd felt in years. I'd wasted so much time looking for a place I belonged, yet it had been here all this time, just waiting for me to discover it.

I wrapped my arm around Gray's waist and laid my head on his chest. "It's perfect."

Later that night, after everyone else went home, I sat in my office, alone. The front room looked like a disaster, but I was happy everyone enjoyed themselves. Everyone seemed pleased about my new adventure, especially my older sister, Laurel. She asked that her divorce be one of my first cases in my new digs. While her husband, Harry, fled after his involvement in David's schemes became public, she refused to remain married to him for another moment.

I happily sighed as I rested my sore foot on my spare chair. Gray came up behind me and dropped a kiss on my forehead. "Happy?"

"Yeah," I sighed. "It hasn't quite sunk in yet, but I think my dad would be proud."

"I think he'd be so fucking proud, Ace."

I swiveled to face him. "So what did Theo pitch this time?"

Gray chuckled, and I couldn't help but do the same. My brother-in-law might not be Gray's agent anymore, but he couldn't help himself. Every week, Theo had a new can't-miss offer Gray had to hear about. He leaned against my desk. "He asked me if I ever thought about coaching."

"Coaching?" I asked.

"Yeah," Gray answered. "Apparently, the league just voted to add on three new teams. One is starting up about an hour from here. They're looking for a new assistant coach, and Theo threw my name into the ring. Said the job's mine if I want it."

"And do you?" I leaned forward and propped my elbows on the desk. "Do you want it?"

"I think I might," Gray smiled. "It's close enough to home that I would be back most nights. Sure, I'd have to travel, but I'd here more often than not. And fuck, Ace–" He sighed, running his hand over his beard. "I miss the game. If I could teach a new group of guys to love it like I used to? Shit, that's the dream."

I stood, hobbling over to kiss him. "Sounds to me like you know your answer."

"Yeah?"

"Yeah," I chuckled. "If you want to, I say go for it. If anything, sign a one-year deal and re-evaluate after that."

He pulled me in between his legs and kissed me. "Might need a good lawyer to look over the terms. Know anyone available?"

"I think I have someone in mind. And from what I hear, her rates are very competitive." I pressed up against him. "In fact, she might just be willing to broker some kind of deal. For husbands only, though." I expected Gray to laugh, but nothing came. In fact, when I leaned back, there was a stern look on his face, one that made my stomach twist into a complicated knot. "Gray? What's going on?"

He shifted me back into the chair and pulled an envelope out of his pocket. I frowned after he passed them to me. As soon as I opened the top, I knew what they were. Tears stung my eyes while I looked at the divorce papers, ones I knew like the back of my hand. In fact, when I read through them, there it was. *My signature.* These were the last set of divorce papers I sent Gray earlier in the year, the ones he never returned. I assumed he destroyed them. But now, they were in my hands, and this time, his signature was on the line next to mine.

"What the fuck, Grayson?" I demanded as I looked up at him.

But this time, he wasn't leaning on my desk. Instead, he was kneeling in front of me, holding a ring. It took a moment for my brain to catch up, ping-ponging between anger and elation. I wanted so badly to give him my words, but the only thing that came out was a muttered, "What the fuck?"

"Okay," Gray smiled. "I can see why that's your first reaction. But let me explain—"

"Quickly," I said, holding out the papers to him.

"I want to spend the rest of my life with you, Devyn. There is no one else in this world who makes me feel like you do. You're my best friend, my favorite person, and the love of my life. I love you so much." He shuffled closer to me, placing his hand on my good leg. "The first time we did this, there wasn't a proposal. And I'm sure when you pictured your dream wedding, you didn't picture Cher officiating." He nodded to the papers. "So those are our chance for a fresh start. To do this right. Not because we were drunk and fooling around in Vegas, but because we want a life together." He brushed a tear away from the corner of my eye. "So what do you say?"

"No." Grays' entire face fell, and I realized my mistake. "I don't mean no to being with you," I chuckled, reaching out to hold him. "I mean no to the divorce."

"Are you sure?" Gray whispered, searching my eyes.

"Yes." I smiled through the tears. "I know our story isn't perfect, but it's ours, Gray. I don't want to change a single thing that led us to this moment." I held out my hand, and he smiled so brightly, it rivaled all the stars. "Because I want forever with you, Grayson Anders."

When he slipped the new ring on my finger, I smiled, recognizing the design. "Braided metals?"

"Yeah." Gray smiled, the tips of his cheeks turning pink. "For our past, our present, and our future. Thought it was pretty fitting."

"I love it," I said, leaning in to kiss him. As his hands gripped my hips, I leaned back, smiling at my husband. "Actually, I have something for you too. Only, I'm not going to give you a heart attack and hand you divorce papers."

"You could try," Gray chuckled as he stood. "You know I have creative ways to make them disappear."

I moved over to my purse and pulled out the business paperwork I'd filed earlier in the week. Gray's eyes tracked me as I moved closer to him. He took the envelope and opened it slowly, but I knew the moment he found what I'd done. "The Law Offices of Winters-Anders?"

"For my dad and me." I shrugged as I stepped between his legs. "Wanted to keep Winters as part of my last name to memorialize him, but I think it's about time I add my husband's name as well." I smirked as his eyes twinkled. "Devyn Winters-Anders has a nice ring to it."

"Fuck," Gray said as he dragged me closer to him. "Got a new fucking kink, baby. You're going to be the death of me."

"Not anytime soon," I chuckled. "We've got a lot of time to make up for, Grayson."

"Looking forward to it, Devy."

ACKNOWLEDGMENTS

I am sitting here stunned because I can't believe that the Saint Stephen's Lake series is over (at least for now) This place has been my world for the past eighteen months, and while I'm excited to venture out to new places, a piece of my heart will always be tied to this place.

There are so many people who made all of this possible, and without you guys, I would not be able to do what I love. So thank you, all of you, from the bottom of my heart.

My family— you guys are my rocks. You support me, encourage me, and inspire me. I love getting to share this journey with you.

My friends—all of you who listened to me talk about Gray and Devyn for months, and never telling me to stop, thank you. You guys made this story so much better with your insights.

Lauren at laurenturnsthepage— I cannot say enough good things about working with you. I love your reactions and questions, and how you push me to make each book better than the last. Thank you for all of your encouragement and Gray love! I can't wait to see what we create together in the future.

To Alexa at Fiction Fix, thank you so much for polishing this story into the best version of itself. Your edits always take my books to the next level, and I could not appreciate it more, especially with this book. I will never trust a lawyer TV show again!

Lemmy & the Luna crew— Thank you guys for your ARC management. You guys take so much off of my plate, and let me focus on writing. I love knowing that my books (and readers) are in such great hands with you guys.

Ainna- Looking at the four masterpieces you've created makes me want to cry. I am so lucky that you agreed to take on this series. Thank you for sharing your art with me and bringing my characters to life.

Books and Moods- There aren't words to express how much I love the covers you designed. You crafted something so unique with each cover, yet they match so well. I am in awe of your designs.

To my amazing beta readers-- Meghan, Katie, Brandi, Maeghen, and Katherine, thank you so much for all of your input and invaluable feedback. You guys are the best hype team, and I love that I can count on you to help me create the best possible version of my books. You guys are the best!!

And last- to my readers. Whether you started your Saint Stephen's Lake journey right in the beginning, or if you are just finding me now, thank you. Thank you for investing your time in my world, and I hope you enjoyed it.

Love you all!

ABOUT THE AUTHOR

K.C. Brooks is an avid romance reader who has always dreamed about turning her ideas into a book of her own. She lives for sunny days, iced cold coffees, and stories that make your heart ache for more. When not living in the fantasy worlds of her books, she resides in upstate New York with her husband, two children, and two fur babies.

www.ingramcontent.com/pod-product-compliance
Lightning Source LLC
Chambersburg PA
CBHW030743310726
48969CB00005B/1300